Also by John Sadler:

Scottish Battles

Border Fury

Clan Donald's Greatest Defeat: The Battle of Harlaw 1411

Flodden 1513

Culloden 1746

Bannockburn 1314

Massacre of Glencoe 1692

Blood on the Wave

A Novel of Flodden Field

JOHN SADLER

LION FICTION

Published by Lion Fiction
an imprint of
Lion Hudson plc
Wilkinson House, Jordan Hill Road
Oxford OX2 8DR, England
www.lionhudson.com/fiction

ISBN 978 1 78264 089 9
e-ISBN 978 1 78264 090 5

This edition 2014

A catalogue record for this book is available from the British Library

Printed and bound in the UK, September 2014, LH26

This one is for Captain Sam Meadows 2RGR

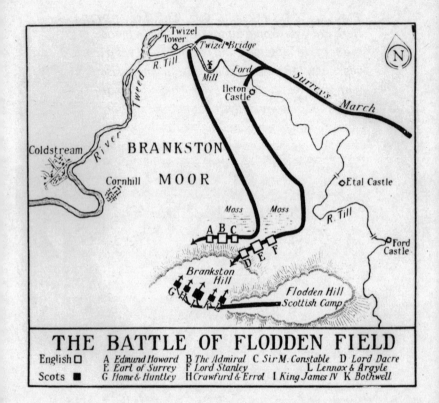

THE BATTLE OF FLODDEN FIELD

English □   A *Edmund Howard*   B *The Admiral*   C *Sir M. Constable*   D *Lord Dacre*
               E *Earl of Surrey*   F *Lord Stanley*   L *Lennox & Argyle*
Scots ■   G *Home & Huntley*   H *Crawfurd & Errol*   I *King James IV*   K *Bothwell*

*Here are two people almost identical in blood...
the same in language and religion; and yet a few
years of quarrelsome isolation – in comparison
with the great historical cycle – have so separated
their thoughts and ways, that not unions nor
mutual dangers, not steamers or railways, nor all
the king's horses and all the king's men seem able
to obliterate the broad distinction.*

R. L. Stevenson: *Essays of Travel*

Dramatis Personae

SCOTS
James IV of Scotland
Margaret Tudor, Queen of Scotland
Alexander, 3rd Lord Hume
George Hume (half-brother to Alexander)
Isabella Hoppringle, lay abbess of Coldstream
Archibald Douglas, 5th Earl of Angus
Alexander Gordon, 3rd Earl of Huntly
Adam Hepburn, 2nd Earl of Bothwell
Walter Scott of Harden

ENGLISH
King Henry VIII of England
Thomas Howard, Earl of Surrey
Thomas Howard, latterly Earl of Surrey and
   3rd Duke of Norfolk
Lord Edmund Howard, Surrey's third son
Sir Edward Stanley, 1st Baron Monteagle
Thomas Dacre, 2nd Baron Dacre
Thomas Darcy, 1st Baron Darcy de Darcy
Sir Marmaduke Constable
John Heron, Bastard of Ford
George Darcy
Lady Elizabeth Heron

Note: The Canonical Hours

Matins – daybreak

Prime – around 0600 hours

Terce – 0900 hours

Sext – noon

Nones – 1500 hours

Evensong – early evening

Compline – later, before retiring

Chapter One: The Quarrel

A prince is also respected when he is a true friend and a true enemy; that is when he declares himself on the side of one prince against another without any reservation. Such a policy will always be more useful than that of neutrality; for if two powerful neighbours come to blows, they will be of the type that, when one has emerged victorious, you will either have cause to fear the victor or you will not. In either of these two cases, it will always be more useful for you to declare yourself and to fight an open war...

Machiavelli: *The Prince*

Bastard Heron picks a fight

It was that sort of spring day on the marches: fat, grey-bellied clouds sagging, peevish rain, wind that brushed the fresh, border grass. Just ahead, a lone magpie started from cover. There was no sign of a mate. Bad omen.

"There's hundreds of them," Lilburn, my new man, exhaled unnecessarily.

"Several hundred," I replied, "but we're all friends today." You know how it is on these days. There are rules, of course, conventions – even laws – but none of those count for too much on the marches, the threapland,[1] the wasteland between two perpetually warring states.

---

1 Wasteland, a contested barren frontier.

I was kitted out in my better finery: slashed jerkin over pinked doublet with fine linen hose. I still carried sword and buckler, of course, and they weren't decorative in the least. Marjorie, my wife, glowed in a fine kirtle, shining nearly as bright as my sister-in-law Elizabeth, whose gown was cut to show off her fine swan neck and dazzling skin. William, my brother, or half-brother I should say, free of the taint of bastardy and safe in acres, looked worried as was usual in my company. I wasn't sure if he feared my greed for his wider estate or lust for his beautiful wife. On either count he'd have been fully justified.

"William, and John." This was from our warden, Bull Dacre, businesslike as ever, dark as a crow, only his fine harness freshly burnished. Despite this being a truce day, the warden would have seemed undressed without breast and back.

'There'll be no trouble today, boys. Mind your manners and – I'm talking to you, Johnny – wind your neck in and keep your temper. Today, we salute our Scottish cousins and remember what good friends we all should be." Sage advice from one not noted for his amiability towards our neighbours. The great red bull banner of Dacre had flown over most border battlefields.

The Scots were closer now, Sir Robert Kerr's flag "The Sun in his Splendour" wafting over. A hesitant sun peeked out and decided, at least for the moment, to stay – perhaps a better sign or just a drier day for killing.

"Has anyone told him we're friends?" I gestured towards the Scottish warden, Dacre's opposite number.

"He'll behave if he stays sober. Best keep out of his way," he advised. "The man hates you even more than he hates me, and that's an achievement, but he won't pick a fight with me because I'm warden. You, Johnny, on the other hand, are a notorious reiver. You've emptied his byres and killed his clients and he's not the forgiving sort – no sense of humour I can detect. So, for God's sake, try to break the mould and be discreet."

All true. As I was only half a gentleman, I needed to steal to maintain my estate. I was good at robbery and still alive, two things guaranteed to annoy Sir Robert Kerr of Cessford. I might be the Bastard but he was utterly vicious, vain, bitter, quarrelsome, and vengeful. Perhaps I'm no different, but I do as I do to survive. He spilled blood for sport and there is a difference.

"The Scottish warden," I suggested, "could be counted as something of an expert on the subjects of thieving and the cutting of throats. There's none of either occurs on his patch unless he's ordered it so and takes his cut."

"True enough," Lord Dacre replied equably. "I'm not asking you to like him, just keep out of his way." Delicacy prevented him from pointing out that he and I had a very similar relationship: I paid him a fee per head for every beast I lifted and never, or mostly never, shed Scottish blood till he gave me the nod. All in all, we were very useful to each other.

"John," my half-brother nagged, trying not to look as worried as he clearly was, "just keep your peace, just for one day. Do you think you can manage that?" I had not come to seek a fight. Only a fool would do so on a truce day when all quarrels were set aside. I had with me only two of my company, Lilburn and Starhead, both quite new and neither with a price on his head. Within my affinity, this was rare. I was here just to see, to observe and to listen, my pouch heavy with English silver, for ale and other forms of tongue-loosening. I had other functions in the game of cross-border politics.

"Do as we're ordered," I told my lads. "Keep clear of any of the Scotch warden's men. Watch both your drinking and your mouths. There's no complaints filed against us. We're as pure as the local virgins." No complaints. This was the cause of the Kerr's fury. He had nothing on any of us; not so much as a willing witness. Intimidation was habitually a game with several players. On this bare upland pass, one of the gateways through the crowding hills, the bigger mummery of marcher justice unfolded. Now was all brightness and cheer, winter and dark nights of a reiver's moon both gone. Our countries were as near to peace as they'd ever been.

On our right, a narrow burn ran alongside, a slash across the dun moor, clear water flecked with brown gurgling over speckled stones as round as shot. As was usual on these occasions, a sudden festival appeared. Ale and wine flowed. Dice rolled and horses pranced, restless. Colour spread lively across the narrow neck of empty moorland, this saddle between England and Scotland. Every man and woman preened in their very best gear. It was only on days like these we got to meet our neighbours other than over snarling lances.

Bright as fireflies, our women chattered in a warming sun. Tables were set up and both wardens took their solemn places, each equal in his station. I drifted amongst the company, drew some nods, and kept my two fellows close. Thieving's a common trade on the marches, defined by name rather than nation. An Armstrong's an Armstrong come whatever; otherwise he may be English or Scots to suit.

Martin Elliot of Braidlee lounged by a conjurer's booth, watching all and nothing, a lean, spare man of middle height. "Your brother's wife is a rare beauty," he confided. "No wonder he never looks easy." Elliot and I were no strangers. "Our precious warden lusts after your blood," he continued. "He's a great practitioner of the arts of hating and you're his current favourite. Loathes you more than he does me; I should be offended."

"I like to think I've given plenty cause."

"Have a care, Johnny. He's bloody minded and determined. He has you in his sights."

I'd already weighed the odds. Tynedale and Redesdale men were there. I enjoyed our warden's protection for what that was worth. Kerr had a dozen men with him, all well armed. I didn't think he'd want a brawl – too far beneath his precious dignity, the ground too public. Our kinds of dealings were best done in darkness. William and his small party ambled over, the women arm in arm, laughing, Elizabeth with her head back, her lissom figure enticing. Her fine, very blue eyes rested on me for a moment, her glance unfathomable, and passed on. William did not notice or chose not to.

"The Treaty of Perpetual Peace," he said to me, "the old king's legacy, near ten years calm or just about." Aside from people like me, he didn't need to add.

"War is always just around the corner," I responded cheerfully. "France and the empire banging it out and our new king's not his father. He's full of high ambition, blessed with a fat purse. He's no time for his brother-in-law, far as I can tell." Now, as you can imagine, King Henry did not discuss grand strategy with ruffians like me. I listened to Dacre who listened at court and had more fingers in more pies than any knew. I said so.

"Our lord warden is a spider sure enough," Will acknowledged. "He has a man at every lord's table on both sides of the line and chooses his agents with a

15

fine eye, which is why you're not dangling from a noose somewhere. He needs you because you're useful, because you ride with the Liddesdale names, because you're his eyes and ears. Get it wrong just once and you're a dead man for sure."

"I'd hate to damage the family name," I retorted, "and I pay my dues." The fiscal aspects of my relationship with the warden went both ways. He paid for information and intelligence received, for lies and deceits put about, while he took a generous slice of my profits from robbery and extortion – a very worthwhile connection for both parties.

"The marches are strung tighter than a lute," Will continued. My nearly brother was not a reckless or a vengeful man – rather more the affable type – but he had wit as well as position. "Our King Harry has the urge to strut a rather wider stage. His careful father bequeathed a realm at peace and free from insurrection, a calmer England than we've seen for decades. These Great Italian Wars provide opportunity to resurrect our ancient quarrel with the French. Nothing goes down better with the English than frog-bashing. You know that well enough. You've done your share."

"And isn't James tied to France, like all before him?" I queried.

"He is that, which means the two must fall out. Henry doesn't give a fig about the Scots and he won't pass on chances in France just to keep the back door to England bolted."

"That will be our job, I assume?"

"Same as ever: England fights France, Scotland fights England. All English eyes are on the prizes over the Channel. We'll be left to hold the line."

"Business as usual then," I suggested.

"As always, which is why we must be careful, taking care not to give provocation," he warned.

"We meaning *me*?"

"You, brother John, in particular; Cessford is James's favourite. God knows why but he has the King's ear and he pours venom. Your name is mentioned frequently. The warden and council receive a litany of complaints against you. Kerr has made you his special project. Your continued existence offends him and, at the same time, diminishes him. How can he claim to rule the march when you wave two fingers at every opportunity? Your presence here is a snub to him and to the Scottish King. You're a very clear indication that our warden, and by implication both King and council, pass water heartily on the Scots."

All this was true, but the arts of peace have little attraction for us paupers. War was far more desirable. Brother Will could shake his lugubrious head but he had a fine house and rents to pay for it. My own was far more modest and its upkeep demanded a more active lifestyle.

"Actions have consequences," he reminded me. "Your actions in particular. So take good care not to poke the hornets' nest today. When the muck flies it generally comes in my direction so you'll understand why I go on like an old maid. They can't find you but they know where I live."

* * *

Trestles had been set up so the wardens could begin their business – or what passed for business. Most, if not all, of the accused were clients of one side or the other. They could trust their respective wardens to cheerfully pervert any semblance of justice as long as they'd been paid. You might say that was really the sticking point. Those who were appointed to uphold whatever law there was were more part of the problem, a very large part. And who am I to preach? No small part of the general enmity was down to me. Our wardens were just rather higher up the pay scale.

Hooves thundered by. Vast amounts of coin changed hands on truce days, wagered on horseflesh. Our mounts hereabouts are important and breeding's a very lucrative business. A decent horse should be able to carry you forty miles in a night and then forty back, and be as adept driving a herd of recalcitrant beasts as in facing an enemy line.

For once I did not bet. My aim was directed to a smaller booth on the periphery, scruffy and ill-adorned. Master Willie Dodds, "Dentatore", had no need to advertise. A queue of sufferers lined up outside, as though hesitating before the abyss. Pained and suffering, they attended upon the barber surgeon's pleasure. I ignored the queue and strode straight in. One of the benefits of reputation is that lesser men tend to give way. On these marches reputation is everything, and mine, I can say without boasting, was significant.

"Master Heron, as ever a pleasure." Dodds was enormous, a great swag-bellied giant with forearms thick as hawsers, jowls overlapping like breakers on the shore, fringed by a great, dark mass of beard. Cowering in the single battered chair was one of the Robsons, Sym of Silkieside, who looked imploringly at me as though I had come to mount a rescue.

"One of the dangers of your calling, Master Heron," Dodds continued, "is that you take your dinner too hot before you mount up or too cold upon your return – if you do return, that is." His expression was mournful, that of a man who habitually expects the worst and is rarely disappointed. "Whilst this is understandable, it plays havoc with your teeth. And you do all seem to like your preserves, sweet and sickly; death to molars."

Beside him on a crude stand lay a selection of his instruments – an array of files and scrapers, rasps, and various diabolical spatulas. No torturer could ask for more, and looking at Master Robson's expression I could see he agreed. "I'm afraid this tooth is beyond redemption," Dodds advised his terrified patient. Swift as a snake he seized and pinioned his victim from behind, his impressive bulk and vice-like grip inescapable. With a mild flourish, he picked up a pair of well-used bronze pliers and speedily inserted them into the patient's gaping mouth. Sym was emitting mewing sounds of mixed pain and terror.

"Ha," the surgeon grunted, finding purchase. With a practised jerk he yanked the offending tooth free, a spurt of blood and vileness running over the patient's jaw. Sym was near fainting. I was feeling a little green myself. "Wild mint and pepper," was the advice, "rinsed around with wine, administered daily. Now be off with you. Sit, Master Heron," he commanded.

"I'm sure my teeth are perfectly fine," I asserted with the barest hint of tremor.

"I'll be the judge of that, laddie, and besides, our type of business is best transacted with at least a semblance of passing trade. Although your teeth are indeed sound, I detect signs of limyness. You do not cleanse them as often as I'd recommend. No need for these, as yet." Almost sorrowfully, he put down the pliers. "But you should try some of this, a physic of my own devising." He handed me a small earthenware jar. "Don't look so alarmed. It's merely a mixture of sal ammoniac and rock salt with saccharin alum, all ground down into a powder. Just rub your teeth daily using a small piece of red cloth."

"Why use red cloth?"

"Haven't a clue but that's what all the great writers say, and who am I to argue? I have the honour, I may add, to be consultant Dentatore to His Majesty King James. The King, I am pleased to say, takes a great interest in my art, and is most learned on the subject. He has read all the great masters – Aetius and de Chauliac etcetera."

"What else interests the King of Scots?" I enquired, poking my head outside the booth towards the pitiful queue of sufferers. Clearly their own pain preoccupied them, their moans and cries certain to muffle any utterances of ours that escaped.

William Dodds spied for England and probably for Scotland, France, and Spain and for any other interested party with a deep enough purse.

"He likes war," my informant continued, "as a drunkard craves liquor. Unlike you, he has never practised in earnest, of course, but he loves the idea of battle, of armour and trumpets and all that martial nonsense. He seeks to build an army that can beat the English in plain field."

"Something of a novelty," I suggested, idly fingering one of Dodds' instruments of torture.

"Times change," sighed Master Dodds with the sure certainty of a man who knows too well they always change for the worse. "He builds harness[2] to protect his men from English arrows. He reads Vegetius and all who write on war. I'm not persuaded he understands all he reads, for – as no doubt you could advise him – the gulf between theory and practice is as wide as the sea. He loves his cannon though. Those are his special toys. Great noisy monsters they are; frighten half of Edinburgh near to death, work of the devil." He shook his head disapprovingly.

2 Armour.

"A potent artillery train nonetheless?" I probed.

"If you say so, but I do mind how His Majesty was thwarted by Norham's walls, before we entered into this new era of peace and mutual love. He may have reflected on how a future siege might be accelerated, should we say. He loves his ships too."

"His navy grows?"

"Prodigiously," he smiled. "You'll recall he launched *Margaret* in the year '06, one of the finest warships afloat. Well, now he is building the *Michael*, which will dwarf all his past efforts... She'll be the greatest ship on the ocean, carry a vast arsenal and scores of men-at-arms. She's cost the Scottish taxpayers all of thirty thousand pounds."

"I'm impressed," I admitted.

"So you should be. Navies are what it's all about these days it seems and so Scotland will rank with the world's great powers. King Harry will have to dig deep into his father's treasure to build a bigger one, though no doubt he will. England's not the only player on the field, not any more. The King is of course admiral of his own fleet, wearing his gold chain and whistle like a schoolboy. The council voted unanimously to give him the job. He was the only candidate, surprisingly."

"Surely this is all just posturing?" I scorned. "Scotland is small and impoverished. The King's grip is only firm on half his kingdom."

"Well, I'm sure Lord Dacre knows better than the likes of us. It's his silver that keeps the pot boiling. As for King James, he means it. He will have his place on the stage like his brother-in-law. He burns to sit on the councils of Europe. Both he and King Harry yearn to be bigger fish in a wider pool and in this they cannot remain friends, for each is backing a different horse."

"Is there talk of war – in the council, I mean?"

"None I can detect as yet but King James encourages his privateers: those Barton brothers, as you'll recall, who care not which flag they plunder and are a pain in King Harry's Tudor backside. You understand all about enemies, though, as you've so many of your own. One of them is scarce fifty yards away."

"Sir Robert and I are not friends," I confessed, "nor likely to be."

Dodds looked at me. If I didn't know him better I'd have thought he was concerned. "The warden detests you," he went on, choosing his words with care. "You are notorious; your lawlessness which is your own and not his embarrasses him. Sir Robert is ambitious too. He seeks a place on the council and the King shows him favour. James is a poor judge in many ways and Kerr is a cunning flatterer. He's already got a plum job within the household and will have more. Bringing in your head would serve him well. He's built you up as the bogeyman, so now he needs to bring you down or look the fool."

"Perhaps I should feel honoured?"

"For sure, and if he brings you down, he weakens Dacre. But the one good thing about having enemies is that they have enemies of their own who may become your friends, at least when it suits them. Kerr is but one warden; the other, Lord Hume, hoards his honours as a miser loves gold. Compared with him, Cessford is a mere novice, a parvenu. Hume has held high office since he helped this King get rid of the last and he won't let James forget that. His power is here, on the marches. Kerr is also on the marches so he's a threat and Dacre pays and plays with them all."

Outside, the sounds of the fair continued, like some distant fairy tale. It wasn't, of course; half the men present had blood on their hands and most of the rest were thinking about it. I could hear my two fellows muttering, cadences wafting on the fitful breeze.

This was a hint that I was due to disburse some of the English warden's silver, though even the satisfying clink of coin achieved no visible cheering of Dodds' demeanour. "I think it's time I thought of retirement," he confided. "If I was you I'd be doing the same."

When I stepped outside the booth, the surgeon's queue of sufferers had evaporated, replaced by a burly half dozen, none of whom needed medical attention and all in Kerr livery. Sir Robert himself, warden of the Scottish March, in finest slashed jerkin and silken hose, stood at their head. My two men looked nervous. In all probability so did I. We had cause. This man was dangerous and breaking the truce was apparently a matter of no consequence.

"Heron," he began, "the Bastard." He and his affinity moved like well-oiled harness, supple, smooth, and all joined up. None had been chosen for his looks or wit. Nothing about them shone but their weapons, which included a brace of Jeddart staffs and a very handy looking two-hander. I and my team carried cross-hilts and bucklers.

"Thief, murderer, and outlaw," the Scottish warden continued, all conversational but his hard, narrow eyes weren't smiling. A big man, Cessford, easily my size and height, a good few years my senior, inclined to paunchiness but still strong as an ox. He'd go for heft and bulk, not finesse; he'd a few jars on board but not enough to affect his moves.

"Scum of the marches" – he was warming to his sermon – "you've emptied barns and byres, left widows and orphans across Teviotdale, yet you dare show your tinker's face at my court."

23

"Not all true," I replied. "I have never struck a woman or child. I've killed a few Scotsmen, of course, but all in fair fight."

"Do you imagine you can parade yourself here, dressed up like a bishop's catamite, and simply strut around, thumbing your nose at my justice?"

"Justice?" I queried, just the hint of a sneer. "I'm not sure your lordship would be too well acquainted with justice. Extortion, murder, thievery and so forth, yes, but not what any, other than you of course, might describe as justice."

The man had a narrow face, a particularly sly breed of malevolent fox, red-headed, with ginger stubble above the pallor of his flesh; I knew I'd have disliked him whatever the circumstances. The feeling was clearly mutual. He was arrogant, savage, and ill-tempered, so sure of his position and sure of the moss-troopers at his back – three to our one at best. It's not always the odds that matter, though; it's how you use the ground. The trampled space was narrow, hemmed by the tawdry booths and straggling guys.

"Damn your insolence," he retorted. "You are my prisoner. See how fast your tongue wags when you're kicking air."

"Need I remind your lordship," drawing out the word, "this is a day of truce? Everyone here is inviolate. You have no bill filed against me or any of my company. I ride with the English warden and insist upon your courtesy."

"Insist? You piece of filth – I'll spill your thieving guts. Give up your swords. Now."

"Come and take them," I suggested, "if you have the nerve for it... if you are not the bag of wind and water I take you for." I heard Lilburn exhale slowly behind me. He was never that bright but he recognized Rubicon as we

24

crossed over. Cessford must draw or withdraw. Neither necessarily appealed. He had relied upon surprise backed by odds. Now we had stalemate, a stand-off. What he proposed was a gross breach of marcher law, even by local flexible standards.

"What the devil is going on here?" Lord Dacre, my brother Will, and a posse of others had arrived, Tynedale men mostly. The odds had just shifted. "Sir Robert?" enquired the English warden, all politeness but with an edge. Cessford boiled, thwarted. "This man, my lord, this Bastard, whom you see fit to shelter, must answer for his crimes."

The English warden seemed to ponder. "Master Heron is not called to answer any charges today, though, is he, Sir Robert? I will advise you that he rides in my company as land-sergeant." This sudden appointment was news to me but afforded some measure of respectability.

"Sergeant!" the Scotsman sneered. "Since when do honest wardens employ gaol-scum?"

"Not infrequently, sir, judging by your own affinity." This drew a laugh and, true enough, Kerr's company were notorious. There's a certain pleasure to be had in goading a bully when he's wrong-footed, though you've really got to be careful you don't push it too far.

"The Scotch warden," I advised loudly to all and sundry, "favoured the odds but a moment ago, come like an assassin in the night, but now it seems his ardour has cooled or perhaps he's less the hero than he'd have us imagine." This went down well, with the English at least. Poor Will went a whiter shade and Dacre a tinge redder. "That will suffice, Master Heron," he chided. Cessford was proper mad, fighting mad. His retreat option had just evaporated.

"This man has insulted me," he exploded, his rodent face as puce as his beard. "I will be satisfied."

"Come, Sir Robert," warned Dacre. "This is foolish and unseemly. Gentlemen in high office do not brawl like broken men. We'll have no feuding at the truce."

"Truce be damned!" he screamed, spittle flying. "Draw that blade!"

I obliged, feeling the steel slide clear, bright with lanolin from the wool lining.

Lord Dacre gave an eloquent shrug, his duty of moderation discharged. Will put his head in his hands. All the Tynedale men brightened visibly. Here was rare sport on a day of alleged amity. Money was already changing hands. I hoped I might carry the better odds. The space around Sir Robert Kerr and me cleared as though by alchemy. We stripped off jerkin and doublet to avoid constriction and fought in bare sarks: a chill, after all, was the least of anybody's worries.

Now a brawl may be murder but duelling is gentlemen's business. Daft, you'll think, and maybe it is. Our raids and forays provide ample scope for getting yourself killed. But there is kudos in the affair of honour, intoxication in the red shift. Blood flows like fire in your veins and the colours all around glow as never before. Spring grass shone green and the brightening sky a deeper blue.

"Vermin," my opponent hissed. Sir Robert Kerr was not a clever man but slippery as an eel and brave enough, heaving with fury. Left or, as we say, Kerr-handed as well, which confers advantage in scrapping. Two of his affinity acted as seconds, Lilburn and Starhead for me. I'm not sure if either knew quite what they were getting into.

Enemies were the one commodity I already possessed in impressive numbers, but this was different. If I killed Kerr – and only one of us would be leaving the stage alive today – then my entire name was at feud with all of his.

Kerrs were very numerous and possessed of very long memories. Poor Will had a right to look depressed. He was at feud with a few names already, thanks to me, but the Kerrs were in an altogether different league. Vengeance to them was religion.

We'd fight with sword and buckler. I took guard, right leg thrown back, blade low and to the left, buckler covering sword arm. His stance was similar. No fanfare or fine sentiments ever preceded a borderers' fight. We had so many; there was neither time nor inclination. I moved first, cutting upwards under my opponent's wrists, shifting grip and springing forwards. He simply stepped back then thrust, venomously swift, aiming for my belly. My turn to step back, parrying with buckler. Clang of steel on steel.

Blades touched again and broke off. Together they made six feet of honed death, controlled by mass of muscle, sinew and nerve, tight as a bowstring. We beat lightly, a dancer's step, flicked away and drew back, his slime-green eyes on mine. We both wore horseman's boots, supple and tied tight; nails gave grip.

Around us the crowd, half-glimpsed, milled and shifted, mutterings on form, shouting odds. I gathered I was ahead, guaranteed to goad my mad bull opponent even more. Fine by me; mad is careless and careless is dead. My turn to swipe at the fat Scotsman's gut, but he skittered back out of reach. I came on, aiming for his lumpen head, pivoting on my left. He side stepped also to the left, and took my blade on sloping parry. The swords scraped and parted.

Overhead a curlew called out its plaintive serenade, oblivious to the madness below.

He was quick, far quicker than his bulk suggested, tremendous power in his blows, like trying to block a falling oak. That was his style: use weight and force to batter an opponent. He turned his parry into another belly-slash, forcing me back on my right, weapons high, balance and protection. This saved losing an arm, though his point flicked blood from mine. A glancing cut, no damage to muscle.

I sprang back fast and low. Keep this ox on his toes and make the idiot sweat, wearing him out. He parried downwards, left leg back, blade down. We closed and he sought to rearrange my features with his pommel, tensing his right leg for the lunge. I beat him back with buckler. Sweat coursed from us in rivulets. We steamed like destriers.

No respite for Sir Robert. I lunged hard, opening a distance, and sent him scattering back.

Swords grew heavier, muscles of wrist and arm knotting against the strain. Bucklers provided play of their own, battering in fast beats. I feinted, he parried too close and I stabbed down into his thigh. He grunted with pain, blood on his fine hose – just a prick though.

"Finish him!" someone exhorted, though to which of us I couldn't tell. Men truly enjoy another's agonies, I find. One of us would die today but there'd be some revels at the wake. It is always the way. He came back, grunting, knuckles up, passing right. I moved left for a circular parry. He'd be sweating harder than me. This killing business is tiring, both of us heaving like blown nags.

This last parry, delivered with as much force as I could muster, spun him round so I could plant his kidneys with rammed buckler. He arched back, swung around, too slow – too damn slow by far – and I lunged straight for his hanging face, taking out one astonished eye and driving clean through bone and brain to burst out through the back in a pleasing shower of bright red.

Sir Robert Kerr of Cessford puked his breakfast, and a good one too, over the new green grass, thrashed like a landed fish, and passed ingloriously into history. It was, arguably, my finest kill to date and I was well proud. To judge by the cheers, my exertions had brought profit for some.

"Get him out of here and be right quick about it." I recognized the voice of the English warden. "Make yourselves scarce, the lot of you, and you too" (this to my half-brother). "Stop gawping like an idiot and get your disreputable sibling on a horse, preferably a fast one."

The rage of the Kerrs beat like a wave. The dead man's affinity howled like dogs – as well they might as I'd just deprived them of gainful employment. Foaming, they looked around for Liddesdale men to back them but saw none. The late warden was no more popular there, and besides, I had some understanding with the riding names.

Marjorie had appeared as efficiently as ever – first aid was a speciality – and was fussing with my sleeve; Cessford's cut had bled more than I'd realized. As the red mist receded, it began to hurt, rather a lot. Will looked fit to weep, yet his beautiful wife looked rather bored by the whole business. I had hoped for a warmer reaction.

"There'll be the devil to pay for this," Will half moaned. He wasn't wrong.

Autumn: at sea. Thomas Howard writes his report to Thomas Wolsey

Most Reverend Sir; firstly my greetings and our hearty congratulations on your recent elevation. It falls to me to report an action at sea, here off the Downs, scarce two days gone, which I humbly beg you may relate to His Majesty and to the council. *The weather was vile, high seas and wind, but the lord admiral and I, engaged upon the fatiguing business of our patrolling, he with his flag on* Barbara *and I in* Mary Barking *did, by chance as it would seem, come up upon two Scotch vessels –* Lion *and* Jennet, *in press of sail and weight of shot our marked inferiors.*

The former we knew to carry Andrew Barton, that most notorious of pirates who has, these many years, preyed upon His Majesty's shipping. They would outrun us, hoping that high seas, strong winds, and fog might give them succour. Swift as hounds we gave chase. A hard-run quarry it was, great crashing waves that seemed ready, by the minute, to engulf us utterly, hampering both hunters and hunted. Our two English vessels became separated in the squall and I, in my smaller carrack, engaged the lesser Jennet *whilst my lord admiral closed with* Lion.

Broadsides thundered over the darkening waters, round-shot crashing. The Scotchman, against whom we were opposed, soon struck and we took possession of her. This Barton, in the larger, would make a fight of it. With the waves riding so high, there was little that longer range gunnery could achieve and the two bigger vessels closed to grapple and board. Barton directed his men with élan. One of his singular tactics was to unleash a heavy boulder or weight from the yard arm to come crashing down onto and through an enemy deck.

My lord admiral, alert to his peril, detailed his most efficient archers to shoot any Scot seeking to clamber up and release this great weight. Two brave Scots tumbled to the bloodied decks before Barton, who had the benefit of harness, refused to sacrifice more sailors and attempted the job himself. A first shaft glanced harmlessly from plate and it seemed the day might yet be his, but a second, well-aimed point shot under the arm, sending that notorious pirate plummeting down upon his own deck, mortally wounded.

Facing death, his courage, we grant, did not waver, urging his men on to continue the fight for as long as he had breath. Once their captain had expired, however, the rest swiftly became dispirited and hauled down their colours. In short, I am pleased to report that the day was ours and I wished my lord admiral joy of his great victory. Both of the Scottish sail are safe, the lesser of a hundred and fifty tons' burthen; the greater, double that, the whole valued at near six hundred pounds and more.

I hope I may have the honour to remain, etc...

Chapter Two: Rumours of War

A prince should avoid ever joining forces with one more powerful than himself against others unless necessity compels it... for you remain his prisoner if you win, and princes should avoid, as much as possible, being left at the mercy of others.

Machiavelli: *The Prince*

The prioress writes to Bishop Elphinstone

Your lordship will understand with what trepidation I enter upon this correspondence, as the drumbeat seems to roll all around us. Here, in my House of Coldstream, the women continue with their daily offices and chores and every hour we pray that God may yet preserve the peace between these our two realms.

Yesterday, some little time after Terce, a messenger arrived from Lord Hume intimating that he fears His Majesty is determined upon war with England. In God's name, why? We have been at peace these ten years and more, and though I was but a girl last time the armies marched, I remember the smell of burnt thatch, remember the scenes of ragged hostages dragged back over the ford here, beaten, chained, and abused. Are we not all God's creatures?

Why can we never learn from all the horrors of the past? The women here in this my House petition me daily for their safety. I wonder what it is I will have to say to them or to their naked corpses when the armies again pass by. Your lordship knows well how men in war become ungovernable and how furious the heated blood runs after battle, so that they may commit any manner of excess.

I am fearful, I do confess, and heartily beg your lordship that you will do all within your power, for I know well how the King values your wise and temperate counsel. Be then our shepherd and our shield; only your strength and wisdom can save us from this tempest. Forgive me when I say I begin to believe God has abandoned us here on this frontier.

Your most humble and loving daughter, etc.

Lord Hume speaks in the council chamber

"Rank folly, rank and *utter* folly, ill-thought, ill-advised, and ill-judged." Angus, his heavy four-square frame stiff in the high-backed chair, powerful forearms braced on the table, spoke with force. Though he also talked calmly, the wildness of that Douglas blood was in his eyes. Some of the younger lords sniggered. Dolts; they had not seen this old man in the vigour of his youth. He looked at me. They all looked at me.

The King's council comprised most of the great lords of the realm. I was chancellor and thus senior statesman, a position far less secure than the description implies. Angus and Bishop Elphinstone represented what was disparagingly the "Peace" Party. Those who preferred subtlety to suicide were not fashionable that summer. Those younger lords – Argyll and Lennox from the west, hotheads like Hepburn, King's favourite and Earl of Bothwell – dreamed of glory and gain. Errol, Crawford and Montrose were with them if for no other reason than they lacked the will to oppose.

"My Lord of Angus is wise to counsel caution," I replied disingenuously. The King had listened to the old man's tirade calmly enough but I could sense his petulance. Dissenters were not welcome at the council table. "Yet, we must carefully consider all of the available options." Some other idiot tittered, that upstart Hepburn. "His Majesty has led our armies right well in past campaigns," I began diplomatically. "Our French allies call for assistance..."

"... and we all know where that got us," Douglas interjected. "Our backsides kicked." All true, but our King would have his war and courtiers need have a care.

"We learn from our mistakes," I replied (and fervently hoped). "His Majesty carefully weighs all matters." Not true, of course: James was as intent upon war as upon life. He was in thrall to the idea of war. Yet this King was no fool. The lessons of the past were not wholly lost upon him – some of them at least.

Light slanted through high lancets, throwing shafts across polished boards. The King sat as though the glow gilded his presence. King James IV was a man of average height, well proportioned, outwardly amiable, and with a fine cascade of red hair to his shoulders. He was also narrow, vain, and impetuous, though – thank God – free of his father's vice. Quite the opposite: his appetite for women seemed insatiable; but at least the stable-boys slept easy.

"Our Brother of England," the King began, "continues to treat us with contempt. He withholds the Queen's inheritance, her rightful portion. He refuses to offer compensation for the killing, the murder, of Andrew Barton and, worst of all, he instructs Dacre to give shelter to that murdering thief, Bastard Heron."

"Bad enough, I grant you," Angus retorted. "Annoying to be sure and in need of remedy, but Your Majesty will allow me to point out that the new Pope continues the policy of the old. He favours the Emperor's quarrel and threatens excommunication to those who support France." This was potent indeed. If James invaded England he declared war on the Holy League and thus upon Rome. Excommunication would be inevitable. Not even kings can ignore the power that emanates from St Peter's throne. The King remained calm but I could sense a storm brewing, a right royal tempest. "Why, even the Queen..." Douglas ploughed on.

"Our Queen," James exploded, colour rising to his face, "does not sit on this council." He was never a man who could master passion. "Nor does she dictate policy. It is the very future of our sovereign state at issue here, Scotland's place in the councils of Europe. This has long been denied us and it is this for which I have striven these last twenty years and more."

Nobody could deny the King's right to govern. For a quarter-century since the necessary disposal of his pederast parent, he had ruled both wisely and well. The nation was stronger now than before, less divided. We had prosperity, mighty ships and trade. In this martial obsession, James was sailing into uncharted waters, or rather, waters we'd foundered in so often before.

"What do your spies tell you?" He shot the question at me.

I've always held that the truth is such a rare and precious thing. It should never be given away lightly, but this was perhaps one of those occasions. "My people tell me that Dacre is on full alert and that no northern men will stir for France. King Henry thinks little of any threat but he won't ignore the basics. He won't leave by the front door whilst the back gate is open."

The King waved a dismissive hand. "Henry will strip England to build his army. He means to astound the Emperor and cow our French allies. He'll take every man with harness and every gun he can find. He knows little of matters in the north and cares less." This was wishful thinking. No king of England, however heartily he despises the Scots, will leave his frontier exposed. We'd tried that one many times before and failed. The ghosts of thousands of our Scottish spearmen could have told us why.

"Besides," James continued, warming to his theme, "whoever we face will only have bows and bills, a handful of guns, no more. We have the finest artillery in Europe and our men will be trained for once, properly trained with pikes. The French are sending us their specialists."

This wasn't good. Happily, Angus said it for me. "Bows and bills, Your Majesty, have sufficed often enough before. The Swiss with their pikes win battles, I grant you, but they've not faced longbows, and those bows have slaughtered our spears on a dozen fields."

James's limited store of patience was exhausted. "Do you imagine I've not considered that? Do you not recall how I have made fresh armour for our men? I will drill them and drill them and drill them till they can march as hard and strike as hard as any poxy Swiss. We will, if we fight, wage modern war with modern tactics. The English are complacent and they're out of time."

On paper this was all good. It was only when these ideas brushed up against reality they came unstuck. I felt that Douglas needed a respite. The posturing of these young hawks, un-bearded, un-blooded, and clueless, was becoming irritating.

"Your Majesty has made great study of the arts of war and has taken great strides in arming the nation, but" (and here it got tricky) "our men, dragged from the plough or the apprentice's bench, are not the Swiss. We do not pay them; they are conscripted. The Swiss fight only for wages. War is their trade. In the time we have, we cannot drill our men sufficiently. The Swiss take years to train their fellows. Their captains are all seasoned professionals and they'll cheerfully hang any loon who doesn't make the grade."

James slammed the boards. "As I already told you, I'm bringing in experts from France. Our men are taught to fight with the spear. It's not such a big jump to the pike. We can do this. We can field the finest army ever to leave Scotland. We can do what we have to for our allies and *still* have no need to fight. I make our men ready to fight if we must, not just because we choose. We cannot fail. We shall not fail."

As epitaphs go, that's not bad. The sycophants cheered and banged the table like a second rate bunch of mummers. Douglas scowled darkly and Bishop Elphinstone shifted uneasily. Clergy are paid to be pious, of course, and to lament any shedding of Christian blood, but the bishop had been around long enough to share all of Angus's doubts. My own were deep enough.

"You choose to forget," the King strode on, "that we've been down this road before. We fought in '96, again in '97, and came safe home."

This was right enough. "Indeed so," I replied smoothly. "Your Majesty conducted two masterly campaigns. Even now the damage we wrought is only half repaired and Your Majesty most wisely avoided battle."

I like "avoided battle"; it sounds so much better than "ran away". The King had postured with that preposterous pretender Warbeck, though they soon fell out, burnt a few roofs, emptied some byres, and slit the odd throat. This might all be fine sport but it achieved nothing.

"Does Your Majesty intend to besiege Berwick?" I asked.

The King shrugged. "We need to be flexible."

This meant he had no plan. If we didn't want Berwick back then what was the point of crossing the line in strength? I caught old Douglas's eye. We both remembered Berwick. Back in '82, when I'd been as green as most of my fellow councillors, I'd followed Angus when he set about straightening out our Scottish polity. He was a younger man then, full of strength and fire.

Our last King, this one's father – a precious, decadent fool – had, six years before his final disaster, dragged his whole sorry entourage to war. This comprised a painted circus of musicians, actors, painters, and pretty boys – His Majesty's entire crop of catamites. Chief amongst them was Cochrane, the King's architect and bedfellow, self-appointed chancellor who'd near ruined us all with his incompetence.

Douglas had led us, flaming torches high, into the brothel that passed for a royal pavilion. We took them all, every one, James screaming and foaming in his degenerate rage. Cochrane, full of drink, sneered as I dragged him to his feet. "Oh, a proper gentleman," he spat at me. I battered his head off the post for long enough till he was shrieking through broken teeth, gibbering in a froth of his own blood. It felt good; can't pretend otherwise. For far too long these degenerates had laughed at us, the gentry, Scotland's backbone, and tonight we'd had enough.

Weeping and mewing we took them out, impotent James ringing curses down on us. Our army had plenty of rope if little else and Lauder Bridge was near. That was where we hanged them. We threw each over the parapet till the rope bit hard and they jerked in their final dance, kicking the air till it was done. A good night's work, cleansing court and nation; we marched no further, mind you, and Berwick was lost. Playing kingmaker as I did later, during that final crisis, has its attractions, but the plain fact is kings do not much care for kingmakers. What is made can always be unmade.

I took a good look around the table. It was pleasantly warm and no fire was laid in the grate. Dust cones hovered in the bright, empowering light. "My lords," I began and they had to listen. I was still chancellor and the King's first minister, Warden of the Marches and shield of the borders. That all counted for something, hopefully. "England will not be unprepared. I doubt the King will take a man from north of the Trent to France. If we march we will face the whole power of the northern lords. We know these people. They do not fear us."

"Yes, yes, Alec, we've debated all this," the King exhaled. "After all, the Earl of Angus has told us often enough." More guffaws. I kept going.

"Why should they be frightened of us? Their fathers, grandfathers, and great-grandfathers beat ours. We have never matched their English bows. Times change, I know. His Majesty has made provision. We have a fine train and our allies to instruct us. We must weigh the advantages carefully in the balance. If we win, then what do we win? If we lose, we will lose badly. Our French allies use us at their convenience. To pin the northern English to their marches for a season, they'd cheerfully sacrifice Scotland."

The King gazed pointedly skyward but I wasn't quite done. "The King of England will appoint the Earl of Surrey to lead…"

"Ha, that old cripple… it'll take him a month to get this far." This from Bothwell, provoking more laughter.

"That old man," I advised him, "has seen more of war than most around this table combined. He will have his Howard affinity and his son the lord admiral with him, which means marines from the fleet, battle-hardened. The northerners may still cleave to their bows and bills, but they know how to use 'em. He will have Dacre, who certainly knows a thing or two, and the Stanleys. He'll have Heron and every free lance on the marches. It won't be a pushover."

"Bastard Heron!" the king snapped back. "That insolent cretin and his boss Dacre laugh at my demands. Every day the English break the so-called truce, such as it is. Heron murdered my own warden in broad daylight and still no redress." James set great store by petty insults. Yes, Heron killed Kerr but in a fair fight, and, let's face it, nobody was going to miss the fellow – grasping, greedy, uncouth parvenu. If I'd been there I'd have slipped the Englishman a purse.

"That same Thomas Howard," he continued, warming to his theme, "killed Andrew Barton; no redress for that crime either." I thought it best not to point out this Barton was a mere pirate and a reckless one at that. Retribution was a hazard of his game.

"I'm obliged to my lords for their full and frank opinions, but I believe the council is now agreed and we will commence preparations, send out our commissioners to begin raising the levies and so forth."

We were going to war. It was decided.

Bishop Elphinstone writes to Isabella Hoppringle

My dear daughter – for as you are ever my daughter in Christ, yet have I always looked upon you as my earthly child – God has endowed you with intelligence, sound sense, and beauty as well. I might perhaps fret as old men do that you have not found a husband but you are a true shepherdess to your flock. Your strength and resolve will be needed in the times to come, for King and council seem determined upon war.

King James remains deaf to reason and entreaties; I fear the business will go very badly indeed. That fragile peace which has endured since the late treaty was signed hangs now by a gossamer thread. This new Harry is a very different man from his father, full of vainglory and bombast, and would intermeddle with the wars of Europe. James is of like mind – both desperate to strut upon a wider stage. The bounds of their kingdoms are not, it seems, sufficient. For these last five and twenty years our sovereign lord has been a good king to us. He has brought law and order where there was none before. There is much prosperity. He has built fine ships that can rival any that float upon the seas.

Yet now it seems he will put all to hazard in this game of princes and courtiers. Much of it is mere puff and posture, but the armourers toil all through the darkness. The King has many new and fine great guns and he would wish them to have employment. Our fickle allies, who would take us up and put us down at their pleasure, pour

flattery into his ear. The Queen of France bids him
be her faithful champion. Her husband sends gold
and munitions. Be assured I shall labour with all
my strength to prevent this cataclysm and shall
ever remember you in my prayers.

Your most loving and affectionate, etc...

Bastard Heron takes his ease

My sister-in-law has flawless skin, texture of silk, cool and sculpted as marble. The halo of her golden hair was spread over fine velvet cushions. Not mine, to be sure; her husband's. I couldn't run to such fine fabrics. Will was away, far away, and for some time I guessed, banged up in that god-awful tower of Fast – a gaunt, unearthly fist of stone rising sheer from the cold North Sea so many feet below. Even I felt the odd twinge of guilt.

"Do you ever feel remorse?" she asked me, half drowsy like a cat, always ready to spring to full alertness. I didn't understand the woman – part of the reason I was so infatuated.

"I should… sometimes I almost do, like I'm sometimes ashamed I'm such a poor husband. I seem to get over the feelings pretty quickly though."

"I'd noticed," she replied dryly.

Her voice was soft and rather low so that sometimes you had to strain to hear her. Not that she had any trouble in retaining an audience. If they were male, they were generally slobbering. Her solar, or rather my half-brother's solar, was well appointed. Tapestries lined ashlar walls. There was light and the smells were fresh.

"Will has written to me again. His writing gets worse. The place is fearfully damp and he says he cannot be free of a biting cough and the sweats."

Well, I'd got rather used to the lordly life but I pitied any man incarcerated in Fast Castle – place was as good as a death sentence. "I'll speak to the warden," I offered. "Truly I will. He had no choice but to give Will up as a hostage for my good behaviour."

"Good behaviour? Your idea of good behaviour is if you haven't killed anybody in the last hour, or robbed them, or had their wife, or any combination of those. Dacre just needs you more is all. He'd give up his grandmother if it helped his politicking. I want my husband back or at least somewhere comfortable. He'll die if we leave him there. You've seen the place. You told me how bad it was and it's all your fault."

All true and no arguing – not that there was ever any point in arguing with Elizabeth. Beneath her cool demeanour she had the haughtiness of an empress and the fire of a tigress. No wonder I loved her. Besides, though my jealousy ate like a pestilence, Will had never done me any harm. Quite the opposite: he'd used his position and influence as a shield. At the end of the day blood, or even half blood, has to count for something.

Because I was in love with her, I told her the truth or near enough. "Will might be better off – not where he is but in safe custody. War is coming; I can sense it. Death and I are old friends. We know each other's ways. King James will likely invade us as King Henry goes to France. Dacre's convinced of it. He's eyes and ears like a fox and they're everywhere. The French are paying for the whole show and James is spoiling for a fight. He's enough big guns to storm Olympus and is just itching to try 'em out."

"Will he attack us here?"

"Depends... He might – this is on one of their favoured routes – or he may just strike at Berwick. Back in '97 he had a crack at Norham, and Old Surrey saw him off. If he has another go now and takes the place, then this area's wide open. I'm suggesting you pack up everything of value, including yourself and your daughter, then head south. Plenty of places you can go. We'll garrison the fort, but, if push comes to shove, I doubt it could be held for long."

She sat up, languor completely banished. "I'd hoped we'd seen the last of this. Whatever happened to 'Perpetual Peace'? Oh, let me guess, somebody keeps breaking the truce and killing Scottish wardens." I assumed she was referring to me; best to make no comment.

"I'm not that important, nor was Kerr. Hume hated the wretched fellow as much as me. So did Dacre. This is all about politics. Henry and James are like two terriers snapping in a cage. Let's see who can bark loudest. King Harry will have his day in France, which means King James must have his day here. On the marches, we've drawn the short straw as usual."

My sister-in-law turned her fathomless blue eyes on me, dusting a tendril of hair away. "What will you do, Johnny?" she asked softly. "What will the famous Bastard Heron do?"

"He'll fight," I answered, "like he always does. He doesn't know any better and there are those who will be depending on him."

"I depend on him," she confided and I so wanted to believe her. "So you'd better damn well come back."

The Dean of Westminster writes to Wolsey

My Lord Bishop,

I write, yet again, to report on the frustrations of this mission which His Majesty has entrusted to me and in regard to which His Grace may, as ever, be assured of my utmost best endeavours. Yet these Scots do frustrate and vex me to a degree which becomes daily more intolerable nor, despite all prodigies of effort, do I make progress. They are indeed a barbarous race, their miserable land at the edge of the world, their speech unintelligible, dress outlandish, manners boorish, and demeanour generally threatening. Daily must I endure their jibes and insults.

My quarters are verminous. Their food defies description – at best a thin gruel or "porridge" as they call it. Their lives, as it seems, revolve around brawling and drinking. They consume vast quantities of raw spirits and box each other most fearfully for sport. The place is damp and my servants most ill-used. The room where I am forced to sleep is not fit for a dog and I fear much for sickness or being murdered in my bed.

As your lordship well knows, my purpose here is to seek an undertaking from the King of Scots that he will keep the peace whilst His Grace, if it be his pleasure, campaigns in France. You did also charge me with descrying such evidence as I might of the state of preparedness of the Scottish fleet. Perhaps these Scots are not the fools we may think, for I am kept bottled up here at Holyrood, scarce able to walk the streets unescorted.

As for the docks at Leith, these may as well be upon the Barbary Coast for any chance I may find. For the King himself, he puts me off with pretty words and bland assurances. I see him but rarely and he confesses himself much preoccupied

*with affairs of state. When I put to him bluntly,
will he or will he not give me the undertaking His
Majesty seeks, he does but prevaricate. He does
not say he will not give assurance but does not
promise that he shall.*

*He speaks obliquely of the ancient amity
'twixt France and Scotland and that he is much
exercised by our present enmity. I remind him
of the consequence of His Majesty's displeasure
and of that of His Holiness under whose sacred
banner we shall fight. Yet he is so frivolous he
makes light even of this. All he will say is he
would not make war but that his herald shall tell
of it first. What we should make of this I cannot
say and he will not be drawn further.*

*It is all most vexatious. I hope I may, my
lord, before I conclude, draw your lordship's
kind attention to my expenses which are now
somewhat in arrears, though I am sure you will
agree my accounting is most particular and exact
and that, without funds, my people and I shall
come to want even for necessaries, for there is
little to be had in this benighted realm. I hope I
may thus expect your lordship's kind remittance
by return.*

Your most humble and obedient servant, etc...

Heron makes a ride and meets with a friend

Berwick was an odd sort of place: half town, half fortress,
the former bathed in squalor and the latter ragged. Most of
the garrison were near mutinous for want of wages, though
the alehouses were obviously free with credit, judging by
the state of most of them. The place had been the bastion

of power in the eastern marches since Longshanks' day, changing hands more times than a pardoner's promise. It was ours now, for the present anyway. Some repairs were in progress, patching of walls and clearing slime from ditches. My score of riders gawped; Tynedale or Redesdale lads, mostly, who had never seen anywhere as big. They'd mostly never seen a town. Few went much beyond their own uplands, at least not during daylight hours. Workaday warriors, no proud guidons; in my line it's best not to advertise. We wore Jacks and sallets, carried bucklers, blade, and lance, nothing too shiny except along the sharp edges.

Towns smell bad. Berwick was no exception. An uneasy place; the necks of far too many Scotch and more than a few English had felt the hangman's embrace hereabouts. They were stretching a few in the market place as we walked the horses by; always draws a good crowd. One of them, a Bourne I recall, made a decent job of it and went off with a flourish. This always goes down well. The rest gibbered and wept, poor sport at best.

The castle stands outside the walls towards the north-east quadrant – great battered sprawl of a place, but there was fresh lime and some new stonework as well. Sir George Lisle was castellan that year, a mean and devious sort of fellow. He'd a shock of black hair and eyes of a buzzard, manner and bearing of a gentleman but something wary about him, not quite right you might say, something of the night. Had a decent reputation, mind you, but he plainly didn't care for half-gentlemen. Still his wine was tolerable.

"What's Dacre up to?" We didn't do much small talk.

"Well, pretty much as usual," I replied. "Keeping an eye on things, putting some stick about."

"I'm sure, but what does he *know*?"

"He knows that the marches are stirring – the Scots are straining at the leash, some of 'em anyway, and that King James wants to be a player on a rather wider stage."

"What about him?" He jerked his head northward so he was plainly thinking of the Scottish warden. "What's that old jackal thinking? He's a fox, just like Dacre, come to think of it, and don't tell me they don't talk. Otherwise you'd not be here."

"I hope I might find out," I responded, "but Hume never gives away more than he has to."

"Perhaps the good prioress will know a bit more. I won't ask but I assume you're heading upriver towards Coldstream. I've warned my watchers not to watch too hard and I guess he's done the same. I'd have a care though, Master Heron: your old friends, the Kerrs, have eyes and ears everywhere. I trust my own men to be totally untrustworthy."

Ah, the Kerrs and their blood feud. When you kill someone from another name, fair fight or otherwise, the rest are out to get you, simple as that: now and forever. The Kerrs were good at this. They'd had generations of practice. I was currently top of their "must-kill" list. I suppose it was an honour of sorts. After I'd dealt with Sir Robert, I'd advised my two seconds to stick close. They hadn't: they'd panicked and run. You can't outrun a blood feud and the Kerrs had found them both – their heads, that is.

We rode out at Prime, the rising sun coming up over a cold grey sea, dull as gunmetal. Once over the line, across the border, all our heads were in the same noose. I wasn't that popular on our side. Over there I was the devil incarnate. We moved quietly and quickly, half a dozen out in front or on the flanks, another handful some way back. Naturally, we stuck to the English side of the water, taking a straight course south-west.

Dodging those sweeping bends in the Tweed, where the brown, foaming river flows by Horncliffe and towards Norham, brought us to the old queen of border fortresses before dinnertime. The place has a long history and had seen off the Scots for most of it. King James had had a go back in '97 and it had to be high in his priorities this time around. We took our rations in the saddle, washed down with a dram, then pressed on for half a dozen miles to Coldstream. By Sext the place was in sight.

The priory is a substantial affair – Cistercian, if I'm right – church, chapterhouse, and cloister all nestled next to the prioress's most comfortable lodgings. The site could boast a sprawling range of ancillary buildings – guesthouse, impressive kitchens, brew house, bakery, and malt kiln – surrounded by ancient burial grounds, orchard, and barns. It looked prosperous and it was, with wide holdings on both sides of the line. Mellowed and permanent, the place had always been rich enough to attract the wrong sort of attention. Like Berwick, the masonry had been patched, bodged, and re-bodged.

Isabella Hoppringle was prioress. In her case this was a lay office, a political rather than religious appointment, so normal fashion restrictions did not apply. She greeted us at the gate, which was cordial and also a means of pointing out she had watchers too. She was of the slender, willowy sort, though it's hard to tell in a wide gown with those overblown trumpet sleeves. Her age I'd have put at perhaps thirty, give or take. She had fair and perfect skin with a mass of dark curls, well hidden beneath one of those vast hoods that look like a church tower on the move.

We dined in her private hall, clean and well appointed, fine ware and silver much in evidence. There are times when a life of piety and abstinence has much to recommend it. My company fed in the kitchens. They weren't a bad lot but you wouldn't let them near anywhere that had glass in the windows. Besides, what was said was not for their ears.

"Tell me about King James," I prompted.

She laughed at that; good teeth, white and even, and rather fine dark eyes, the sort you could easily lose a regiment in, particularly if you'd had a drink or two. I don't see the need to stint when the liquor's abundant and free.

"His Majesty hates you, Master Heron. You are his very own pet hate and he is impatient with Lord Dacre, who will not give you up."

"Is my brother not good enough for Scottish justice? At least he's from the right side of the blanket."

"The King doesn't like half measures and refuses to be bought off with a pawn when he could have the knight."

"I'm not even a knight," I reminded her, "and I can't see anyone coming forward with the honour anytime soon."

"Perhaps you're more famous than you imagine," she suggested. "How's the wine?"

"Excellent as ever," I replied, and meant it. We were drinking a rich ruby claret. The prioress kept an excellent table and a very fine cellar – better than I could afford by far, even while I was making free with my brother's ample stocks.

Monastic fare, at least what we were eating, ran to rather better than bread and gruel. We had an abundance of fish, mackerel, herring with roast eggs, some really good mutton in verjuice and a rich almond marchpane – plenty of it too. I like to fill up when the opportunity arises. In my business you never know where your next meal is coming from or whether this one is your last.

"Rents still coming in then?" I enquired. "Income holding up?"

"Times are tolerable," she answered with a dry look, "but if our King has his way that may change."

"He plans to make war upon England, then?"

"It would seem so and he will be thorough: a full levy of every able-bodied man, new weapons, new tactics, and lots of big guns. Why can't you men stick to hunting and gaming?"

"Both are admirable pastimes, but war is the test of a prince, or so I imagine King James would say."

"You've been listening to Lord Dacre," she smiled. "He knows the King, of course."

"He does indeed," I confirmed. "I think he quite likes him, for what it's worth. Might I ask what Lord Hume has to say?"

She pushed a thick bundle of correspondence towards me. "That's what he thinks," she continued. "A friendly letter from one friendly warden to another, all in the interests of keeping the peace, naturally."

"Would peace-keeping include details of the Scottish artillery train by any useful chance?"

"It very well might and it's impressive, even I can see that. There won't be a safe fortress in the border. The King's guns alter the whole balance of power, or so the warden thinks, and he'd know."

"What's his first target?"

She shrugged rather elegantly. "I'm not sure, but likely Norham – that's a set of walls the King would very much like to knock down. Most of his ancestors tried and failed."

"He tried and failed," I reminded her.

"So he went home and got bigger and bigger toys. They work too; he's forever blazing away at bits of inoffensive wall. It's not subtle, is it – war I mean – just a stupid game of soldiers?"

"The blood is real enough, trust me; I've seen a fair bit."

"You mean you've spilled a fair bit."

"With me it's business, not the sport of kings, and only when the need arises." Not quite true perhaps but near enough. "I just fight wars; I don't begin them."

"War seems to have kitted you out fairly well, though. For a notorious bandit, you're well turned out; clean fingernails too. You must have a good woman. In fact, I know you have; she must be verging on sainthood."

She knew all about my liaison with Elizabeth and that my improved circumstances were by courtesy of my absent brother, dispatched into purgatory on account of my numerous transgressions. "War is much about reputation," I advised. "It's the same for kings as for commoners; our respective monarchs just need a bigger audience and they've deeper purses."

My fingers were resting on Hume's dispatch, as were hers, and very shapely, strong and tapering they were, certainly not marred by slaving in the fields. I did wonder about Isabella; I liked to think she might wonder about me. I knew this really wasn't the time but there's no harm in speculation.

"I'm not quite sure what's in all of this for Hume, though. If he told me it was raining, I'd go outside and check for myself. He's no cause to love the English."

She had clearly been thinking along similar lines. "Love isn't really a word he uses," she pondered. "He thinks about power, his own, and little else. He thinks how he can maintain his influence and extend it. Beyond that he doesn't care."

"Sounds like someone I could admire, but how does betraying Scotland help him? He's the warden. If his side are beat, we'll be over there faster than hounds, a regular free-for-all."

"That's the point: it's about the balance. That's why he and Dacre have so much in common. Between them, they're the pivot on the marches. If they're level, the balance is maintained."

"And if they're not?"

"Then everything falls apart. Can't you see? If James invades and wins, Scotland is stronger, so he will depend less on the power of the Humes. Our warden is diminished by victory. If your people win, then the Merse, Hume's land, is wasted. So he hedges his bets. He gives information to Dacre so that, if the English win – and you usually do – his ground will escape the flames and the King will need his strong hand on the marches more than ever. Whoever wins, he doesn't lose out. Dacre's in the same position. Help yourself to some more wine."

I did, and she was right. It was as simple as that. Our two grand rulers could wave their silk pennons in the air, but the lord wardens stuck in the real world. They had to. Well, that was fine by me and I'd have to be careful not to take on board too much of the fair prioress's drink.

Across the courtyard a door banged open, noise spilling from the opening, raucous, jarring, and an intrusion on our quiet intimacy. Someone dragged the heavy boards to and the racket was swallowed.

"You'll see Lord Dacre gets those papers," she reminded me. "They're worth their weight in gold." That was true enough. Big guns were the currency of princes. No lord or magnate was safe behind castle walls any more, not as long as the ruler could afford powder and shot. The great fortress of Norham, for all its fame, was not safe.

Now she changed tack, a trick that clever women have. "Do you ever ponder on *your* immortal soul?" she asked. Quite where this came from I couldn't discern. She clearly wasn't one for small talk and I flattered myself she was interested.

"God and I have an arrangement. I don't trouble him and he leaves me alone, most of the time."

"You don't wonder where his will fits into all this? What's the point of it all – nothing but violence and death, despair, hunger, and loss?"

"It's the way of things," I replied cagily; this was not the sort of discussion I was used to having. She was looking at me in that direct way of hers, her bright intelligent eyes on mine. "I'm not sure God really cares. He leaves us to get on with things, to make a mess as we choose. We're good at that."

"And a fearful mess we make," she retorted. "Widows and bairns go hungry. They end their short, miserable, fear-driven spans in want and squalor. God gave you free will, Master Heron; gave you wit and strength, looks, and, yes, a measure of charm."

"Just a shame he didn't furnish my mother with a wedding ring."

"Did she love your father?"

"I believe she did and he did provide..."

"Did you love him?" she pressed on, her dark eyes glowing now. Though she wasn't in holy orders, she was pretty close – otherwise I'd have sent for the Witchfinder. This was getting tricky. I don't get confidential as a rule, but she was compelling and I was in drink to some degree. "Yes," I responded, "I did, and he loved me in his way too. Had to be careful not to show it too much, of course; Will was the son and heir."

"I will pray for you. The nuns here will pray for you and for all who will bear arms in this wretched war you're all so keen on. We'll pray for all the women and children left behind or dragged along, for the hardship, toil, and sorrow they'll endure. Don't lie and tell me you'll do the same." She became silent.

"What will you do?" I prompted her. "When it begins, I mean."

"Sit tight, like we always do, close the doors, and pray rather hard – pray we don't get burnt out. Pray our tenants survive. Pray we're not all raped and slaughtered by whichever army happens to be passing through."

No use pretending these things don't happen; I'd made them happen too often to argue and no point in any gallant offers of protection. She knew the odds too well.

"Stick close to Hume if you can," I advised. "The warden has a genius for survival. If it all goes badly wrong, ride for Ford. The gates will always be open. If they're still standing, that is. If not, make for Berwick. Use my name; use Dacre's for that matter. The warden doesn't forget his debts."

With this helpful advice I and my company took our leave. The afternoon had waxed warm, with just the lightest breeze to ruffle white feathers on the Tweed. Despite the good food and even better drink, I was uneasy. Not with the entrancing prioress – I was almost prepared to trust her – but I'd sensed eyes on us during the morning. Those watchers had had time to report, and Kerrs weren't far away. They never were.

Our return journey to Ford was a handspan of miles and no more. Once over the wide and somnolent Tweed, we'd strike east through Crookham. I still had scouts out ahead but had beefed up the rearguard by thinning the centre; put Crookback Will Robson in charge.

If I hadn't been this careful I would never have made it past puberty.

The ground was level and innocuous with just enough undulation to make it interesting. Crookham was your typical frontier settlement, a huddle of crude huts and bothies with some stronger peles,[3] and a warren of lanes and middens. A few sullen, ragged males greeted us with weary caution. That line between friend and foe is pretty thin up here at the best of times. These were not the best of times.

Our outriders had just topped a shallow rise, lost in dead ground (well named) for an instant, when the ambush was sprung. A mite too soon – I'd have let the vanguard pass first – but no matter. I think I heard, rather than saw, the bolt strike, then a wild cry from one of my scouts and he was down. The rise ahead was suddenly very busy, a ragged line of horsemen, light catching harness, lances poised for business.

The man on my left exhaled and swore, a succinct summary and pretty accurate.

"Lances!" I bellowed. "Close up, stirrup to stirrup, keep going and go in hard!" As tactical briefings go, this was quite limited, but neither fate nor the Kerrs was disposed to allow much more. Our options were also limited. We were too few to stand, too close to run. In such a fix, I'd always go straight at them, keep tight, and rely on heft, bulk, and speed to get you through. I'm not saying it will work but it's probably still best.

More bolts whizzed by. They did no harm. Shooting on the move is near impossible. We crashed into them. One of the Kerrs – I vaguely recognized him, despite the contortions of rage and hate – came for me, lance levelled. I made no attempt to parry, just shifted to let the point pass, straightened, and returned the compliment, my blow

3   A pele is a fortified tower, sometimes referred to as a "bastle".

jarring to the shoulder. The lance snapped off. No matter, the better half had pinned him beneath the arm, driven clear through so he was skewered, bouncing on the turf. One down but plenty more were readily available. At least one of my chaps was in a similar distressed condition but the rest, on both sides, appeared to have come through unscathed.

"Wheel!" I yelled. They were already turning, bunching up. They were quick learners. One of my scouts had come up; no time to worry about the rest. Crookback timed it perfectly, came thundering up as they were half turned. So they milled for a fatal moment while we struck them front and back. More saddles were emptied, the fight breaking up into knots of brawlers, lances giving way to swords. Their leader, nobody I knew, singled me out; ambitious scrapper hefting a very nasty-looking flange mace, sharp as a razor.

He swung fast and very hard, screaming obscenities, foaming spittle. I wasn't sure if that was pure bile or part introduction, but the blades skimmed my jack,[4] sheering off the plates. I rammed my point forward, going in under the rim of harness. He grunted, twisted free, a satisfying spray of blood gushing over his hose – a very nasty wound, I liked to think. He dug spurs and cantered off, bending low over the pommel. The rest followed, streaming away towards the Tweed and safety.

I'd guess the fight lasted a couple of minutes and no more. We had two dead and numerous hurts, none fatal as far as I could see. They left a pleasing quartet behind. We stripped them, took heads, and left the carcasses for the crows. I decided I'd leave the scrap out of my report

---

4   The jack is a padded protective garment with metal plates sewn into an inner lining, to give additional strength.

to the warden. Nothing, I was sure, to do with politics, purely personal.

That's the trouble with reputation.

Chapter Three:
Notes of Preparation

When the Swiss start out to war, they swear a solemn oath that every man who sees one of his comrades desert, or act the coward in battle, will cut him down on the spot, for they believe that courage and persistency of warriors is greater when they, out of fear of death, do not fear death.

Milanese Ambassador to Switzerland 1500–04

Lord Dacre makes his report to the Earl of Surrey

Your Grace will, by now, have received that packet of letters which earlier I sent containing Master Heron's report and correspondence from that Other Party. Whilst John Heron may be a notorious rogue, who presently struts over his half-brother's estate and tups the man's wife, he is nonetheless an Englishman and, in the matters we must now discuss, completely trustworthy. Moreover, he is one marvellously well acquainted with these marches and everything that stirs. The Other is, of course, well placed, rather more so than any we know, to impart such intelligence.

His position is unrivalled and unchallenged. Besides, we have had many such dealings in the past and he has never played me false. Your Grace will readily understand what this does import – that the King of Scots intends to invade His Majesty's realm, as soon as our army is deployed in France. Of this there can be now no doubt. Your Grace has wisely enjoined me to discretion and to make no outward show of preparation for fear we reveal our hand too soon. As Your Grace does well know, I have oft betimes been at cards with the Scottish King. He is a rash and impulsive player, believing he may win because he wills it so and that fortune must surely favour him. Yet these preparations show him to be most thorough. He has considered all the many ills which afflicted his forebears.

Consider this: he turns out harness by the cartload so that his spears may not fear our bows so greatly. His train must count as the mightiest in Europe, near a score of great guns with weight of shot far exceeding that which we have seen before. Master Anislow, Your Grace's captain at Norham, sends me word he is fully victualled and that he is plentifully supplied with powder and shot. He is full of salt and swears the King of Scots may hammer at his gates till Doomsday and not gain admittance. I will tell you truthfully, Your Grace, I am less sanguine by far. Besides, this King does import officers from his French allies who shall daily drill his foot loons in the manner of the Swiss or Almain.

As ever, Your Grace may be assured of my best and most urgent endeavours...

The abbess ponders

I wouldn't have said I was the Queen's confidante. We spoke, she complained a lot to me, believing she had much to complain of. The King always treated her with respect, though he generally took his pleasures elsewhere, like most husbands, it seems. She did feel the need to suggest suitable matches for me. My office does not preclude a marriage alliance. None of them appealed, I freely confess. Whether she just lacked imagination or deliberately sought to demean me I couldn't be sure, but those she nudged were of the solid, scholarly sort or the meaner, mercantile type. Not the kind you'd recommend to your friends. Perhaps she was jealous, perceiving I had position, independence, and remained free of a husband's control.

She would not have considered Master Heron as a contender; then again, not many would. He was dangerous, wild, and *the enemy*, whatever that means. He was also married and conducting a very public liaison with his outstandingly beautiful sister-in-law who, I suspected, wouldn't welcome competition.

I looked in the mirror this morning. While I don't consider myself unduly vain, I'm glad I'm not in orders. The kirtles are purely functional and most of the sisters tend to homeliness – the older ones, that is. We do have a couple of nubile teenagers. The woman I saw was tall with a fairly slender shape, decent carriage. She had a good face. I think I can say that without unseemly smugness – a regular oval with large hazel eyes, good, high, well-defined bones, and a sensitive mouth. She could afford to dress well, so she did.

What I should say now is that she owed her appointment to the crown or, more prosaically, the warden, he being my uncle by marriage and general benefactor. Lord Hume looks out for his own if for no other reason than he builds an affinity to strengthen his hand. He knows I spy for the English and for money. Indeed it was he who suggested it and arranged the whole thing. He does not view this as treason, though a judge might disagree.

Then there's love. It's all very well for poets to drool but I prefer to hang on to the strong-room key. War, though: I can't understand the fatal attraction. I might be hard but I'm not heartless and I hate to see suffering. Life here is hard enough for ordinary folk without having their throats cut. I'm not the warden. My survival to a degree depends upon him, but I still have position, authority. The King never showed much interest in me other than using my house as a convenient diplomatic haven on the marches.

My house of Coldstream wasn't just a religious foundation. I'd negotiated diplomatic status, agreed by both wardens. This suited everyone. It meant my house was respected by both and, on paper, immune from harm. Everyone knows how fragile any such notion is when the guns begin to sound but it is a lot better than nothing and, when your acres straddle the line, it can be the difference between peace and ruin, between life and death.

Thomas Howard writes to his father

Your Grace did kindly enclose the correspondence from Lord Dacre in your letter of the 14th inst. As we know, I have the highest regard for the warden. England never had a truer or more valiant servant. Dacre places much reliance upon Heron for whom I conceive he has some fondness, despite the wildness of his ways. I met this Bastard when last we faced the Scots in the year '97, and whilst his many actions are reprehensible, yet he affects the manner and bearing of a gentleman, is lettered, and devoid of neither wit nor learning.

His intelligence, I feel, may be relied upon, together with that of the Other Party with whom we have had such frequent dealings in the past. Right well do I understand your fears that the manifest malice and jealousy of that schemer Wolsey will deny us our place at His Majesty's side in the forthcoming campaign and that the wretched parvenu means to see us relegated to patrolling the marches. I further and readily comprehend how this might vex Your Grace, who has given a lifetime of loyal service to the crown, to see our family, the noblest blood in the kingdom, supplanted in His Majesty's affections by a lowly upstart.

Do not vex yourself further, for I fancy Your Grace may yet see our banner raised high again when the parvenu overreaches himself, for you know how it lies with the King. He is fickle in his loves and when a person should fail him or disappoint, then shall he be readily cast aside. For every flatterer with His Majesty's ear, a dozen more wait in line behind, all with poignards[5] drawn. This matter of the frontier might yet play to our credit and advantage, for it is sure the Scots would rather fight than the French, and if it be we who beat them well then our star will surely ascend the heavens.

Your most loving and affectionate son...

---

5   A form of thin bladed dagger.

Heron grows reflective

Have you ever looked into a mirror? It's different from a reflection in water. The image is so clear it's as though you look into your own soul. My sister-in-law has a very fine mirror, bought for her by my besotted half-brother. I've never found one near half as good to steal. I wondered about the man I saw. He still has a decent head of dark hair, if inclined to unruliness. In the better light outside, I can discern the odd greying strand. Well, that is to be expected. I am nearer forty than thirty and I think my face more lined, more hollow. Soon, if I live, I will be old. The warden must be the oldest man I know; nearer fifty, I'd hazard.

"You are as vain as a peacock," my sister-in-law observed, mid-summer light catching the tawny perfection of her skin. "It is an obsession with you swashbucklers. You cannot begin killing each other till you're dressed up finer than any princess." I should say here that, in my half-sibling's unavoidable absence, I had assumed full management of the family estates, strictly on a caretaker basis. Marjorie was perfectly competent to run my own rather more modest holding at Crawley.

In part, and as ever, Elizabeth was right. I was wearing a new slashed doublet with just enough colour and style to avoid vulgarity, paid for primarily from my own endeavours but with a welcome contribution from my brother's rents. This reminded me I must earn my keep at Ford.

"I've spoken to Dacre. He has undertaken to speak to Hume and arrange more comfortable quarters for William. The Scottish warden quite likes Will and assures his lordship he will come to no harm. After all he's not the enemy."

"No," she replied, "the malefactor is buying new clothes and looking rather grand. You might at least feel sorry for Will. He is your brother, never did you harm.

Quite the reverse as you know. He interceded more than once when you overstepped the mark, wherever the mark actually is."

"I'm an erring sibling," I confessed, omitting to comment on her own marital failings. "You won't deny me a few moments of luxury, a chance to experience what it's like to be born on the right side of the blanket?"

She shot me a look, the sort that pierces like a lance. "You really understand nothing," she said, in sadness far more than anger. "It is Will who has lived, still lives, in the shadow not you."

Now here was a thunderbolt. "How so?" I queried. "Can't possibly be. He gained everything, I nothing. He has a name, title, lands and," I added quickly, "a beautiful wife."

"Well, you do have a very handsome wife too," she responded, "though you treat her abominably." It seems women always stick together regardless of who is in which bed at any given moment.

"You also have an estate, if less grand. You are the famous Bastard Heron, the marchers' Achilles, ever-valiant, never bested. You have reputation. Most of the gentlemen hereabouts would trade their acres for your name. Besides, Will knows your father loved you best, loved your mother too. That's hard for him. He strove to be the dutiful son – obedient, sober, learned, and respectful. You fought, drank, and fornicated for all England and the old man adored you for it. That's terribly hard for him to bear, worse because he loves you too and you're an ungrateful idiot. You have sons too, whilst I could only provide a daughter."

Elizabeth was crying and I'd never seen that before. I had wit enough to realize that she would not have spoken thus if she did not have some love for me, and I was moved to tenderness by it. That occurs but rarely, so I held her close, stroking the lustrous curtain of her hair, the fine curve of her spine.

I'm not sure where this moment would have led – into even more dangerous waters I suspect – but I suddenly became aware we were observed by my niece, another Elizabeth. Now this young woman was the image of her mother – same colouring, with her height and carriage, a rare beauty.

Seeing her watching us I was suddenly jolted by the fact that my coltish niece was no longer a child. She had undergone that swift, mysterious, and magical transformation into womanhood, thus becoming eligible in the marriage stakes. She had the elder Elizabeth's looks and style but her father's quick intelligence. We had always got along famously and I'd treated her as one of my own. I'd bred so productively that one more hardly seemed to matter. So far she had accepted the fiction that my regular visits here were in the guise of protector rather than usurper and cuckold. That might not endure.

It was near noon, the warming sun climbed high. "Time for dinner," I suggested.

John Heron receives a visitor

Father Thomas Bell, the rector of Corbridge, arrived around Nones, a big, raw-boned ox of a fellow, his habit as scarred and weather-beaten as his face. He used to tell the old tale of Robin-in-the-Hood – always used to delight me as a lad – and his accomplice Friar Tuck. Well, Tom Bell was cast in the same mould and had probably winked at a good deal more mayhem than his legendary predecessor.

Priests, as a rule, were not often seen on the marches, where it had long been thought God had moved out a while back. But there were some, cast in a fairly rugged mould, dirt poor and much abused; half of them unfrocked and the other half illiterate. Tom Bell was of the sterner sort, a learned man and hard enough. He'd knocked down big Geordie Turnbull in Hexham one day when the fellow had sworn at him for seeking alms. Most folk were wary of Geordie but the priest laid him out cold.

"You're a long way from the Tyn, Father," I greeted him. We were old friends. My parents had paid him to mentor me and Will and he'd stuck to the job with stern resolve. I for one had cause to remember the strength of his arm. "Well, laddie, I hear you live in some splendour these days, whilst your poor brother is in a state of some distress."

"Just keeping an eye on the family silver," I parried.

"I'm sure Will sleeps the better for it, if he sleeps at all. I hope Lady Heron is well?" The good father had long since abandoned any hopes of keeping me on the straight and narrow. I knew he'd always liked me. Couldn't see why; observance was not amongst my few virtues.

A priestly vocation in Northumberland necessitated a degree of licence. Those vicars who thrived usually did so at the expense of others' flocks. Though Tom Bell was forbidden by virtue of his cloth to bear sword or lance, he was very handy with a mace. Like most clergy, he lived in a sturdy tower house adjacent to his parish church.

It had rained again and the cleric was mud spattered and sodden, and his palfrey gave an almost audible sigh of relief as he slid from the saddle. His thick, dark hair, which scarcely ever saw the offices of a comb, was shot through with grey and he moved stiffly after the long ride. "Not as young as I was," he confided, "and God's work is never easy." Last time I'd been to Corbridge the rector had found a buxom widow to act as housekeeper and whatever else his calling might require. His pele had often been the objective of Scottish riders, though none had ever succeeded in breaking in. You can't blame 'em really; the place was stuffed full of their silver.

I'd had a fire lit in the great hall, despite the season, though it tended to smoke abominably. A glass of my brother's best claret sufficed to restore the good vicar. "This is better than your usual vinegar," he noted. "I knew my journey wouldn't be wasted." We chatted amiably for a while as politeness demands, but this wasn't likely to be a social call and Tom was far out of his own parish, though parish boundaries did have some degree of fluidity.

"The warden sends his greetings" – Dacre and the rector were deeply entwined – "... and his orders for you. He wants you to step up your patrolling – no provocation, of course; not that you'd ever provoke anyone. Your last correspondence from the fair abbess made most interesting reading."

"She's an interesting woman."

"Aye, lad, and she's far too clever for you. If you think you can add Isabella Hoppringle to your list of conquests, impressive as that may be, you're mistaken."

"I didn't mean in that sense," I clarified. "I meant intriguing, deep. You know."

"I do," he replied. "In many ways an admirable young woman. Born a Scot but that can't be helped. She's more than half decent. Not too bothered about poverty, I suspect, and, as for chastity, I wouldn't like to say. If I did I'd be looking towards that old lecher Hume."

"She asked me about God," I blurted.

"What of it?" he enquired. "High time somebody did. Given your propensities he could be asking you himself any day now."

"I couldn't answer her," I went on. "I felt I'd let her down; that she was looking to me for an answer and I'd no idea. None at all," I added lamely. "I've been fighting for so long I never thought to ask what it's all about. Is this what God intended for me, for us, for her?"

"No good asking me," he replied equably. "I gave up trying to divine God's purpose years ago. But there is a purpose, of that you may be assured. There'll be a time when you answer to a higher authority. Higher even than Bull Dacre or His very high and mighty, far away Majesty. In your case it should be a most interesting conversation.

"Nonetheless," he continued, "you're probably about to embark upon a war, far bigger and likely to be far worse than any you've seen before. Do you ever think that if you believed in God you might be less worried about living and dying? After all, violent death and you are of long acquaintance. What I might hope you would ask is: Is it right? Is this war *just*? I can't pretend I've made you much of a student of morality but I would like to know whether you believe fighting war is right."

"Ah, now you're asking, Father: *Bellum Iustum*, the 'just war'," I translated, just to show his efforts had not been entirely wasted. "If it is, does that get us off the hook?"

"'*What is here required is not a bodily action, but an inward disposition. The sacred seat of virtue is the heart*'," he advised. "Or at least that's what St Augustine tells us. He also tells us that whilst we should not be overly hasty in drawing swords ourselves as *individuals*, God allows us to do so in defence of both church and state. God embodies kingship with virtue and seals the crown with holy oil. If the King declares the war to be just, then so it is, and there is no sin in killing our enemies, and so on and so forth, provided we don't actually enjoy ourselves too much. That wouldn't do at all."

71

"Never that easy," I countered. "If God allows kings to decide when a war is just then what happens when two rulers decide differently? King James is no doubt thinking he's fully justified in having a crack at us, while King Henry reckons we can have a go at the French and the Scotch and presumably still be on the side of the angels."

"Oh, you're right. It's all quite easy in a scriptorium, less so outside. For you and me, and every other Englishman, the fact good King Henry wills it is all we need on the credit side of the ledger. Most Scotsmen will feel the same, of course, but at least we have not begun this war. King James may curse you for a murderer and a villain, but whilst you might have played the one you've never strictly been the other. And that's not why he's raising an army of thirty thousand and plays Lucifer with his diabolical toys.

"This is all about power," he went on, warming to his theme. "About which of these peacocks shall strut across the wider stage, whose vainglory and ambition will carry him into the councils of Europe, who will dine with the Emperor and sup with His Holiness. It surely won't be the likes of us."

"I'm glad you mentioned that," I chimed in. "Isn't it the job of the vicar of Christ to stop Christians killing each other?"

"They do say so, though we see precious little evidence of it. His Holiness feuds with France and sides with Maximilian, as slippery a toad as you'll find. He lavishes praises upon King Henry, who drinks the saucer dry and bleeds the treasury to feed his vanity. He's now excommunicated James so we can truly say we fight for God as well as England, a reassuring thought in itself."

"So God allows King Henry to fall for Rome's blandishments – that same Rome as pits one prince against another and now brings the Scottish plague upon us. Thirty thousand, for God's sake; we can't field a third of those numbers."

"Well, as to that, the King is sending the Howards and Old Surrey will raise the north-land. We may never be as many but I pray we'll be enough." He grimaced here, an eloquent comment on the likely odds. "You worry about your pretty abbess," he said, with a look as near to a leer as befitted a chaplain, "and the plain fact is you cannot help her. If you sweep her off now, gallant knight to the rescue, her countrymen will know she has played them false and she will lose everything. I wish the lass no harm but I hope she and her women are busy at their prayers."

Thomas Howard sees King Henry cross the Channel

A fine evening for the King's great adventure, the waters a sheet of beaten gold, sun like a benediction hanging in the evening sky, still warm with just enough breeze to cool the blood. His Majesty was in full harness, the god of war embodied, even if there wasn't an enemy in sight. Light dazzled from burnished plate so that it was too much for the eye. As circuses go, this was a cracker. I'm not just blowing my own trumpet. Master Wolsey, *Bishop* Wolsey, I should say, sanctimonious little cretin, was making sure I'd have no trumpet to play. No, I want to describe King Henry, ready for a second Agincourt, or so he hoped.

I was on the quarterdeck of *Barbara* and had enjoyed the privilege of transporting His Majesty with certain of his household. This honour owed much to King Henry's fondness for my late brother, dead this past year in the King's service. His badge of lord admiral now hung around my neck. This was as much glory as might be expected, for upstart Wolsey had ensured we, the Howards, would win no glory in France. He poured not so much poison – too clever for that – as doubt into the King's mind, fickle at best. Being left behind would be dressed up as the greater honour. So it was with bitter gall I witnessed the joyous revelry aboard my ship and sour was the wine the King forced upon me.

"Never seen anything like it; this will put the wind up Froggie." This from Maurice Berkeley, one of my best skippers, awed by the vast fleet gathered around us. It was a marvellous sight sure enough, a score and more of heavy carracks, forests of canvas and silk, banners trailing like fireflies, a shoal of pinnaces clustering thick as herring around the great ships.

"The pomp and majesty of England," I replied. "Even the Pope is on our side." Any irony was lost on the good master, so entranced was he by the panoply.

"A sight such as Neptune never saw," he gushed.

Calais, England's mailed foothold in France, was ablaze. Flags and pennons streamed from every house, prosperous streets lined with cheering crowds. Wolsey was never mean with the King's coin. The city is a fat merchant's palace, adorned with fine buildings, pristine ashlar, and well-wrought timber, the streets swept to a fine polish to welcome the King.

Henry did not disappoint. Sweating in immaculate harness, he rode a white charger through the crowded avenues, the spectators driven to excess of jubilation, as far as St Nicholas, where King and court pledged themselves to God and to war. Most of us, the lords who followed in his train, had put on armour for the show and damned uncomfortable it was too. I was lathered by the time we entered the cool cavern of the church, soon overheated by the sweaty press.

Next day, when the fumes had cleared and crowds departed, the council met at Guines, sentinel of the Pale. Around us the flat wetlands glittered in bright summer sun and light filtered through the gauze of water into the confines of the great hall, a rather drabber and more purposeful assembly. Fat little Wolsey opened the proceedings.

"My lords, we are met to decide upon the course of His Majesty's campaign, alongside our illustrious ally Maximilian."

I was feeling reckless, perhaps driven by the vestiges of drink. "What of the Emperor?" I asked. "Has your lordship yet heard as to when we might expect his forces to join us?" I let this sink in, and then added, "As they are sworn to do." Sniggers at this; I wasn't alone in hating the man but the bishop was immune to sarcasm, secure in the King's affections. "His ambassadors are expected any day now, my lords," he smoothed. "Meanwhile, we must plan our advance."

The King nodded and took over. Henry was as addicted to finery as the cock pheasant loves his feathers, yet he could carry it off better than any man I ever knew. His height and breadth were impressive; the auburn hair falling about his shoulders seemed to glow like deep, beaten gold. He was pretty as much as handsome, I'd say. You'll think me jealous, dark and slight as I was and some years his senior, but he did have charisma. The dark and bitter side of him, petty and malign, was hidden then beneath the glow. He looked every inch the Christian prince and perfect knight.

"Our first goal is Therouanne. I'm sure the bishop can give you a full history of the place." Some tittered at this but Wolsey soaked it up. "Fact is we had it once, then it came to the Emperor till the French unkindly relieved him of it.

Now our job is to get it back. Of course anything we find on the way, we can keep for ourselves."

Laughter now and much thumping of the table. "Light horses will lead with heavies behind, guns and baggage in the centre, bows and bills around, more cavalry following behind. Let's keep our fellows sober as we can and make sure they don't fall out with the Emperor's hired staves. Keep their ardour fresh for the French."

"Will they fight, sir?" one asked.

"I surely hope so. Be a shame to get all kitted up for nothing. If they don't we'll burn their kingdom down around them. After all, the Pope says we can!"

Now applause exploded, some of it genuine. These lords had come to France to fight. All their fine show masked serious intent. They craved victory as surely as Henry. The King was gilded, his coffers were full, but he was unblooded. Without laurels, his crown stayed hollow.

After dinner – chicken, mutton and veal, washed down with small beer and a little good wine, not bad for campaign rations – the inner council met. I was emissary for my father as Lieutenant of the North, those drab, distant and profitless marches where we would play policemen whilst the rest unleashed their steel in France.

"I don't trust those Scotchmen, my whining brother-in-law least of all," the King began. "Soon as our backs are turned, they'll be across the line and after Berwick again."

"My lord of Surrey," Wolsey replied, nodding at me, "is aware of the seriousness of his mission. Indeed, who better, Your Majesty? He knows the marches and he knows the King of Scots."

"Yes, but what does my esteemed brother-in-law intend? He's been canny enough to hedge his bets, tells our ambassador less than nothing whilst he consorts openly with our enemies. Those Scots are all the same: can't wait for any excuse to get out of the place. Can't say I blame 'em. What does Dacre say?"

This was to me. "He says, Your Grace, that the Scots make preparation, that talk of war fills their council, that the King has ordered up his levies and that the French send men and cash."

"Could this be mere posture?" quipped Wolsey, leaning forward, his bloated frog face intent. "Fear of invasion is as good as the thing itself and costs nothing. If the Scots persuade us to deploy an army on the marches, they drain our resources as surely as if they crossed over."

Much as I loathed the little man, he wasn't daft and had firmly nailed our quandary. The survival of our family, precarious enough at best, might depend on how I answered. Undue certainty and an excess of caution were equally dangerous. "For my part," I began carefully, "I think he will come. I and my father the earl, with Dacre's agreement, think he'll strike first at Norham and then perhaps aim for Berwick. We know his artillery is formidable, far more so than back in '97. The border is where he can hit us hardest, where it's most difficult and costly for us to defend."

"And what does the earl intend?" demanded the bishop.

"Having taken leave of His Majesty at Dover, my father now musters his household men and affinity. He is organizing his staff even as we speak. Grain, powder, and other stores are already being shipped up to Newcastle."

"I worry about guns," the King confided. "The best of our artillery is here in France. We'll need every gun, of course, but that does mean we don't have much left to face the Scots with."

I'd thought of this. "Sir Nicholas Appleyard will command the earl's gunners. We've still got good men and those guns we have are lighter, more readily transportable, and handier in the field. He doesn't fear the Scotch guns or their gunners. Dacre confirms that most of King James's professionals are with his fleet."

"Ah, the fleet," queried Wolsey, "and what of the Scottish fleet? King James has lavished a fortune, several fortunes, on his new warships. I can't see he'll leave them sitting idle in port."

I decided for once that candour might have its place. "We're not sure as yet but odds are he'll attempt to unite with the French and attack us at sea wherever they can."

"Would they dare?"

"They very well might. Combine King James's capital ships with those of the French and their weight of shot could easily match our own. Besides," I continued, seeing no reason not to remind them of Howard victories, "the Scottish King still smarts over the defeat of the Bartons."

"You're right, Thomas," the King replied lightly. "The damn fool keeps writing to me demanding I do something about you. The sheer temerity of the man; I keep reminding him that the depredations of a bunch of pirates are no business of princes and that my officers will deal with such criminals as they see fit, and good riddance."

As the meeting broke up, the King drew me aside, out of earshot of the others, even the hovering Wolsey. "You know, Tom," he began, "I loved your brother as I would have loved my own." This much was true. Edward had been the King's favourite. His looks and cavalier bearing, his fondness for the tilt yard, had fitted the chivalric ideal to perfection. Edward was outgoing, charismatic, and a born courtier. I was none of those, very much a poor relation in the King's affections.

"The thing is," he continued, "I worry about your father." We had progressed to the parapet walk, leaning out over the battlements, looking across the serene marshland, the narrow gulf between what was ours, won by the sword, and France proper. Silence hung heavy in midday heat; light glanced from placid water disturbed only by the bright flash of gulls, wheeling and darting amongst the reeds.

"No king ever had as loyal a subject," he continued, "nor one who did better service for longer."

I waited. "Yet I do worry about his health. Your brother's death was a cruel blow. I know what it is to lose a son – nothing could ever be worse. Your father is not as young as he was; indeed, many would have gone into honourable retirement long before now."

The King was all solicitous but his meaning was plain enough: the old man wasn't up to the job. "I'd feel easier if you were with him, Tom, like a chief of staff – share the burden and ease the load, that sort of thing. Will you do that?"

Princes only ask questions when they've decided on the answer. It paid to show enthusiasm. "If it be Your Majesty's command," I replied, "then I am more than willing. It would be a great honour."

"It's decided then. I'm obliged, Tom; I and the council will sleep much easier for it."

Lord Hume in the council once more

The jackals were yelping again, trying to drown out the bishop. This tactic was not without success, for the worthy cleric was foundering. William Elphinstone, with Douglas, was the core of opposition, a generation and more senior to the braying, wet-nosed hawks with their hunger for glory or the grave.

"We owe the French nothing," he continued. "They ignore us mostly, then flatter us when it suits. The plain fact is we are not so indebted to them or so hostile to England that we should chance all upon a war to suit the King of France's convenience."

King James was tolerably tolerant this morning, no petulance or princely tantrums. Indulgence was a luxury he could afford. The matter was decided. "You're crazy, old man," laughed the idiot Hepburn. "This pious cant flies against our best interest and the ancient ties of obligation. The King of England ignores the truce and daily flouts our honour. Now, he makes war upon our ally France. Are we supposed to just sit idle?"

I'd be damned if I'd see the "old" man so publicly abused. Besides, he wasn't much older than me. "You will extend that level of respect to which the bishop is entitled," I tartly reminded him. "You would do well to consider that making war on your former countrymen is no mere afternoon's work. The future of our, and now your, nation hangs on this debate." That shut the weasel up. Hepburn hated being reminded that his family were English immigrants, freebooters and opportunists. Most would say the same of me, of course, but I and my name had been here for very much longer.

James now intervened, all reason and light. "It's like this," he began. "One way or another we are pushed into siding with somebody. If we do nothing then I might as well hand over Scotland's crown to my brother-in-law and accept I'm his vassal, along with all of you. We sink or swim here. The decisions we make now will define us and this country for centuries. The French ask us for our help; it's a yes or no answer, and it has to be yes."

"Why?" the bishop battered on. "Why should we not

send our own representatives to King Henry and persuade him to desist? He won't want a war on two fronts."

"Doesn't work that way, I'm afraid." This came from Huntly, which made it worth hearing. I never knew a Gordon who didn't carefully weigh the odds. That's how he's so immensely rich. "I doubt King Henry has given more than a passing thought to Scotland; nearest he's ever been is York. I heard he sent for a map to see where Scotland was. He'll do what England always does: focus on France and keep the back door well bolted. And it will be well bolted, as we've found out so often."

This seemed like my perfect cue. "King Henry will appoint Surrey to lead. He's his most experienced lieutenant and Wolsey will want the Howards as far from the centre of power as may be decently arranged. The appointment is perfect."

"Just how old is this very old man?" Hepburn quipped.

"Old enough to have beat your father and grandfather and wise enough to see to you," I replied, as evenly as the circumstance would allow. "It is unlikely the earl will come alone. He will have his household men and every lord north of the Trent, including Stanley. Very likely his son, the lord admiral, will join him, bringing marines from the fleet – chosen men, crack troops. I'd put Surrey's likely muster at not less than twenty thousand bows and bills."

That bought a moment's silence. "What guns will he have?" the King asked. "We know King Henry has taken his entire train or near all to France. Our artillery is the best in Europe. We have men to serve and beasts to draw. How will the Earl of Surrey answer that?"A good point and hard to counter. To my surprise it was Huntly, leader of a horde of highland kerns and who'd never seen big guns in action, who answered.

"I suggest that the King will leave Surrey with a mobile train. The guns that have gone to France will be heavier pieces intended for siege work, as are the bulk of our own. To accompany the army north he'll have field guns, nothing above a six-pounder I'd guess, lighter and handier by far. Our guns will do very well for knocking down castle walls but perhaps less well on the battlefield."

This was sound. "All the more reason," I urged, "to avoid a contest. The mere thought of Your Majesty's train will suffice. You may meet your obligations to our allies without stirring across the Tweed. The fact we are mustered and ready will oblige Surrey to march north with all his power and at great cost to the exchequer. This war of King Henry's will not prosper. It's all show, mere bravado. King Henry postures whilst at the same time he must rely on Emperor Maximilian, who is any man's fair weather ally. The union will not endure. Promises will not be kept. King Henry will soon gobble up his father's gold. He merely strikes a pose. Let us do the same."

"It won't do," the King replied equably. "To achieve, to *earn* our rightful place in the councils of Europe, we have to be proactive, not merely passive. We have to show we can muster large forces *and* deploy them. We have to do more than merely scratch at England's walls. We have to knock them apart. King Henry has given us the perfect chance, handed us a golden opportunity. It will not come around again. We must act now and we must be seen to act."

"Does Your Majesty then intend to offer battle?" I asked deliberately. This was the very core of the business. To advance, take up the country, and withdraw was no great matter. We'd done so before and got away with it. To fight was another prospect. The King could have his war but did that mean he had to have his battle as well?

He paused in his reply, as well he might. "I say we have to go to war," he began, "but not that we must fight. I do not, will not, seek battle. On that you may be reassured. I will fight only if I am attacked and only if I may not safely withdraw. But if I was not ready to fight, then I'd be a fool to stir."

"*Si vis pacem, para bellum*," intoned Huntly, to show us he'd had the benefit of a classical education, and then translated, "If you wish for peace, prepare for war," for the benefit of those who had not. Elphinstone and I looked briefly at each other. He was no more convinced than I was. His face was lined and leaden, partly from the battering he'd had and partly from the knowledge that James was committed to a fight. I probably looked very similar.

King James writes formally to his brother-in-law of England

25th July

Your Majesty will know with what perfect hatred we must embark upon a course that may lead us fully into war. Your infamous conduct has left us with no remedy but to issue you with this our edict resolved in council and borne by our right trusty and beloved Islay Herald. If we do not receive from you full assurances, returned with our said herald, that you shall forthwith desist from attacking our ally of France and refrain from these lamentable and unchristian slaughters and depredations then we shall consider our realm of Scotland to be at war with England.

Further, we are aware in what low esteem you have held the accord between us, of the wrongs

we have endured and have yet received no redress.
How you did allow that notorious outlaw John,
Heron, the Bastard, to foully murder our dear
servant? You have ignored our pleas for justice.
Now you have unjustly deprived our right noble
and beloved Queen of her rightful inheritance and
you have further refused redress for the murder
upon the seas of our subject Andrew Barton.

As you love God and your honour you must
now cease from further assaults upon our dear
brother of France, abandon that false and
unbecoming amity with perfidious Maximilian,
whom some call Emperor. Return to your city of
Calais with all your power, horse, foot, and guns
and from thence to your realm of England. Should
you fail to heed our just and lawful entreaty then
all that may flow from this wicked intransigence
may rest upon your head. Widows and orphans
will have cause to bewail the folly of their King
who chose to reject the hand of peace and throw
down the gauntlet of war!

James Rex, etc...

King Henry replies to King James

1st August

We have received Your Majesty's letter and send
back our reply by that same herald. You will know
that we, and our right noble ally the Emperor,
do make just and holy war upon that wicked,
perjured, and unchristian wretch who styles
himself King of France, a realm which, as His
Holiness does award, is ours by right.

Therefore we pursue our just quarrel and shall do so to the utmost of our power and with God's blessing until, by his grace, we shall be victorious. Therefore it ill behoves you, our mere vassal, for know you we are the true and rightful owner of the realm of Scotland which you hold of us, to issue threats and dire predictions. Further if you shall break your solemn oath to us, we shall deem you false and traitorous and shall not hesitate to use our power against you.

If you would see your realm, which is our realm, laid waste, your towns reduced by fire and sword to ashes, your subjects slain, their wives and children left as destitute beggars who will curse your name for evermore, then persist in this folly. England fears Scotland as the lion fears the jackal. Think well before you let slip the hounds of war. It will be your very flesh and bones which they devour!

Henry Rex

Chapter Four:
Towards Rubicon

I say at once there are fewer difficulties in holding hereditary states, and those long accustomed to the family of their prince, than new ones; for it is sufficient only not to transgress the customs of his ancestors, and to deal prudently with circumstances as they arise, for a prince of average powers to maintain himself in his state, unless he be deprived of it by some extraordinary and excessive force; and if he should be so deprived of it, whenever anything sinister happens to the usurper, he will regain it.

Machiavelli: *The Prince*

Lord Hume inspects the Scottish guns and takes notes on the matter of drill

Impressive. Not a word I use often but the royal artillery, Scotland's pride alongside the King's fleet, was mighty impressive. My guide in the mysteries of the gunner's art was Robert Borthwick, the King's master-founder who would lead the train. "These *murtherers*," he enthused, "weigh in at 6,000 lb, 6½ inch bore throwing a 36 pound shot." The master-gunner was a four-square stocky sort of fellow, thickset and ruddy, around my age I'd guess. His hands, ingrained with dirt and oil, were huge and strong.

"They're called the Seven Sisters," he went on, "as there are seven."

"Really so," I replied, but irony was lost on Master Borthwick, a slave to his devilish art and a very fine craftsman. Edinburgh Castle, our great, gaunt, ancient fortress, was alive with hubbub and purpose, the outer ward crowded with bustling soldiery and mountains of gear.

"These handier pieces," he gestured at the range of lighter guns, "we mount on wheeled carriages – far easier to shift that way – but these bigger fellows we still fire from fixed platforms and move the great heavy sods by cart. Needs three dozen oxen, mind you."

I could see what he meant. These guns were enormous – some of iron, others cast in bronze. Their great, long, perfect barrels shone in limpid light; a merciful break in the clouds. The castle yard was a hive of activity. Guns aren't just weapons; they're an industry. There's the gunners themselves, their mates or matrosses, labourers, and pioneers by the score, as well as carters, carpenters, and farriers.

There are smiths and joiners, wheelwrights and coopers, vast sulphurous barrels reeking with the stink of powder. Small wonder it's called the Devil's Invention. There are gun-stones, gabions by the score,[6] women fussing over rations, naked children screaming and running like a pack of ferrets.

"I was trained by the best," my guide continued. "Foreigners, of course, but they knew their trade, masters of their art. Half of my lads are Dutchmen or Flemings. When the King's ships sail, they'll carry my guns and I may

---

6   Wicker baskets filled with earth and stones.

say you'll not find better in Christendom. Nor better hands to man them; best we've got." He stuck his chin out as he spoke, a regular bantam cock, but he did right to be proud. His guns were magnificent and awful but, as ever, a worm of doubt was nagging.

"Your men, then," I asked carefully, mindful of my companion's sensibilities, "those who will accompany the army, they too are well trained?"

For the first time a flicker of doubt. "I've done my best," he began defensively, hesitating, "but I haven't had much time. The King was planning to use his fleet, as your lordship knows, so I sent my best crews…"

"Perfectly right," I commended. "No point in having first-rate men o'war, state-of-the-art ordnance and second-rate gunners."

He visibly relaxed. "Your honour understands; what I have left I've trained well, trust me."

I did but the plain fact was we would go to war with untried crews. The English would not.

"I'll lead them," he repeated. "Nobody knows these babies better than me; cast most of them myself." The man's pride was at stake and he had much to be proud of, but the plain fact was both guns and crews were untried. Nobody enjoys having his professionalism questioned. "I mean, I know how to knock down a fortress wall," he blustered on. "Show me any set of walls in England and I'll show you a pile of rubble, once my beauties get at them."

I still didn't doubt him but what worried me was what would happen, not in the stately ritual of the siege but in the inferno of battle when there would be enemy gunners shooting back. These enemies might be better versed and nimbler on their feet, unafraid of crashing round-shot, and then what?

From the rearing cliff of the grey-stone castle, dominating the ribbon of city, I rode down and out beyond the walls onto the open expanse of Burgh Muir. Normally, this was empty heathland, rough grazing, but today it housed what appeared to be a migrant horde. It is probable that the armies of the old kings such as Attila or the Mongol khans looked like this, a vast sprawling anarchy. None too clean either; the smells that greeted me were numerous and varied, the distilled essence of crowded unwashed mankind, smoke and roasting, sweat, wet wool, and human waste in abundance, pretty evenly concocted. A squalid township of bivouacs and rough bothies streamed away over the moor, hung with smoke, garnished with filth.

"Quite a gathering," Huntly greeted me. "The King has been as good as his promise. The provosts reckon we've got near thirty thousand. That's without your marchers of course." These figures were substantial and my own men were indeed mustering nearer the line.

"It would be more impressive," I observed, "if their order matched their numbers." Huntly made a sour face but nodded. This was not an army but a rabble.

"I'd be happier if they looked enthusiastic or even busy for that matter."

They looked neither. Screaming sergeants were trying to shuffle bodies of men into some kind of order. They no longer carried their traditional spears but the eighteen-foot pike, cumbersome enough in the hands of one who knew what he did. This lot knew not what they did or were expected to do. The women chattered on in groups, laughing at their men's clumsiness.

"Never seen pikes in action before," Huntly continued. "The Swiss sweep all before them, I'm told, as relentless as Alexander's phalanxes. Not so sure about this lot, though.

It's a tricky beast: nose heavy and damned unwieldy. Get 'em all in line and pointing the right way, they'd stop anything on horse or foot. Keeping them moving, though, that's a different art."

Directing this carnival were a group of French officers and drill-instructors. They looked like they knew what they were doing but hurling abuse in French wasn't going to win the war. "It takes years to train the Swiss," I went on, "and they expect to be paid. This isn't a business for conscripts. They know how to use a spear; best leave them to it."

"Right enough," my companion replied, with the calm detachment of a man surrounded by his own highland affinity who needed no lessons in fighting. "Yet our spears could never beat bows and bills. The pike just might. If the front ranks are well harnessed against the arrow storm and the ground is well chosen, who knows what we might achieve? But ground will be everything." Huntly knew a thing or two about ground. "The Swiss choose theirs with great care, advance in the hollow, fight on the plain. They attack in echelon, you know: left, centre, and then rear; bang, bang, bang." He smacked his hand as he spoke to emphasize the effect. "It's really all about ground."

"The marches aren't that flat," I observed somewhat sourly. "Not flat enough for thirty thousand massed pikes."

"There is that of, course," he conceded.

Gordon's affinity lounged around, their elite status granting exemption from mundane drill. They were an altogether different company, whippet-lean and hard. Most wore their long saffron shirts, a few with aketons[7]; none

---

7   A form of padded undergarment worn under chain mail to absorb the shock of blows.

was wearing mail, the badge of their calling. These were Huntly's household men, professionals. They did not sow nor did they reap. Their weapons were their trade. One pair were practising with their fearsome double-handers, moving as gracefully and powerfully as rutting stags. The long blades, flicked and locked, parted, flashed, and parried. The combatants moved with speed and precision. They looked as though they could continue all day without tiring. I began to feel very old.

"Handy enough, aren't they?" Huntly had seen me looking. "They'll do you good service on the day, if the day should arise. The Swiss, I'm told, send swordsmen in on their flanks for cover, with commanded parties ready to break into an enemy line. Well, you'll have this lot. They may not be Swiss but they'll do."

I didn't doubt him for a moment.

Lord Dacre writes to the Earl of Surrey

As Your Grace knows and my spies do daily report besides that intelligence which Our Friend imparts, the King of Scots makes preparation. Bullion and arms flow into Leith from the King of France who sends yet more captains for the instruction of the King's levy. From every shire they gather upon the Burgh Muir which, as Your Grace will know, lies just beyond Edinburgh's walls.

We hear they are forty thousand strong, some say sixty thousand. That is too many, and they will be sufficient to do us great harm if they can be got into order. Lord Hume has his muster within the march and it is from here we should apprehend the most immediate danger. It is certain the warden will make a raid upon us

within weeks if not days; the season advances,
wet and horrid as it is, so the King may not long
delay if he means to attack us. When he comes I
avow he will come by Coldstream and the Tweed.
As you know, Our Friend there keeps daily watch
and Master Heron brings me her reports.

Touching upon the business of Norham, which
I know is dear to Your Grace as the gateway to
the marches, I have sent Master Heron to make
inspection and report privily to me. John Anislow
there breathes fire and laughs at the mention of
Scotchmen but I confess I share your doubts as to
his readiness. Heron can be discreet and though
a ruffian born, he has seen some service in the
Italian wars and may be counted upon for his
judgment of castle walls. In short, Your Grace, we
must brace ourselves and prepare to do our duty
to His Majesty as right well we shall.

This will be a sharper testing than we have
had before, for this King of Scots will have his
war and, should the chance offer, his battle too. I
know it is in Your Grace's mind to fight, for while
the Scots are bound to serve, our fellows are
all waged and a great drain upon His Majesty's
purse. If we must have at them, then it is best
done sooner before the season advances further
and autumn be upon us...

I have the honour, etc...

Heron takes a tour

"'Queen of Border Fortresses': isn't that what they call the place?" Master Anislow was not pleased to see me. To be fair, most people feel the same way. It's perhaps as well I lack sensibilities. "I've written to the earl," the castellan persisted, just to remind me one who corresponds with magnates need not be over punctilious with almost-gentry. "This place is pretty near impregnable. We've food and ale, powder and shot for a month. Surrey will be with us within a week of any leaguer. We are ready and I am ready and that's it, all of it."

Norham has had an eventful history. The place stands high above the Tweed, its ancient keep a massive donjon that rises sheer as a cliff. Both wards are strong and in good repair. The outer yard sprawls beyond the moat, studded with towers and hugging the contours to best effect. Our ancestors had an eye for defence.

"I'm not sure what Lord Dacre intends by your visit, *Master* Heron." A barbed reminder of my standing. In other times I might have been tempted to teach this fat, beer-sodden sack a lesson in etiquette. He may have had sufficient wit to realize he was pressing close to the mark and attempted to be more relaxed. "Look here, look around. You see how well found we are. This place has never fallen. Does Dacre forget the year '97? We saw those Scotch savages and all their King's guns off then and we're stronger now."

This was right enough but the Scottish guns were far more numerous, far heavier, and a damn sight more potent than before. "You're cavalry," he continued, "our eyes and ears. They cannot then surprise us. Besides, that many men and guns will kick up enough dust and be heard clear to London. Sieges aren't for horsemen," he continued, being careful to rob the words of offence. "It's a different type of war."

"I wasn't always cavalry," I confided. "Saw some action in the Great Wars which included laying siege to Naples and being besieged there; saw what the newer breed of guns could do to the strongest of walls. Norham was built centuries ago before the enemy was that ungentlemanly. Your walls are thick but they're also high and you lack bastions for your own ordnance and outworks to keep the enemy from laying his batteries close."

That shut him up. As I made to leave he asked, "How was it you were with both the besiegers and the besieged?"

"Oh, I changed sides," I replied. "You're quite right: life behind castle walls under enemy fire is no place for a horseman."

The Earl of Surrey writes to his son

Now we have August and the weather is constant – high wind, pelting rain, and cold. The sort that leeches into your bones, and mine, I fear, have seen too much of campaigning. This gout galls me abominably, even worse than the Scots whose muster I am informed continues apace and we may expect them upon our doorstep within a couple of weeks at most. King James does not mean to trifle with us or to stint his ambition. His attention will first be fixed upon Norham: I am convinced of it and Dacre agrees. Anislow remains bullish and bids me not to fret but fret I do as old men must.

Not all are as confident as our castellan that his walls will stand the weight of shot our enemies will throw at them, for it is certain so wondrous a train of guns has never yet been seen and their power would shame the devil. Our own guns I have sent forward to Newcastle so they may be ready to accompany our advance. Still I

have not been idle here in Pontefract. I have met
with Stanley and sundry gentlemen who are full
of resolve and draw forth their muster. My clerks
are scribbling furiously to see indentures drawn
up and I am confident we shall not want for able
men, well harnessed and ready to do His Majesty
good service.

We need to strike fast when the time comes,
for the Scots will have the advantage over us
in both men and guns. Moreover their supply is
certain, ours attenuated. The Bishop of Durham
writes daily to worry over his fine castle of
Norham and to remind me our borderers are
not to be trusted. This I know well! Still, Dacre
promises his own lances and those of his man
Heron, together near fifteen hundred marchers.

I do freely confess within the bounds of
these pages that I sorely miss your strength and
guidance and will be much relieved when you
come up with us. This burden that I bear and
which His Majesty has imposed upon me is a heavy
one. And damn that perfidious Scotch whoreson
King for a villain. I shall, if it be in my power,
ensure he shall fully rue this insolence and live
long enough to rue the day he set foot on English
soil.

Your loving father, etc...

The abbess attends upon her Queen

The marches were humming with tension. You could feel
it. Borderers are like foxes. They develop an instinct that
senses the hounds before they're scented. It was as though
we held our breath. Wars are like floods. Once the dam

breaks there's a fury that sweeps all before it, denying reason and humanity. It engulfs all in its path, relentless and insatiable.

In Holyrood, all was bustle and all the talk was of war. Silly women preened with their sillier menfolk, as eager and witless as schoolboys. The Queen received me in her private chamber. "I'm glad to see our abbeys aren't totally succumbing to poverty" – her sour greeting. I had made an effort, best gown and all. If I was the point-scoring type I was a good head taller than she and a tree's width narrower in the waist. I had tried and failed to warm to our English Queen. She had some good qualities but remained petulant and irritable. Dumpy and rather plain, it seemed her royal brother had all the looks and, of course, all of her father's inheritance, which could account for her ill-humour.

"I support my husband fully," she announced, as though it was in doubt. Given the strength of anti-English feeling, which hung like contagion in the streets, I could almost sympathize. "I would also avoid war if it was possible," she conceded. "Scotland has rarely won against England and my brother, though he has provoked the whole business, is no fool." I couldn't think of a reply. The peace party, those few there were – Douglas, Bishop Elphinstone, the Queen herself – were like nuns stranded in a brothel.

"You speak to Lord Dacre." This came more as a statement than an accusation. "If he could persuade the Earl of Surrey to write to the King and request a further embassy, offer even the merest concession – some recompense for the violations of the truce perhaps – this might suffice?"

We were not alone in the Queen's chamber, which was well and pleasantly appointed, hung with fine tapestries. When the young princess came north she brought her own ladies-in-waiting. One of these, Alice Musgrave, was in attendance.

A west marcher, her brother served as pathfinder to the King. Alice was tall and fair with the strong determined bones of her Viking ancestors and if she wasn't already on Dacre's payroll, I'd enter a nunnery myself. Now she said nothing, calm and serene, a perfect companion to the mercurial Queen. Whatever Dacre was paying her it would be hard earned.

I was bidden to sit, and Alice served us with wine, cheap and nasty, typical royalty. Margaret's main weakness was her total self-obsession. I suspect she'd been indulged as a child and a few more beatings might have been in order. "The King's cause is just," she repeated. Perhaps, if she said it often enough, she'd believe it herself.

"Yet it is a dangerous time, our son a sickly child, though with another on the way. At least he finds time to attend to the safety of his dynasty." This was a barb aimed at the King's numerous mistresses which, I'd wager a year's rents, included the strong-limbed Alice. She'd not be short of stamina and Dacre would always pay extra for pillow talk. "I've already lost two sons and two daughters. The prince is not strong. If anything happens to my husband, then what will become of his kingdom, his line?"

What she really meant was what would become of her if the King failed to return? Her position could become precarious and depend upon the survival of her one remaining child. No wonder she was so keen to go on breeding.

"Madam," I began, "if it is within your power to persuade the King then you must do so. However strongly he prepares, England will not be caught unawares. I have heard", and I needed to phrase this carefully, "that the northern army is mustering, that half of England will be marching."

"How do you know?" she asked sharply, then answered her own question. "Many travellers pass your doors, I know, so you must hear things. I assume you share this gossip with the warden."

"With Lord Hume, most certainly. He maintains a very efficient watch on the marches. He is the King's eyes and ears."

"The King doesn't trust him." She flicked a look at me. "Did you know that? He thinks Hume is a schemer, out for himself. He's your uncle, isn't he?"

"Well, you could probably attach that label to any courtier," I countered.

Her Majesty wasn't in the mood for facile attempts at humour. She didn't really possess a sense of humour as far as I could detect, so wrapped up in her own injustices. "His Majesty thinks his warden is far too thick with Dacre, talks too much to him."

Care was needed here. This might be more than idle chatter. Hume had more enemies than Caesar on a bad day in Rome. "Lord Hume is careful," I replied. "He has to work with Dacre day to day, else the marches would degenerate even further. He may have to trade information to gain more. There are plenty who criticize but few who could do as well or for so long."

"Hmm," she grumped. "He sees the Merse as his own kingdom, and his family has been there long enough. What does he say to you?"

"Well, I'm just a woman, so he wouldn't bother." I caught a flash of approbation from the blonde Amazon, clearly an avid student in the game of deceit. It worked as well. The Queen moved on to other complaints. The moment passed and we were still at war.

As I left, the oak panelled door swung shut. I still heard the Queen's parting aside to her buxom maid: "Stuck-up cow," she muttered.

It was near Evensong when I returned from Holyrood. The roads, as ever that summer, were foul, stinking, sunk in slime and with ruts the depth of ditches. If His Majesty had been disposed to spend as freely on his highways as he did upon his guns and other war toys, the country would be a great deal easier. I was in poor humour when I trotted through the archway – muddied, perspiring, and still smarting at the stupidity of our plump little Queen.

A smell of rising bread emanated from the bake house, a freshness that always raised my spirits. There I found young Ellen Turnbull, one of our novices, a well-made red-haired child, sixteen I think, but with the kind of abundant curves that even a habit cannot disguise.

Her shining red-gold mane was loosely gathered at the neck. She was pounding dough with a fierce concentration, and barely looked up as I entered. I was too amused, perhaps entranced, to trouble too much over etiquette. Besides, why should she bob to me? I'd failed to offer that measure of protection these walls should have offered.

"Ellen," I began, "I think that dough is completely vanquished."

I was not to be saved by small talk. She shot me a fierce young glance. "Are we safe here?" she demanded. "There will be war; we all know that. What will happen to us?"

She was angry but frightened too, looking to me as a child does to its mother for reassurance. But the well was dry; I had none. The girl's lovely, fierce green eyes were fixed on me; platitudes would not suffice.

"I'd love to tell you it will be all right... I'd like to tell myself and everyone here the same," I went on. "I'm not going to lie to you, though. There will be, there is, danger."

"What will we do?" She was frightened now and the need in her twisted the sinews of my heart.

"We will pray," I replied. "Pray for God's protection and guidance, and we are not altogether without friends. The warden will look out for us."

"And if the English come?"

"We even have a few friends on that side as well. We must pray it will be enough. We must have faith." I'm not sure whether I was trying to convince her or myself.

She was still looking at me – that steady, knowing gaze the young and innocent have. "I've seen the English come before, when I was a child – can't remember why. We hid out in the mosses. We were there for days. My little brother, he was already sickening, died. When we crept back, cold and hungry, there was nothing left. I remember one woman, an aunt; she had been caught. They'd raped her, then killed her and left her body on the midden. I remember how she looked. Her hair was very dark and around her face. She lay on her back, her eyes wide open and as dark as her hair, almost as though she wasn't real."

The child was weeping now and my eyes gave me away. I could not speak but held her close.

First blood to the Bastard

"Ah, Johnny," the warden greeted me, as near to affection as I was ever likely to get. "Sir William Bulmer," he gestured to a hefty-looking type on his right, "High Sherriff of Durham, no less, sent by His Grace to bring us aid."

From Dacre's tone it was impossible to work out if this was a good thing or not. We needed reinforcement but the warden was touchy concerning his fiefdom. He didn't like interlopers or interference. This was his patch, after all – his and nobody else's. "Two full companies of bows, he brings us; can't say they're not needed." This meant it was all right.

"Needed they certainly are," I confirmed, "seeing as we're expecting visitors."

"When?" queried Sir William. His tone was entirely affable, always reassuring to one of my touchy sensibilities. He was, after all, a full gentleman, with a straight line back to Hastings and enough acres to prove it. "Anytime soon," I replied. "Hume will lead for sure. He's completed his muster in the Merse; could have as many as seven or eight thousand spears."

Sir William exhaled, uttering an expression one rarely hears in church.

"We likely won't see the whole lot; too many for a raid. He'll be probing our defences." I left the "such as they are" in the air; we all knew the march was wide open. Wardens have sensibilities too. "My guess is he'll bring a thousand riders down the Till, find out what he can, steal what he can, and torch what he can't."

"You're sure that's the way he'll come?"

"Bound to be," Dacre grunted. "Johnny here is too polite to tell you the area is wide open. Half the towers are roofless since the last time in '97. Norham is the key. If James can take the place then he'll gobble up Etal and Ford. Best get your stuff ready, lad; you may need to move back home." For Sir William's benefit he added, "Master Heron here has been so good as to look after his brother's estates while he's away."

Bulmer was too polite to comment.

It was August now, high summer – not that you'd have noticed. We were in the great hall at Ford, a damp, chill wind gnawing at the few hangings not yet packed.

The place did look pretty sparse. I'd sent Elizabeth and her daughter away with most of their people, those *bouches inutiles*,[8] as the French would say.

"How many men do you have?" Bulmer asked.

"Well, there's a score or so of my own affinity, more from the able-bodied tenants hereabouts, and more from some of the other names. So I'd say a full company, mounted and reasonably well harnessed, and they know how to fight."

Sir William nodded. "Can we fight Hume?"

"Yes," I replied cautiously, "if we are careful."

"Johnny always says yes," the warden guffawed. "He has a taste for killing the Scotch."

"Good," Sir William replied. "Looks like there will be enough to go round. How might it be done?"

"Not as they come but as they go; hopefully they'll be less wary. We can't take 'em head on. Not enough of us. Hume can afford a few empty saddles; we can't."

It began to rain. Nothing new there; it had rained all through this truly awful summer. Like the flood – though God's wrath was now called Scotland. Rain came down in great sheets, drenching already sodden fields, spilling over the burns. Skies were leaden and grey. There was no warmth. Bleak roofless towers stood stark and bare. People were restless and furtive. Consensus was things could only get worse. Plenty remembered the raids of '96 and '97. Lucky ones still bore the scars.

"I hear King James desires your head," Bulmer noted. "He blames you for breaking the truce, even cites you in his correspondence to King Henry." He grinned. "You should be honoured."

---

8 Literally, "useless mouths": those who would be expelled from a besieged castle or city as useless to the core defence.

"We won't get much warning," I advised. "Hume keeps the march as tight as a nun's bodice. He's an old hand at this, after all. He'll strike hard and fast, be gone as quick as he can. My lads and I will shadow his every move. You, Sir William, if you will, keep your fellows in reserve but handy. If we get a chance it will just be the one and the offer won't be repeated."

Bulmer was prepared to take my lead and the warden concurred. The Scots would be three or four to our one. I'd best get it right. Sir William's bows would keep their muster at Wooler whilst we stayed all eyes and ears. That evening, as the shades of grey settled into dusk, I received word from the abbess that Hume and his marchers were on the move. It was time for me to earn my retainer. Perhaps, if I survived, I might negotiate a raise, though Dacre parted with the King's coin as though it was his own. He was a peerless knight but a most parsimonious employer.

Next morning, before dawn, we were in the saddle. In the half-lit stables, our garrons were skittish. Horses aren't as daft as their riders; they know when trouble is in the wind. As another colourless dawn crept over the hills to the west and rear, light shifting over the long bulk of Cheviot and hunchback Hedgehope, we saw them come – a thousand at least, maybe more in front, a cloud of hobilars,[9] skirmishers, spread out and watchful. Then the vanguard, heavier men on heavier horses, a dull glint of morning brightness picking out harnesses and sallets.[10] Behind them, the main body, strung out in a dense column, Hume's pennon and a flowering of others the only splashes of colour. Flankers fanned out on both sides; a strong

---

9   Light cavalry.
10 A form of fifteenth-century helmet with full neck protection; can be with or without visor.

rearguard and more hobilars behind. This warden wasn't taking chances.

"There seems to be a sufficiency," Crookback Will observed on my left, unnecessary but true. We were on the west bank of the Till, on the pimple of Pace Hill, the broad sweep of the river and fat valley bottom below and eastwards. The Scots fanned out like contagion. Their path, on that brightening morning, was marked by sparking thatch and ruin of meagre crops, the bellowing of beasts and ewes beneath prodding lances. We were no more than fifty strong, strung out along the ridgeline. The Scotch prickers knew we were there but gave us no trouble. They preferred easier game.

Hume's scourge passed down the valley, wasting everything in its path. I guessed he'd advance no further in than Coupland whilst his scourers swept the area. He'd not linger but would fall back next day. That's what I'd have done anyway. I sent Will on to Wooler to raise Sir William and the marchers there. "Take them up the old Roman road to the east," I instructed. "Get across at Heaton Ford and we'll muster at Fishes Steads below Flodden."

The long summer's day brightened considerably before waning into afternoon and evening. My lads were still shadowing the Scots and I was right: that night they camped by Coupland. The castles themselves were safe enough. This was a raid, not an invasion; hit and run. Hume had come for learning and loot, not to fight. We'd see about that though.

The settlement was a huddle of bothies. In terms of the prevailing squalor, it scored pretty well. The people were gone, melted west into the hills, taking everything with them: beasts, rations, bedding, pots and all. The Scots were never particular. They'd nick anything; even take the doors and windows if they were worth lifting. The place was as empty as a pardoner's promise, so left plenty of room to hide. I was guessing they'd leave the hamlet alone – not worth torching. We hid our horses in the bothies and bedded down without fires.

"What's the plan, boss?" some of the lads asked.

"The plan is we hit them very hard tomorrow," I replied. "So wind your necks in, get some kip, and generally keep quiet." These were the sorts of commands they understood. Sir William Bulmer demanded rather more. He and his archers filtered in before dawn, most on ponies or sturdy garrons. Will had led them well and they'd been marching all night. No complaining though; clearly I had more in mind than a shared breakfast. Most were in dead ground to our rear. The innocuous green hill sloped down to the river in front.

Bulmer was in full harness, along with some additional gentry. The rest were plain in sallet and jack, their staves unstrung. "Well then," he said, "I hope I missed supper for a reason?"

"You did," I replied. "Look down there towards the river. The broom grows thick on the west bank, below where we are now." I saw the light go on in his eyes. Surrey hadn't sent us anybody's fool. "If your men deploy, using the bushes for cover, there's a good chance we'll catch them unguarded. Let the scouts and van get clear. I'll send Will with a strong commanded party round towards Crookham to give 'em something to think about, and Geordie here," I indicated Master Armstrong lately of Liddesdale on the Scottish side, "will slip between the main body and rearguard."

"Doesn't he mind fighting his own people?" Bulmer asked.

"They're no mine," Geordie responded. "Just a bunch o' Humes an' Kerrs an' others."

"Liddesdale folk don't care much for outsiders," I amplified. Nor much for each other when you think about it.

The plan was laid, the ambush set. We made ready. Bulmer's bowmen slipped down into the canopy of broom which spread like a carpet. The covering was dense and so ordinary as to pass unnoticed – so I fervently hoped anyway. The sun rose higher in the morning sky. Lads sweated in their harness. It became warm. Close and humid too, a wash of light over the valley floor just smudged at the edges by smoke from yesterday's burnings.

We weren't kept waiting. Hume needed to be safe across the line. His prickers came first, strung out and still wary, though perhaps not as wary as the day before. We left them unmolested; their surprise lay further on. Next the main body: a vast, dust-shrouded, mud-garnished caravan of beasts and bleating ewes. They had goats, swine, and chicken, saddles groaning with gear, hostages drawn like stumbling sacks behind.

"Wait," I cautioned as I sensed archers tense, that first pressure on the string. "Loose only on my command and not before."

We let them come on. Hume's banners fluttered in the centre, surrounded by a knot of his household men. It was time. I nodded to Bulmer, who nodded to his sergeant and the orders rapped out, "Nock, draw, loose."

You've heard of the arrow storm, of course. Well, this was perhaps more of a sudden squall than a tempest, but it did the job. The Jocks simply didn't see it coming and the shafts thumped home gleefully, dropping a score at the first draw. Hampered by the fruits of their own pillaging,

Hume's men were off guard, unprepared, and very, very surprised. For a full, glorious, mad minute our yeomen drew and loosed, punching men from saddles, pinning them to screaming garrons.

Time to close. My lads swung into the saddle, their lances levelled. Longbow men drew swords and laid on. We came thundering from cover and smacked into the struggling mass. Hume's sergeants were bellowing for the men to close up but the very abundance of their own harvest defeated them. We picked them off, a brace of archers here and there tackling a harnessed man – one to block his parry, the other to hook behind the knee and pull him down. Whether a man was rich or poor then determined his life expectancy: any man worth a ransom could be expected to live; if not, he very likely died.

Riders closed around the warden's flag, forming a compact mass, ready to bludgeon their way through. Hume would have quickly worked out we'd keep both vanguard and rear busy so it would be every man for himself and a bad day for the tardy. I brained a couple of nobodies for the sport then moved to intercept a well-built knight, encased in decent-looking harness. He carried his own banner – Hume's brother George. I could find use for a warden's brother.

George was disobliging, coming at me like a mad bull, trusting to fine Italian plate. My lance sheered off. His came uncomfortably close. I recovered and swung the war hammer I was wielding. I'd come across it at Ford – probably belonged to my father or grandfather. It was a bit last century but still potent and hefted well. I used the hammer end in a wide swing to clout George about the head, leaving him a bit groggy, then the beak to tip him from his saddle. Give the fellow his due, he was trying to rise as I dismounted, so I fetched him another. That fettled him for the moment.

By now the fight had spread out in an untidy sprawl over the plain, knots of terrified beasts swirling as my riders sought to gather them in. The Scots had mostly gone, galloping off northwards. Many others, a satisfying number to judge by the heaps, had gone to their maker, their twitching, blood-laced carcasses sprawled pallid in the limpid light. Our fellows were whooping and cheering with that exultant rush of men who have escaped death and tasted victory.

My captive was stirring and I unbuckled his sallet to let him have some air. He was trying to focus. "You bust my damned skull," he complained.

"Don't think so," I responded, "but you were being troublesome." His eyes were clear enough and I didn't think there was any permanent damage. Good; I wanted him alive and functioning.

"You're Heron," he croaked.

"Indeed I am," I replied, "and you're my prisoner."

"You'll get your ransom," he managed to bluster. "The warden's my brother."

"Oh, I know, else I'd have hit you a good deal harder. Thing is he has my brother, and now I have his. As long as my brother thrives so will you." I left the alternative unspoken.

Heron and a matter of faith

"Synod of Whitby," the Rector of Corbridge exhaled. "Remember that?"

"Not personally," I replied. "Something about haircuts, wasn't it?"

"The tonsure was discussed and a few things more, but the fine abbey you see before you was Wilfred's church

109

and it's stood here for centuries since, despite the frequent, best attentions of our neighbours over the line. That ruffian Wallace sacked it long time back, in Longshanks' day – blamed his men for it. At least he had the decency to apologize, which you wouldn't have expected."

For any building, especially one this tempting, to endure so long on the Northumbrian marches was no mean feat. The great church reared above the west flank of the square, sweeping and serene, crowded by the rows of tenements that rose rather more unsteadily around. The castle, now behind us and from where we'd just emerged, filled in the eastern aspect. Hexham is a good strong site. The town dominates a bluff above a lazy curve of wide water. We weren't sightseers but here to report to the warden on the affair at Crookham.

"They say," my guide continued, "the ancient Romans may have had a fort here beforehand – plenty of their stones to be found."

"Doesn't surprise me. If I were them I'd have done the same – dominant position above the ford, long view, easy to hold."

"I'll bow to your superior knowledge, John, where warfare is concerned. So would most men, I imagine. Speaking of which, this market place itself has seen its share of bloodletting. More or less where you are standing, the Duke of Somerset was executed back in the old days of Lancaster and York, and more than a few with him. That was in the time of the present King's grandfather, before even I was born."

"Well before my time, though I think my people were all Yorkists – when they weren't being Lancastrians, that is." I was diverted from reflecting on ancient torture by the current version. A bunch of artisans were constructing a pyre in the centre of the square, surrounding a single stake. Judging from the quantity of fuel, it would be a decent sized blaze.

"A spot of witch-burning?" I enquired.

"Heretic," the rector muttered in reply. "Poor devil. A Lollard no less – first of those I've heard of in a very long while."

"What's a Lollard?"

"One who denies Christ, or more properly, denies the authority of the church."

"Is that a greater sin?"

"Yes, as far as Bishop Ruthal is concerned. Come on, we're bidden to attend."

Thomas Bell was always outwardly respectful towards his superiors, even though he might have a pretty low opinion of them. Where the taint of heresy was concerned, it was best to tread warily. The prince bishop was a stickler for burnings. Lord Dacre was entertaining his guests in the great hall, well hung with tapestries he'd looted from somewhere, the blood-red banner of his name prominent, just in case anyone forgot who was running the show here. Bishop Ruthal was a plump, moist man whose vestments could easily have cost a king's ransom, his fat little fingers nearly hidden by a blaze of bejewelled gold. He was waving his short arms as we came in.

"But what if Norham is attacked?" he queried, all petulant. "They will come – you've told me they will come – and then what will happen?"

"Master Anislow has assured me, has assured the Earl of Surrey, that he can hold out and that is all that can be done. I have no men to mount a relief and no more guns to send." Dacre was on his best behaviour but I could tell the bishop's whinging was beginning to grate.

111

"Church property, sir, *my* property and such a drain upon my slender means as fills me with despair. If the place falls I am sure the loss will be so mortifying, it will quite carry me off..." The warden didn't reply. A most eloquent silence.

"Master Heron," Bull Dacre continued, "my lieutenant" – here was another promotion – "has been to Norham. He has taken assurance of the castellan. His light horse will shadow the Scots' every move. We are prepared, Your Grace; as prepared as we may be till the earl with his power is come up. There is nothing more to be done. See to your witch-burning and be done here. Leave the business of the Scots to me."

"Er, not a witch, my lord," corrected a tall, spare fellow, as cadaverous as the grave – the sort you'd not notice but it would pay to keep your eyes on, a clerk or a lawyer. "A heretic, sir, a Lollard. There are few of the devils who have escaped God's punishment, but when we do find one..."

Dacre cut him off. "Witch, heretic, whatever, just get the job done and don't hurry back."

"Never seen a real heretic," I confessed to Thomas Bell. "Do they have forked tails and stuff?"

"Not that I've noticed, but if you've the stomach for it and sufficient curiosity, I'll introduce you. I've a mind to deny the bishop and his crew their sport if I can but persuade the fellow to recant, though I'm not sure him seeing the likes of you will help."

* * *

Kempson, the man was called, and frankly he was a disappointment: a mild, inoffensive sort of fellow, all humility and politeness, not a pair of horns in sight. His clothes were of the ordinary workaday sort, much darned but he'd tried to keep them clean, a tradesman I guessed. His family must have had some means or his wife was good looking, for he was accommodated above ground in the gaol. Most, particularly those of my calling, went straight into the undercroft below, often till they rotted in their own waste.

He stood up and bowed as we came in – a novel experience for me at least, as most folks generally run, fight, or sneer when I turn up. I knew the rector to be a decent man with a care for other men's immortal souls – he'd told me often enough – nor was he one to mince his words when out to salvage souls.

"Look here," he began, "there's chaps busily employed outside constructing your funeral pyre. They are very much in earnest. And sit down, for God's sake, though I am here on his behalf or so I fervently believe."

The man lowered himself gingerly into a chair, wincing as he sat. Clearly the bishop's agents had attempted persuasion of a different sort. Leg irons, I guessed, or I'm no judge of a spot of professional torture.

"Do you imagine God wants you to die, to throw away your life, beggar your family, and erase your line upon a point of doctrine?"

"It's rather more than that, though, isn't it?" he answered respectfully. "God wants me to be true to myself."

I butted in: "Couldn't you be true to yourself and just not tell anyone – render unto Caesar and all that?"

"Caesar may order my flesh but not my soul. The church tells us she speaks for God but she does not. Rather, she stands in our way. Where in the Bible does it say we need priests to intercede for us?"

"His Holiness," Thomas Bell explained, "is the vicar of Christ. His authority derives from St Peter, handed

113

down through the apostolic succession. The priest is the shepherd of his flock. He intercedes with God on their behalf, not for himself."

"Did God intend that the Pope, cardinals, archbishops, and bishops should live like princes in their great palaces while his children go hungry; that they should deny Englishmen the right to read the Holy Bible in their own tongue? Did God decide priests should be paid to sing masses for the dead in chantries paid for by lords to assuage their guilt over their killings? Did God ordain that we pretend the wine and wafer become Christ's flesh and blood? Did he ordain his priests should live an unnatural life of celibacy?"

As you know, I'm not a great reader of the Holy Scripture, nor, for that matter, was the good rector any shining paragon of celibacy. He now changed tack. "Look, the church has its failings, I'll admit, even if not in front of the bishop, but we cannot endure without her. The church is all that brings order into the world. Without the Holy See there is only chaos. If every man were to decide for himself how he dealt with God and with his fellow men, where would we be? There would be no order – just anarchy and death."

"You'll forgive me, Father, but is there not already anarchy and bloodshed enough? You come with Master Heron here, who, I hope I may say, has shed some blood in his time and produced his own fairly effective versions of chaos. No offence intended."

"None taken," I replied. I rather liked this fellow – a sparky little character with more salt in him than his tradesman's threads and calloused hands would suggest.

"Then what of you, Master Heron, the soldier, reiver, widow-maker?" He turned his mild gaze fully upon me. "How does your conscience stand? How do you deal with God, and where is the order in your world?"

The honest reply would have been I didn't think much about conscience and there was no order I could discern, particularly in my world. I came from a broken frontier. Admittedly, I'd been responsible for much of the breaking.

"I follow the advice of the rector here," I replied, news to both of us. "When all comes to all, we need a priest to set things right, hear our confession. Though," I admitted modestly, "I'm not as regular in my attendance as I should be." The rector had the decency not to comment.

And so it was left. Master Kempson bid us not to worry on his part, for he was bound for a better place and the painful means of passage was but a brief trial before everlasting glory, etc. Some men wear a taste for martyrdom like their livery. We may deride them but this small man had a kind of sublime courage. There was irony in this. Many have been martyred for the church; he was about to be martyred by it and damned as a heretic to boot.

"God wills us to try our utmost," the rector wearily concluded as we left.

Our business, or at least my own, in Hexham was not yet complete. On the floor above the defiant Kempson was kept my own prize, George Hume. He lived rather better, and why not? His welfare was important to me, and my sister-in-law had already shown her approval in a most stimulating manner. As for Hume's bread and board, the cost all went on his brother's slate, added to the ransom. He was eating chicken and drinking an indifferent wine but otherwise was well housed and cheery. As I entered, he rose in greeting and motioned me to join him. Such small courtesies are important between gentlemen.

"How are you doing, George?"

"Can't complain, really; head still aches a bit but the grub is pretty good and the drink's plentiful. I do rather better than I would at home."

Like many second sons, this one lived as a mendicant off his brother. I could not see the Scottish chancellor being an easy man and said so.

"Oh, you know," he replied, "he has a lot on his mind – affairs of state and what have you. He's not a bad fellow really. Thing is, he just doesn't see lesser folk. They're not in his thinking, if you see what I mean. He only worries about folk grander than himself and he doesn't acknowledge too many of those. Quite likes you though."

"Me?" I was surprised "Only half a gentleman and an outlaw to boot?"

"You killed Robert Kerr. I know; I was there at the truce in fact, watched the whole thing and, before you ask, I wagered on you. Most I've ever won. Alex was happy you topped Kerr. He hated the fellow, saw him as an upstart, a boor, and a bully, pushed me into nettles once when we were boys, just because he could. We Humes were leading the cheers when he went down. And, seeing as you mention it, there's quite a few of us almost-gentlemen around. We haven't all done as well as you."

I've had worse endorsements. George enquired if I would attend the burning next day. I said not. "I will, I think, if you don't mind. My parole's good, of course, and I've never been to a proper burning. It's only a shilling – should be a good show."

Wishing him joy of his sport I made to move.

"I don't suppose I could trouble you for the loan of the shilling, could I? As you can imagine, I'm a bit short."

"Not staying for the fun then?" Lord Dacre asked as I

took my leave. Thomas Bell was to administer the last rites to Master Kempson as he mounted the pyre.

"I prefer honest killing to ritual murder," I replied.

"I know what you mean," he grunted. "It leaves a bad taste, and not just the smoke."

Lord Dacre writes to the Earl of Surrey

Your Grace will be pleased to learn that your lieutenants have beaten those Scots who recently crossed our border. My Lord Hume had intended to take up his fill from His Majesty's subjects in Glendale and prepare the way for King James who will follow on with a far greater force. Master Heron and That Other whom I will not name here have provided me with much intelligence, which I believe to be good. It is said the Scottish army is forty thousand strong, well furnished with ordnance and other warlike stores, and that all the great lords of that realm are come in with all their affinities and that the commoners do rally in their thousands.

Yet though they be many and we few, first blood has gone to us. Hume is much discomfited and Sir William Bulmer, whom you sent to me, has done right good service. He, Heron and their fellows have laid half a thousand of these boasters lifeless and taken many ransoms, whom I now do hold here in Hexham gaol at His Majesty's pleasure. When you and your power are come up, then do I trust we shall be a match for the Scots, for, though their numbers be great, I wean their hearts are not fully with the business. The commoners are dragged from their

117

*ploughs, harnessed, and drilled after the Almain
fashion, yet do I wonder if the work of days can
accomplish that which should take months.*

*Their guns be many and strong, yet their
gunners and matrosses are but new trained, the
rest being with their fleet, of whose actions I have
previously acquainted Your Grace. I tend to the
view, and the letters which I have received do
confirm, that the Scots will attempt Norham. The
prince bishop is much vexed over his grand castle
and fears for the ramparts should the Scots attack.
If he were to petition God for the safety of the
men within, rather than for the maintenance of
the fabric, I'm sure I'd be much comforted. As it is
Master Anislow makes good report and swears he
can hold. I will be free and confess me that I have
some doubts. I know what great store Your Grace
sets by this, our great bastion. I will assign Heron
with his light horse to provide his best support and
I have charged him that it shall be his best support.*

I hope I have the honour, sir, etc...

Isabella and notes of preparation

It was now the third week in August – high summer if you
could believe it. Rain chucked down from lowering skies,
driven by cool winds that whipped the rich green grass
by the river, which flowed frothing and fretful. More rain
spattered on the slates and made waterfalls of our gutters.
The harvest would be late and sparse, if any was there to
reap, that is.

I had gathered the sisters in my hall just after Terce.
They were a dozen in all, mostly older; only red-haired
Ellen and another, rather timorous, fair girl whose name

I could never seem to remember formed a more nubile element. My recent brush with Ellen suggested this was not necessarily an ideal calling – not that I was in any position to criticize. The rest were mostly well past that; perhaps I was too. If I was still alive in a year I would be thirty, an old maid.

They all looked to me. I was responsible. Ultimately the decisions rested with me. I wore a magenta gown that day – not quite the thing for one of my station but I felt like making a show. Though I ranked as abbess, I'd never been in orders. My authority came from the King in Edinburgh rather than the Pope in Rome; not that any gang of marauders would be bothered by such a fine distinction.

"It is like this," I began. "The army of the King of Scots approaches us, a day's march and no more. The warden's men muster nearby, as you know. Tomorrow they will cross the Tweed here, past our door, at least thirty thousand strong, maybe more." Most looked blankly at me; they'd no idea how much humanity that actually was. Neither did I, really, except it was an awful lot. "There will be nearly as many women and followers. They're likely the bigger menace, at best light-fingered. We have to nail down all the hatches against pilferage."

"But surely the warden will protect us?" someone asked uncertainly.

"He has given me that assurance," I responded, "but he's likely to be rather busy. He has offered us an escort to Coldingham on the coast; just lock our doors and run for cover till it's ended, if it does end. What will remain when we return is another matter."

"What must we do?" another asked.

"I've thought very hard about this, thought of little else. I say we stay put, keep our nerve, and trust in Lord Hume."

"And in God," the same voice, one of the older women, chided. "We must place all our trust in him."

"Yes, naturally," I half snapped. "We will trust in God. He too may be busy in the coming days, however, and I feel we should ease his burden. See to your offices. Look to your tasks. Keep an eye on the servants and make sure the gates are locked at all times. Admit none but on my instruction."

The sisters departed. There was plenty to do. Just Ellen and her wide-eyed friend remained. They were holding hands.

"There's something I'd ask of you," she began. "If they come for us, I mean." Why was it I found this girl's shining eyes so hard to meet? I knew she could set me blubbering again and that wouldn't do at all. Still, with her gaze upon mine, she took a dagger, some ancient scarred rondel, from the folds of her habit.

"I know you'll save us if you can but if they take us, please promise me you'll kill us first." The knife lay between us. I could not speak. I could no longer look at her. Just the thought of driving the sharp, pitted blade into her, through that flawless skin, her bright blood jetting over me, brought bile to my throat.

"I could never harm you, Ellen," I somehow managed, "but I promise I will die to protect you if I have to." Yes, I meant it.

Chapter Five: Castle Walls

All Lancashire, for the most part,
The lusty Stanley stout did lead.
A flock of striplings strong of heart,
Brought up from babes with beef and bread.

The Earl of Surrey writes again to his son

25th August

My dearest son,

You will know by this and other letters I have sent
you that I am now at Pontefract, that old grey
fortress, somewhat dilapidated but still the bastion
of the north. Lord Dacre sends me news of the
Scots and we know for sure the King of Scotland's
great army is on the march. Damn the petulant,
cringing cur and damn all his unwashed horde for
we ken well they mean to do us great harm and
shall have the marches at their pleasure till we are
come up against them. By this precious assembly
of tinkers, thieves, and ruffians we are denied
our proper place in France. Where will we find
honour here, let alone profit? Full oft betimes I've
campaigned in these wet and barren wastelands.
Our marchers are indistinguishable from
theirs. Each would as cheerfully rob all mankind

and slit your throat as eat his dinner. It sluices down every day, soaking man and beast. The vileness of the season adds greatly to our daily labours. The traffic of ordnance and warlike stores is much delayed; foodstuffs are hard to come by and ever dearer to buy. Besides, the wet and cold causes this damnable gout to flare worse and worse. I am so enfeebled I can barely hold in the saddle and perforce am transported like some diseased hulk or aged Turk in a light carriage which does vex me greatly for I would not have our people see me so reduced. If they are to hazard their lives against the Scotch, they can at least expect to be led by one who can stand on his own two feet.

We have much to do. I have sent out summons to all of the northern lords and I know they will not fail me. Within the next two days I shall advance such forces as I presently command (mainly our own Howard affinity) to York and thence to Durham. The Abbot of St Mary's has collected funds to pay for our muster and right welcome they will be; the drain upon the King's purse is prodigious. By God's good grace and my best endeavours we will be in Newcastle before the month is out and there we shall complete our muster and order the army. Then we will go a-hunting, for it is my intention to seek battle at the first opportunity.

Only a trial of arms can suffice. If the Scots merely thumb their noses at us and run, as they have done before, then we are confounded. I cannot keep such forces in the field past the

season and it is very late even now, as you know.
If we can but manoeuvre and bring King James
to battle, then we may yet have some glory from
this miserable campaign. Meantime, I fret about
Norham, our chief strength in that march. As you
know, our captain there does assure me we've
nought to fear, but Lord Dacre is less sanguine
and I've that whinging fool of a bishop who
writes to me daily, fearful for his acres. Well, we
shall see.

Your ever loving father...

The Scottish warden takes stock

Let me be candid: it was a mess, pure and simple. I'm too old a hand to be caught out by one of the oldest tricks in the book, but there it was. I'd screwed up. Master Heron had been one jump ahead and now he had my idiot brother to bargain with. Of course, I still had his.

We'd gathered up the stragglers and such wounded as could be saved. It was best to deal with the worst cases straightaway, a kindness really. That's why I dislike war so much: too many uncertainties, and when things go wrong, they go wrong very fast and generally there's not much you can do about it. There might be a lesson in this for King James, if he was of a mind to learn, but he is not of that sort. Besides, my own after-action report would present a rather edited view.

I was in the abbess's capacious and well-appointed private solar, sipping her excellent wine, a salve for most troubles, I find. She sat opposite, in plain kirtle, her rather glorious hair pinned up and hidden under a muslin cap. Her dark eyes were enormous. Her fine skin was pale and slightly ragged from lack of sleep. She and her women had laboured all day and most of the night with the injured. Most had done well. Inevitably, a few had not. I'd seen her in tears, which I'd never witnessed before, and even I'm not so cynical as to remain unmoved.

"So this is the face of war?" she asked when she'd recovered sufficiently. "It's even worse than I thought. Was it worth it?"

"No," I replied. "Your friend Master Heron got the better of me. He was ready and I was not. The fault was mine and those poor fellows you are tending to have suffered accordingly."

I'd guess we'd lost several hundred and all the gear, of course, but nobody that mattered, thank God – just the usual toll of marchers, broken men, and disposable scum. "We were beaten, fair and square, out-thought and out-fought. My report won't say that, naturally; I'll refer to a successful deep reconnaissance and say that we fought our way clear against stiff odds with a heroic sacrifice by the rearguard."

That's the other problem with military action: if you're in command, the buck stops with you. It's near impossible to find a decent scapegoat. No wonder I prefer politics – you choose your own ground, you prepare, you can control the timing, and you've always got someone in mind to carry the blame if things go wrong.

"No gentry were lost, so the council won't care. My enemies may read between the lines but they'll keep their conclusions to themselves. The King, bless him, won't be interested. He doesn't want to know that the English are ready; that's the last thing he wants to hear."

"This is just the beginning, isn't it?" she went on. We both knew the answer. She spoke evenly but her eyes were brimming, her normal cool demeanour under siege. I felt a rush of affection for this feisty young woman – my niece, after all – and added to my resolve to keep her safe. "It will get worse, won't it?"

"Oh yes," I replied. "No point in pretending otherwise. I've decided to leave a company here, chosen men under one of my better captains, Willy Hume, a second cousin or some such. He's a steady fellow and his men are to be relied upon. I'll billet them here or hereabouts if you've no objection. On paper their job is to guard supply lines but Willy's orders will be to take special care of you and the sisters here. If things get bad or worse than bad, his orders will be to evacuate all of you to Coldingham. Make sure you are all ready to move at a moment's notice. Should that moment come, then time will be of the essence. Not that I need to labour the point, of course."

She nodded her thanks. She was exhausted and more vulnerable than I had ever seen her. I rather liked that. I'm not the sentimental sort, but, were I younger and were she not family, Mistress Hoppringle would have been tempting. I like women, always have – not with the random, priapic excess of our noble sovereign, but I have an appetite. I've tended to the view, though, that entanglement is dangerous. Women are good at keeping accounts and once you're firmly on the debit side, their demands can prove embarrassing.

Generally, I find it's easier just to pay for pleasure beyond the marital bed. I could have made an exception for the enigmatic, dark-haired abbess though. Briefly, and with a silly pang of jealousy, I wondered about her and Heron. I could live with being bested in the field – such things must happen – but beaten to the bed-chamber as well seemed downright unfair.

"Your friend," I continued, "now has my brother, as I have his. There I owe the Bastard an apology. Poor Will has not been as well cared for as I would have intended. Distracted by affairs of state, I have allowed his accommodation to be seen to by others. They're not used to having gentlemen, you see. I wouldn't put a dog into Fast Castle, not even the meanest mongrel."

"Will you do something for John's brother now?"

"I meant to anyway. I need to make amends. After all *he's* not the criminal, merely a surety, and it's very bad manners. Besides, Dacre will want him back and I hear George is well-enough housed. He's always cost me a fortune."

"What happens now?" she asked wearily. I was jolted from my almost amorous reverie, watching the agreeable motion of her shapely bosom. I was tired as well and she looked somehow even more beguiling without her customary armour of finery.

"The army will march. It will be quite some army too, I can tell you; the grandest that ever stepped over the border. Horse, foot, and guns – a great many guns, in fact, with a monstrous weight of shot and prodigious killing power; King James is about to rewrite the rule book. No fortress, however grand, will be safe once Norham falls – and it will. James is right; this won't be a repeat of '97. Then, that accomplished, the central corridor is busted wide open. The rest – Wark, Etal, and Ford – will collapse like a deck of cards. Master Heron may have to find fresh pastures. I'm sure he will."

I spoke a mite sourly perhaps but the fellow had just humiliated me, taken my brother – a burden, like most illegitimate offspring, but blood just the same – and, I suspected, stood quite high in my handsome hostess's affections.

"I don't understand any of this." There was a fresh tremour in her voice and I felt another stab of guilt for embroiling her in the dirty laundry. She'd been well paid, though, I reminded myself. "It seems like madness," she chided.

"There's some method, at least," I replied. "King James will march his grand army into a salient, a balcony if you like, blasted into the English march. His left will be covered once we have Norham and the chain of forts; his right is protected by high hills, and if he digs in wisely and deeply, his front will be impregnable. He can fly his banners and snub his nose at the Earl of Surrey till autumn comes. Weather's bad enough now; it never stops raining and it's as cold as a witch's pap."

"And that will be it," she persisted. "A stupid game of soldiers that will beggar Scotland, waste half the border, and accomplish what?"

You know women: grand strategy is a bit of a closed book. They think more in tactical terms.

"What King James hopes to achieve is a strategic stalemate. His incursion will compel King Henry to send Surrey north with all his power. My guess is he'll have twenty thousand men, maybe more. We will have numbers on our side, so if the earl is to fight – and he will be looking for a fight, no question there – he will need to fight on favourable ground. If we deny him the ground, manoeuvre and dig in so we bristle like a great fortress, he will not shift us. Every day we buy for France costs England dear. Surrey's men are raised by contract, not levy, so he has a hefty wage-bill day on day. Our fellows serve because they must."

I could see she understood. She had the quickness of a sparrow hawk. "Scotland buys time for France, then bleeds the English treasury. I can see that but does the King – ours I mean – intend to fight a battle? The way you explain it he doesn't have to."

"No, you are perfectly right; he does not. Rightly, battle should be the last thing he intends. With our flanks covered, the English cannot move to cut us off from the Tweed and thus from safety. Surrey will have no mandate, nor a deep enough purse, to mount an invasion of his own."

"Yet you have doubts?" Women might not do policy but they understand male vanities.

"King James is un-blooded. Oh yes, we crossed the line in '96 and '97, but that wasn't war, not really. We bolted as soon as Surrey came up – best thing too." I chose my words with care, knowing they'd be repeated to Dacre before the day was out. "The King has sufficient wit to understand the risks involved in offering battle. The ghosts of several of his ancestors could tell him why the tactics failed. Objectively, he understands our main weakness – that our men will fight with unfamiliar weapons using untried tactics. Admittedly, well-tried weapons and tactics have usually failed."

"And subjectively?" she persisted.

"Well, there is my chief worry and it sticks deep. In his heart he believes that on the right ground we can win. Perhaps he's right, but Surrey's a very old hand at this, was wearing harness long before James was weaned. He won't fight unless the ground suits, and he'll manoeuvre all ways to find that ground. He'll have Dacre and Heron, who know these marches like I know my own. All we need is a single mistake and we're in trouble, seriously deep trouble."

With that helpful conclusion, I made my excuses and rode out towards Edinburgh. I needed to get my report in before anyone else provided a more colourful, perhaps even accurate, version. The wounded were in good hands, and wounds, after all, are an occupational hazard for reivers. It's bad when you lose men but at least what spoils we'd salvaged would go further and keep the rest content.

The abbess now giving her version (earlier that day)

The warden is a hard man to fathom. He has lived so long in the shadow of deceit that he is forever a closed book. At times he seems to look upon me as a species of daughter – we're related after all. Yet, at other times, I catch a glance of an altogether different kind of interest. But that's all, just the suggestion. He is too much in control to let earthly temptation get in the way of policy. He is all about policy, about burnishing his name with fresh titles and a swelling estate. He has no thought for anything else. His pursuit is so refined he's almost an ascetic.

Dacre is subtly different: hard as flint, pitiless as iron, but ever the good servant. He's served several kings and each one well. He keeps a miser's grip on his own marches, keeps some semblance of order so his private enterprises are winked at. He has John Heron and a few others to do the real dirty work, so the crown winks at them also. Here am I, head of a religious house, taking money from both sides, selling secrets like a market vendor and getting hot at the thought of the most notorious of outlaws.

I was taking time out for this reverie in our physick garden, which is on the south side nearer the river, drawing on the richer, alluvial soil. It's been here for generations, based, I'm told, on an ancient plan from St Gall. Surrounded by a wicker fence and entered via a trellis, the garden has a series of raised beds. We've culinary herbs such as lovage, thyme, sage, and dill. Then there's a bed for medicinal plants, *Artemesia*, betony, plantain, comfrey, southernwood, and hyssop.

Ellen was bounding over the field towards me, lithe and lissom as a deer, her curtain of hair flying. "Quick," she exhorted, "you're needed!" I briefly wondered what part of our discussion on decorum she'd forgotten. "It's really urgent," she gasped, grabbing my arm and yanking me bodily. I gave in and followed.

She had not exaggerated. Our courtyard was already a shambles, like the aftermath of battle. It clearly was the aftermath. One of the warden's sergeants, Davy Little, I think, was in charge. He looked appealingly at me. "We've wounded," he announced unnecessarily. "We were cut up by damnable Bastard Heron and English bows. God knows how many we've lost."

Already there were dozens, some still mounted, though barely; others limped or stumbled on foot. "We've more coming in carts," he went on. "Can't say how many – lots." Ellen and the other women, along with half the servants, were gawping. Time to take charge; they were waiting for me, all of them it seemed.

"Right," I snapped at Master Little, "I want the able-bodied to help with the injured. I want the worst cases into the hospital, the walking wounded in the refectory. Ellen, clear the tables. Get the servants to draw straw for palliasses. Someone bring my medical chest and surgical kit, and quickly. Get a move on!" I yelled as they stumbled into action. More casualties were swelling the congestion in the courtyard. "Horses to stables or just hobble them outside; we don't need more muck inside. You," – this to my steward – "clear one of the barns."

"What for?" the dolt queried. Before I could answer, a youngish man stepped forward, plainly dressed in jack and sallet but with the air of a gentleman. "Giles Musgrave," he introduced himself. At once I saw the likeness to the Queen's buxom companion, her brother, an officer in the King's service. "Let me help," he suggested. "I'll sort the worst cases; Master Little here will organize the minor wounds."

By "worst" I knew he meant those who were beyond hope. Anyone might think this callous but we couldn't hope to save them all and that's the plain truth. A number would die whatever we attempted, so our efforts had to be concentrated on those who had some chance at least. It's the arithmetic of war, so utterly hateful.

"Take them through into the nearest barn. Margaret," I motioned to one of the older sisters, a steady matronly type, "make up some potions of hemlock and henbane to ease their pain. We'll need plenty."

Confusion reigned. The broken and maimed were streaming in faster than we could shift them, the walls of the yard already slick with blood and faeces. I left Musgrave in charge outside. He had a purposeful air and the habit of command. I knew I'd do most good in the hospital. All religious houses have hospitals, we have done for centuries. Ours was airy and well appointed. We cared for the sick and the elderly, for pilgrims seeking spiritual solace as well as earthly cure. Our present emergency was on an altogether different scale.

The place was solidly constructed with high clerestory windows that bounced light from whitewashed walls. I insisted it be kept clean. We strewed the flagged floor with wormwood and meadowsweet to combat insects and evil humours. Now, I cannot claim to be a physician. Very few women were allowed. But I'd been able to observe dissections in Edinburgh, I'm a skilled herbalist and reasonably competent with minor surgery. Besides, there was nobody else. But a lot of the surgery wasn't minor.

Our neat hospital was filling up, the aroma of herbs giving ground to blood, sweat, and ruptured intestines. Most with stomach wounds would be laid out with the no-hopers. Ellen was fussing over a young man, very young, no more than a boy, who'd sat down in the middle of the floor. He was the colour of marble but with no visible hurt. She was attempting to help him remove his dented sallet. "No! For God's sake, no!" I yelled. Too late: she'd wrested the thing off and now his brains were spilling down his doublet, a viscous bloodied ooze of grey matter and bone. His mess was soon accompanied by Ellen's dinner.

He died and I dragged the shocked girl to her feet, shaking her roughly. She was on the edge of hysteria. I wasn't that far behind. "Don't let me down, Ellen." I shook her again, bringing her back to focus. I wanted to hug her, to shield her from all this, but we were way past all that. "Carry on," I told her, "just carry on. I need bandages. I need water, all the herbs from the garden. Organize a couple of porters to move the dead out to beyond the barn and cover them up."

My calm and dignified house was suddenly a sea of suffering. I was completely out of my depth. I had watched physicians, even read Galen and de Liuzzi. I'd assisted with operations, carried out a few myself, but never on this scale of severity. Four fellows heaved another onto the scrubbed boards. He was a Hoppringle, a cousin, younger than me, terrified. An arrow, probably, or, so I hoped, a bodkin had punched through the visor of his fashionable armet and lodged in his face. Someone had tried to extract the point, clumsily, for it had only snapped the shaft.

The lad was thrashing about a fair bit so I had to get the others to hold him down, to unstrap and remove the helmet. He'd fouled himself and the stink of fear and bowels clung to my nostrils. He was conscious, eyes wide with terror. The bodkin had struck at an angle under the cheekbone, driving deep. It had missed the eye but must be lodged very close to the brain. Whichever idiot had snapped the shaft had left only a stub, not enough purchase to drag the point free without doing God knows what damage.

I administered henbane for pain relief. He'd need it. From my kit, a fair selection of saws, probes, and knives, I selected a finely threaded worm which, with infinite care, I could screw into the stump of ash to gain a purchase. My patient's companions watched in awe. Other people's sufferings are always fascinating. At last I had a grip and, with a swift prayer and sharp tug, jerked the point free in a gush of very bright red blood. I called for honey and cobwebs to pack the wound and could leave the dressing to one of the women. There were plenty more casualties to go round.

Around Nones, Hume's physician, George Beaton, arrived. The family have been healers since the days of Bruce. The good doctor's forebears had been physicians to the Lords of the Isles. This one was a stocky, rubicund fellow, modestly but expensively clothed in sober grey. He looked like your prosperous sort of innkeeper but I knew him to be a master of his profession. A team of barber-surgeons in plain hoden cloth rode on mules laden with chests of instruments and remedies.

"Daughter," he greeted me, "a joy as ever and you've brought me some trade, I see." His wiry ginger top was greying at the edges and a well-stocked belly bulged, but his eyes, fast and shrewd, were everywhere. A series of curt commands set his team in motion as slick as well-oiled tack. "Seems we've had quite an affray. That's the trouble with my calling, you know: either feast or famine."

I felt such a rush of relief at his familiar, infinitely confident presence that I could have wept. "Now then, my dear, let's have a look on the ward and see what you've brought me." He was very quick for a bulky man, his fingers nimble and strong. He moved from man to man, rapping out orders to his acolytes, steering the women. They'd come in from the town. Many had kin or friends amongst the wounded. They needed little direction from me. They'd all done this before. He glanced approvingly at my own efforts. "Admirable, my dear young lady, most admirable. If you'd been a boy, this should have been your rightful calling. I wish half my students had listened as well as you."

I was relegated to the rank of assistant and was heartily glad of it. By now, the tide of human wreckage had begun to ebb and whilst many remained untreated, the initial flood had subsided. "This will be the end of it," Beaton confirmed. "Any left behind will have been dealt with by now." The handsome Master Musgrave, who'd moved from chief scout to porter at death's hall, was still in charge of the worst cases, all discreetly removed to the barn and their condition eased as best we could.

He and the doctor had a hurried, muted conversation. He spoke, Beaton listened, and then when the marcher was done, he nodded curtly. Ellen, who had regained her composure and, bless the girl, had worked like a Trojan, made to follow as Musgrave went out. "Stay with me here, child," Beaton gently urged. "I and your mistress have need of you. Master Musgrave will see to the rest." Ellen merely nodded, clearly content. I knew what had passed between the two men and felt bile rise in my throat. Such things happen in war but not here, not under my roof – God's roof, I should say.

The doctor looked calmly at me. "It's best the lass doesn't see. She's had enough growing up for one day." I was about to speak; he motioned me to silence. "We'll say nothing and continue," he said. "It's for the best. Master

Musgrave is a serious young man who knows what he does. He is not without compassion."

"There must be something more we can do," I blurted, even though I knew he was right.

"It really is for the best," he repeated. "If we could help those poor fellows then we would, but it is beyond our power. They are in God's hands now. He will not judge you. Any man in their condition would ask for the same. No man deserves a lingering and agonizing death. Now help me with this fellow whilst I get the leg off."

It was still dark when the warden rode in. He was paler and more drawn than usual but outwardly unmoved. He made a quick tour of the wards. Some of the minor cases had already been sent on their way, some discharged to family, but the whole place looked like a charnel house. Discarded kit and harness was everywhere, blood and excrement in abundance. I'd several baskets of assorted hacked-off limbs and the whitewashed walls were no longer white. I'd not looked in the barn. Cowardly, I know, but Musgrave had set burial details to work discreetly out of sight.

"I am sorry for your trouble," the warden confided. "I would not have wished this hell upon you for the world." He may even have meant it; with him you could never tell. He steered me away from the carnage into my solar, which had largely escaped the onslaught. "Your women can do the ministering. You are utterly exhausted." He sat me down and poured a generous measure of decent liquor. "I can play the servant this once," he continued. "Your people are otherwise engaged. All have done good work today. The King shall hear of your ministrations."

For some reason, that unleashed the floodgates. I wept, I cried, I howled; horror, grief, rage, and frustration, fear as well, I suppose. I'd not blubbered like that since my pet rabbit died as a child. He sat next to me, probably as near affection as he'd ever get, one hand stroking my hair. "My poor, poor child," he soothed. "What have I embroiled you in?"

The lord warden now accompanies the Scottish army upon the line of march

In the streets of Edinburgh all was noise and excitement. The army was about to depart and convention demanded we put on a good performance. After all, we might not look as pristine when we got back. We might not get back at all.

"Not a bad show," Huntly offered, "as such things go." I understood the Gordon. Like me, he didn't give much away and his remarks were always cautious, careful, and chosen. There's no such thing as being among friends at court. He was right, though. King James was an average politician, probably a poor soldier, but a first-rate showman. Amongst princes, that tends to matter. Both he and Henry had an eye to dazzle. Radiance is good as long as you're not the one who gets blinded. "They march well enough," my companion continued, "and those guns are mighty impressive."

Again, he was right on both counts. Our fellows were stepping out neatly, their harness burnished to a brilliant shine, the long pikes shouldered. We both knew the march would soon degenerate, as dust, filth, and tiredness took hold and aching feet sapped ardour. Was there any ardour? I wasn't sure. I felt none but I'm old and cynical. The young lords fluttered like fireflies, their gleaming plate and proud banners a testament to their purses. His Majesty was resplendent, in gorgeous armour in the very latest style and never scarred by blades or campaigning. His royal arms and badge of office lent a fine gloss. He was wearing his lord admiral's chain, though as far as I could see, we weren't going anywhere near the sea.

"You need have no fear where your fellows are concerned," Huntly advised. "They're almost a joy to drill; took to their staves like true professionals."

"Did you mention loot?"

"I may have done; that seemed to encourage them no end."

"Usually does; my marchers are like your caterans..." These, I should say, are your wilder highland types – uncouth but effective when sober. "Fighting is a job to them, and as long as there's profit in sight, they won't grumble too much."

"I'll tell you what I've done. Well, you've seen the drill, of course. I'm using my handier lads as swordsmen to protect your flanks, put some bows out there too. I've got some squads of axe-men; you know how the Swiss use their halberds. My chaps carry their long-handled axes, very similar if not quite as smart. I'm putting them into the front ranks, so if your pikes are held up, my boys will clear the path and keep things moving. They're good at that."

As ever, I didn't doubt him. He'd thought our tactics through carefully and, like me, had taken a long hard look at what our Swiss teachers were doing. It was all about beefing up the line. If momentum slowed, his kerns would see it got going again. I wondered aloud if anyone else was doing the same.

"Not that I can see."

A succinct assessment but one laden with meaning; the Swiss did nothing by accident – never had, never would. They were very good at fighting. They got very well paid for it. Conscripts are a different thing altogether. A man who fights for wages knows why he's in the line and knows he won't get paid unless he wins. For most of King James's subjects this did not apply.

"Master Borthwick," I yelled out, competing with the fearful racket of the great guns. The master gunner was fussing over his ponderous great charges as they groaned and swayed through the city's gates. Each of the monsters was hauled by a long trail of oxen. Difficult brutes at best, guns and oxen both, the beasts shuffled and harrumphed as the drivers beat them on. The biggest ordnance required thirty apiece. Borthwick acknowledged our salute.

It was scarcely Prime and the morning cool but he was already sweating, stripped to oil-stained shirt sleeves. We ambled over, our palfreys flinching in the waves of noise. "Hot work, my lords," he confirmed, "damnably hot work. Be easier once we're clear of the streets, of course. Confound it, man, mind my supplies... Idiots, half of them," he continued. "I mean, I knew it wouldn't be easy – so many great guns, such a weight of powder and shot and so forth – but you can't train monkeys to dance; not in a fortnight anyway."

This was the matter I'd broached before. Most of the King's trained gunners were off with the fleet on a wild goose chase upon the seas, posturing with our French allies, pretending we could mix broadsides with the English fleet. We had what was left and what could be found.

"The guns are only as good as the men who serve 'em," he confirmed. "It ain't a trade; it's an art, and high art at that, even if I do say so myself. I'm not boasting, your lordships understand, but it takes me a good five years to train a handy crew. They need skill, strength, dexterity, and agility. Above all, they need nerve. None of these have seen a shot fired. Won't matter if we're rearranging castle walls – won't matter a toss. You've all the leisure you need. It's the poor sods inside who are taking the hammering. In the field, though, it will be different."

Master Borthwick looked at us both. He knew what he was saying would read badly in certain quarters. Most of those gaudy fireflies leading the army had no ear for bad news. He judged Huntly and me to be different. We both respected him and it was plain he told no more than the truth. Now, some might say I'm a stranger to the truth. Most times they'd be right, but war is different. In politics you can dissemble, shift your ground to suit, but war, and particularly battle, is the test of harsh reality. The harsh reality here was that our guns – magnificent, awe-inspiring, etcetera – were poorly served and that was a very bad thing indeed.

An army is a living organism, a vast, trailing serpent. It's never like you expect, aside from shows such as this, a circus for the cheering masses. We had marched from the Burgh Muir, the bulk of the foot had passed outside the walls, but the King, his officers, and the better-dressed rankers had paraded from the castle, down the high street. The banks of jumbled houses, crowding and spilling onto the overhung streets, were adorned as though for a saint's day. Flags and banners were everywhere. For once that miserable summer, the sun actually shone and the sky was clear, a perfect dusty blue with just a few high, languid trails of cloud.

The deeper into the lower town we marched, the worse it stank. The King had the common touch or at least would have it so. Today, the people loved him, thrusting their scruffy, scabby urchins up for a better view. I've no love for the commoners, but I can be civil enough. It goes with the job. I don't like the unwashed herd; they are as uncertain as the wind, fickle and inclined to savagery on the merest pretext. For preference I'd chain them to their slums and only feed 'em when taxes are due.

Trapped by the lofty tottering tenements, noise beat from the walls, the remorseless, regular tramp of thousands of marching men, the wild cheers of the crowd as thick as starlings. Once we were finally clear of the city, and it took till dinnertime, strung out along the line of march, slogging towards Dalkeith, the tempest of sound receded, swallowed up by countryside. Some watched us still, by the roadside, insofar as the milling swamp of a track could be so described. These were country-folk though and far more wary. They knew what the passage of armies meant. Friendly or not, doesn't matter: an army tramples, consumes, pilfers, bullies, and abuses. It's best to keep out of the way altogether. As marshal, my job was to keep things moving, put some stick about, cantering along the great sinuous serpent of the army.

I was summoned to the royal presence at the head of the column, unsullied by dust and muck. "Well now, Alec, what do you think? Are we sufficient? Will our enemies run like dogs before us?" James was in high good humour. He liked playing soldiers. I'd noticed I was increasingly excluded from his inner circle. Doubters weren't welcome and I knew there were mutterings. James continued, "This is the finest army Scotland has ever mustered – not just the biggest, the best. Our guns would be the marvel of any army. I hope your fellows are ready?"

"Indeed, Your Majesty," I replied unctuously, "ready and willing." That much was true. They were keen to be off and over before anyone else could pick the place clean.

"We will be forty thousand strong," the King kept on. "Imagine that. How many can Surrey muster? Less than half, I'd guess, and all the scrapings." I did not reply but merely nodded sagely. We had had this discussion. I had made the point tirelessly that the enemy we faced would be far from second rate.

"Then let the damned soothsayers mutter," the King went on sourly. "Divine warnings my backside. Who believes that nonsense nowadays?"

You, for one, I thought.

Before we'd set off, James had encountered some rather strange characters who had issued dire warnings about invading England and entertaining loose women. The Queen was, I suspected – in fact I knew – behind all this daft mummery. She knew her husband though. Inside this great and mighty prince there lurked an uncertain schoolboy, unsure mostly of himself. All he did now was in order to prove his manhood, as much to himself as the rest of us. Well, the invasion was on regardless, and as for women, there were none on the borders now safe. Such appetites as men have are sharpened by war.

Strung out, the army had rather lost its lustre. Now it was altogether more workaday. A mounted vanguard with prickers beyond was strung out a dozen miles in front, and the great, winding tail of camp and followers stretched for another dozen behind. I'd already spurred past the massed brigades more than once. Our great lords with their household men looked smart enough, most mounted, the foot loons rather more shambling, muddied by the miry track, trailing their cumbersome pikes. I know these can win battles but they're awful heavy on the move. Most were marching in their everyday gear, homespun doublet and hose. Some had harness, others jacks, but many had nothing more than a crude sallet with chains sewn onto their kit to afford some measure of protection.

Our rear echelon, if so formal a description could suffice, was enormous, biblical. A population greater than any town in Scotland straggled behind the army: sutlers, vintners, carpenters, joiners, labourers, farriers, smiths, armourers, bowyers, fletchers, quacks and apothecaries, wives, campaign wives, women, all their wild children. We had cattle and sheep, goats, pigs, geese, and fowl. The King had forbidden free quarter this side of the line, so what we ate came with us. Carts carried all the gunners' stores, spare harness, medical supplies, tents, and pavilions of the gentry. On through the long summer's afternoon we toiled, still blessed by the light.

"Can your fellows shoo Heron and his moss-troopers away, I wonder?" asked Huntly. We were walking the horses, just to the rear of the vanguard.

"He'll be there," I replied. "Dacre has eyes everywhere; besides, this lot aren't something you can easily hide. Let 'em look, I say. The sheer scale of our forces might just make them think twice."

"Perhaps, but you don't believe it?"

"Not for a moment, I'm afraid. Surrey wants a battle even more than James. He can't afford to keep an army here just to watch us through the autumn. It would bankrupt the treasury and his King is unforgiving." I let the implication hang in the air. Kings are naturally unforgiving. That is why my own place, seemingly secure, was anything but. If there's one thing a king really hates it's a kingmaker. I'd served his father – badly, I admit – and I'd been instrumental in removing him. This had been good for our James but he'd always be looking over his shoulder.

Once you break your oath to royalty, it can easily become a habit. Old Warwick, the great maker of kings, had shown that. He swore to serve one king, broke his oath to make another, then betrayed that king with his own brother. After that didn't work, he swore a fresh oath to the king he'd helped depose, and, further betraying his second oath, put the old man back on the throne. It got him killed in the end but that's a lesson for kings and kingmakers.

My own muster was at Ellam, where my division would join the main army. Next day we'd cross over the Tweed at Coldstream, Scotland's Rubicon. Once across, we were really at war, no more posturing. Not a prospect I relished.

John Heron makes an assessment

"I will concede that things aren't going quite as well as I'd hoped."

I've heard many understatements but this was a pearl. Master Anislow's haggard features were an eloquent confirmation. His confidence had sagged like his jowls. He was puffy, grey, and unshaven. I didn't blame him. If we were not in hell we were in a pretty fair facsimile. Norham's walls stank like the plague; a black, sulphurous fog clung to the place like a leaden shroud, courtesy of the Scotch gunners. We were in the great hall, stripped bare of all adornment.

The formidable keep, vast monstrous pile that it is, rocked to its foundations when another smashing round-shot hammered the walls – or what was left of them; the outer ward was breached in two places. His French officers had probably advised King James that the breaches were practicable. They weren't, as a mound of dead could testify – not this time, anyway – but there were an awful lot of Scotsmen outside.

"You did try to warn me, but I was over-confident. I am sorry if I appeared discourteous," he went on wearily. "But I was sincere, you understand; I really thought we could do it. The bishop won't be at all happy." The prince bishop's worries were the least of the castellan's concerns. Thousands of impatient Scots and a dozen and more great guns were altogether more pressing.

"Look here," I said. "Your powder and shot are almost gone. The walls are crumbling. Dacre hoped you'd hold for a month, at least, but you aren't going to last the week. We both know that when the Scots offer terms you will have to accept. Nobody will blame you for that. No point in sacrificing your men for a half-witted point of honour, and, if James takes this place by storm, he'll likely string any survivors up."

Now what the devil was I doing inside the fortress? My job was to keep an eye out, not get stuck in. Well, Norham is an ancient hold. Like most, it has a network of passages which lead in from secret entrances outside. This isn't legend or myth. When a garrison is under siege you need to be able to get messages in and out, same with supplies. You have to be careful, of course: the enemy has lookouts. Most of the Scottish army were encamped by the river and there were an awful lot of them. I'd not seen armies this size since Italy and I'd guess there was fully thirty thousand fighting men and a sprawling hinterland of followers.

"It's those guns, you see," Master Anislow continued. "I've never seen the equal. I mean, I knew they had cannon, naturally, but nothing like this. It's the work of the devil."

It's odd how many fellows see Lucifer's hand when they're losing, but this was no time for recriminations. I even felt sorry for him. There wasn't really anything he could have done. His great fortress was redundant. The 'Queen of the border' had just been dethroned. Times had changed. He had not.

I had a couple of my steadier lads with me. The rest were lying up to the south, keeping watch on our back door. Even Crookback Will, who'd seen a scrap or two, jumped every time one of the monsters belched. I affected nonchalance. It's what's expected, and besides, I'd had some experience.

Then, there was a shout from the ward. Our visitors were getting restless and the trumpets were blowing. "Will you stand with us?" Anislow asked plaintively. "Having one like you amongst us will give the lads heart. They need it," he added unnecessarily. I bang on about reputation and honour – the only assets I had – but I will tell you plainly, my instincts were to run. We tumbled out into the inferno of the inner ward. As the guns fell silent it seemed like deliverance. It wasn't. This was the calm before a different storm: they'd be sending in the infantry.

I've never liked this type of fighting – close up and very nasty. Doesn't matter how well you handle a blade, how nimble or alert, survival is random. It depends purely upon fate. There would be several thousand Scots in the attack and we'd be a tenth of that. They were fresh and rested; our chaps were half starved, ragged, knackered, and many already had wounds. Still, hard to say no.

I heard Crookback swear loudly and inventively as we ventured into the ward; the outer had mostly gone. We held what was left of the towers and precious little else. They came on like a steel-tipped avalanche. Banners floated, adding colour to the miasma. The smell was even worse: sulphur, blood, death, sweat, urine, faeces, and fear – war's potion. On the walls and what was left of the parapet, our men manned their guns, mere toys by comparison, and only a few rounds apiece. One man, who could easily have been my father judging by his age, limped by, his hose torn and bloodied, calf crudely bandaged, clutching his bill.

Up to the parapet walk we went – best seats in the house. "Right, lads," I yelled above the din. "Here they come. Your fathers and grandfathers kept 'em out. Let's see if we can do the same. Be of a good will and ready to be at them. We don't want those tosspot southerners saying we couldn't hold the line without them, do we?"

Not much of an oration, but all those grand speeches you may have read were written long after any fight. Men about to die have little need for playwrights. They just need to know they're not alone. We were alone, of course; about as alone as it gets.

The roar came louder as the forlorn hope struggled up the rubble.[11] Now, it might be obvious but any decent gunner will batter a wall from the bottom up. He wants the masonry to fall outwards and form an orderly ramp, so his infantry can close. That's the theory anyway. It's rarely the same in practice. The noise was like a hurricane, beating over the shattered walls, a rampart of furious sound that swelled with the chorus of drums, trumpets, and those infernal braying pipes the Scotch seem so addicted to.

Well harnessed, their levelled pikes a forest of staves, the Scots came on. All in good order; these were chosen men, so our time here would not be wasted. The more we killed today the fewer we'd face later – if we lived, that is. They clambered steadily, not in a rush, keeping close order – well, as close as you can. The ramp of tumbled stones was an obstacle in itself. Our fellows had thrown up barricades, lined by our shot. Archers filled the walls.

---

11 "Forlorn hope" is the first party to assault the breach, a place of honour and great danger.

They were waiting for me, our chaps. My name and Dacre's commission gave me authority. Gentlemen, sons of gentlemen, almost-gentlemen, and commoners waited upon my convenience. I made a show of cleaning out a random fingernail, ever so casually. Then, as they were perhaps twenty yards distant and no more, I gave the nod.

Hellfire and brimstone, our volley thundered. Smoke belched out, instantly blotting the assault party. Fire ripped them apart. Men were lifted bodily and flung back, blood spraying out in as many fountains. The attack wavered as though struck by lightning. Our bowmen drew and loosed; almost every shaft found its mark against such a press and at virtually point-blank range.

King James had made armour for his men: munition-quality stuff to be sure but serviceable enough. It would do at a distance but close up was more of a hindrance. Shot punched straight through; our men's cloth-yard shafts sought out weak spots, drove through visors, struck at the shoulder or groin. Men were screaming. One fellow, shorn of both arms, thrashed noisily on the blood-slick stones till he bled out.

These affairs are always bloody, so many compressed into so small a space, so much fire directed at so few. But they came on, clambering over their own dead, kicking flailing bodies clear so the lifeless and dying formed mounds of their own. I'd borrowed a crossbow – not one of our horsemen's latches but a hefty piece, spanned by a lever. It was devilishly slow compared with our bows but hideously effective at such short range.

I sighted at an officer, a big burly fellow in a nicely chiselled breast and back. If things went well, they'd be mine. As he raised his sword arm to encourage his lads, I shot him, the short stubby bolt driving through to the heart. He went back without a sound, stone dead. No comfort, there were plenty more behind.

We must have killed or maimed scores of them, with few hurts on our side as far as I could see. Their numbers impeded them. The thicker the press, the slower they struggled forward and the better the target they presented. They wavered; I could feel it.

A battle is like a kind of dance (not that I'm much of a dancer). You have to sense your partner's moves, be ready to respond to the merest nuance. It was time this reel was ended. They had got close enough for our bills to strike. Their order was gone and the pike, supreme on the field, was no match in a melee. Our fellows could wield a bill; it was in their blood. Less so in mine but I grabbed one anyway and got stuck in. There are times when being only half a gentleman has its compensations.

Killing them was easy. Their long staves could not be swung, their puny points hacked off. They lacked order. There was no cohesion, no momentum, left. We chose our stance and fought them – killed and kept killing, our bows still shooting into their flanks. Finally, they were gone, like an ebb tide racing out, falling back, mainly in good order, I'll confess, but beaten nonetheless. We sped them on their way with loud huzzas and a storm of shafts. The mound was no longer splintered, whitened stone but a heaving carpet of dead and dying. Glossy strings of spilt intestines garnished the wreckage, steaming in the foetid air.

Norham was saved and for a good hour at least.

Both my chaps had come through unscathed and, true to their calling, were amongst the first stripping the dead. Our situation overall might be hopeless but old habits die hard. I reined them in. "Time we were elsewhere," I suggested. Getting out was as easy as getting in. The Scots were too busy licking their wounds and loading their cannon for another storm. We slipped southwards like wraiths, dodging patrols, hugging the contours. This was how we lived, after all – half a day's ride back to Percy's bastion of Alnwick where Lord Dacre kept a temporary headquarters.

"A right fine, royal, and total mess," the warden growled. His lordship was lording it in Percy's vast citadel, not stinting himself when it came to the earl's stocks, though the dram he grudgingly shoved towards me made you think it was his own. "That fool Anislow; I knew the fellow was a fool. Don't even think about telling me you told me so." It was wisest to remain silent and let the squall blow itself out. He slumped at the board. "God knows what I'm going to say to Surrey, and that tosspot cleric will see me sacked. What's to be done?"

I'd been wondering this myself and none of the answers I had would give much comfort. "James has Glendale in his hand; he's punched a hole in our defences..."

"Such as they were... I hope you finished your packing?"

"I'm not being too optimistic there. My sister-in-law is writing to King James to broker some kind of deal and get my brother back."

"Well, I wish her good luck but you know it won't work. The Scotch cretin will burn you out and Manners at Etal too, and then what?"

"He won't stay at Ford. I've heard there's typhus in the camp already."

The warden grunted. "Let's hope that pestilence takes the whole lot of them off, but it won't, you know. Surrey is no nearer than Newcastle, his muster nowhere near complete. I've perhaps fifteen hundred lances, no more."

"The Scotch," I continued, "have lost men at Norham, more now to sickness, and they'll soon be deserting in droves. James can't keep such a huge force in the field indefinitely."

Another grunt from my employer: "He's not just going to turn around and go home. That would be failure; makes a joke of all his preparation."

"I didn't say he'd run. No chance of that. He'll dig in and dig deep."

"Where?"

I'd thought about this too. "It has to be along Flodden Edge, west to east. It's the obvious place. Some of my lads saw what was probably a pioneer detachment moving up there yesterday – well screened by cavalry, of course. If he throws up earthworks and he has plenty of engineers and sites his guns properly, he'll create a natural fortress. He has a clear field of fire over Millfield Plain in front, high hills to his left, the river downhill on his right. He is secure on both flanks; plenty of room for his army, straight road home behind him."

Lord Dacre swore fluently and at length – didn't add much to the tactical assessment but summed up his mood and our prospects most eloquently. "Surrey will really love this," he snarled. "Scotch thieves, got us by the short and curlies. All they need do is sit there, nice and dry, whilst we dance around them and then slope off back home when it suits. They keep our forces in the field, win the eternal gratitude of their garlic-eating Froggie friends, then wave two fingers and run for the hills when it suits 'em. How the devil do I put all this to Surrey without losing my job?"

"Perhaps you should just say the tactical situation remains fluid."

"Yes, maybe I will. Quite like that in fact: say little, tell nothing. If you ever decide to swap murder and robbery for murder and politics you'll do well, Johnny." That got me a bigger dram.

Lord Dacre now reports to the Earl of Surrey

1st September

Your Grace,

It is with a heavy heart that I must report the fall of Norham Castle to the Scots. That outcome which I did daily dread is now certain and they have possession of the place. Our officers and all our company within are now their prisoners. The facts are plain enough and just as Your Grace did fear. The Scots' guns are wondrous mighty and their weight of shot far exceeds anything we have seen before. It was said a base traitor from our people showed the King of Scots where to lay his guns. Be that as it may King James did hang the fellow for his treachery, or so it is said.

The siege lasted five days and both wards were breached. Our fellows gave a good account of themselves, and three times the Scottish spears were repulsed. Master Heron, upon my instruction, did enter in and fight alongside. Though the Scottish dead were piled high in the breaches, our men were forced to capitulate through want of powder and shot, having used up their stocks at a prodigious rate. Whilst I could curse Master Anislow for his neglect, Heron assures me he is blameless and did as well as any man might, discharging his duty till all became hopeless. In short the cornerstone of our defence is taken. King James can now proceed upon our marches at his leisure. Master Heron and the light horse remain in contact with the enemy, who has now summoned Wark and Etal to surrender.

These will not hold, no more will Ford. As yet I cannot fully discern what the King of Scots intends. He allows chance to dictate much, I ween. Our Friend can tell us no more, for the King keeps his counsels close. Though he has high office, as you know, our Friend is not within the King's circle of intimates. He is mistrusted. Master Heron is of the opinion, and I concur, that the King will not pursue his advance past Wooler; rather, he will seek out high ground and thereupon dig in, fortifying his camp and emplacing his guns so as to render his position inexpugnable.

This will be greatly to our disadvantage, for in such country Your Grace's army will struggle to come at them. King James, a novice in war, yet has good advisors, French and Italian, well schooled in the art of fortification, whose efforts may gravely embarrass us. With his flanks secure and a supply corridor across the Tweed and through Coldstream he will be well placed to defy us till the season be out. I pray therefore for Your Grace's swift march north so that we might raise our banners and send these devils post haste back to hell.

I have the honour, Your Grace, to remain, etc...

The English camp by Wooler; the Bastard solicits information

"Now look," I cajoled. "There really isn't any need for any of this unpleasantness. I don't enjoy playing the villain. All you have to do is help me and then we're done, *comprenez-vous*?"

Passable French was about my only bonus from the Italian Wars – that, and a few additional scars. The fellow I was addressing was indeed French, or I was pretty sure he was. He'd come into my possession the day before, had been with a patrol of Scottish horse, having a snifter down by the river – the Till, that is. We'd moved camp up towards Wooler, pulling the army together. As ever, we were eyes and ears. The Scots were dug in to the west, along the high ground as I'd anticipated, and mighty industrious they'd been. Just how industrious is what I needed to know. They had the place fenced pretty tight; no chance of us getting within a mile.

"What I need from you is very simple. I just want you to draw a nice sketch of the Scots' earthworks and camp. Dead easy: you don't have to speak, you don't have to write. Nobody will ever know, will they? I mean, I'm not telling, you don't need to, and these chaps here don't get to the French court that often. The only court they're ever likely to see deals in rope's end."

They'd thought they were safe with the river between us; I'd some of my chaps milling on the east bank. A small patrol of chosen men were with me on the Scottish side, hidden in the lee of the bank. As soon as Francois (my christening) and his pals were in reach, we'd jumped 'em; jumped 'em good and proper. The Scotch had done the sensible thing – dug spurs and belted back up the hill. My captive and a mate attempted the honourable thing and made a fight of it.

He was a fencer to be sure – well enough trained but had never encountered the border shift, that alarmingly effective manoeuvre of tossing the blade from hand to hand to confuse your opponent. The very large bruise on the side of his head testified to its effectiveness. The other one hadn't been so lucky, depending on how you define luck, that is.

"I don't like this thuggish stuff, you know. It isn't gentlemanly; even the scoundrel in me doesn't like it." True enough, I'm not naturally an advocate of what you'd call torture; it's nasty at best but sometimes inevitable. "You'll see our warden has left the tent; he doesn't want to see what we do here. I don't blame him; it's not nice. It's very painful and terribly degrading – for you, that is. Master Robson and Master Armstrong here may lack the finesse of your Dominicans but they make up for it with their enthusiasm."

He understood me. I could tell. Too aloof to say a word, he was a bit more shop-worn than when I'd captured him. His fine dark doublet was messed up and laced with blood, all his own. His pale, aquiline features were a bit less regular since the lads had softened him up, a few teeth gone, one eye closed by swelling, cheekbone busted. You know the sort of thing – ignoble, downright nasty but, from time to time, inevitable and necessary.

My tone was the epitome of reason, as though we might agree some half-decent compromise. "*Vous-avez une femme, les enfants?*" He didn't answer, just glared, but a flicker of the eyes told me he had both, which was a shame as they would soon be widow and orphans. You think me cruel? If you go to war you have to live with the consequences. Our backs were very firmly against a very flimsy wall and so courtesy went out of the window.

"It's easy," I continued. "Just a sketch is all I need. I'm not expecting you to sign it and it won't be hanging on anybody's wall. We'll pretend we got the information from a deserter – plenty of those, we've seen 'em slinking off. After that we'll get you cleaned up, say you had a nasty fall or two – happens all the time round here. Your Scottish ally has a whole parcel of our chaps he bagged at Norham. You'll be exchanged within the week... I give you my word as an officer." Don't sneer; I was an officer and had risen to the strictly temporary status of deputy-warden. Hopefully, he might believe me. He must be thirsty. He'd glanced at the pitcher of water standing on the warden's table.

"Master Armstrong," I commanded, "I think our guest could use some lubrication." Water: it looks innocuous, yet it's a cheap and effective tool for loosening recalcitrant tongues. I could see a look of almost gratitude in his almond eyes as Christie's Will hefted the jug. Any anticipation was short-lived. He was soon gagging and thrashing as they emptied the contents.

As I said, water-treatment is a cheap and very effective way of gaining someone's cooperation. It produces all the horror and agony of drowning and can be repeated to suit, the subject being pulled back from extinction every time. First, you cover the victim's face with a hood – it robs him of his usual senses. He's strapped down to a wooden plank, angled downwards. Next, you place several layers (I find three is best) of cloth over the hood and begin to pour. Initially the water goes up through the nostrils and the instinctive reaction is to breathe through your mouth. All that does is pull the fabric tight against your face. The result is as much due to panic as drowning.

We gave our Frenchman three good doses till I judged he couldn't take much more – gagging, mewing through his broken teeth, retching up from an empty belly fit to bust. He still wouldn't play, though. No matter; it was time for

Sergeant Carleton to make his entrance. Lance Carleton is one of Dacre's henchmen. They're a tough bunch but you wouldn't turn your back on them if you understand me. Certainly not on Lance who, with a suitable flourish and before our guest's terrified gaze, produced his absolutely favourite toy, the pilliwinks.

These are better known as thumbscrews. Our Frenchman recognized the gear all right; he began rolling his eyes and twisting against the bonds. "For God's sake, lad," I murmured consolingly. "Make it easy on yourself; think of your wife and bairns." He was nearly with me, I could tell, and when Master Carleton, as swift and terrible as a hawk, clamped the screws upon his thumbs, I could see he'd lost the will. He messed himself. I'd have done the same.

Again, this is just a technical note. The pilliwinks are very simple, like most good tools. They're formed of three vertical bars. The thumbs are placed between. A wooden slat is slid down along the bars, pressing flesh against the base. A simple screw then exerts pressure on the bar, crushing the thumbs with exquisite slowness and unendurable agony. If I hadn't been so busy otherwise, I'd have found time to admire our man's courage. I'd have blubbered everything I knew long since, and they call me a hard case.

It's not so much the noise of your subject screaming – I'm used to that and we'd gagged him anyway. No, it's the grinding, rather liquid sound the screw makes as it bores through the soft flesh and tissue and begins to crunch up the bones – a sound that conjures up a sea of pain.

A couple of expert turns sufficed. Lance looked disappointed, as though he'd anticipated some more fun. He wanted a few more notches for sport, but I demurred. I needed our man to have the use of his fingers. He was weeping and cursing – in French, of course. I got the lads to clean him up a bit, then put parchment and ink down. "Draw," I said. "Rely on your knowledge and not your imagination, for I will know the difference and it will come back to bite you. What you've had today is just a taster. We can do much worse, trust me." I could see that he did.

He drew quickly, if rather shakily, giving me what I needed. When he'd finished I looked at his plan. It was pretty much as I'd thought. His sketch of the central redoubt reminded me of fieldworks I'd seen on the continent. "*Trace Italienne*?" I queried. He nodded wearily, now shivering uncontrollably. It's often the case. "Take care of our good friend here," I ordered the boys. I translated into French; it seemed polite. The last words a man hears should really be in his own language.

Dacre had vacated his tent for the space of my interrogation. Being fully a gentleman he could hardly be associated with such crude nastiness. Crookback and Christie's Will had soothingly removed our guest. Borderers are the world's most accomplished liars.

"Well?" he snapped. The lord warden wasn't strong on small talk.

I spread out the sketch, which I'd had time to annotate. "What the devil's this?" He pointed to the bastion.

"State of the art," I responded. "Latest thing in Italian design; essentially it's a defended gun platform, strong, stable, all round fields of fire and solidly built, reinforced with gabions."

"What are all these?" The forward slope of Flodden Hill was studded with the same symbols.

"Those are the guns," I explained. "Lots of them, well dug in and sighted. Anybody who attempts to come up that hill will be shot to pieces. We'll never get near. If we do and we can take the punishment, their pikes will finish what's left. The King may be a novice but his professionals aren't."

"Damned foreigners," Dacre muttered. "They'll damn well wish they'd stayed at home by the time I'm done. This is our land, laddie, and nobody takes up residence without asking. How the devil do we see 'em off though? Aside from ground they're two to our one at best."

"I'm glad you asked me that. I have an idea."

The Earl of Surrey writes once again to his son

2nd September

My most dear and beloved son,

It has gone as I feared and Norham is fallen, with it the gates to the march, and the King of Scots will soon, if he is not already, be so surely entrenched that we shall struggle to evict him. More likely he will simply slip away upon news of our approach and leave us looking like fools. The weather has taken his part, for I was near drowned between here and Durham. Our guns at least are come up and we have stores enough for now but once we march north of Newcastle, our supply becomes daily more difficult.

There are scarce any roads worthy of the name; those there be are rutted and waterlogged. The borderers live like jackals. That we be their fellows will count for nothing; they will despoil us as best they may and that's the one art they have mastered. Northumberland is a dank and miserable place. It bears all the scars of two centuries and more of strife. What habitations there are remain poor, scattered, and miserable to a degree you would scarcely credit. Sod huts and bothies cluster around towers and castles.

Even the gentry are mostly thieves, for they all live by robbery here. They rob the Scots and each other with a fine impartiality. They are, I grant, skilled in arms and nimble upon their horses. They cannot be trusted, though, for all are too cosy by half with the Scots, inter-married and inter-bred; all laws to the contrary are more honoured in the breach than the observance. They know no law, and for the most part they worship no god. They are much addicted to drink and their form of vengeance, which they term "the feud" or "feid" as they call it. If one of their name is injured by another, then they will all take his part and return worse for like. So it goes on, for time out of mind. They will slaughter each other, hewing their victims in pieces for a long forgotten slight in their grandfathers' day.

These then will be our companions. But all is not darkness and gloom. At Durham I collected the old flag of St Cuthbert, the greatest talisman of the north. How many times have our people beat the Scots, succoured by the saint? You'll recall that old story of Alfred I used to tell you and your brothers. How, when all seemed lost in the wet marshlands and the larder was as bare as the muster roll, an ancient pilgrim called and the King gave him his dinner as a courteous man should. How again that night the old man came to Alfred in a vision, saying, "I am Cuthbert, a soldier of Christ, and I am your shield." Well now it is we who will have that shield and perhaps it is as mighty as ever and we shall deal with these boasters as Alfred did the Danes!

Your most loving father...

Chapter Six: Councils of War

We are but warriors for the working day;
Our gayness and our gilt are all besmirch'd
With rainy marching in the painful field.

Shakespeare: *Henry V*, Act IV, Scene iii

Old Surrey writes again the same day

2nd September

My dearest son,

Newcastle is fit to burst, which is why I move the army towards Alnwick. We need to instil some order and ready our fellows to face the Scots; already we've tripled the size of the population here. From all the miry lanes and highways of Lancashire, Cheshire, and the Dales the men keep coming in. Sir Edward Stanley has raised some six thousand and more of his people who, having mustered initially at Hornby and Lancaster, came up to me beneath the banners of the Earl of Derby and St Audrey.

At Skipton in Craven they were joined by two thousand more under the colours of James Stanley, Bishop of Ely, commanded by his bastard. No fewer than twelve hundred more have come up from south Lancashire and Cheshire. Scrope brings his bows and bills from Wensleydale and Swaledale. The north riding marches behind Conyers whilst Clifford has mustered the flower of Craven.

Old enemies, too, some of these. The northern burgesses have sent their quotas, men from Hull and a company from York, led by the sword-bearer and carrying their city's standard of a red cross with five golden lions. I know these men, you see. I fought with their fathers, aye, and a few grandfathers, and they know me. They know us Howards. They know, as their fathers knew, that I am a plain-speaking fellow who will not play them false nor will be careless with their lives. When I beheld them in the great hall of the old castle here (even though it is called "new"), old Marmaduke Constable was there – must be near as ancient as me. They are straightforward men and their fellows are of a like.

Ours will not be a "modern" army such as the King of Scots may boast, but I'll warrant no truer company ever set out. When I beheld them – these plain men from the working day with their battered and bruised harness – it was then I viewed our task in a different light. Let Wolsey and the rest of his creeping toadies sneer as they will. Let them say they have humbled the mighty Howards. But I tell you this: it is we who shall have the honour from this war. I see it now. It is, by God's grace, we who shall have fresh laurels. Our cause is just, our company noble. I yearn now for our coming together, for we shall have much work to do.

Your ever-loving father, etc...

The abbess pursues her new vocation

"Vermin, dog-leech," fumed Dr Beaton. Death in all its forms, sickness, pain, and anguish did not dent his professional detachment, but an attack upon his art and livelihood was guaranteed to enrage.

"You vile horse-gelder, tinker, vagabond, scum: you would pass yourself off as a surgeon, you would have the same wages as my fellows here who have spent years learning their skills. You profess to treat wounds, and with what?" He brandished the offending potion. "I'll tell you with what – with a foul concoction of shoemaker's wax and rust. Rust, I say, scraped from old iron."

The object of his ire was a scruffy, diminutive, one-eyed, slack-jawed, raggedy-man, caught masquerading as one of his staff, drawn by the lure of wages and perks of the trade – excused fatigues, drill, and the like. The little man was terrified, spittle hanging. Hume's provost was happy to carry out Beaton's sentence, a flogging the best he might get away with.

"Be off with you," the doctor commanded, most leniently in the circumstances. "Do not let me see you again or it will be the whipping post. Get him out of my sight."

We did have more pressing concerns. My house had become a town, a city of canvas and bothies. Since Norham was first besieged, wounded had been coming in by the cartload. Hume had sent the sisters from Coldingham to swell our auxiliaries and put me in charge – not, I knew, on the basis of seniority or merit but simply because there was no one else around.

I'm not squeamish and I've seen the consequences of many a foray, but this was just sheer waste on an enormous scale. "Why do princes assume their conquests will be bloodless?" I asked. "Did King James imagine he would fight a war without loss?"

"Such matters do not feature highly in the thoughts of princes," the doctor replied, his customary equanimity restored. "They tend to think in terms of policy, and assume others, lower down the pecking order, will see to the bandages. Generally never happens in my experience, though to be fair our European allies and indeed their adversaries – and I've worked for both – are adding more surgeons to their forces every campaign. More and better, I should say. Look at this."

He produced from his kit an intricate-looking tool, beautifully constructed, and seemingly worked by a series of transverse screws. "I'm not sure if it's a medical instrument or a device for torture," I answered.

"Oh, it's rather ingenious," he went on. "Only thing wrong with it is I didn't invent it. This is what's known in the profession as a goose-billed bullet forceps. We've had devices for removing the nastier, barbed kind of arrows forever, of course, but this is new, designed for extracting lead balls from gunshot wounds. State of the art, I can tell you. Ah, and here we have a customer."

A wounded man was carried in by four orderlies; the warden had assigned me a score of his older men, unfit for combat. They were happy enough with their lot, easier and safer than the front line. The injured man was laid on his side. By his dress I could tell he was a gentleman, a cousin of Scott of Buccleuch, I found out. At first he looked unhurt. As Beaton and I moved to turn him over, we saw the mess spurting through his doublet on the left side of his chest and shoulder.

The remains of his coat were already saturated with blood. Either round-shot or a heavy harquebus ball had punched a hole so deep the lung was fully exposed. Cloth from his torn doublet had been driven into the gaping wound. Those ribs over the heart collar bone had been shattered, showing gaunt and splintered. The muscles of his chest had been ripped into long strips, torn apart and grotesquely knotted together by the force of the impact. His left arm was attached only by the torn, ragged sleeve and then tendrils of flesh.

"No need of this little fellow," the doctor observed, laying the bullet-extractor aside. "A potion of henbane, as strong as you like, and we'll commend him to God's care."

A young lad was hovering by. He was the dying man's brother. "There must be something you can do," he expostulated.

"I'm afraid not, laddie," Beaton confirmed sadly. "He is beyond my help. The abbess will see to his spiritual need. He will feel no more pain."

Administering the sacrament was becoming second nature and I was pretty near word perfect by now. Even the most potent herbs can only reduce the pain to a degree. This young man would die in unendurable agony unless Master Musgrave or someone else eased his passage.

I'd become hardened to this. There were so many wounded that we couldn't hope to treat them all. Such medicines as we had were running desperately short. Fresh supplies had been requested from other houses but these took time to arrive. Bandages were washed and reused till they disintegrated. The handsome captain helped out when his scouting duties allowed. Ellen, I could see, was smitten. I thought it was probably wisest to get the girl married off – best for both of us – and I very much doubted her true vocation lay in the church. She was born to breed if ever anyone was, and, looking at the carnage around, the nation's bloodlines would need re-stocking.

"I know you think me cruel," Musgrave once said as he assisted on my interminable rounds.

"No," I replied honestly. "I'm just not used to the logic of war. I'm not judging you. I understand Dr Beaton has instructed you in this. I know I'm being squeamish, that there is no choice, but my order is dedicated to preserving life, not extinguishing it, and I hate the whole awful business. Being so helpless, knowing these men cannot be saved, causes me to despair."

"You'd best take that up with King James and King Henry," he observed drily. "They're the ones who made this happen. The rest of us just do the best we can."

"I'd like to believe that," I replied, laying my hand on his arm to show I meant no offence. "Yes, princes may begin quarrels, but men love to take up the gage. You adore your banners, your armour, your swords, your imaginings of glory and great deeds. This is the result. You know that perfectly well but you never learn. You don't seem to want to. You are obliged to serve, I understand that, but the call to arms is never unpopular."

"Well, a second son like me cannot advance but at the whim of a greater man. As gentlemen we can hardly venture into trade. Who wants to live off the scraps from his brother's table? Our only skills are in our swords. We can't all be priests after all."

"I can't really see you in a cleric's habit, Master Musgrave," I answered.

Doctor Beaton had more need of me. This time he'd found employment for his novel extractor. "Haven't used this in a while," he beamed. "Now do lie still... there's a good fellow."

A ball had entered the patient's right shoulder, travelling upwards. He'd apparently been shot while trying to climb up a scaling ladder. The man was conscious and bleeding profusely. "Now the bullet has entered cleanly enough but remains in the flesh. If we leave it, the wound will fester and mortify. Thus we must extract." I administered some pain relief to calm the whimpering casualty, whose terrified eyes rolled in the marble mask of his face.

"Nothing to worry about, dear boy," the surgeon enthused. "Done dozens of these and some of my patients have even lived!

"Speed," he confided to me, "is always important: go in, and get out as quickly as possible." Putting theory into practice, his experienced fingers probed and searched as delicately as those of a lover. The bullet-extractor proved its worth, its flattened, blood-slicked prize plopped noisily into a dish.

"Now your Frenchman, or Dago even, would have me cauterize the wound with boiling oil. That's what writers like da Vigo advocate and he's widely followed. There the great man and I disagree, though. I side with the Italian physicians. I much prefer to cleanse and irrigate the wound with wine – like so – then some neat and perfect stitches. That, my dear, as ever, is your job. You are most nimble and accomplished. We will use the balsam dressings again, if any are to be had."

Later, as we grabbed what bare rations we could before another wagonload of maimed and dying added to our collection, I asked about victory and defeat. "At first I thought we must have been beaten at Norham. The wounded were coming in faster than after the debacle at Crookham."

"All battles are messy," Beaton replied, "sieges endlessly so. Most commanders now tend to avoid battle if they can – too uncertain, too risky. Campaigns are fought out with endless bickering over city walls, or so it seems. I'm no strategist, mind you; I just try to clear up after the event. As far as we're concerned, the face of victory and the face of defeat look remarkably alike – lots of broken bodies."

He paused, and then went on. "Defeat, by which I mean a major disaster, would be worse though, very much worse. All our orderlies and followers would disappear like snow off a dyke. They'd loot whatever they could. The wounded would be abandoned without medicines, aid, or hope. Men after battle are ungovernable.

"They descend into a state no wild animal would ever enter. Their fury, their bloodlust, their cruelty, is beyond our worst imaginings. If that should occur then you and your women must flee too. On no account should an enemy find you here, for nothing then would save you. Forget ideas of sacrifice, just get the devil out. I'll be right behind you, if not in front."

As though on cue, the rain returned. It came down in waves, washes of shimmering wetness. It was cold too. The wind carried an intimation of impending autumn. We were not to have any glorious fading of a hot summer – that quiet, mellow warmth easing into the cooler season. It had been autumn all year. For our bleeding, groaning charges, this brought fresh misery.

Those under canvas shivered in their thin blankets – the ones that had them, that is. For those left outside, wet and cold would carry more off each night. In the dank mornings, we'd find them, stiff and crooked, waxen, glistening with dew. It was a good year for grave-diggers.

The Earl of Surrey writes to King James

5th September

To His Majesty King James IV of Scotland,

I am sending this letter by His Majesty's herald Rouge Croix, under my seal as King's Lieutenant in the North. His Majesty is aware you have invaded his realm contrary to your solemn oath to him and that you persist contrary to all honour and conscience in cruelly murdering, oppressing, and despoiling his subjects. You will know by his previous letters to you that King Henry is the true owner of that realm of Scotland which you hold from him and that it is contrary to God's will that you now take up arms against your prince. Furthermore, you have entered into treasonous and unnatural alliance with His Majesty's enemies against whom, according to the will of His Holiness himself, he now makes just war.

King Henry, then, through me his servant, orders you forthwith to desist, to summon your forces now engaged unlawfully within our realm and to retire immediately behind your own borders and that, furthermore, you will make full and due payment of such compensation monies as His Majesty's commissioners may duly determine in respect of the slaughters, depredations, and destruction of property which your aforesaid forces have committed against His Majesty's realm and subjects.

I am empowered, should you fail immediately upon receipt to heed this summons, to come upon

*you with all my power which is assembled here
beneath His Majesty's banner for the defence of
his realm. If you shall persist in these unlawful
and perfidious treasons then I, as His Majesty's
lieutenant, do summon you to assemble your host
upon fair and even ground by 9th September next,
when we shall both submit to a trial of arms.*

I have the honour to remain, etc...

Lady Heron also writes to King James

5th September,

To His Majesty King James IV,

*Your Majesty will know of my present distress
that due to the exigencies of war Your Majesty's
army with vast superior force now occupies
my husband's fair castle of Ford. I know Your
Majesty to be a just and honourable prince and
do therefore beseech you to refrain from wanton
destruction of my husband's property. You will
know, sir, my husband, a just and honourable
man, is now a prisoner of your lord warden,
not on account of any crimes or alleged crimes
committed by him, who is indeed blameless, but
because, directed by conscience, he did willingly
surrender himself as a surety for his half-brother,
who is the true party so accused.*

*I propose, therefore, that in consideration
for Your Majesty undertaking to safeguard my
husband's property, his goods, livestock, and
sundry chattels I will prevail upon Lord Dacre to
agree to an exchange of prisoners, which matter I
know has been raised between the lord wardens.*

For my part I should expect my husband to be
amongst those captives exchanged whilst, for his
part, Lord Dacre has intimated he is prepared
to exchange Alexander and George Hume, Lord
Johnson, and William Kerr. Furthermore, sir,
as a wife and mother I throw myself upon Your
Majesty's chivalric mercy, etc...

Sir Thomas Howard comes up with his marines

Have you been to Newcastle? It's not much. The place lives off the river and off its coal, the staithes forever groaning with black gold. "New" Castle, which is called new only because it came later than the "old" one there before, looms over the crossing. They say the ancient Romans had a bridge here too and one of their forts on the spur. Presumably, the pestilential Scots were troublesome then too.

We supped in our lodgings, my captains and I, the place no more verminous than others and the ale tolerable. Our chaps were billeted throughout the town, in lurching tenements lining the waterfront and crowding the steep rise towards the castle. I'd declined to lodge in the fortress itself as I needed to oversee the offloading of kit and supplies. The Earl of Surrey with the bulk of our forces had already marched out northwards towards Alnwick. We were to follow on next day.

Maurice Berkeley from the *Mary George* was with me, of course. I had Sidney of *The Great Barque*, Echyngham from *Spaniard*, and King who skippered *Julian of Dartmouth.* These men I knew, I knew them well, and there were other masters whom I knew. Each commanded his own company of marines, all in our green Tudor livery. I had sailed with these men and I'd fought with them. I had no doubts of them and I prayed they had none of me. We were an easy company, a brotherhood. The bond between father and son is scarcely stronger.

"This place is a cesspit," someone stated.

"Don't know... the beef and ale pie is all right," Maurice answered. Good old Maurice; always looked on the bright side.

"Will they fight, sir?" another asked.

"Let's hope so," I replied. "Be a shame to come all this way for nothing. It's the army council's job to make 'em fight if we can."

"Won't they just ride off again, soon as we come close?"

"They will try, for sure. If we can we must move around 'em; cut off their retreat. Won't be easy. Dacre tells me they've punched clear thro' the armour of our defences; the castles fall like skittles. Now, they're at Ford, leastways they were. That's been James's way in the past. Draw us on then slip back over the line, suck his thumb at us, damn him."

"How will they fight, assuming they do or we give 'em no choice?"

"They always used to rely on their spears, massed formations. They would come on, time and again, in the same old way; our bows would shoot them down, and our bills would finish off in the same old way."

"Very obliging of them."

"Aye, but they've learnt new tricks this time. Now they're aping the Swiss or Germans, using pikes, better harness, and bigger guns, much bigger."

"Sooner the better," was the universal response.

Next morning it was wet, a chill damp mist rising from the river, mingling with the steam and murk of crowded humanity. It felt like a dank autumn day. Officers and sergeants were hoarse with bellowing. Organizing a thousand men who are more at home at sea than on land, with hobbies and garrons, pack animals, tentage, and all manner of gear into a marching column is damned hard work and, had we been able to see it, the sun was well up by the time we were free of the walls.

Beyond, a sprawl of slums and bothies, a dismal landscape of bell pits and workings: King Coal ruled there. The road north was a rutted trackway, potholed and awash. My chaps were not impressed. "You're into the marches now, boys," I laughed. "See what two hundred years of war has achieved? It will only get worse from here."

My prediction was only too prophetic. All of the earl's army – horse, foot, guns, baggage, and supply – had passed this way. We walked on at a snail's pace, our mounts slowed to slowest walking speed as we were providing an impromptu guard for a convoy heading towards the muster at Alnwick. The sutlers complained loudly of the need for protection – that the locals would rob indiscriminately. Friends or foes, all were easy prey.

I took a moment's leisure to curse the Scottish King once again. It was on this man's account that I was adrift in this barren wasteland, the end of the world, relegated to the role of mere gamekeeper. I was in poor humour as we trudged north, slopping, slipping, always with one eye open for predators. Sometimes we saw them, grey -black shadows flitting by the roadside, crows waiting for pickings.

"The earl's castle, I assume?" Maurice asked me as long, exhausting hours later, daylight already slipping, we stumbled into Alnwick. "It's damned impressive." That at least was true: Northumberland's castle is vast, a great frowning fortress of warm sandstone, the power of the Percy family written in ashlar. You have to admire them.

They've been up and down more times than the Howards and we've a fair track record. The army wasn't here, though, but encamped a few miles west by a village called Bolton in Glendale. I'd never heard of the place, just another scruffy border hamlet. Now, it was rather busier than usual.

"Stab me," I heard one of the lads mutter in awe.

I was with him on that. The earl's camp was the largest I have seen, spreading like some vast, wondrous – if not overly clean – caravanserai, swamping the huddle of shacks and tiny chapel. In the grey, dismal dusk, a forest of banners caught the feeble embers of light. Gaudy pavilions of the northern lords, miles of plain canvas, men, guns, stores, and beasts, spilled over the open moor, the northern host, and England's buttress. In that instant my spirits lifted. I could sense the stiffening behind, as men squared shoulders and braced themselves. They were mightily cheered. So was I; this forgotten war might yet yield dividends.

"I'm heartily glad to see you," the earl confided when we were alone. "I know the King thinks I'm too old. That's enough of an insult – worse because it's probably all too true."

My father was still bluff and bellicose but fraying at the edges. His blunt features were rimmed with fatigue. "This damn gout is killing me. The infernal climate will do for me just as surely."

"What about our uninvited guests?" I enquired.

"Presently at Ford, we think, though they won't stay long. Lady Heron negotiates to save her property but Dacre won't budge on his prisoners. Now's not the time for bargaining. His man Heron, who's been making free with his brother's estate, and other benefits I hear, is sure James will shift his whole force to high ground, Flodden Edge.

Dislodging 'em will not be easy." Outside, the late summer darkness was already descending. Torches flickered in the bland half-light; canvas creaked and shifted in spasms of uneven wind.

"We're already into September," my father went on. "Feels more like November. If Jamie-boy holds his ground even for a week and we can't get at him, we're sunk. He can come or go as he pleases whilst we fritter away our time and treasure here. I can't afford to keep on paying this lot for much longer."

So to bed: a seriously hard cot but free of wildlife at least and I slept the sleep of the dead. Next day, fifth of the month, we went to work. Our muster-roll showed we had five and twenty thousand men enlisted. Most, particularly their captains, were old hands. When I say "old", a number were venerable. Little Sir Marmaduke Constable was easily my father's age, though just as full of fight.

Bows and bills – English armies had carried these for centuries. Times might be changing; we would have to change, but perhaps not just yet. I would not have deployed our army as I did if we were to fight on the continent, but this was not Italy – no great wide plains, no dazzling spread of jewelled cities with their bastions and ravelins. This was the land over which these fellows, their fathers and grandfathers, had fought for generations. We faced the same enemy. He might have some new tricks but his men were still conscripts, his captains un-schooled, their King and general untried. We could beat them.

It was mid-morning when Dacre rode in with Heron and a score of their fellows. A mean looking bunch for sure, they rode as though born in the saddle, weapons included. Of these they had plenty. This Heron is a tall, well-made fellow with the manner and speech of a gentleman and the grace of a cavalier, handsome enough if a bit knocked about. This fight was clearly not his first.

"Now, he can really handle a blade," my younger brother advised. "He's the very devil in fact." We Howards come in two varieties: focused, energetic, and dynamic – or not. Ed was of the latter inclination. Always affable, liked by all, gainfully employed by none, he had Edward's build and looks, was universally popular. He was addicted to dice and pleasures, could handle himself well enough – very well, in fact – but he would never be the sort whom men might follow. I wasn't altogether happy over this sudden intimacy with such a notorious brawler and vagabond, but I could see where it came from.

Master Heron, like most of his kind, possessed charm enough and an easy manner, courteous but never obsequious. He was very quick and clever, knew the ground like no other, and was equipped with a first-rate grasp of strategy. War does make for odd bedfellows, and besides, Bull Dacre relied on him, trusted him implicitly. That doesn't occur too often.

"It's like this…" Heron was now giving his report to the council, eighteen in all: all three Howards, Stanley (more of him later), and the other captains. "The Scots, as we feared, have shifted their whole army up onto Flodden Edge." He produced a sketch map of their dispositions. We all craned to look. Heron was not exactly the equal of any man here in terms of status. He had little or none. He did possess an ability to lead, however, an easy authority. If some of that rubbed off on Ed, I'd be happy.

"They're dug in, well dug in. James's French advisors know their trade. Their central redoubt is a masterpiece, bang up to date. They've trenches and earthworks, guns emplaced, protected, and laid. Both flanks are well covered."

"How may we approach?" I asked.

"As things stand, it would have to be a frontal assault uphill from Millfield Plain below. Their guns would decimate us, and the ground is perfect for their pikes. No Swiss or German captain could have selected better. Their fellows are only half trained but it won't matter. They'll flatten us with round-shot and I'm guessing they've plenty of lantern rounds for close up." This was all very depressing. Lantern shot is very nasty – a potage of stones and lead balls crammed into timber casings that burst on leaving the barrel, spraying their deadly cargo. You really don't want to be within fifty yards, more probably.

"I've sent a challenge to King James," the earl advised. "I've asked him to come down from his hill and fight fair like a good 'un. He won't, of course. Nobody's that stupid. Meantime we need a plan and we need it quick. The Scots aren't invulnerable, and if their ranks aren't already thinning through sickness and desertion then I'm the King of Spain." This was true enough of them but true of us as well, naturally. Cold, hunger, boredom, or fear of infection saps men's ardour very quickly indeed. Being permanently wet and tired doesn't help.

"We've got eyes on their camp," Heron confirmed, "day and night, but they've plenty of patrols out and outposts along the flanks. Difficult to slip through and meddle with their supplies but they cannot make any serious move without us knowing."

"Intelligence is always good – vital even," Stanley commented. "Now, how good are you with miracles?"

Nobody laughed.

Sir Thomas adds a letter of his own to his father's correspondence

To King James,

Sir – you will know that I am the lord admiral of England, come from sea to land. On the former, as you are aware, I bested and slew that notorious Scotch pillager Andrew Barton to whom you, notwithstanding the fact the base fellow was but a common pirate, had shown much unnatural favour. Be it known to you never did the service of my King ring so sweet to me as when I rid the seas of such vermin and took his ships as prizes. As I did chastise your base-born privateers so will I now chastise those forces which you have unlawfully unleashed upon our peaceful realm. Oft betimes you have complained to the King's council that you are lacking in redress for the loss of this petty pirate.

Well, sir – I am now come here unto you and you may have such remedy as God determines, for it is my intention, if you will fight, to meet you at any appointed place and there we will see who shall have redress for the greater wrongs. Know also that, as lord admiral, I should have chosen to fight your ships, yardarm to yardarm, but Your Majesty's vaunted navy of which we have heard much declines to fight and has run away to hide behind the skirts of the French. Know also, Your Majesty, that we, all the captains in the English army, are resolved to punish your people for the great wrongs which, in clear breach of your oath, they have perpetrated against His Majesty's

subjects. None, regardless of his blood, may call
upon us for quarter, for he will receive none.

Signed, Thomas Howard and the captains of
the fleet...

Lord Hume surveys the Scottish encampment

Massive. That was the only word. I'd never seen the like. Our camp was a city, a fortified citadel. It stretched out like some fabled fortress of old. Troy comes to life in Northumbria. It's not often I'm lost for words. The bowl beneath the rise of Flodden Hill was a sea of silk and canvas surrounded by the crude shelters of the commoners. The King's seat, as befitted His Majesty, floated in a lake of banners at the highest point, removed from the stink and squalor below. For once it wasn't raining.

"It would be epic if it was not for the smell." My companion on that morning was Lord Lindsay of the Byres, a smooth, eloquent man and something of a cynic. Fellow after my own heart, this was code for – it's a grand show but all smoke and mirrors.

"A fine sight," I replied carefully. "Our defences seem fully in order."

"Indeed they do," Lindsay replied. "Nobody will have seen the like this side of the water." That was true. The King's French engineers had constructed a magnificent redoubt, low and wide, built for firepower with angled bastions that meant every inch of the ashlar walls was covered by guns, state of the art by anybody's standards.

"We will do well enough if we bide here," Lindsay ventured. "No army in Europe, not even the Turk, could come up that hill. Our flanks are surely secure?"

This was rhetorical. We both knew our breach was sealed in. The Cheviots to our west were impassable to large forces. You'd never get guns anywhere near. East, the slope down to the river was covered by more guns. We'd eliminated the English garrisons, neutralized Norham, and set up a series of outposts. Our patrols ranged freely.

Lindsay looked at me. "We've sickness, you know: always happens, of course, and more men slip away each night. No point trying to stop the flood; half the time the provosts defect with 'em."

"It's always the way," I replied. "Our blokes are unwaged. They fight because they're obliged. Once they've got whatever loot they can filch, they're off. It's a bad business but nothing you can do about it."

Any Homeric images were dispelled by the smell. "Largest town in Scotland," Lindsay observed drily, "and the foulest-smelling – no mean accomplishment!" If our army was still, say, thirty thousand strong we must have had half as many again followers, tradesmen, and the like. Most had no tents; our commissariat didn't run that far, so they made do with mean bivouacs hacked from branches.

There was no sanitation for the camp, and the latrine trenches created their own pungent miasma. If you think that a large city, such as Edinburgh, might hold ten thousand citizens, King James and his host were at least three times that number. To keep such a population in bread and cheese was a herculean undertaking in itself. Armies are a plague of locusts. They strip the land bare.

The mood in council had shifted. I felt I was no longer so much at the margins. The hawks had rather run out of steam. Norham had fallen. Our strategic aims had largely been met. The question was "What now?" and nobody seemed to have an answer. King James had got his way. He had his war, he had humbled mighty Norham and now held Surrey in a stalemate. "So far so good, you might say," Lindsay offered.

We met after dinner; little warmth in the uncertain sun but at least it stayed dry. The King was in a good mood. He was pleased with himself. "Well, Alec?" he shot at me. "What about all you doubters now?"

"Your Majesty has achieved much," I toadied. "Our allies will have cause for thanks."

"I should damn well think so," he went on. "Surrey leads half England – the northern half at least. My brother-in-law is deprived of twenty thousand men and more. They must be costing him a fortune. Every day we pin them here drains his treasury."

"Just so, Your Majesty; and what now?"

This was the nub of the matter. James had created an impasse; built a land fortress, but boxed himself in at the same time. The season was late. Men were thinking of their harvest. If Surrey couldn't attack us, we couldn't get at him without throwing away all our present advantages.

"We must weigh the options," the King responded sagely, though our options were limited at best.

Lindsay was uncharacteristically blunt. "We should withdraw – before our army is thinned by pestilence and more desertions, before the English find a way round our flanks."

"Nonsense, man." James was always short on patience when he found himself in a cul-de-sac. "How can they come at us here – Master Borthwick?"

The artillery commander merited a seat at the table. His prestige had soared since Norham, though he spoke only when spoken to as befitted his station. However brilliant a technician, he was still only an artisan. "The guns are emplaced and each piece is fully sighted. Our ranges are perfect. My gunners are become nimble in their work. Your Majesty's engineers are most helpful too. Nobody can come at us from the front or flank but that my guns will shred them to pulp."

This was all sound but it failed to answer the question of what now. "We should consider Berwick," the upstart Bothwell chimed in. Other young lords whooped and thumped the table – idiots. The King said nothing. Huntly and Lindsay said nothing; their expressions, however, were eloquent. I said it for them. "The season is very late, the weather abysmal, and it will only get worse. To march eastwards would expose our flanks and Berwick is a tougher nut than Norham. Surrey will never let us leaguer."

Answer that, I thought sourly. Nobody did. There was no sensible argument for an attack on Berwick, at least not this season. As it stood, James had achieved all his goals. With Norham smashed, Berwick was exposed. Retaking Berwick, which his pederast father had let go, was one of his chief aims. With this fine artillery train it was doable, just not this year, not with so many English troops on the marches.

"The war will likely go on," I continued (though I was far from convinced). "The French will have further need of us next year. With King Henry still bogged down, we can focus on Berwick. The time would be ripe."

There were sagacious nods from the older lords; even the hawks looked uncertain. I could see James was thinking. Don't get me wrong, the man was no fool. He knew we couldn't achieve much more as we were. If he withdrew now, he could claim a victory. If he stayed, the laurels would begin to tarnish. The god-awful weather, sickness, desertion, and autumn would thin his army down to the bone, empty his coffers, and get us nowhere.

"We can't move till the 9th," he cautioned. "Surrey's challenge expires then. If we retreat now it will look like we've refused to fight him. Once the ultimatum runs out, he's the one who is humiliated. We haven't run away; we're ready to fight."

This was a tricky one to argue. I just wanted to be up and off – leave the English wet, cold, hungry, and frustrated. Humiliation is a bloodless victory and leaves things otherwise much as they were: fine by me. Chivalry is important, though, in the games of princes. You have to be seen to play by the rules. So far we had. Nothing in the conventions said you had to make the enemy's job easy. The fact we were dug in was perfectly acceptable. Getting to grips was Surrey's problem.

"That's decided then," the King concluded. "We stay put. We don't advance. We don't retreat. If the Earl of Surrey wants to fight, then he can just come straight up the godforsaken hill."

There's an expression I've heard – you'll know it. Goes along the lines of "it seemed like a good idea at the time".

The Earl of Surrey writes again and for a final time to King James

To King James IV of Scotland,

Your Majesty will see that I, as the King's Lieutenant, and all the captains of my host have signed this, our final letter to you, for I warn you we will brook no more of your delays but will have you advance your banners in the manner of a Christian prince and meet with us in open field when God shall be the arbiter between us.

To skulk as you do, in the manner of a Turk or
heathen, behind your great defences, does you no
credit, for you know, placed as we are, we cannot
come at you and decide the issue by a fair trial
of arms as custom and chivalry dictates. We will
have you fight by the afternoon of 9th September
or be seen to forfeit all honour and know that you
are no true prince but a mere brigand who scorns
to face the fruits of his temerity. Know you again
as oft we have said, it is you who has summoned
up the piper and now we both should dance the
reel.

Signed, Surrey et al...

Heron and a bickering of heralds

Let's face it; you don't see many proper heralds in these parts. Our brand of brawling doesn't leave much call for chivalry. Higher up the scale I can see they have their place. Doesn't mean you have to like 'em. This one, Rouge-Croix, was pretty far up the ladder and very pleased with himself. A long, spindly, ultra-supercilious type, he had no time for almost-gentlemen; anyone beneath a baronet barely merited a sneer.

"So, you are my *escort*?" There's a kind of artistry in summoning so much contempt into an everyday phrase. Looking down his long nose, his perfect, regular features, I'd a mind to rearrange these so he fitted in better with the locals. You can't smack a herald, though; not even if he's on the other side. They're inviolate – that's the rules – and I'm a stickler.

"Your duty is to take me as far as their outpost, where their *officers*," clearly implying I was not quite officer material, "will conduct me to His Majesty. There I shall deliver His Grace's final ultimatum and we shall see if these Scotch barbarians have a mind to fight like gentlemen."

"Nobody in his right mind is going to come down off that hill," I decided. "You and that Scottish peacock are just window-dressing. You're the jokers on before the curtain lifts. James is not going to fight."

"Well, I'm sure the King of Scots keeps you privy to his plans," he huffed. "You are mentioned to be sure – you, or rather your head. His Majesty does not much care for *outlaws* and other riff-raff."

I gave our herald a stare which I hoped conveyed the reality that it is a very long way back to London, on very bad roads, often in the dark, and let him ponder what that might imply. He looked away; message received and understood.

He wasn't really even that annoying, just silly and tedious, a bit like our mission; we all knew this whole business of courteous exchanges was a charade. The real business was all pragmatism. I had a dozen riders, all my own lads, and was dressed up as befitted my role of ever-so-temporary deputy-warden. My breast and back were burnished to a glittering sheen and I'd added a plume to my sallet for effect, a regular mountebank.

Wooler lay behind us, our camp now by the banks of the Till. The river flowed rich dark brown, heavy with peat washed down by the rains, as swollen as you'd expect in spring or perhaps autumn. The earl's camp was a brave riot of colour in the dull ochre of workaday landscape.

We plodded over the sodden plain. Ahead of us Flodden Hill surged upwards, the rolling green turf churned by the Scots' defences. We were a good mile off and their vedettes would never let us get closer. Even from here you could plainly see their massive guns, surrounded by fresh earthworks, lines of trenches running like scars over the slope. As if on cue, several cannon thundered at once, blank rounds and all for bravado. Our horses skittered at the noise, which, even at this range, cracked like darkest thunder.

The Scottish warden was waiting for us. As befitted his higher (and more permanent) status, he paraded a full squadron, well turned out and all in his livery. Hume himself was in black, as ever, as far above me as I the beggar at the gate, fine harness chiselled, gilded and gleaming.

"Master Heron," he greeted. "Another miserable dawn but my congratulations upon your promotion." All this without a trace of irony. I don't think the warden ever really attempted humour in any form; it wasn't in his nature. He was all pure purpose. I returned his courtesy and I suspect our precious herald was surprised at the easy way the Lord Chamberlain of Scotland conversed with a mere border reiver.

The warden bowed in the saddle to our popinjay – perhaps he did do irony after all – and the herald was led, suitably blindfolded, up the hill by a brace of marchers. As though by unseen agreement, Hume and I sidled off whilst our fellows chatted. We might be enemies but certainly not strangers: half were related to the other half – and the rest, probably, if they'd ever been formally introduced to their fathers.

Hume produced a flask; the liquor was top notch too. "I hope your man knows he's on a fool's errand."

I nodded. "Well, *I* know we're wasting our time; not sure about him though. He seems to think he has a function. Someone should have told him."

"I'm not sure any of us has a function other than to mind each other." The warden was all casual and affability itself but he never spoke without meaning, and whatever he said to me was intended for Dacre and not necessarily for anyone else. "The armies are marshalled and in the field. The musicians are ready to play but nobody wants to dance."

"Perhaps that's for the best?"

He shot me a glance and a rare smile. "I'm sure the Howard clan might disagree – the earl, his elder and younger sons. You've become quite friendly with Edmund Howard, I understand?" This was a moderately subtle way of reminding me I wasn't the only one with eyes and ears.

I changed tack; his point had been well made. If we moved, he'd know of it. The very last thing the lord warden wanted was a battle outside his front door. "How fares the fair abbess?" I enquired mildly.

"Very well," he replied, "though much put upon. Her house is somewhat less tranquil but she adapts. She's a remarkably courageous and highly intelligent woman. Her knowledge and application of medicine is astonishing – for a woman, I mean."

Something in his tone caused me to start slightly. I'd never thought Hume might have a personal interest in Isabella. I'd rather thought I might have a clear field. This time he smiled broadly. "No worries there, Master Heron. If I was thirty years younger then, perhaps, we might fall out over the lady's favours but I'm too old for all that, thank God, and she is my niece, my favourite niece, after all."

The morning wore on, almost like a truce day, though my track record with those wasn't perfect. Our man was away for a couple of hours, no more. He was hustled back by the same pair and his blindfold only removed when he was handed over.

Master Rouge-Croix was a trifle out of sorts.

"That man, this *King* of Scots, was positively rude, ranting like a fishwife. Wouldn't even see me to begin with then launched a tirade about not being commanded by the whims of a *mere* earl." He shuddered. "These people really are barbarians; place stinks like a cesspit."

"Most armies are generally un-fragrant," I reminded him. "Tell me what you saw."

"Well, the tent fittings were all very fine but a bit prone to ostentation. You know what I mean – all rather *vulgar.* Not what you'd expect to see in the Earl of Surrey's accommodation, say; too much rich colour and jewellery, downright ungentlemanly, like a travelling brothel."

I doubted our herald had ever been in a brothel; not one staffed by women anyway. "Look here," I said. "I don't expect you to report on the decorations. I'm interested in stuff like how many guns there are and where they're located, what reserves of food they have – that sort of thing."

"Oh, didn't see any of that; sorry. The blindfold was too tight and those brutes positively manhandled me through their camp. It's really not the way, you know..."

So much for fresh intelligence and no chance of the King being obliging enough to leave his prepared defences; you couldn't blame him. He seemed to hold all the aces, except for the one I had up my sleeve.

Ahead of us a curlew lifted off, dipping over the moor, lilting its mournful dirge; dusting off, I thought – smart bird.

Isabella faces a fresh challenge

Never think the worst is past. It's not; it's always just around the corner. In the sprawling tented township that had been my quiet house, some semblance of order had been achieved. We couldn't do much about the mud,

188

and my precious herb garden was a wasteland. Most of the wounded were comfortable, though my makeshift cemetery continued to expand; it covered a couple of acres at least.

Doctor Beaton was looking worried. That alarmed me; his calm confidence was the single balm in our sea of pain and suffering. "You'd best come," he motioned to me. Ellen, whom I'd made my assistant, made to follow. "Stay here, girl," he commanded, never loud but with total authority. Ellen plumped down sulkily. She was a good nurse, quick and tireless, her youth and looks always considerable assets. The quicker I got her wed and away from here the better. New-born infants we did not need.

"We've contagion in the camp," Beaton explained as we walked. "It was inevitable; pestilence follows armies as the sot runs after ale; been the way forever, as far as I can see. We've cases of gaol fever now, though, and that is most worrying."

"Gaol fever?" I queried.

"Aye, came from Spain I think and spreads like wildfire. We'll need to set up separate wards. There's a dozen or so at present but soon we'll have hundreds."

"What causes it?"

"We don't know but I'm guessing filth and waste are involved. The longer the army is static in one position, the worse the odds. Ah, here we are..."

A couple of Beaton's assistants were looking after a full spread of patients. None of these men and a handful of women bore any traces of injury. They stank. "Their bowels void continuously," the doctor continued. "They develop a raging fever and acute pains in the head. They become supine and listless, often delirious. You will observe that some develop this red rash and sores. These can putrefy." The stench was the worst I'd experienced. I felt the bile rise and had to stumble outside to draw in some cleaner air. It took all my will to go back, cursing my own cowardice.

"You'll need one of these." He was referring to the outfits his assistants were wearing. These were both bizarre and ominous. From a patient's perspective, nothing could have been less reassuring. "The gown," Beaton explained, a glistening, voluminous form of habit, "and the mask," a weird bird-like beak, at once both ludicrous and terrifying, "provide protection from the evil humours, or so we hope."

"How much protection?" I asked, cravenly I admit. I was terrified.

"I'm not altogether sure. Some, certainly, but I suspect not that much. Not a great deal we can do for any of them, I'm afraid. We can try bloodletting but I'm not convinced. Around half will die; the other half will recover. We can only make them as comfortable as possible."

There was faeces everywhere. Most couldn't move so they just spurted where they lay. Many had signs of the red rash Beaton had described. What I cannot describe is the smell and vileness oozing from those whose sores were infected. Their skin seemed to bubble and crack as they shifted in their delirium, hideously discoloured and emitting an unutterably foul odour of death and decay that clogged your nostrils and assaulted the senses.

"We can use herbs," I offered. "Some I know can ease various fevers – crushed lavender for one. There's Belladonna, Wolf's Bane, and Henbane to ease their suffering." I could feel a ripple of hysteria. I'd actually thought the worst might be over; that we wouldn't continually be needing more pasture for fresh graves.

Tiredness washed over me. None of us was getting much sleep. The sense of helplessness that had dogged me since the first wounded started coming in felt ever more palpable. Whatever we did was a drop in this endless sea of pain, anguish, and despair.

I allowed myself a private moment to rage against my King in particular and princes in general, to curse his doltish ambition, blind self-obsession, petty pride, and greed. I prayed for strength to face whatever nightmare was to come.

That done, I went back to work.

"You take too much of the blame upon yourself," the good doctor continued over our dinner, a sparse affair and only ale to drink. "You take responsibility by nature – even when you were a girl I observed that – but you are not responsible for all this."

"Someone has to be," I retorted. "There has to be someone, and aside from physicians such as you, and thank God for you, it's always the women. The sisters and the wives from the town, the women from the army, look to me. They understand I'm obliged by birth and calling to do the best I can – the best we can – and it's not enough; it's nowhere near enough."

The doctor smiled at me. "You do so underrate yourself, my dear. All these poor fellows adore you. They think you are their guardian angel. They see you upon the wards, so outwardly calm and serene, a word, a smile for each of them, and they love you for it. You show them kindness. That is a rare thing, rarer still in wars."

"They still keep dying," I almost snapped, the hot prick of tears building again. I really couldn't afford any more shows of emotion.

"Again, that isn't your fault. It might occasionally be mine, though I like to think I save rather more than I lose.

Besides, you have what I'd call the healing touch. It's not just a matter of knowing how to change a dressing or what potions to administer. It's a gift for caring, for giving hope. I'd best be careful or I'll get us both accused of witchcraft. You're mighty pleasing on the eye, too, and that helps a bit, like that red-headed young acolyte of yours. She's learnt a lot from you."

Howard hears of a bold plan

"What in the pluperfect hell are we going to do now?"

Edward Stanley was the Earl of Derby's fifth son. Not easy being that. I was the second, with my older brother dead, and it was still hard enough. Half the other Stanleys were in France, Sir Edward here with us by Wooler. He was already a decade older than me and still waiting for his hour to arrive. Today, that prospect seemed unlikely. It was wetter and colder than ever. Our supplies were steadily failing and rations had been cut again. There was still plenty of drink, though, but liquor and an empty belly are dangerous companions.

Stanley was better at asking questions than answering them – not that I had any answers myself. All of our captains, or most of them, had looked at the Scots' position. All were equally downcast. Clever ideas were in short supply. Only my younger brother still seemed cheerful – that's one of the prime benefits of having limited intelligence. I signalled for more wine.

The earl's tent was crowded. Rain streamed off the canvas and leaked insidiously through a dozen tears in the fabric. The cold was palpable. Dacre and Heron came in late, fresh from more scouting. The marcher was indefatigable in his reconnaissance. I respected his professionalism. Both men took the offered dram gratefully.

"I hope, gentlemen, you've come to tell us the Scots have advanced down onto the plain and now bare their backsides at us."

"No such luck," Dacre grunted in reply.

"Then we're truly lost," Stanley added unnecessarily.

"Not necessarily," Heron added conversationally. "There may be another way." My father was looking haggard; gout and helplessness were taking a mounting toll. Now he straightened.

"Speak out, lad," he urged. "We're all ears."

It's odd, you know, a man like Heron wouldn't get past the front door at court yet he had half the chivalry of England hanging on his every word. He had presence, no question, and a reputation. "It is like this," he began. "We know we cannot attack them as they are. We know they will not budge." This was all obvious stuff but we knew there was more. I should add Master Heron was a natural showman. If he ever did get to court, they'd love him.

"The lord warden and I are in agreement," he continued. "Our plan is that we break camp tomorrow and cross the Till here." As he spoke his finger traced a route on the map he'd drawn, rather nicely done too. "We march north and east, passing Doddington by the old Roman road. The Scots will see us go but they won't know where to."

"Are they just going to sit there while we run rings around them?" Stanley again; he was beginning to grate but did raise a bit of a laugh. There was a new tension in the sullen air. I could feel it, a quickening. After days of frustration, the Scots several moves ahead, we might just somehow level the field.

"I've thought of that," Heron continued, unruffled. "I'm planting some deserters amongst the Scots who will say we're moving up to shield Berwick and then maybe jump

193

the Merse. Hume will be for retreat but James will want to be sure before he moves. That may buy us a day and a night and that's all we need."

"You did ask for a miracle," my brother quipped at sour-faced Stanley. Sometimes he wasn't such a fool. I realized with a bizarre jolt of jealousy that he knew about this already; Ed was in on the performance. Dacre and Heron were actors on their own stage and they were well rehearsed.

"We spend the night at Barmoor, and then move on next morning. It will be hard going, I'm afraid – no way round it. Then we swing wide to the west; get the guns back over at Twizel Bridge, the foot to cross at these fords here, a bit further down."

"Hang on." This was Stanley again, very annoying. "Won't they have patrols out and surely they've covered the bridge?"

"Good point," Heron replied, equably. The Bastard might be only half a gentleman but he was a match for Sir Edward. "Most of our march will be screened from the enemy by high ground here." He indicated where. "Our scouts will keep their patrols at a distance, so no worries there. They've planted a detachment in the ruins of the old fort at Twizel but they'll be taken care of."

"Are we going to cut their throats?" Ed asked excitedly.

"We aim for their purses," Heron replied. "The company, and they're only a dozen strong, are Liddesdale men. We have an arrangement." No more need be said, nor need it be pointed out that the warden was mighty familiar with the Scots' most notorious reivers.

"All right," Stanley grunted. "What next?"

"We march south till we swing west again into the valley of the Pallinsburn. Once we climb out of the dip onto Piper's Hill, Branxton Edge stands in front. Above the ridge, the land slopes into a saddle a mile or so wide, and the reverse slope of Flodden Edge with all our Scottish friends is dead ahead."

"They'll be on to us by then."

"Yes, but they will have to marshal their army, wheel everyone around. They'll have to dig out their guns, harness them, cart their powder and shot all the way over the saddle to Branxton Edge."

"Look, this is a bold plan no doubt, but surely they'll beat us to the top of Branxton Hill? They'll still have the high ground. We'll still have to attack uphill." I was getting tired of Stanley, but he did have a point.

"You are quite right. By the time we march out of the Pallinsburn valley I'd be expecting our guests to be lining the ridge above."

"Right, well, I'm not local. Don't know the ground. You do; no argument there, but how are we better off after all this?"

"We are between the enemy and the border." This was Heron's masterstroke. "He cannot run when he chooses. If he wants to get home, he has to come through us. If he won't fight we've bottled him up and his supply line is cut."

There was a pause but, like a true actor-manager, he wasn't done. "Besides," he added nonchalantly, "we would prefer if they attacked us." He let that sink in. "Consider this: their ordnance will not be ranged in nor will the guns be protected. Master Appleyard is confident his gunners can prevail when it comes to a duel." Our master gunner who said little but knew his art nodded silently. "Once their guns are quietened, our shot may play upon their ranks. They'll be a perfect target, a gunner's dream. Then it is they who must come to us, come down the ridge and try to see us off."

It was my turn for a question. "This is all good – very good in fact, breaks the deadlock, and gives us back the initiative. We're overdue there. But if the Scots come down the hill, assuming their training holds, won't they just sweep us aside? After all, such ground would perfectly suit their Swiss mentors, wouldn't it, nice easy slope and all that?"

"It would," Heron replied with a smile. This man was an accomplished seducer. "They don't *know* the ground though. You'd have to live here for that."

He sketched a further section, showing the slope of the hill and a burn that ran at the base. "The angle seems fine, ideal even, but the view from the top is deceptive. Two things: firstly, when you reach the base, you're not on level ground – you must now advance *uphill* again to meet your enemy who is deployed here at the foot of this little mound – Piper's Hill.

"Now, that's no great thing in itself and the burn looks passable enough. The first few ranks will cross easily but if you've driven beasts over that ground you'll know the more weight you try to get over, the more the water rises. It's like a sponge. First rank may get their feet wet, the second their ankles, the third their knees, but the fourth will be up to their waists."

He paused, letting that settle. "Masters, you know that the Swiss rely upon momentum, a relentless forwards movement. They rely upon the ranks sticking together in close order. They need speed. King James's men will lose all of these."

"That's cracking," said Edmund. I scanned the faces of the men I was to lead. Not a novice in sight. They knew what was being asked of them. It was a very great deal. They had all had enough of shivering, impotent, in the rain whilst the enemy laughed at us. They were ready.

"Gentlemen," I said. "Time for the vote; we must be unanimous on this. It's a job for volunteers only."

"Do we have any other choices?" Stanley asked.

"None whatsoever," I replied. "We do this and win through or we skulk back home with our collective tails between our legs."

"That was easy enough," Dacre commented after the rest had left. Tomorrow would be a busy day.

"We've faith in you both," the earl replied. The old man had cheered visibly; nothing like the prospect of action. "Besides, you didn't give 'em any choices. It's for the best, I find; last thing we need is that idiot Stanley leading a flaming debate. It does bother me though – will the Scots just sit there while we dance around them? If I was James I'd scarper back home the moment we strike camp. Besides, won't his scouts have warned him about the risks at Branxton?"

I answered the first of these. "He won't want to do that till he sees our intentions. Master Heron's plan keeps him guessing. He knows we're short of supplies and it's logical for us to move over towards Berwick. If he thinks he's not threatened, his own corridor is safe, he'll sit it out and see what we do. As for the scouting, I can't answer that."

"I probably can," Dacre offered. The warden was a man of few words but his experience was enormous, the web of his affinity immense. "James's chief scout is one of the Musgraves, a west marcher, clever young fellow, went north as part of the wedding package and has done very well for himself."

"So he doesn't know the area?"

"Oh, he's a good enough scout, one of the best I'd say. He should be – trained him up myself."

"Now even I didn't know that," Heron exhaled.

"Nor does King James, happily." That's how Dacre had lasted so long, always an ace up his sleeve. James's chief scout was his own protégé.

Chapter Seven:
The Long March

War should be the only study for a Prince, and he should see peace only as a breathing space, which allows him time to contrive or gives him the wherewithal to execute his military designs.

Machiavelli: *The Prince*

Sir Thomas Howard writes to the Regent, Katherine of Aragon

7th September (evening)

Your Majesty,

As ever it is my humble duty to report upon the doings of Your Majesty's forces. My father, the earl, has entrusted me with the duties of Chief of His Staff; thus it is my task to see to the general ordering of the army, to appoint and instruct the officers, maintain discipline, and so forth. Your Majesty will know what tribulations we have endured, how this barren country and its secret, rapacious, and difficult inhabitants seem sworn to confound us daily. If we sleep, they rob us; if we move our supplies, they rob us. Whatever is not nailed down and guarded they will rob.

Whenever they sell us victuals, they rob us; their merchants and sutlers rob us.

Truly, I would rather our northerners were with the Scots, for there they could do us some service by treating the enemy as they do their friends! There, I have complained enough and Your Majesty may, as ever, be reassured that we Howards will do our duty whatever the obstacles. Tomorrow, we shall embark upon a bold plan. The King of Scots with his host is presently entrenched upon high ground above us. He has created a fortress where, should we seek to enter, all would be lost, for mere valour will not serve against such defences. With God on our side, he shall not escape us. We have formulated a plan to march our army around his flank, which we may do screened from his sight, and place ourselves between him and his escape.

Then he shall have no choice but to fight. The ground may still favour him but not as much as before. He will be deprived of many of the advantages which he now enjoys. Our brave Englishmen are much fatigued by their hard marches, their rations are thin and barely sufficient for a dog, yet they remain determined to close with these Scotch boasters and do them much harm. I pray that when next I write to Your Majesty it shall be to report of our great victory.

Your most humble subject, etc...

Heron leads the march

The ancients thought that still waters were the gateway from this world to the next. As I watched the rich brown waters of the Till, laced with a swill of froth, drag sluggishly by, I could see why. The water is both a mirror and unfathomable. Thoughts of impending mortality might have been uppermost in many men's minds that early morning. Before Matins we were on the march, tents struck in the pre-dawn, wet blankets of dew clinging to soaking canvas.

"This will be something to tell your grandchildren," Dacre observed. By his standards this was philosophical. "If you live long enough to produce any," he grunted. The camp was bustling: shelter and supplies, though we had little enough of either, were being loaded, fires doused, harness and kit hefted and fastened, fingers clumsy in clammy air.

"I wonder if they'll give us a salute?" the warden enquired. As if on cue, the Scotch guns obliged, crack and roar splitting the dawn; great tongues of fire belched like flaming dragons' breath. Way out of range, of course, but the warning was impressive. Fountains of turgid water sprouted in sudden geysers from the river; horses bucked and whinnied in blind terror.

This was bluster. The enemy had no real idea what we were about. I hoped to God I did. This was all happening on my say-so. The fate of the army, of England if you like, hung on my initiative – quite impressive for one who wouldn't get past the servants' entrance of most of the officers who were cursing and bawling at their shuffling minions.

"You've gone up in the world," Dacre divined my thoughts. "Let's hope it's not just a temporary engagement." The old fox was enjoying himself. The English warden was more a man of action, of reflex. That we were at last on the move with the enemy in our sights was all he asked.

By Prime, we were fully on the move, an endless column of men and beasts. I'd patrol out front, on the flanks, and at the rear, to keep our Scottish guests guessing. The dawn had risen like a grey shroud lifting. Swag-bellied clouds bumped overhead, blending into the greens and browns of the moor. An old Roman road, which locals call the Devil's Causeway, rose ahead of us, slicing over the upland but partly screened by low hills to the west that distanced us from inquisitive eyes.

"You'll have the sods guessing," Dacre chortled. "They'll be wondering what the devil we're about."

"I've given them some ideas," I replied. "A couple of our more accomplished mummers have gone over, trading news for rations."

"Hume won't buy it. He'll have sensed what we're about."

"Probably not, but others might. If they stay put for today that will suit us just fine."

Enemy patrols would be hanging on our shirt-tails but my lads would keep them well at bay. They needed to be kept wondering for a while longer yet.

The ground was empty, bare of men and animals, the few silent hamlets deserted. War is like the plague; it strips everything away, sucks out the life. All ordinary folk fear armies, regardless of which flag they're under. You can't blame 'em. Who wants people like me calling round?

Dod Law is a broad, flat hill, crowned by one of those weird concentric forts of the old people, its overgrown ditches and banks a mute memorial to some forgotten chieftain. "Odd business." Edmund Howard had ridden up to join us. "Imagine how long it took to build this – months at least, I'd say – and yet nobody knows or cares who did it. Makes you think, doesn't it? All this enormous sweat and effort, and history might never know who we were or what the devil we were about. What are these?"

He was gesturing at some inscribed rocks. Circles and depressions had been cut into the sandstone, clearly in a pattern. Not just one or two but a whole series, all very cryptic. "You keep finding them around," I explained. "From ancient times; nobody has a clue what they were for. All sorts of theories from blood sacrifice to calendars, or boundary markers."

"That is what I meant, really. Those who carved them knew what they meant. Presumably, it all mattered to them. You remember Caesar?"

"Not personally."

"One of the stories goes like this. He was moving up through bleak mountains, the Alps I assume. The army passes through some miserable poor villages, high up, people no better than savages. Someone asks if, in this godforsaken hole, all the same politics and jealousies occur as exist in Rome itself. Caesar replies that he would rather be first citizen even in this dismal privy than second in Rome."

"If I remember my history correctly, he should have taken his own advice."

"The point is that it's all vanity and, at the end of the day, means next to nothing; that all the glory, if there is any, is an illusion; it doesn't matter and we'll soon be forgotten. I wonder if future generations will hear of us, will know how hard we fought and for what."

True enough, I'm sure, but more immediate considerations were pressing. "Let's leave that to the balladeers for now. If we're alive this evening I'll recite the old song of Douglas and Percy at Chevy Chase – bags of glory and no survivors."

We had to move twenty thousand men and all their baggage and gear over to Barmoor by Evensong. Strung out in column, the army looked the very opposite of the chivalric ideal: unkempt, for the most part unwashed, and now very much underfed. But they were by no means downtrodden.

Banners and colours furled redolent with odours of wet wool, leather, and humanity. Women and camp followers in a great, stumbling, bedraggled tail. Tradesmen, tapsters, sutlers, women, and farriers all needed to service this great beast in the field; gunners, sweating matrosses, and begrimed pioneers laboured together. Moving even our lighter field guns was a tough assignment over such ground and in such dismal conditions.

The road wasn't much to begin with. The Romans knew how to build. Their monuments are all over. The line of their great wall across from east to west cuts like a scar over the high ground. People still think it had to be the work of giants. Thing is, nobody had done much in the way of maintenance since and this constant wet didn't help.

Thomas Howard halted the column at Sext and we ate dinner, a miserable affair as there was little to be had. Happily, my lads still had a dram or two left in their flasks. A puckish wind chipped fitfully over the crown of the moor, buffeting the tussocky grass climbing over the old fort. It had brightened. Patches of blue drifted among the grey and you could see far out to the east towards the sea. Westwards, above the low hills, the higher mountains rose, hunched and inscrutable with the indifference of infinite time whilst we scurried about below in their shadows.

Crookback came puffing in. His men had been in the saddle since the early hours.

"Any movement?" I asked.

"Seems not," he exhaled in reply. "Lots of runnin' about an' shouting, but nothing gives. Guns still where they were; plenty of prickers about but nowt else. They're staying put."

"So far so good," Edmund commented cheerfully.

This was my chief worry. If the Scots realized what we were about, they'd just up sticks and be off. In their place that's what I'd have done. Meanwhile, on the line of march, Thomas Howard was everywhere, a damn good chief of staff. "How far from them will we be tonight?"

"I'd say just over four leagues."

I respected Thomas even if I couldn't like him. He was always courteous, his natural haughtiness refined by good manners. With his status, he could afford them. He was as different from his easy-going brother as chalk from cheese. A born leader, meticulous, tireless, and decisive, his father was, I suspect, content to take something of a back seat. He'd ridden up with his son and motioned me over as Thomas questioned my scouts.

"Do an old man a service, would you, lad? Give me a hand down."

I did as requested and he leant heavily on my shoulder for a moment. "This climate ain't kind to old bones," he confided. "Do me another favour too, if you could. Keep an eye on young Edmund. He fancies himself as a swashbuckler. His older brother, God rest him, was just as vain and got himself killed on account of it. Will you do that for me?"

It's not something you could refuse, and not often an earl begs a favour of you either.

In the afternoon, as we trudged down towards Barmoor, skies thickened and we had more rain, stiff, blustery showers scudding in from the east, blotting out the coastal plain. Barmoor is an old tower, built by the Muschamp family, a bit dilapidated but it had escaped the previous best efforts of our Scottish guests. It stands next to a dense wood, twisted bog oak and myrtle. This was the best, or least bad, shelter for so large a force. Senior officers would find shelter in the tower; the rest would, in the usual way, fend for themselves.

Sir Thomas Howard pauses to take account

"He wasn't such a bad fellow, really."

We had ridden to the top of a wind-tossed hillock, Watch Law, I think Heron called it. Though we were several leagues distant, I could see the Scotch encampment far more clearly than before. Dacre and Heron were right. Their army was vast, filling the side of the hill like ants, King James's banner floating serenely from the highest point. From the south, the place was impregnable.

I digress: my father was referring to another king altogether.

"Our Tudor bosses will tell you King Dickon was a villain. I daresay he was in his way, though most of the people he killed were Woodvilles. The rest of us said good riddance and that fellow Hastings was a dreadful oik. He maybe went too far with his nephews but that's politics for you."

The old man hadn't lost his marbles; he'd been reflecting on the risks of leadership and we were, for the moment, out of earshot. "I remember I said after the battle – Redemore Plain, the one we lost – that if parliament had put the village idiot up and called him king, I'd have served. Complete nonsense, of course, but my neck was rather on the line and old Henry needed the Howards, thank God, or you'd have been fatherless. His son does not need us, not so much anyway, so we must beat these Scotch brigands or go under. I backed the wrong side that time. I, or rather we, can't afford another such mistake."

"Let's hope we can persuade King James to oblige us. Will he, do you think?"

"My guess is he will. Princes need glory. He can retire now and his French friends will be perfectly happy with the outcome. He's done a damn good job for them – but not enough for himself. No Scottish king since Bob Bruce has given an English army any kind of thrashing. His own desire for immortality will carry him beyond mere tactics."

"Then can we hope to beat him?" I was reflecting on the odds. You couldn't guess at numbers over such a distance, what with all of the followers and hangers-on mixed in, but I'd say they were two to our one at least. Dacre rode up with Heron and George Darcy, the saturnine Yorkshireman and, like all our senior officers, no virgin in arms.

"Well, gentlemen," Dacre began, bluff as ever. "There they are. Will there be enough for us, do you think?"

"Like ancient Philistines," I replied, "a nation on the move."

"You can see how the ground lies from here," Heron interposed. He was always punctilious but never overly deferential. I could see why my brother had formed such an instant liking. "This side of the camp, lying north, is the saddle. It can be very wet, and in this weather even more so."

Though the day had, as ever in these dour, sodden hills, been wet and blustery, a timid sun had now broken through, piercing the prevailing grey with lancets of late afternoon light. It was after Nones, our chaps were due to make camp, and a miserable wet bivouac it promised to be. The vast tented city of our enemies stood in a golden halo, like the Mongol horde. It was too far away for us to smell them. Their guns paid us a loud compliment, the huge bark of cannon bashing through the blanket of damp air, clouds of black sulphurous powder blossoming: the devil's very own good afternoon.

"Silly sods," Darcy grunted. "They're wasting shot."

"Yet sending us an eloquent message," my father noted. "Telling us they know where we are, that they've powder to spare, and their position is as strong as ever."

"That's where they are wrong," Heron interjected. "Helpful of them to think like that, naturally, but you can see that beyond the saddle, which is really quite shallow, the ground falls away, down that gentle ridge above Branxton, or what's left of it."

"You intend we make them come at us down the slope?"

"That would be my advice, as you know."

"It looks harmless enough," Darcy said. "Even the little burn looks pretty innocuous. Good. If I was a German and didn't know the ground I'd think I'd found an ideal battlefield. John, if we get through this, I'll be first in the queue to fill your glass."

Below us, our Englishmen were shaking out from the line of march. "It's unforgiving country," Darcy went on. "Tomorrow will be further and harder, with the prospect of battle ahead."

"Personally, I'm looking forward to it," Dacre confirmed in his usual incisive monotone. "High time this bunch of Scotch tinkers was sent packing." I looked around at the rest. They clearly thought the same.

On the way down the hill, the old man said to me, "With this lot behind us, we might just beat them."

Barmoor Tower was that and very little else, patched and mismatched, solid sandstone chipped and blackened from previous batterings. I'd summoned the war council to meet in the knights' dingy hall, crowded around the single worn oak trestle. The chamber was full. Light faded, dusk was approaching, and I'd ordered torches to be lit. Their uncertain, smoke-incensed light masked the heavy dank odour of the unwashed.

We opened with our indispensable frontiersman, Heron, reiterating his earlier briefing on ground. This would be critical. "Our plan," I reminded my officers, "depends on us offering what appears to be a perfect field; too good to resist, especially if our guns are flaying their ranks."

Next, I asked Darcy to explain enemy tactics. Like Heron, he'd fought on the continent, had seen these invincible Swiss in action. He wasn't the sort who wastes words either.

"You'll not have seen anything like it," he began. "They'll come down quietly, none of their old noise. That's how the Germans do it. It works; makes 'em seem more terrifying. And they are. Their columns will be broad and deep, a forest of points. Looking at 'em, you'll think they're unstoppable – on the right ground they are. That's why so many Swiss are now rich men. But if they lose their forward rush, if their ranks and files fall into disorder, their plan of attack collapses. That's why they're so choosy over ground."

"How will they deploy?" one of my skippers asked.

"In three principal divisions: van, middle, and rear; they'll attack in echelon – that is, one unit follows another down the hill. They aim to strike three great blows – bang, bang, bang." He drove fist into palm to add dramatic impact. "My guess is their third or last division will be the strongest."

"Who will command there – the King himself?"

Darcy shrugged. "Can't say. Might be James who'll lead. If I was him, you couldn't stop me, too much fun to be had. Besides, and here's a point, Swiss generals lead from the front. That and the rope is how they motivate their blokes. You don't get to command unless you've the courage to be first. I can't see our Scottish hero sitting it out on the sidelines. Can you?"

I couldn't. "James leads a nation in arms," my father advised. "His realm is not united, never has been. His stupid Jock subjects are mostly at each other's throats when they're not annoying us. If he expects them to follow, then he'll have to lead. I remember a conversation I had with the Spanish envoy whilst I was a bored guest at our right royal wedding. You remember, when they swore undying peace and amity. Well, never mind, the Dago told me he'd seen James in action: brave as a lion, no question there, and daft as a brush – throws himself into any breach in sight."

"So I've heard," some comic quipped.

This was good: flippant you might say but our officers were not afraid. They knew the size of the task ahead. They knew they would be heavily outnumbered, that their marching tomorrow would be long and hard. They knew their men; they knew their bellies would be damn near empty but that their spirit was ready. That's as good as it gets, trust me.

Lord Hume as ever is cautious

A storm was brewing, inside the gilded canvas rather than out. King James was about to launch into a right royal tantrum, but for once, I wasn't doing diplomacy.

"Retreat," I said bluntly. "Retreat now while the path is open." All the earlier choruses of derision had died down. There was silence, then Lindsay said, "I agree." Huntly said it too, as did Argyll and Lennox, the two highland chieftains. As anticipated, this advice was unwelcome.

"What is the matter with you all?" the King snapped.

210

"What are you so frightened of? Are the English on our backs?"

"Not quite yet," I persisted, refusing to be browbeaten, "but by tomorrow they may well be."

"They're marching away from us, for God's sake, not towards – Master Musgrave..."

"All the signs are they're heading north and east..."

"Towards Berwick," the King finished for him.

I'd taken the precaution of having this conversation with Musgrave beforehand. "That's not a given," I persisted. "There's time for them to re-cross the Till and try to turn our flank." Musgrave said nothing; a most charged silence followed.

"Pure supposition," James exploded. "Never heard the like. How the deuce are they going to turn us? They've got to get more than twenty thousand men back over the river. Their only crossing for the guns is Twizel Bridge and we've got that covered. Then they have to march all the way south, cross bad ground, and try to get up the northern ridge so they're behind us. We'll see them coming from miles away, man."

Perhaps I'm too hard on James. This is largely because I never liked him – vain, shallow, and silly. Now he appeared to be right. It did seem like a very tall order. Still, I persisted: "Surrey has to bring us to battle by the 9th tomorrow. He cannot fail. If he lets us go and slinks home, Wolsey will see the Howards are ruined at court."

Finally, I could see these witless sycophants were getting my message. "The English *must* fight us tomorrow. After that we can up sticks and saunter home with a jaunty air. We've won. The Howards cannot allow that. They mean to come at us even if they have to pass through the gates of hell to do it."

This bought a moment's silence. Lindsay, right on cue, chipped in with a change of tack. "Your Majesty, if we fight and beat Surrey, what has England lost? An arthritic old earl that half the court wants rid of. If we fail, then we hazard your own person, the very jewel of our kingdom, Scotland's prize. The risks are wholly disproportionate. They risk little, we everything."

It was nicely put: pragmatism and flattery combined. I couldn't have phrased it more cleverly myself. Clearly, James disagreed. He turned the full, impressive weight of his anger on Lindsay.

"You'd have me play the coward and run away, would you? Turn tail and flee like a frightened virgin, bring shame upon Scotland, upon my crown. Do you imagine..." his voice was rising, practically to a shout, "do you imagine I brought this great army into being, brought us here with our honour intact, just so I could run away at the first hint of danger, the first time some yokel yells 'St George'! I will hear no more of this talk, my lord, from either you or any of the rest of you. You veer very close to treason. Be advised and choose your next words with care."

"Treason!" Lindsay yelled back at him. "If it's treasonable to care for the life of your king and the safety of the kingdom, then I'm the meanest traitor alive. If hanging me will keep Your Majesty safe, I'll tie the noose myself!"

"My lords," I cautioned. "We all speak honestly and plainly here. Your Majesty has no more loyal subjects than those who sit around this table. I for one would stake my life on any and all." Not entirely true: half of them would cheerfully see me swing and most of them I wouldn't miss, but I needed to make the point.

James lapsed into sullen silence but would not be budged. We'd stay where we were.

The evening, uniquely it seemed in that vile summer, was unusually warm with that timeless dying of the light we often get here, an echo of the fading summer. Those dun-coloured western hills glowed. Once past the noise and squalor of camp, the green saddle below the high hill stretched invitingly. Lindsay, Huntly, and I rode out with Master Musgrave and Borthwick the gunner, one born to the saddle, the other most uncomfortable. I needed to know about those guns though.

As we cantered northwards, we were crossing a slight depression that separates Flodden Edge from Branxton. If you imagine a plate, dished in the middle with a rim around, the distance is barely a league. The northern approach is similar to that from the south. The ground slopes quite easily and Branxton village – well, what little our army had left of it – lay below, scorched and roofless, as though ripped apart by some malevolent giant's hand.

"I don't get it," I said to Musgrave. "If they come at us from here, how are they better off?"

He shrugged, clearly perplexed. Now I didn't trust him, of course. He's a west marcher. They're more inbred than a nest of foxes. But I could see he was genuinely at a loss.

"If they come, then they have to cross the river higher up. Only the bridge would do for their guns, I'd guess. Then they've got to march back again along the west bank. See that stream, over beyond this little ridge below? It's not much but it's an obstacle; the ground there isn't easy, be the devil of a job."

"Then they've got to get up the hill," Huntly observed.

"Suppose they don't," I persisted. "Just suppose we have to go down to them..."

Musgrave pursed his lips. "I've not seen pikes in action

– not for real, I mean – but that slope looks ideal. Isn't that the sort of ground you'd be looking for?"

"Could be," Huntly confirmed. "What about this burn here, at the bottom of the slope?"

"It's nothing... well, it's a wet gap of course, bit boggy and what have you, but you'd only get your ankles wet; shouldn't be that much of an obstacle."

I was missing something. I could feel it. I detected Master Heron's subtle hand in this. Wrong side of the blanket or not he knew this ground like no other. Not the Howards, not even Dacre, came anywhere close. They were listening to him. They had to be and the Bastard knew something. Something I suspected that was blindingly obvious.

"Something isn't right," Huntly echoed my thoughts. "They're making it too easy. What of your cannon, Master Borthwick?"

Our master gunner was troubled, I could see. He'd spent days sorting his present positions, had every angle covered. "Well," he began, "I can bring the guns around. It's doable – damnably hard work and it will take hours – but we can do it. Looking at the ground, I say we'd drag the guns round the rim of the saddle behind us, not into the dip. It's further that way but the gradient is easier and it's drier."

"That seems fair enough," Huntly replied, "but there's a 'but', isn't there?"

Borthwick gathered himself. "The 'but' is we won't be as ready. All the guns are both sighted and dug in as they are. All our fields of fire are covered and with solid earth around the crews. They're safe from counter-battery fire. If we have to move we lose both those advantages." He let that sink in. "We throw them away in fact. Their guns are lighter, much handier; I'd be worried."

I already was.

Now Lord Hume writes to Queen Margaret

8th September

Your Majesty,

By these instruments I do communicate as I undertook privily and to keep Your Majesty appraised of the affairs of our army. It is like this. We are encamped upon a high hill with the King's power all around. We are fairly placed and strongly posted for, as we are now, none may approach us. However, there is disquiet amongst the lords, even amongst many of those who were cock-a-hoop at making war upon England whilst they sat safe in council. Here, they grow less bellicose and the counsel of such old men as Huntly, Lord Lindsay, and myself is listened to. His Majesty, I fear, does not listen.

He will not budge from this place till the date appointed by the Earl of Surrey, for the giving of battle is past and our honour secure. Yet to tarry here is rank folly, for even now the English army is on the march. As to their purpose, we remain uncertain. It may be they are intending to safeguard Berwick, yet we do not threaten the town, and the season is now too far advanced for fresh manoeuvres. It is my conviction and Lindsay's that they somehow mean to outflank us and place themselves between us and the Tweed. The King's scouts say this cannot easily be achieved. His Majesty is pleased to rely upon Master Musgrave, a smooth chancer like all of his people and not to be trusted.

*There has been much heated talk in council
here and I have pressed as hard as I dare but
His Majesty will not be moved. We shall sit here
upon our mountain, believing ourselves safe,
till, all of a sudden, we find we are not and that
the English have humbugged us. I know this old
earl. His bones may ache till they crack but he
means to fight us. He needs this battle as much
as King James desires his. His Majesty believes
that he is ready, that we are ready for this trial
of arms. Yet I am far from certain. Daily, we lose
men to desertion. There is much sickness. I send
cartloads back to the abbess at Coldstream, now
a city of the lost.*

Your most humble and obedient servant, etc...

In the dark wood

"It's your lot again. It has to be, an' I'm heartily sick of
it." Ritchie Graham, general sutler, thief, and pimp, was
complaining.

When Dacre promoted me he hadn't explained that
this elevation involved a delegation of his own chores,
particularly acting as provost-marshal. You know what the
job involves, keeping the fellows in line, stopping pilfering,
kicking the whores out of camp, banging heads together –
a watchman's lot.

"Poacher turned gamekeeper," young Howard
guffawed. "Just the job for you, Johnny; I thought you told
me the warden has no sense of humour. I'd say it was
very funny."

"Perhaps I was wrong," I acknowledged sourly. "He
must be laughing now."

"What about me pans? They're me best, finest

copper – you won't get pans like that up here from any other trader, I can tell you." That's the thing about the Grahams: once they start there's no deflecting them; money is sacred.

"That's a fair point," chorused Edmund. "Master Graham is concerned for his livelihood; perfectly reasonable. Your chaps are pretty light-fingered, you know."

I can't think I need to warn you about the Grahams. They're west marchers and sit on both sides of the line in every sense. Ritchie of Brackenhill ran the biggest protection business on the border, the envy of us all.

"How do you know," I asked, as politely as I could bear, "that it was my fellows who thieved your pans? We're in an army of twenty thousand or so and I command two hundred at best."

He smiled craftily. They do that, the Grahams. When it comes to criminality, they've got all the angles covered. Master Graham squared his hefty shoulders and looked me in the eye. "It's the spoons, see; the spoons. That's how I know." His point made, he stood back smirking.

"I'm getting a bit lost here," Edmund confided. "Why are the spoons so significant?"

Trouble was Graham was right and we both knew it. "The spoons," I explained wearily, "are made of wood, dirt cheap, and as plentiful as the pox." Ed still looked nonplussed. To be fair to the lad he wasn't local. "Master Graham is pointing out that only a borderer would bother to steal the spoons as well. Anyone might nick his precious copper pans but that level of finesse indicates local talent at work. We're known to be thorough like that."

"Rob the very shrouds from corpses, they would," our complainant continued. "It's true; I've seen it." As he was a Graham I didn't doubt it for a minute.

I've encountered death in many forms; slow killing by tedium has to be one of the most pernicious. "Master Sergeant," I addressed this to Crookback, who'd enjoyed an unexpected elevation to respectability, "go forth and address the multitude. Let it be known I'd be very much obliged if Master Graham's property could be returned, undamaged, to him at someone's earliest convenience. Explain that should I have to come and personally *search* for these items, then I should really be very displeased indeed and someone is likely to feel my official boot up his thieving backside."

There was plenty more like this. The irritating petty complaining of human life continues regardless of circumstances. Ours were bleak. We'd camped after the hard day's march by Barmoor Wood. Senior officers had passable billets in the old tower. The rest of us made do. There were few tents; we travelled light.

"Have you heard of that old Scotch king, Macbeth?" Ed asked me. "He was pretty famous. Well anyway, a witch told him he'd be safe as houses as long as Birnam Wood, I think it was, stayed where it should be. I'm not exactly sure of the story but his enemy, Old Siward the Dane, cut down all the branches for cover and used them as a screen; must have been the devil of a shock, seeing a whole great, teeming wood coming at you."

"It's usually dry in stories; not like this at all." It was chucking it down as ever, a steady, relentless drizzle laced with cold. The brief flurry of sun we'd seen had disappeared beneath the gathering clouds. I could see what he meant, though. We'd near stripped Barmoor Wood for shelter.

"I don't think a few trees are going to bother King James too much and we're a pretty average-looking army."

"Ah well, we don't want him taking fright, do we?

218

That's your brilliant plan. Be a nasty surprise for him; that's what happens when you upset the Howards."

"Ed," I said, "and I mean this as a compliment, a bit back-handed perhaps, but if your lot had been born up here, you'd have made first-class reivers."

I should tell you we were playing chess at this point. I'm addicted to the game, as was Dacre. I think that's half the reason my neck has never felt the weight of my boots, as we say. Edmund Howard, for all his affability, is a ferocious player.

"You know that chess is listed as one of the seven skills a good knight must aspire to," he told me when we first started to play. "The church often seems to disapprove – too much money being wagered, licentiousness and drunkenness, and so forth." He had a finely crafted miniature set in ivory and thrashed me on a regular basis.

"An odd business, this gentility," he mused. I was bent over the board, wondering how to get out of the fix he'd neatly led me into. "I mean, it doesn't really amount to all that much."

"It does when you're not quite there."

"Well, that's the bonus of war – if we live, anyway." I looked up at him. "If we come through this, see the Scots off and come safe home, we're made for life. The old man will get his dukedom back and that will really upset Wolsey. There's a peerage at least in it for Tom, me too if I'm lucky, and a knighthood for you. God, if we win, I mean really hammer them, you could hope for a baronetcy."

"Bastard to baron," I reflected. "Quite some elevation." He was right, of course, and I won't pretend I hadn't thought of it. Yes, I hated the Scots; they'd burnt down my house – well, my brother's house. Happily mine was still standing but Dacre had made it plain this war could be my path to proper gentility.

"I was lucky," Ed went on. "I was born legitimate even if I'm the poor relation and I don't have ambition. I'm the runt of the litter, not as dashing as Edward, nor as clever as Tom. The King loved our older brother, just his type, the very ideal of knighthood. Tom's spent his whole life trying to catch up. Now that Edward's dead, died gloriously fighting the French, he's no chance. Edward, bless him, was no brighter than me, older and braver, yes, but not as..." he searched for the right word. "Not as assiduous as Tom, not as considered. Tom does nothing by chance or on a whim. He thinks about everything and he's clever. You're ambitious too."

"Am I?" I pondered. I've never thought of myself as ambitious, not in that sense, the political sense. I'm ambitious to stay alive, naturally, and that's generally a full-time job in these parts.

"If you'd been born your brother, title, castles and all, you'd have still been a brawler, though you'd probably have been warden rather than gentleman-outlaw."

"I'm not a proper gentleman."

"You're every inch a gentleman. I wouldn't be pouring this good claret for a mere commoner. No good staring at the board by the way – that's check."

"Chess, now there's a thinking man's pastime." I should have mentioned that Father Bell had joined the army. He was, more or less, the warden's chaplain unless they'd fallen out. Always a good man in a crisis, his bare arms and tattered habit didn't mask his natural authority. Besides, most priests enjoy a decent war – makes for a captive congregation. There are no heretics in a scrap.

"Set the board up, lad," he enthused. "Don't be wasting your time playing against dolts like Master Heron here. I couldn't even beat the beginnings of Latin into him. He's got no hope at chess." War makes for odd companions:

the nobleman's son, the outlaw, and the rustic priest. "His wine's better than yours too," our spiritual comforter advised, awarding himself a generous measure. "A thirsty business, all God's work, and still so much to do."

"Best fetch us another bottle," Edmund directed his squire.

And so to bed – not much of a bed and very little repose, rain filtering through the denuded canopy of trees, already tinted by autumn. The faded hills around were draped in low-lying mist. No marching camp is ever silent. Some will while away the fretful night by their sputtering fires; light and liquor keeping fear at bay. Fear and fear of fear are demons in the darkness. They stalk you, can catch you unawares; your bowels turn to water, your sinews shiver. Real captains make their rounds then. It is the test of an officer, that little reassurance, a joke here and there.

Small things, you may say, but they matter. When all the pomp and pretence is stripped away, and men – cold, hungry, wet, and fearful – know tomorrow's march may be their last, such little tokens matter very much.

Meanwhile the abbess continues her ministry

"Hippocrates wrote about this, you know," Dr Beaton informed me. "In fact, he left us precise instructions which Galen echoes and amplifies. Very obliging of them both, though, I'm bound to say, it's not really as hard as it looks. Sponge, please."

I assumed he was referring to the doctor's rather than the patient's perspective. Mine looked frantic with terror. He was one of my own grayne,[12] a Pringle, fresh-faced and strong, at least until somebody had bashed his head in, or half bashed it in, I should say.

---

12 An element of a clan or family.

"Depressed fracture," Beaton had diagnosed straightaway. "Trepanation's the only thing for it, I fear. You'll be pleased to hear survival rates amongst my patients are encouragingly high, all things considered."

My township of half-rotted canvas and squalid little bothies had expanded to urban proportions as the numbers of sick increased. Around half died. We no longer buried them separately but had moved on to a form of industry, digging great yawning pits where the dead, huddled in sack-like anonymity, were laid in rows: men, women, and more than a few children, heaped together, a community of the forsaken; whole families and piles of dead strangers, all doused in a cloying blanket of quicklime. War strips us of our humanity so quickly that casual indifference becomes the new norm.

"Now then, preparation." Our patient was strapped upright; Ellen held his head steady. She was a fast learner and nursing seemed a natural vocation. Her pale oval face was set in a mask of concentration.

I'd used a sponge liberally laced with opium, mandragora, and hemlock, one of Beaton's patent recipes, to knock the patient out. A few seconds under his nostrils and he was away.

"First stage," the doctor intimated to his acolytes, all suitably wrapped in awe of the great man busily at work. "We've shaved the area of the wound, which you can plainly see." A depressed fracture is just that: an area of discolouration, clearly indented, about the circumference of a decent apple. "So we begin, as you will note. We make four swift incisions into the skin, just so – remember, speed as ever is of the essence. We wouldn't want the poor fellow waking up, would we? Then we draw back the flaps of skin, just like peeling ripe fruit."

The glistening dome of the skull was starkly exposed. "Now we arrive at the more technical part. Pay close attention, gentlemen, and ladies too, of course." He beamed at us. I often think doctors are like lawyers, part professional and a larger part actor. "The trepan if you please, my dear." I passed the implement. This was the hardest part to watch. Well, not so much watch as hear: the grinding of the saw-teeth through bone. Even Ellen, who'd got pretty hardened, flinched. She wasn't alone.

"And so." There was a kind of viscous sound and a noise of bubbling even as the trepan was removed. "Air bubbles," the doctor confided, "running under the bone. Ah, there we are. See the offending fragment?"

The trepan held a disc of bone. The patient's skull was open, grey matter of tissue and brain clearly visible, pulsing softly away. I was beginning to feel queasy – surprising, as I'd thought my diet of horror pretty much complete.

"Now, I prefer silver, though bronze will do." With a flourish Beaton produced a flat, gleaming disc and inserted it into the hole. "You will see that as we've relieved the pressure, our patient's condition is very much improved. Now, all that remains is to seal off the wound, thus."

Having inserted the disc he pulled the flaps of skin back over. "You may finish up," he instructed me. "Our abbess has become a most accomplished seamstress. Very fine work as ever and quick, as you will note. Never forget speed, gentlemen. It is the catechism of the successful physician. If you dawdle you will lose patients and that will do your reputation no good at all. This young fellow should do well enough."

It wasn't just the sick, the dying, and the dead who passed through. Others, in increasing numbers, were slinking away. The King's army was shrinking by the hour.

Hume's men, nominally acting as provosts, simply looked the other way or, if the fugitives were particularly burdened with loot, would help themselves to whatever they fancied by way of local taxes.

I didn't see defectors as any of my business. The men were conscripts, forced to fight. If they preferred to see to the welfare of their families with harvest time drawing on, then, frankly, I didn't blame them. They were the sensible ones. I was having enough trouble feeding my own swollen household. Some rations did arrive. The warden had not forgotten us, but my barns were emptying fast. I tried not to think of winter.

Before Evensong, one of Hume's riders cantered in, his garron foam-flecked and steaming. "The English are moving," the scout gasped, "heading north-east." He must have seen my look of sudden alarm. "Not coming here though; doesn't seem like it. Likely they're headed for Berwick; maybe anyway."

I'll confess to a moment of near panic. I'd hoped the whole campaign would just end, that King James had made his point and would be content to retreat. What if he was now forced to fight?

"What's going to happen now?" I asked plaintively.

Nobody knew. I could feel my shallow equilibrium slipping away. Seeking solace in drink wasn't going to help but I got a decent dram down my neck regardless. "What now?" I asked nobody in particular. The women were no wiser. Beaton shook his head. "I'm not much good on strategy," he replied, "but I suspect we'll be getting more customers, perhaps rather a lot."

I realized I knew nothing about how battles were actually fought. Men died; that I understood, but little else. "We'll need to be ready," he went on. Nothing may happen, of course; most times nothing does. Everyone huffs and puffs, then gets bored and goes home. That's the best kind of outcome. Everybody waves his tool in the air to show who's got the biggest, then puts it away again."

"What about the other sort?"

"They can be messy – very messy in fact. Both armies, as we know, are large. We and the English have a long history of killing each other, often in considerable numbers. The dead are not our concern. They are commended to God and grave-diggers. But there will be many wounded, always are. So, if there is to be a battle, our place will be behind the front line, at a respectable distance naturally, so we may deal with our customers while their wounds are fresh. We'll need a team here while we send out a field unit. I do hope our fellows choose somewhere level for their battle. I really can't abide climbing hills."

I was near-retching with fright. With considerable effort and a further generous measure – who was counting? – I pulled myself together. I was desperately tired. "Right," I ordered. "Let's have two carts made ready. Ellen, I want you, and you, and you..." I selected the youngest and fittest. "We'll load supplies, whatever we can spare; yes, I know we've got very little. Dr Beaton," I glanced at him and he nodded, "will be coming with us. You," I gestured at the warden's man, "find half a dozen blokes, preferably sober, as escort. We'll get started at first light."

The sisters were going to war and I was sweating with terror.

Chapter Eight: Trial by Battle

Between two valiant Kings there is always one weak in mind and body. This has been so since Arthur, and most true it is.

Froissart: *Chronicles*

The Earl of Surrey addresses his troops upon their approach to battle

Morning, 9th September

Englishmen! Today, all of your gruelling marches will be ended, though the hour of our greatest trial lies ahead. We are soon to stand between our enemies and their road home. They must fight us or flee like dogs and be at our mercy. Their numbers are great, we fewer, but we march with God and Right on our side and by his almighty grace we shall prevail. The fight will be hard. I will not hide that from you. For my part I would not have it otherwise. I would have none say that we triumphed so easily but rather that we met the enemy point to point and sent him tumbling home.

For he who takes my part today, which is the King's part, I promise this. None that bears the name of Howard or wears my livery shall flee

*this field today. We are determined that we shall
gain the victory or die striving. Before us stands
our ancient enemy. Fear them not, for at your
shoulder as you fight this day you will find the
shades of your fathers and grandfathers down
through all the ages past who, when they were
tested against this same foe, did not falter nor did
they flinch.*

*Time and again our forefathers laid these
boasters low, stripped them of life and honours,
recovered from them, aye and with interest, all
that had been stolen. So, be the men you are
today, bear your staves steadfastly, deal them out
with blows till none be left standing on our land.
See them off. Give them such sorry hurts that
all Scotland may curse their menfolk for their
folly. Lay on, give no quarter nor seek any. King
and court and country attend upon your arms
today. Let it be the case that those in France, not
so workaday as us yet might our laurels glow
brighter, may yet curse themselves they did not
stand here with us. Cry God for Harry, England,
St George, and all the riches that lie within the
Scotchmen's camp!*

Thomas Howard earns his salt

I'd like to say for posterity that a glorious, sun-gilded dawn
heralded our great enterprise. It's never like that, of course.
Morning crept in like a mist-shrouded thief, a filtering of
black towards lightening shades of grey. It had rained most
of the night, the ancient trees of our bivouac heavy and
dripping. Breakfast was sparse where there was any to be
had. Despite this, my rounds passed cheerfully; our men

were ready and willing and their discomfort merely honed the urgency of our getting to grips with the detested enemy.

Heron's riders were already in the saddle, scouting towards Twizel and campaigning freely with the King's silver. Dacre's chaplain, a big, raw-boned fellow, battered jack over his equally shop-worn habit, was busily frying bacon. The prince bishop had provided for his clergy's more physical needs and no doubt I'd be billed in due course.

"A plate for our general," the vicar boomed. He was ragged but radiated authority like a crown. I took the proffered fare without dismounting, and damn, it tasted good. The prospect of a fight makes me ravenous. "And a dram." The raw spirit, more refined than I'd expected, slid down warmly. "Bishop Ruthal's best," he confirmed. "Normally reserved for those in holy orders but I'm sure he'd approve of the exception."

"I'm obliged to you," I confirmed. "Where's Master Heron?"

"Ah, well, I'm to tell you he's scouting up around Twizel, making sure our fellow travellers there depart with good heart and heavier purses. No fears there. They're Liddesdale men; never get their priorities mixed up."

"What about the rest of the party?"

"Sleeping sound as babes; they've not moved. That won't last, of course, but gives us a head start."

George Darcy was with me; he was acting as the old man's chief of staff. "You'd at least expect that, as God's on our side, he'd get the sun to come out, wouldn't you?" I liked Darcy, a good man to have at your side, though he did take things a bit far at times – full of the fires of faith and all that, regular fanatic.

"Well, if I'm to move in plate, I'd sooner be in the shade," I replied. We were fully harnessed up. Plate is heavy and chafing but it's reassuring too; besides, mine was new and needed wearing in.

"Nice gear," George commented. "Italian, I assume?"

Well, anybody who wants to be somebody wears Italian, or perhaps German, armour. "It's incredibly expensive but the prize money from Barton's ships has paid for mine, so reminding King James seems like a good idea."

"Do you actually hate him – personally, I mean?"

"Never met the fellow; the old man has, of course, and Dacre too. My father says he quite liked him – bit vulgar perhaps but that's the Scotch for you. Apparently he likes to wear his seaman's whistle, badge of office and all that."

"Which is why you're wearing yours?"

"Yes, and another reminder. I earned mine by killing Scotch pirates!"

By now the army was beginning to move, like some mythical monster waking from a long slumber. Not that many of us had got much sleep.

"You know the drill," I told George. "I've got Edmund and his blokes out in front on the right, Sir Marmaduke on the left. I'm taking the centre, you and the earl the rear. I've beefed Dacre up as rearguard with some bows and bills. Your boys in good heart?"

"No complaints there; aside from your father's affinity we're nearly all Yorkshire men. Stanley's men are all from Lancashire so it's just as well we're marching separate. Will young Edmund be all right?"

"Well, he's not short of courage, nor of daring, even if he's as green as grass, but Stanley's men, those I put with him, aren't too happy. You know what they're like: if they can't fight under their own banner, they sulk. I've sent Maurice Berkeley, one of my best skippers, with two companies of marines to stiffen their backbones."

I'd arranged for two large divisions, my own as vanguard or first and my father's as the rearguard. Numerically my division was much stronger and I'd posted smaller, brigade-sized units on each flank of the larger formations. The Scots, inevitably, were playing by a different rule book but we'd drilled our chaps in just these units, keeping the pals' companies together. Men fight better with their mates around. Nobody wants to be the fellow who lets the local side down. That's why we fretted about the Cheshire men with Edmund. It wasn't that they didn't like him; they didn't know him. It's nice to be on at least nodding terms with the man beneath whose banner you are possibly going to die.

"Do you suppose Alexander's army or Caesar's looked as knocked about as this lot?" George asked.

"Probably," I answered. "I suspect the world of gleaming armies only exists in some painter's fancy. The reality stands before us." We had swung westwards as the morning grew, angling back towards the Till. Today we did at least look like soldiers. Most of everything was left in camp. The men carried nothing but their kit and personal weapons. Food wasn't a problem, as we had none. Horses and what baggage we had all stayed at Barmoor. We proceeded on foot. This was my manifesto. We came back as victors or not at all.

George trotted back towards the rearguard, though I was presently joined by Ed. "Odd bunch, Stanley's lot. Can't understand half of what they say. Thanks for your marines, though. They, at least, look the business. God, what a dump."

We were passing through a village called Duddo, the gaunt spire of its tower, blackened and skeletal, a relic of the last incursion. The place was empty, bothy and byre equally deserted. "What's this?" Edmund gestured to a ring of ancient stones just outside the settlement. "More from the old folks, whoever they were?"

Whoever they had been, my thoughts echoed, this empty circle of monoliths as inscrutable as the stars. They'd stood there for God knows how long, all trace of their people and purpose lost. "It's odd," I said, "at a time like this, when we seem to be surrounded by great events, that none of it is new. If I live to chronicle today's battle, I'll make damn sure it isn't forgotten."

"Yes, be a crying shame if it was – all this trouble and effort we've gone to, best gear on and all that. That kilt of bases you've got on is rather good; wish I had time to get one made. Of course we don't want to end up looking like twins." Mine was red velvet decorated around the hem with crosses from our family arms – my own design and pretty neat, I reckoned. I can face death but I expect at least to be properly dressed.

We had a full two leagues (or six miles, if you prefer) to march before we got to the bridge at Twizel. I'd some fourteen thousand men marching with me, plus all of our guns. No army ever moves silently. The crashing of so many marching feet, hobnails, and armoured sabatons, plus the clatter and cursing of the guns (we had twenty-two), together with all their supplies and warlike stores, was apocryphal.

It was nearer Sext by the time we reached the bridge. I'd not seen it but the rather fine arch looked serviceable enough. We, with the vanguard, would cross here, the only place practicable for cannon, then we'd retrace our steps another two weary leagues before we reached Branxton. The old man, with the less encumbered rear, a couple of thousand fewer than us in number, would use some handy fords downstream. Heron's troop awaited us, as mean-looking a crew as you'd find this side of hell's front door, their lance-points glinting.

"How-do, Johnny?" my brother enthused. "Do we have to fight our way over?"

"Don't be in such a hurry," Heron answered affably, grinning that easy cavalier smile of his. "All's well. The Elliots have cleared off. King Henry's silver is as good as anybody's. They've had a decent little war, all things considered." The old hall above the river crossing was as silent as the grave.

"Let's get them moving," I instructed and we began the job of spooning so many men and guns over the high vaulting span. Below, the heavy waters of the river, swollen and browned by the rains, white froth riding, flowed sullenly. It was well past noon by the time we'd got everyone over and begun the reverse march down the western bank. We'd have the river on our left for most of the distance. To our right, the high hills rose. In front, the enemy waited.

"I hope they're damn well waiting," I confided to Heron. "If they've rumbled us and run off, we're going to look like a complete bunch of jokers, all dressed up and no party to go to."

"That's worried me from the start," he confessed. "They've still time till we cross the Pallinsburn." To keep up morale I ordered our banners unfurled and the drums to beat. It was an odd sight, these sudden gorgeous bursts of colour blossoming in the drab green wilderness. The King's great dragon banner, set with the cross of St George, garlanded by Tudor roses, spilled out for a good eight yards, dwarfing the pennons of the lords. Our own square flag, lions both couched and rampant on a red background, complemented the ancient talisman of the northern saint with its glaring crimson cross.

We'd marched for a league or so when one of Dacre's patrols rode in, his mount steaming and near-blown. "They're stirring," the heavily bearded, scarred ruffian reported to Heron, ignoring me. This was no time for protocol though. "Lots of movement; we were south of the burn, could see their fellows milling about on top of the ridge. Couldn't be sure – they were well screened – but I'd swear the King was there. Had a fancy coat on over his harness, looked like the lion badge – couldn't swear to it though."

"Is their army on the move, man?" I pressed.

"No sign of it, your honour; just looked like a scouting party," he shrugged. "No hint of infantry and guns and stuff."

I looked at Heron and he glanced at me. "Looks like we'll have our battle after all."

Queen Katherine writes to King Henry

7th September

My beloved husband,

I hope all goes well with Your Majesty's great venture in France since last you wrote to me. For our part here, the Earl of Surrey has advanced his banners to bring those insolent Scots who have invaded Your Majesty's realm to battle and to account for their impiety and impudence and to make redress for those great wrongs they have done here and the hurts they have inflicted upon Your Majesty's subjects.

I am assured that, with God's blessing upon Your Majesty's cause, our Englishmen will acquit themselves right well and do you good service. I hope then I might write to you and very soon,

*to advise you of our great victory won here to
add fresh laurels to Your Majesty's renown in
France. In the meantime the Bishop of Durham
has written to me loudly (and at some length)
complaining of his loss at Norham. He fears the
shock may hasten him to an early grave yet he
has found the strength to make a most careful
tally of his losses with interest accrued to date
(and accruing daily), which he has sent to me,
expecting, as I imagine, the treasury will provide
full recompense. Freely I will confess to you I had
no idea castles on Your Majesty's borders were of
such expensive construction...*

Your ever loving and affectionate Queen, etc...

King James at last is made aware of his peril

Dinner, which we ate at Sext, was some decent beef
(sourced locally as we could have said), washed down with
an offering from the King's travelling cellar. His Majesty
was minded to celebrate. He seemed to have won the game
– it was noon and the English had not appeared. Not yet,
anyway. I'd had Musgrave out since first light to watch
them and some of my own fellows to watch him.

"Well, Alec," James beamed. "What of your fears? No
sign of any English bogeymen and their time is up." He
drained his glass and signalled for another. I was being
abstemious. I usually am. Drink loosens tongues and I'd
a feeling my wits would be needed. As though on cue,
Musgrave came clattering up the short rise to the King's
pavilion. In my experience bad news always travels fastest.

"Majesty, lords – best come and see."

"Look like you've seen a ghost, boy," quipped His Majesty.

"The English are coming."

If King James saw a ghost in that instant it was his own, and the ghosts of most of those around the table. Horses were called for and we trooped back over the soggy saddle towards Branxton Edge. Below us, the view had not changed, but to the north, there was movement, the odd flash of banners stirring in the light wind, the glint of harness – and the noise. Like a distant storm, the racket of thousands of marching feet came to us. Noise ebbed and flowed, partly swallowed by the hills. But noise there was and an army was coming. And they were coming to fight.

Someone said something pithy and unrepeatable – as neat a summary as we'd get. For a moment the King sat rooted in his expensive saddle, his gold, emblazoned surcoat a dash of gaudy finery along the long green ridge. You remember the old caution – be careful what you wish for. James had yearned to be tested in battle and Old Surrey had obliged. We must now fight. The enemy would be between us and the Tweed. Our range of available options had just shrunk clean away.

"Well, gentlemen," the King exhaled. "It seems you were right after all, Alec, and they mean to be at us. How long, Master Musgrave?"

"A good couple of hours at least, I'd say. They've still a league or more to cover and they've got to get all their people across the Pallinsburn, that stream that runs along the next valley. It doesn't look like much but it's very wet around; like I said before, be the devil of a job to haul their guns over."

"I imagine they've thought of that," I advised. "Whatever they propose, it's been carefully worked out."

"Are you sure?" James asked. He wasn't being clever; he clearly couldn't fathom exactly what our enemy intended. Neither, in all fairness, could I.

"Will they try to get up this slope?" I demanded of Musgrave. He looked at me uncomprehendingly. If he was an actor, he was a damn good one. I was pretty sure he had no idea.

"If we stay where we are," the King answered, "then they surely will and come at us this way. Our redoubts, our ordnance, our whole strength is facing the wrong way. Clearly we can't have that. We have to swing the army around, haul the guns, and form our line along this crest. Agreed?"

This was faultless; nobody could argue with the logic. "Right then, we need to rouse our fellows for a little light exercise, brace our gunners for some rather more vigorous work, turn the whole army round, and form here. We have two hours at most. Let's not hang about. You all know your stations. Let's get moving."

A very big job indeed, you'll think, and yes it was; perhaps less than you'd assume though. Our camp was laid out by divisions so all had pitched according to their station in line of march. That now had to be reversed and the columns shaken out into line. We'd practised enough; our centenars and vintenars[13] knew their business.

I left a skirmish line of cavalry to hold the ridge and sent Master Musgrave off on his travels again to find out what his countrymen intended. I hurled orders at my subordinates, the other commanders doing the same; for us, a hurried council of war.

"We've been through all this," James began. "Alec, you're on the left; you three" – Crawford, Errol, and Montrose, all young and eager – "go next. I'll take the centre. My Lord Bothwell, you'll command the reserve, and you gentlemen"

---

13 A "centenar" is an officer commanding a company of 100 (*cent*), whilst a "vintenar" commands a sub-unit of 20 (*vingt*).

– this to the two highland chiefs – "will hold our right. Master Borthwick, Alec suggests your place should be on the left of his column – gives you less ground to cover – agreed?"

Borthwick was flustered. His careful plans were coming unstuck and he'd be forced to improvise. Gunners dislike this. They're methodical by nature and he was all too aware of his Achilles' heel: his men were untried in field operations. Presently, they were cursing and heaving to lever their monstrous charges from the sanctuary of their present positions. They were sweating to load powder and shot, tools, kit, and everything.

It was Lindsay, as ever, who broached the obvious question. "Does Your Majesty intend to lead the centre division *himself, in person*?" He loaded his words with incredulity.

"Of course," the King replied. "What were you expecting?"

I had to back Lindsay. "Majesty, we were hoping you would appoint one of your officers to lead the tactical unit whilst you yourself retained strategic control." I liked this. It implied that surrendering unit command was policy not poltroonery. And indeed it was.

"Look," James replied, "I know you fellows speak from the heart and I'm mindful of your concerns." He shrugged. "The fortunes of war can be fickle. But if I'm asking near thirty thousand men, drawn from across the kingdom, and most of them don't want to be here, to risk their necks on my account, then the least I can do is share the risk. I've studied our Swiss masters. Everything depends on timing the assault, on momentum and impact. These will be critical. Having the fellow who wears the crown in front loads the dice. It can and will make the difference. We'll debate no more."

That was that. James had decided and would not be deflected. Part of me admired him and there was reason in his analysis, yet my heart sank. A king is not a captain. He can send others to lead while he keeps tight control of the battle from a safe vantage. Generalship isn't about bravery; it's all about common sense.

"I'd rather they came to us. Let them struggle up the hill while we keep our feet dry and our guns pound them. For once we'll not be plagued by their bows."

"I've thought of that, Alec; you know I have. Our front ranks will all have decent harness. Our tactics depend upon our taking the offensive. The Swiss don't just wait for the enemy. They control the fight by initiating the action, as shall we."

Fact and theory: they look good together on the page, but in the field it's all rather different. Plain fact was we were losing control of the campaign and being forced into a battle our enemy wanted and we didn't; damn.

"Right," I yelled at my officers. "Get everyone moving, full kit and gear, take water, weapons and harness check. When I say now I mean yesterday!" Like a giant beehive, the army began to stir, to shake out by platoons and companies, dragging itself from the midden. "Now," I instructed my stewards, "get the women to pile everything spare and combustible and get some decent blazes going – more smoke the better."

"Are you assuming they've eyes on us, even here?" Huntly enquired. "Can't be too careful, I suppose." I should say that fixing a smoke screen was a well-tried tactic. Yes, the English would know how we'd be likely to deploy but no need to make it any easier for them.

Grumbling, cursing, and fumbling in the time-honoured way of soldiers, my column began to take shape, a great forest of points rising a dozen feet above a sea of burnished sallets. Huntly's caterans fanned out on our flanks in a colourful slew of plaid. We borderers would lead, the three earls' division swinging into line behind, next the King's grand phalanx, and then more wild highlanders under Lennox and Argyll. We filled the plain and shallow valley between the two ridges. To the west Borthwick and his sweating teams were manhandling their great and cumbersome guns around the rim.

"I don't like this ground," Huntly muttered. "Too much damned water everywhere."

"Now I'd have thought you'd be used to that, at least," I replied. "Couple of times I've been up your way, it's never stopped raining."

"True enough, but see the effect." This was noticeable. As the ranks tramped over the lowest point, those in front got over pretty much dry shod but those behind sank deeper, till, say a dozen ranks in, they were struggling up to their knees. "The ground's a quagmire. What you've got is a series of watercourses underground. Once you apply a lot of pressure, water spills up like a fountain. Plenty of spots like this north of the Great Glen, trust me."

Something struck me just then, a random thought, but it vanished as quickly; something that jarred. I was diverted by the sight of Isabella and the medical train bringing up the rear of our contingent. She was riding a fine, light-boned mare, her dark mane streaming behind. Her slim elegance was a marked contrast to the lumpen bulk of harnessed men tramping over the wet plain, the noise of marching feet tremendous.

A cool wind blew over the empty bowl of land, chasing the morning's cloud so ribbons of blue shone through. At least we'd fight in the dry. I wished fleetingly I could have remembered that thread of thought I'd begun and lost – happens when you get old. Because I couldn't fathom it, a lot of younger men marching today were heading inexorably to their deaths.

The prince bishop writes again to Queen Katherine

8th September

Your Most Gracious Majesty,

I do not doubt that you have heard by several posts both from the Earl of Surrey and Lord Dacre. The warden is a most valiant knight, though inclined to be neglectful of order and to my mind is occasionally too free and easy with those of the rougher sort.

I hear that Heron now acts as his deputy and sits upon the earl's council of war. Whilst I acknowledge that war makes strange bedfellows and I willingly grant the man has abundant experience, I do wonder if our gentlemen should be so free with such outlaws and people of the lesser sort. I fear it is most unseemly. Why, I myself once met the fellow, a most impudent swashbuckler, upon the streets of Hexham where he was quite ribald at my expense; nobody of worth took proper offence and many others simply sniggered.

Truly the marches are a barren threapland. That their lordships will tolerate such impudence fills me with deep misgivings. And what of the King of Scots, who has raised his hand and his army so cruelly against us? That boaster disports himself upon our marches with the greatest insolence I have ever beheld, deaf to all Christian

entreaty. As for my castle of Norham, the jewel
of my estates, it is quite slighted, ruined and
reduced to a mere pile of stones. The pain of this
great loss as I have several times communicated
to Your Majesty will, I fear, be the end of me and
I shall shortly be called upon to make account to
our maker.

On the matter of accounts, might I draw Your
Majesty's attention to my own which, as Your
Majesty knows, remains outstanding. Though my
surveyors dare not yet approach Norham they
have advised me that the cost of rebuilding will
amount to some six thousand, one hundred and
forty-three pounds, seven shillings and sixpence
(depending on variations in the cost of local
stone, fluctuations in labour rates, etc.). As I feel
the tug of mortality press ever harder upon me, I
should pass happily if I could be assured the great
work of reconstruction, for the safety of Your
Majesty's realm and the diocese, was already in
hand and that funds were available.

Might I therefore entreat Your Majesty, etc...

The Scottish women

I was completely knackered. We all were. The march up from Coldstream was hard work; it was cold, wet, and somehow hostile, as though the beast of war was summoning us up onto his ground. I rode. I'd not been on horseback for a while, tied to the campus of horrors my house had become. The mare was skittish and excitable, flaring her sensitive nostrils at the strange smells. I'd decided to pull rank and avoid footslogging, thinking time in the saddle might prove calming. It didn't.

The night was raw and smelled of dank autumn, whorls of leaves already dancing in the bladed wind; the great broad sweep of the Tweed rushed and frothed, wide and swollen. The blackness swallowed all beyond. We knew the way, skirting westwards to avoid any patrols. There were none, or if there were we didn't see and they chose not to deter us. I'd loaded a cart with the meagre supplies we could spare. Dr Beaton rode uncomfortably next to me; Ellen, a dozen other women, and a couple of orderlies trudged behind. Our guardians, the warden's men, ranged ahead and on our flanks.

"You've not seen an army encamped before?" the doctor asked, shifting in the saddle. "God, I do hate riding; not built for it; does fearful things to haemorrhoids."

"No," I said. "Skirmishers, raiding parties, that sort of thing, escorts and stuff but never a field army. I imagine it will smell pretty awful."

"It will indeed," he confirmed.

He wasn't exaggerating. We smelled the place long before we got there. I'd taken us up onto Branxton Edge by the easy gradient to the west. Our horsemen had already made contact. We were expected; shapes of riders, their lances fingers of shadow in the glimmer of early light, loomed and receded. Lord Hume's division was encamped on the right at the base of the higher ground. Some were under canvas, most in rough shelters, hacked from denuded trees. The women looked at us curiously; they didn't get many social calls.

"God, it stinks," Ellen shuddered as we nestled in the lee of our cart, partly for the pathetic shelter it offered but more to stop anyone from nicking our precious supplies. We were huddled together, a blanket draped over us. I could feel the heat from her supple young flesh. Noises and flickers of movement coming through the damp shroud of dawn suggested others were engaged in more carnal comforts.

"The fires are pretty though," Ellen added. The wide bowl beneath the ridge was alive with countless fireflies of light. The camp was truly enormous. That steady stream of wounded and sick, the deserters filtering through in ever increasing numbers, didn't seem to have made a dent in the numbers of the King's great army. They filled up the whole landscape. The girl was dozing with her head on my shoulder. I stroked her soft and lustrous hair.

Dawn was merely the lifting of a damp, grey shroud. The camp stirred, smells of cooking competing with the core odours of stale sweat and ordure. Nothing much seemed to be happening. We stretched and ate our own fairly sparse rations. If this was an army preparing for battle, then it was all very relaxed.

"Any sign of the English?" I asked the sergeant from our escort, one of the Kerrs, I think, not noted for friendship with the warden, or anyone else for that matter.

The man shrugged. "Not sure, ma'am. Nobody tells us anything but there's no action anywhere, far as I can see."

I received an invitation to breakfast with the warden. As you might imagine his lodging was somewhat further up the hill and altogether smarter. For all his notorious parsimony, Lord Hume lived pretty well. A capacious silk-lined pavilion was set aside in his own compound, no shortage of silver and plenty of servants on hand. Plenty of food too, and I admitted to being ravenous. A steaming plateful was produced and I devoured the contents with gusto. The warden, dark, immaculate, and inscrutable as ever, merely watched, his odd half smile giving nothing away.

"I'm sorry you've been so inconvenienced," he began. "I've heard glowing reports of the work you're doing, positively eulogistic. Depending on what happens today, you might have more custom."

"Will there be a battle?" I asked mid-mouthful.

"Haven't a clue," he replied, "but Surrey hasn't marched all this way for nothing. He has a plan, to be sure, and I'd lay good odds your friend Master Heron is at his shoulder."

I said nothing.

"Isabella," he continued, "contrary to the evidence, I do care about your welfare, but if there is to be a fight, I need someone to take charge of the women and baggage, not to mention providing for our wounded."

I didn't reply. I couldn't think of anything to say but this news filled my heart with lead. More responsibility was not something I was seeking, especially so heavy a burden.

My face must have given me away. He raised his hand as though to calm an outburst but I had none left.

"This is merely a contingency," he soothed. "It may not happen." Lying snake – he knew it would. One thing I did trust was his instinct.

"Should the worst actually occur, take your medical team and place them to the rear of my division. Use whoever you need from the rank and file. All the rest – the useless mouths, tradesmen, tapsters, whores, and all – get them formed up in column behind the army, ready to move off towards Coldstream, should the need arise."

"You mean, if the English look like they're winning?"

"Just so: you'll not be alone. I've men enough to spare; I'll give you a mounted troop and a company of foot loons. Can you do this, Isabella?"

"Are you offering me a choice?"

He shrugged. "Of course not. Nobody is going to volunteer for this and you're by far the best we've got."

* * *

"There's an honour I could live without," I confided to Ellen. "The warden's not giving much away, not that he ever does, but I'm sure he thinks it will come to a fight." Yet the overcast morning passed without much activity. It wasn't until past noon that the alarm went up. Knots of horsemen were scattering about purposefully as we set about the muster.

"It will be a heck of a job, I can tell you. We've got the provosts, of course, and half the women will be ready to march with their men. Does that surprise you?" I asked Ellen. "Battles are not just for boys only; women trudge onto the field as well – not because they're after martial glory, undying fame or any of that nonsense but because someone has to bring water: harnessed men will become dehydrated in minutes. Another someone has to get the wounded off the field if they're to stand a chance. That particular someone has to have a working knowledge of first aid treatment for wounds, and yes, they need to be pretty strong. If things go well, they'll scavenge the dead; if not, they'll be the ones getting scavenged."

"Does that include us?" she queried.

"Broadly, yes; we'll have the warden's men as protection but they can always run faster, so I wouldn't be too hopeful there."

Those women with the baggage and their squalling, ragged imps of children were a mob – a surly, resentful, and disorderly mob. "Right," I bellowed. "I want tents struck and loaded onto the carts, rubbish piled and burnt, gear stowed, lines ordered, and the whole lot of you ready to move off behind the reserves." Not much happened. I had to send the provosts around to kick some life and response into my new charges. Sluggishly, with aching slowness and endless complaining, the column began to take form.

"You can leave that behind," I snapped at a fat bruiser of a highland woman. I'd no idea if she understood – their dialect is impenetrable – and she reeked to high heaven, shapeless kirtle straining against a sea of vast uncontrollable bosom, arms like hawsers. She was trying to hump a decent-sized chest onto one of the carts, probably representing her accumulated loot.

Her reply, though half unintelligible, was succinct and to the point – as was my reaction. I swung a fairly decent left hook at her. I had grown up with a gaggle of boisterous older brothers and could punch above my weight. She didn't see it coming and snorted like a shot deer when I connected, dropping like a sack of turnips, face down in the clarts. Now I was talking their language, one or two even looked impressed. The pace improved, and besides, I felt better – I'd really needed to hit somebody.

"A fine sight," one of Hume's men said, indicating the army, marching off by divisions, the King's great standard flapping in the cool wind.

"They're in good order; even I can see that," I replied. And they were. It was impressive, all the manhood of Scotland, their banners raised, sudden trails of brilliant colour against the dun-shaded grasses. To the west our artillery train was inching around the rim, great guns harnessed, oxen straining, shouts and curses of the gunners carrying clear.

I felt a sudden rush. There were so many of us. Surely so great an army could never be defeated. But Surrey's men would be marching with the same thought and they were ready. I had struggled to put all thoughts of John Heron out of mind. Nobody here was the enemy, really, since I took gold from both sides, but my thoughts had little to do with policy.

"You fancy him, don't you?" Ellen had once asked without sounding censorious. "Have you let him, well, you know?"

"It's always more complex than that," I answered cautiously. "There are consequences. There always are."

I'd sent the medical team ahead, at the rear of Hume and Huntly's companies, while I attempted to get the rest in order. By the time Bothwell's reserves had tramped by, wild clansmen bounding alongside, saffron and plaid flashing, we were more or less in order. The rubbish pits were fired and we moved off as smoke thickened and eddied. The distance across the saddle was less than a league. The army filled the space like Israelites on the move, the great lurching train of baggage slewed behind. You'll ask me how many there were and you'll hear God knows what numbers mentioned, but I'd say there were ten thousand women and their broods, maybe more. There were provosts bellowing all along the line, like frantic sheepdogs.

At this point I was dismounted and I'd recruited a few of the brighter specimens to act as auxiliaries for the medical train. They'd be needed, and as we straggled over the soaking peat, at times calf-deep in well-churned mire, a few more came up and volunteered. One was a slim, dark-haired young woman, my age I'd guess, though probably younger. God loves us all, I know, but he seems to love the rich best. She was pretty, with good skin, unmarked, tanned and freckled, reasonable teeth too and a ready smile.

"I'm Jen," she confided, not awed by protocol. "My man's with Errol's – though he's just a cobbler, never handled a flaming spear in his life, plain conscript, just like all the rest. What about you?"

This was forthright. "I mean, I know you can't, well you know, with men, you being in orders an' all... yet you're not bad looking." She didn't realize that not all who ran religious houses were wedded to the cross, so this could have become an interesting conversation.

"Thanks," I replied. "Well, not all of us are in holy orders for a start. I'm not and I'm head of the table. It's just that there can be other priorities."

"You're not married though, no bairns?"

"No to both," I laughed.

"Mine are back home with me mam. I'm glad they're looked after, wouldn't want them here, but I've got to look after him. God help us if the great loon gets himself killed."

Her tone was light but her fears were deep. "If he doesn't come back, we'll starve. The King wanted him to sign up, but if that gets him knifed what then? Can't see us getting a pension. Can you?"

No arguments there.

"I told him – I said get ourselves away while we can, plenty have." She looked half defiantly at me as if she expected me to argue. Well, to the devil with that; in their position I'd have been gone days ago and left King James to enjoy his battle.

"I hope it works out for the best," she ended lamely.

Not much more to say really. I reached out and took her hand as we plodded on, marching towards extinction. Then it was time for me to mount up and go forward to the medical train. I'd a feeling we'd soon be very busy.

Heron formally goes to war

"At least it's fared up," Father Bell observed, "God's sun shining on our arms. On theirs too, of course. King James will be pleased he's to have his great fight after all, damn him. Or perhaps I should curse you, as this was all your idea."

It had brightened, though the ground beneath still slopped. Howard's division, in remarkably good order, was strung out behind, the guns and their carts trundling over the uneven ground. Appleyard and Blakenhall, the gunnery officers, were everywhere, chivvying their blokes and ministering to their precious charges.

"He summoned the minstrels; I'm just providing the tune," I reminded. "We'll just have to see who dances best."

We'd picked up Surrey's brigades, splashing through the fords. They fell in behind us with Stanley's fellows bringing up the rear. I wasn't worried that the Scots would attack us on the march. I'd pretty much assumed, and the Howards agreed, that they'd stand fast on Branxton Edge, surmising it was our intention to storm the ridge.

"Remind me how far off we are?" Bell asked.

"A couple of leagues, more perhaps. We'll march with the river on our left, then swing westwards into the Pallinsburn valley."

"Much of an obstacle?" he queried.

"No, nothing really. There's a narrow crossing for the guns; otherwise it's only a trickle. Then we scramble up the hill, Piper's Hill that is, and the ridge will be in front."

Dacre came up, black as a raven, his harness fitted as though he'd been welded in. Unlike much of the armour around, his was scuffed, ragged, and dented in places. "Now then, Johnny," he began, with a nod to the vicar, "you've brought the sun out and our friends are stirring. I've had reports of smoke. They've fired their camp for sure. It's an old trick of theirs. That means they're on the move."

"They'll make the higher ground before us then?" Bell asked.

"For sure, horse, foot, and guns, and a fine sight it will be; might unnerve a few of the lads, especially once their guns get started, be a hell of a racket."

For a moment, I fervently hoped Isabella was not with them. I knew she was running the hospital at Coldstream and I prayed she'd stay there. I wanted to see lots and lots of dead Scots today but there had to be at least one exception.

"If things go our way this afternoon, we'll send your pretty prioress a load or two of new customers," Dacre went on, somehow guessing, clever old sod – wasn't as bluff as he seemed. He passed his flask around. "In case I don't get the chance to say so, good luck to all of you. We'll be up against stiff odds, however it goes. Howard's a good commander but once the music starts there's nowt most generals can do."

"Where will he place the cavalry, do you think?"

"My best guess will be on our right but in close reserve, probably behind young Edmund's brigade. They're our weakest and those shifty Lancashire men can be truculent. They'll fight like blazes if your name's Stanley but do nowt for anyone else."

The ground was pretty level, rolling moorland with the odd patchwork of in-by fields, most bare and stripped, the sparse settlements empty and hollow. The only life on the plain wore armour. We had no purpose other than fighting. Plenty of those marching now would not be marching back. It took time to get the army down to the Pallinsburn. A good couple of hours must have elapsed, plenty of time for the enemy to get into gear.

I'd said the burn wasn't that wide but weeks of rain hadn't helped, swelling the modest stream and spilling a quaking wet mass around. Some will say it was just a "step-over" but you'd have needed damn big boots and a long stride. As it was there were only two viable crossings, Branx Brig to the west and Sandyford further east.

"That isn't a bridge," Appleyard the gunner boomed at me. "It's a miserable excuse for a plank. Do you think me guns can fly?"

I had thought of this and we agreed the ordnance would cross via the fords with the earl's division whilst we at the front used the tiny bridge.

"Can't see a damned thing," Thomas Howard groused at me. "Where precisely is the enemy?"

"See this small hill in front of us, over the stream? Well, we climb up there and there's a bit of a drop in front, fifty, sixty feet, no more, down to the next watercourse, then Branxton Edge climbs up from there. I imagine our guests will be lining up to cheer us in."

"Let's find out."

As the army filed over the narrow planks, we spurred up the steep reverse slope of the higher ground – Piper's Hill it's called, and any tunes that it ever inspired would only be laments.

As I mentioned, the hill is just a pimple; the ground falls away down a gentle gradient to the burn then rises again to the ridge. It's no great height, mind you, three hundred feet maybe and an easy slope. Normally it's just a bare tussock-coated line, stirred by the wind and little else. Today was rather different.

Late summer sunlight was touching the valley. More light was glancing from the vast forest of spear-points opposite. The Scots army faced us over the drop, rank upon serried rank, their tall staves seemingly without number. Their harness shone; their banners fluttered proudly.

"There's thousands of them," some idiot observed.

"What did you expect?" I snapped back. "We came here to pick a fight and there it is."

"I make it five divisions." Howard was at my elbow. "They're deployed in deep columns – what would you say, a bow shot apart? Oh, for God's sake..."

I followed his gaze. He'd turned to see how the earl's division were closing up from their passage from the ford. They weren't – for a good mile there was no sign of them. Ahead of us, the Scots were barely a quarter of that distance.

He turned to me. "If they hit us now we're done for; they'll pick us off one after the other." He pulled his heavy chain of office, the Lamb of God, from around his neck and chucked it to me. "Ride, Johnny, ride," he ordered. "Let the earl know what a fix we're in. Get those fellows moving whatever it takes and for pity's sake bring those guns up."

To underline the urgency the Scots' big guns began to fire. The noise was terrific; half our horses near bolted. The ground shook. Vast clouds of diabolical smoke billowed out, blotting out the ground, merging with the creeping grey cloud from the burning camp. You could see the enormous shot arcing over. Well over, I'm happy to report. They were shooting wide. The cannon balls, as big as boulders, screamed over our heads and smashed impotently into the swollen mire behind. Great geysers of slick mud spouted into the air. Many of our fellows got a thorough dousing but none was harmed, Scotch clowns.

By then I was pelting down the long slope eastwards, past Branxton Church and the front ranks of our men as they shook out into line, flinging chunks of turf as I galloped flat out towards Sandyford. George Darcy was at the head of the column, hurling curses at the laggards struggling across.

"I know, I know," he lamented, even before I'd got a word in. Surrey was there too. Despite his gout the old man was in full harness. "Right, lad," he bellowed at me. "You've come to tell us to get moving, and move we shall and swiftly. Getting the guns over has been a flaming nightmare. Now, where do we want 'em? God, those Scotch heathens are making a racket."

"On the hill, my lord, if we can. The lord admiral is deploying his men forward of the crest so from there our gunners will have a clear shot."

"Right, that's it then. Now, you idle toads, this is where you finally start earning your wages. Get marching and double time."

As the men finally filtered through the ford, the bottleneck was easing and they were beginning to shake out, closing the gap. The guns went trundling west towards Piper's Hill. I cantered back ahead of them.

"Looks like we got away with it." Thomas Howard breathed relief. We were yelling, for the Scottish guns kept up their barrage, though, thank God, their aim was still off and, in that short time, our men had got used to the noise. Most had anyway.

Dacre rode up in a foul temper. "Run off, bolted like a bunch of milkmaids. God help them when this is over." I gathered he was referring to the two squadrons from the east march, Bamburgh and Tynemouth men. "I never liked them anyway," he muttered. "Pain in the butt bunch of whingers. That's the trouble with fisher-folk – not enough to do on winter's nights; all that incest saps the blood, you know."

It was now late afternoon; roughly our line extended

nearly a mile, with Edmund Howard on our right, the lord admiral in the centre, and Surrey on the left. We'd spread out to conform to the massive Scottish columns towering above us. As always, our boys were hurling taunts and abuse but they stayed silent, awesomely so. Clearly, this was part of their new drill and all the more terrifying. Whoever had carried out their training hadn't been wasting his time.

Behind me, our guns barked into life. This fresh assault on the ears was deafening, percussive waves of noise beating like an infernal drum roll. I'd stayed with Howard for the moment, the rest of the cavalry were down below, and we'd a brigade of foot in reserve with them. Smoke from our guns blew back in our faces but their line was still shrouded by their own.

Time is an odd business in battle. Things seem to happen either very slowly or very fast. I couldn't tell you how long this gun duel lasted but I'd guess it was only a matter of minutes, for it was soon obvious that the fire from their side was slackening and then it ceased altogether. A loud huzza rose from thousands of English throats as our gunners, first task complete, switched their aim.

"Now we'll see some sport," Dacre chuckled. "Let's see how they like the taste of our old iron."

I doubt our gunners had ever been presented with such an inviting target: vast bodies of formed foot, easily in range and completely inert. Rounds began falling on the packed ranks, grazing over the wet ground to slice and eviscerate. We could see them striking, shearing, and toppling men like a hammer breaking skittles. Great gouts of red erupted as the lines shivered and closed. If they hadn't been Scotch I might have felt sorry for the poor sods.

The worst that can happen to infantry is to be caught in the open, packed like kippers and nowhere to hide. Their guns made no further reply. Our fellows had made short but sure work of them. A severed head sailed high up from one of the central brigades, spilling a bloody tail. "This will do nicely," Howard beamed. "Get some ale up to our lads on the guns, seeing as they're doing all the work for us."

Our men were screaming at them now, baying like hungry wolves as the balls smashed home, punishing the enemy, hurting them. Their formidable great array was now a death trap, an abattoir. It was good for our lads to see the enemy suffer. For too long we'd danced to their tune. We'd slogged and sweated for the best part of two days just to get here while they'd sat warm and comfy. As every round crashed home, as every file was pulped, our blokes' fury rose another notch.

"Old men and boys, eh?" Dacre grunted. "That's what King James called us, but who's calling the piper now? Seeing all this Scotch blood flying around is working our fellows up good an' proper. There'll be no holding them."

The same thoughts must have occurred to our opponents across the way. Their men couldn't soak up much more of this punishment. Then, suddenly, on their left, they came down the hill. Hume's division I'd guess from his banners, a cloud of hairy Jocks on the flanks. Scarcely a moment later, that big division opposite us followed on, tramping down the easy slope. I could see they'd mostly cast off their shoes – smart move given how wet the ground was. Despite the battering they'd had they kept good order, not a sound from them.

Our archers nocked and drew.

This was it.

Bishop Ruthal writes again to Queen Katherine

9th September

Your Most Gracious Majesty,

It is, as before, with a heavy heart that I must write to you again pertaining to these matters which I have raised before and pray that I might in early course receive Your Majesty's reply, for I fear my time here on earth is nearly spent, worn down by the cares of my high office and sorely oppressed by these Scotch rogues who have wrought such damage to church property. When I did under previous cover send to you my list and estimates of costs accruing from the depredations of these impious devils I find now that, in my anxiety and great concern, I omitted to include certain ancillary but necessary costs, now pointed out to me by the diligence of my clerks and to which, with greatest respect, I now direct Your Majesty's kind attention.

Whilst I had taken full account of the necessary repairs to the fabric of the castle I plain forgot the matter of ransoms which will be due for Master Anislow and several other gentlemen, captured and held by the Scots, plus of course the cost of their lodging and victuals whilst they are held. Here I am quite at the mercy of those rapacious Scots who will never turn aside from any course that involves yet more larceny and extortion from my overstretched diocese.

The insolence of these people is intolerable, yet what else is one to do? Added to this there is, as I have now been made aware, the cost of replacing all the ordnance that was taken, not forgetting that quantity of powder and shot that was seized, together with all manner of tools and general warlike stores and then there are the bows and bills that were lost, much harness and gear... Your Majesty will see how dreadfully I am vexed and how my only hope of comfort is Your Majesty's understanding and early remittance.

I have the honour to remain, etc...

Chapter Nine: Nemesis

We shall say nothing of those who often come home crippled from foreign wars… They use their limbs in the service of the commonwealth or the king and their disability prevents them from exercising their own craft, and their age from learning a new one.

More: *Utopia*

Lord Hume fights his battle

You know things aren't going too well with the artillery when your gun commander's severed head lands at your feet. It's pretty disconcerting and I'm an old hand. Master Borthwick's face still bore a look of astonishment or fury or indeed furious astonishment. His headless torso was thrashing and gouting blood yards away.

"Everything he feared," I bellowed at Huntly. "Every damn thing we feared." Our guns were ill-prepared and worse served. Ranging downhill is pretty difficult at the best of times. This was not the best of times. The English cannon were firing from the small hill to our right front. They were well prepared and very well served. The noise was terrific, louder than the fiercest storm, a rolling thunder of noise and smoke.

I suspect the gun duel lasted for minutes and no longer. Their shot came thick, fast, and very accurate. One clanged off the barrel of a culverin, ricocheted into the flank of my right-hand brigade, and took both legs off a pikeman. The gun sagged, crushing one of the gunners, whose screams kept up a regular accompaniment. "Put that poor devil out of our misery." I gave the nod to one of Huntly's caterans, who shot off fast as a hare and the screaming stopped. "You can always trust a proper highlander to make a decent job of cutting someone's throat," his employer cheerfully confirmed.

"I'd like a chance to show off this harness," he continued conversationally, as though we were trotting down a quiet lane. "Cost me a fortune and her ladyship belly-ached for weeks... just a tad conspicuous at times."

We were already in trouble. My lads were drawn up in two brigades, lining the lip of the ridge. This might be intimidating for the enemy below but a dream come true for their gunners. A whistling round-shot smacked, grazing just right, and caught several of our frantic matrosses as they laboured over their unwieldy ordnance. It cut the first neatly in half and eviscerated the one behind, who went hurtling backwards, trailing a bloody slime of steaming intestines – hot tripe on the battlefield.

The fight was totally one-sided and ended with Master Borthwick's head. Those who survived simply bolted. They abandoned their expensive charges and scattered off westwards. The artillery fight was over. It would now be an infantry fight, what they call a "soldier's battle". With our guns silenced, we were horribly exposed to theirs.

I should have said that we were at the extreme left of our line, facing a weak English brigade – couldn't call it a division. I recognized the Howard banners and supposed this was the younger brother. Isabella and the medical team were behind our right-hand formation, the three earls to our left, then the King's vast phalanx with more highlanders beyond.

There was a moment's lull as the English gunners shifted their aim. Our own great cannon, abandoned and forlorn, stood like beached wrecks on some distant shore. "Now we're in for it," Huntly commented, motioning his own men to lie down. This was sensible. We knew what was coming. The great mass of spears ranked around us did not. "This will be truly disagreeable."

None of my affinity, seasoned reivers many of them, had ever been under artillery fire before. For a foot soldier that's about as bad as it gets. We were a perfect target, a great regular mass, obligingly lined along the skyline. A posse of lasses could have blasted us and these weren't novices. Shot, fast as meteors, hurtled up from the smoke-shrouded valley, grazing or bouncing from the lip and flensing our files. Men were flung aside and stunned, just by the force of balls battering the air. Others were disembowelled, decapitated, shorn of limb. One ball bounced too soon and rolled towards the line. Some idiot stuck his foot out as though he was playing football. He wouldn't be playing again.

As befits a commander, I had stayed mounted between my two brigades. That's the trouble with nobility. You have to set an example, in this case one of rank stupidity. Below us, in the intervals between salvos, we could see the enemy lines, heaving and swaying as their men jeered at us. Their morale must be soaring, faces howling, demonic, screaming curses. Their officers could barely restrain them.

"I fancy our chances against that lot." Huntly indicated Howard's division. Of their formations, this looked the weakest, perhaps three thousand bills I guessed. "We're three to their one. That's the sort of odds I like and the ground favours us."

All true. We just needed the order to attack. To my immediate left one of our leading ranks was struck in the midriff by a two-pounder. He doubled up like a folding jack-knife, bizarrely staying on his feet, though his innards must be completely smashed – very disconcerting. "Look at that!" someone yelled. There's nothing like someone else's disaster. Sergeants were bellowing "Close up, close up!" as the English shot winnowed us. The lads wouldn't take much more. We needed the order to advance. I decided I'd give it regardless when we saw the flags signalling from the centre.

Off we went.

The slope in front of us was gentle enough; the burn which flowed further east, along the foot of the ridge, had petered out. The English guns had inflicted casualties on us but not that many. The damage was mainly to our nerves. We were pumped up, the red mist thickening. Our advance swiftly brought us in range of their livery bows. The English yeoman with his cursed bow had scourged our armies in a score of battles. These Cheshire and Lancashire men, if I guessed right, nocked, drew, and loosed as we came on. The arrow storm: deadly bodkins – hardened steel piles to pierce the best harness, vicious barbs to skewer through jacks.

Our fellows had heavy timber shields in front, a devil to manoeuvre but effective. Those behind did at least have some harness. Many did not. The wind was blowing stiffly and a hint of wetness still hung in the air. The shafts struck home like the devil's rain, lifting men from their feet, punching like sledgehammer blows. One man might be studded with half a dozen points whilst his neighbour escaped. Though the force is terrific, the arrow blow doesn't kill cleanly. Victims shudder and writhe, their screams adding to the mounting crescendo of sound.

Speed I knew was of the essence. Come to contact, get in fast and hard. And we did. We swept downhill like the wrath of God, our great forest of points drooping towards the front. Huntly's kerns and caterans skipped alongside, stripped down to saffron shirts, mail for those as possessed any. We stayed silent.

I'd sent my horse to the rear (not too far back obviously) and was leading on foot – it encourages the lads – and I'd picked up a half-pike, quite long enough for a gentleman in my position. I could feel the enemy wavering as our phalanx swept on. Our pace was brisk. Our drill was right and we had crucial momentum. "They won't stand!" someone yelled and he was right. The English line wavered, milled, and then broke.

Now, rot never starts at the front. Any man there is too busy trying to stay alive, and besides, where can he run with another twenty pushing behind him? That luxury is reserved for faint-hearts at the back, the sort who'd naturally avoid the front. The English deployed in lines. These can beat columns, such as ours, but only if everybody holds his nerve. This lot didn't. They just fled.

A single English knight, well harnessed, failing to rally his company, charged full tilt into us, buying time – a brave gesture if a foolish one. I saw him hack down at least one of our own gentlemen and a commoner or two before one of Huntly's swordsmen felled him with a backward swipe from his double-hander. He sprawled and a bevy of thrusting spears finished him off.

"Well, that was easy enough," Huntly observed, as his wild highlanders went sprinting after fugitives, dragging men down like deer. "No point trying to outrun my lads; they're awfully quick on their feet."

"It's not over yet," I cautioned. Howard's banner was

still flying in the centre. His household men were ready to sell their lives as dearly as they could. That was only a matter of time. "Where's Dacre?"

This proved rhetorical. No sooner had I wondered than that great Red Bull banner came dipping and flowing past the gaggle of deserters. They were all mounted, Heron's pennon there as well, more foot behind. Huntly swore in Gaelic – lost in the translation but spot on in the circumstances.

"Charge to horse!" I was bellowing. "Come on, you idle shirkers. Start earning your pay" (the few of you I am paying, I could have added, but it was the galvanic effect that mattered). "Charge to horse..." This is a manoeuvre whereby spearmen, dismounted, jab the butts of their staves against their instep and level the pike about chest high for a horse. It's a remarkable deterrent and no cavalry can get through.

Dacre had his men well in hand. None of them were amateurs, foot forming on his right flank (our left). The secret of a decent charge is to keep the line steady, stirrup to stirrup. As with pikes you need mass and momentum. Huntly's caterans were skimming back, not abandoning their loot, of course, but moving damn near as fast as garrons.

A fight was still raging in the centre. Howard was proving hard to capture. Heron's troop dug spurs and rode into the melee. This was inconvenient as Edmund Howard's ransom would have kept me in bread and ale for a year or two. "Reform!" I yelled. "Come on, back into line, form up." Officers and sergeants took their cue from me, dragging our boys back into some semblance of order. I'd the impression of quite a few bodies around where the scrap had raged, but otherwise losses on both sides seemed negligible.

The English warden's horsemen were practically upon our lines. I say practically because they didn't venture closer than a spear's length, partially as our pikes wouldn't let them and equally because they weren't trying all that hard. It was a stalemate in every sense. They couldn't get past our points but we weren't about to launch another charge. There was no momentum and, frankly, no need. We'd won our fight, taken our ground. All in all we'd done quite enough for one afternoon's work.

Huntly came up – sensible fellow, he'd not dismounted. He just ignored the arrows. "Look over there." His face was set, not the look of a man content with his labours at all. I looked over to my right where the earls' division had marched down from their start line and felt my bowels loosen.

"You remember what I said earlier," he continued. I now recalled that fleeting thought which had come then flitted clean way on the march, all the more galling as it was so screamingly obvious. I'd noted the way the ground filled with water in the depression now above us. Well, my thought was that if it was bad on top it would be worse below. Indeed it was – much worse.

"This is what Heron and Dacre intended all along," I muttered. "Damn the pair of them." Our pikes came down from the high ground and attempted to step over the little stream, flowing all innocuously. The first ranks barely faltered but then, progressively, they began to sink. Most now were up to their waists. The attack slowed and stalled. A few huddled corpses dotted the hillside where the bows had found a mark but now, barely fifty yards from the English line, their archers were having a field day. "Nock, draw, loose": for how many thousands of Scots had that been the last set of commands they ever heard?

Momentum was gone, as was cohesion, and morale was evaporating. Worse, if there could be worse, the view from the top was deceptive. The ground from the base of the hill was not level, far from it. In fact, it rose quite steeply towards the English lines. And those ranks of hungry bills, eager as jackals, weren't about to attend on our convenience. They came forward. I could hear the centenars bawling, "March on, march on."

And on they marched, in perfect order. Howard had his crack marines forming the first ranks. They came down as though on parade, a desperate contrast to the struggling mass they faced. Our men still floundered. I could see Scottish gentlemen, mired in the weight of their own harness, trying to get the men forward, themselves having to be dragged out of the mess. Behind them the ranks huddled largely motionless. Arrows came in thick and fast, men dropping.

I said before that the rot begins at the back. You need your stoutest lads up front. This leaves only the dross behind. "They're wavering," Huntly confirmed. And they were. With English shafts coming in like hailstones, the doubters were getting set to disappear. What begins as a trickle soon swells to a river and then a flood. Dozens, then hundreds, were dropping their staves and scrambling back up the ridge.

"Naff all hope of rallying that lot."

I agreed. "Right, let's disengage. Pull all our lads back. Your chaps cover the flanks as before. Withdraw in good order, nice and steady, slowly does it. I want us halfway back up that hill."

Dacre was happy to let us go. Some of our men poked ineffectually at some of his. A few of his had edged closer but they weren't serious. They made no move to follow as we shuffled back. We retreated a hundred paces or so, not much more, but it gave us the advantage of the slope. I was mindful our medics were just over the lip and that great fat target of the baggage train not far behind. Otherwise it was a perfect stalemate. Nobody was going anywhere.

It was time to take stock. As I said we'd not lost many, but one of my sergeants, bloodied and breathless, reported on casualties from the fight with Howard. "We killed a good few," he noted. "We lost some as well though."

"Who?" I demanded. My half-brother Davy had commanded a company in that fight.

"Sir Davy," he mournfully confirmed. "Howard himself did the killing. The idot also did for your cousin, Cuddy." I hardly had time to digest this bitter harvest – just time to damn John Heron and Edmund Howard together.

As we withdrew uphill Thomas Howard's men laid into those from the earls' division. They hefted their old-fashioned bills with the ease of masters and sliced into our shuddering pikes. None of our Swiss mentors had ever encountered the English bill. If they had they'd be rewriting their manuals. The axe blade enabled the marines to sweep aside our points then step in to engage. Our men had to drop their staves and draw swords. Now they were outreached, and whilst I'd back a single blade against the bill, it doesn't work against numbers.

"We're beaten," Huntly grunted.

Right enough; our people were being sheared like corn stalks, and those who'd struggled over the moss had nowhere to run. Nobody was taking prisoners. One of our officers, might have been Montrose himself, was making a brave effort to rally survivors. One billman engaged his blade, trapping the point. This one's mate – they worked in pairs – used the hook to catch our knight behind the knees and send him crashing or splashing into the mud. The other then thrust his long spike blade into the helpless man's genitals. Lunge, shove, twist, and pull free. God knows how many times this one-sided drill was repeated; presumably till we ran out of gentry.

"What's happening?" someone, I forget who, asked shakily.

I addressed my reply to Huntly and kept my voice low. "Unless I'm wrong, now that our next division is gone, Howard will swing his men around onto the King's flank."

I should have said that the King's vast phalanx, an acre of spears, had swept down the hill in fine style. They'd stumbled in the bog but had somehow regained their momentum, surging forward and seeming to hurl the old English earl's division back, a fair way back.

"That will sort them," somebody yelled as our fellows cheered.

Huntly, near me, visibly groaned. "They're not breaking. They're just giving ground to draw James deeper in. Howard will hack at his flanks and if their rearguard ever shows up, the King's division will be surrounded. No room to manoeuvre, nowhere to go."

I stood the men down. We kept a hedge of spears facing Dacre but he wasn't moving. As our countrymen fought their last frenzied battle we kept up the stalemate. Many have called me callous, or worse, but when a sweating rider came up an hour later bringing a demand from the King that we advance again, I demurred. Huntly winced but did not argue.

The messenger was a young man, a Crichton I think, one of the pretty young things from the household. He was practically crying, his nice new harness splattered, dented, and bloodied. "You cannot abandon your King," he wailed. "For pity's sake, you've ten thousand men, hardly a scratch.

You can turn the tide. For the King's sake, for Scotland's sake, come up, come up," he blubbered.

Stupid boy. I looked at him. "We've done our bit," I replied coldly. "We've done all that was asked and all that can be done. We've won our ground and we hold it but we cannot advance against the weight of enemy horse. On open ground they'll chew us to bits. Somebody has to cover our withdrawal."

The lad glared at me, stunned. He still thought this fight could be won. That's the trouble with getting old: you know better.

The Bastard Heron fights his battle

"Right," announced Dacre, "off we go." The warden was in high good humour. Nothing agreed more with him than a decent fight. We had one to look forward to. His opposite number had led his landslide of pikes down the slope with commendable élan. This was our weakest point. Ed had far fewer men, temperamental types at that, and was attempting to hold terrain tailor-made for the attacker.

"They're running," someone gasped. And so they were. Our side didn't even wait for contact. They sheered off like rabbits. Tom Howard shot us a glance and we spurred down the easy slope. The warden treated his horsemen to a brief oration: "Right lads, here we go. Keep the line, don't mess about. Lay into them."

Not one for the history books perhaps but Dacre still knew how to lead men. "Cavalry will lead and foot loons follow on, form on our right."

Many will tell you that the charge is a grand affair of thundering hooves, going hell for leather. Well, that's more what happens in a race, at a truce day say. In war it's different – measured and sedate by comparison.

We moved off by squadrons. Most were mounted on sturdy cobs or garrons, rather more squat and workaday than your knightly steed. Caesar, my own grey, stood just fifteen hands, yet taller than most and finer boned. He was ready and eager, gathering for speed; he'd be disappointed. From no faster than a walk, we quickened to a trot. Much faster and you can't hold the line. Infantry were spilling out behind and moving right to cover our flank.

"Now then, Johnny," Dacre instructed, "once we smack their line, take your boyos into the thick and get your chum, young Howard, out of it, preferably alive. We don't want to be paying any exorbitant ransoms." Noise, a tornado of sound, drowned further words. Besides, I knew what was expected. My score and more of riders were geared up and ready. Knots of fleeing infantry, shocked and dazed in their own panic, milled out of the way. They weren't beyond rallying.

The enemy was bracing himself. Officers were bullying men into line, wild highlanders falling back. The dense wood of sharp points began to coalesce, tightening up, a bristling hedgehog of spears, solid as a castle wall. I was heading for the centre where the white prancing lion posturing on the long, red Howard banner still flew defiantly. The scrap was so mixed the Jocks couldn't break off. I dug spurs just slightly and we cantered ahead of the main body. Lances levelled, we pelted into them.

Dead were everywhere. However fastidious our horses, we trampled on lifeless flesh. Edmund and his few survivors were reduced to a beleaguered knot beneath the standard. We bulled through, lances lunging, using our mounts as rams. I dismounted a third of the boys, throwing reins to the rest. There's no subtlety in any of this. It's just brute force and momentum, a mix of scalpel and sledgehammer. The enemy wasn't expecting us, focused on their valuable prey. That's one of the advantages of nobility. Your life equates to a cash sum – in the case of a Howard, a very hefty sum. Sound beat against us in great waves of noise, damp grasses slick with blood.

"Close up!" I bellowed at my company. A platoon of the enemy turned towards us. Our comrades, those still mounted, loosed latches, pinning a few. As they hesitated, we punched through. Some big, square Scot, anonymous in imported German harness, just wolverine eyes behind a bellows-faced visor, came steaming in.

He lunged wildly, relying on force. I parried lightly, stepped back; he swung. Instead of going back, I stomped forward as I blocked the cut. The blades were locked but I pushed the long spike of my rondel dagger through the glaring slit and deep into his wild eye then pulled it free with an obligatory twist, spilling great spurts of fresh red blood.

There were more, swiftly recovering from the shock of our rude arrival. We were dragged into the melee. Another, one of their great hairy types, bare brawny shanks and ancient coat of mail, wielding one of those formidable long blades, chopped one of my blokes then hacked at me. I parried again, cut in close, using the dagger a second time, thrusting beneath his red-bearded jaw, smelling his rank, sour sweat, driving up to where a brain might be.

Suddenly, or so it seemed, the press began to thin, the enemy skittering back, hauled into their reformed main body, as immobile as a fortress. "You took your time," Edmund reproached cheerfully. He didn't look too good. His harness was bruised and battered, grimed with layers of blood. Most wasn't his but enough was running out between the joints. When I eased off his armet, his pale eyes were wide and already glazing; ribbons of red ran down one temple. "My head hurts."

"Not surprised," I grunted. "Gentlemen shouldn't play with rough neighbours."

"I think I'd quite like to lie down for a bit."

I got a couple of my boys to help Ed towards the rear, what was left of his household men gratefully stumbling after. They'd certainly earned a respite. From tempest to calm, the situation had changed. The Scots were all in formation a few yards from us. We were also in our line, mostly still mounted. They weren't bothering us, though, and we weren't much bothering them. Dacre's charge had saved this wing from folding and now Hume's whole division was pinned in a stalemate.

It came to me then that none of this was accidental. He and Hume had clearly sorted the whole game beforehand. Both did their bit with little or no loss to either side. The balance was kept. I was jerked from this happy reverie by a lancing pain in my right calf. I yelped and stumbled sideways. It's wise policy in the field to make sure all your enemies around, those without cash value at least, are dead. One clearly wasn't and had attempted to geld me with a ballock knife.

"Scotch toad," I chirped while, more usefully, someone staved in his head.

"Ow, ow, ow," I hobbled. The blade had, happily for me, been deflected by the thick hide of my horseman's boots and my assailant's failing strength. I could feel the shoe filling with blood as Crookback yanked it off. "Stick to thieving," I grimaced. "Nursing's not quite your thing."

"Just a scratch, man; a girl would let on less." Nobody could say my lieutenant had finesse but his blunt fingers were quick and skilled enough, forming a rough tourniquet. "I don't suppose you'll be heading to the rear?"

Attractive as the prospect was, I shook my head. "Lots more sport to be had yet." He dragged the boot back on and I was able to hobble. Later, it would ache for England but the red mist, that shift-changing intoxication of battle, still pounded through my veins.

Dacre had dismounted. I was summoned. "You can still ride?" he joshed. Concern for my welfare dispensed with, he rapped out further orders. "Right then; we're all quiet here. Nobody's interfering with anybody else, which suits me just fine. Get over to those foot loons yonder and find 'em some gainful employment. They could weigh in on Tom Howard's flank. He's got that parcel of Jocks pretty much beaten but the real fight will be in the centre. See if you can put some fire into the laggards as well. You've preserved his kid brother so he's already in your debt. Help him win this battle and he'll want to marry you. Get going."

The good father, Thomas Bell, detaching himself from the warden, rode, or rather ambled, on a knock-kneed palfrey. In battered jack and sallet, he looked as much like a reiver as any. "You don't often get to meet real bishops," he confided. "We rural priests are pretty much beneath the salt." The senior cleric in question was Bishop Stanley, with more Eagle's Claw retainers braced by a stiffening of Westmorland archers.

"This is pretty much a doddle, scarcely worth getting dressed up for." His lordship greeted us equably, proffering a welcome dram. You have to hand it to the church – they don't ever drink vinegar. The liquor went down, smooth but with a tongue of fire. Reverend Bell took a prodigious swallow. Such bounteous hospitality from his seniors was awfully rare.

"You've work for us," the bishop surmised. He was a typical Stanley, four square and tall, dark and rough hewn with great black beetling brows that added an almost demonic look. "These lads are steady enough, won't bunk off like the others. I've sent chaps to drag 'em back. God knows where they imagined they were running to. Lancashire's the other way; only place up there is Scotland."

He was right. Knots of stragglers, whey-faced and shameful, were being herded back to the jeers of their affinity. So much the better; they now had something to prove.

"I imagine you'd like us to do our bit in the middle?"

"I'd be obliged."

Orders were given. The men turned from line into column. Only the archers remained to form a screen, with a few companies of bills as a stiffener. As we mustered, I naturally deferred to the bishop but he would have none of it. "You lead 'em," he invited. "Looks like you've earned it. I'm supposed to be saving souls anyway." Behind us the Lancashire men trooped on, their own sacred talisman, St Audrey's banner, raised high. Hume's men watched us go. They didn't even look that interested.

"Stand by heaven's gate," Tom Bell boomed. "More trade on its way."

Howard's marines were less prissily colourful. Their pretty slashed hose, green and white livery now bore a more distressed finish, slashed all ways, laced with blood and tissue. They didn't look unhappy though. I could see why. All of the ground down the slope to the bog was stacked higher than a lumber yard with Scottish dead, easily in their hundreds, probably thousands.

I'd never seen so many enemies deceased in one place and most pleasing it was. The pile was a mountain of suffering. It writhed and groaned in myriad choruses of private agonies. It bled and it cursed, it wept, begged, fouled itself continually. Men called out for their wives and mothers but none that cared would ever hear. Though some, even many, still breathed, these were all dead men.

One of the liveried sailors threw some casual banter in my direction, but his south country accent was so strong I'd no idea what he said – seemed friendly enough though. Thomas Howard, as businesslike as his affinity, was marshalling the lines, his officers straining and bellowing, dragging their fellows from easy plunder.

"There's still work to be done, my brave boys," he was shouting. "One last effort and this field is yours." The effort involved would be considerable. A few hundred paces further east and the fight still boiled. King James of Scotland had led his own division, by far their strongest, army within an army, against the earl's banners. The old man had given ground and the Scotch King, like the fool he was, thought he was winning.

Our archers were already letting fly. The compact mass of spears was particularly inviting, swelled by their rearguard which had marched up to add more weight to the scrum.

"I'd wager they outnumber Old Surrey by at least two to one." For a man of the cloth Thomas Bell had a fair eye for tactics. "Time we evened the odds."

So we did. Howard had the division march on, bows and bills. Our Stanley men had recovered from their fright and flight. They'd not run a second time. Our combined brigades now fell upon the left flank of the Scots. Bowmen were standing back to thump flight after flight over our heads. It would be impossible to miss. Still they were so many; a great snarling beast that scorned our arrows, regardless, it seemed, of how many hit their mark. This battle would be decided the hard way.

It was furnace hot in the valley. Great clouds of steam rose like a shimmering haze from armoured men, sweating rivers in harness and jack. As ever, there were women on the field. Both sides needed water, life-blood of battle. Convention was you didn't target the water carriers. The women's second role was to get wounded men off the field to the surgeon's lines. You left them to get on with that as well. Your turn might well be next. As for the physicians, theirs and ours, they'd be very busy indeed.

We crashed into the Scots like a tidal wave that beats relentless against the solid cliff. We hacked and clawed at their flanks. Howling and raging, we pulled them down. Their long pikes were useless, more a hindrance as they tripped and cramped their owners. It was sword against bill. If the English bill was not already a famous instrument of destruction, that day alone would have been sufficient to make it so.

The more there were, the harder we fought till the curses died in our parched throats, deaf from the cyclone of sound. We killed to the left and we killed to the right. We killed to the front; we trampled and gutted those left in the rear. We were creatures from hell, no longer human. Pain and exhaustion shed away. We exulted in the killing, straining for fresh slaughter, deluged in blood.

Trying to describe the course of a battle, trying to measure time, is like counting sand. You just can't do it. By now, the afternoon was about gone, long past Nones. It was edging towards Evensong, though in our lurid corner of hell the minutes meant very little. The fighting eddied and swayed. We scrabbled and bit like wolves, then parted, gathering ourselves.

Someone gave me water. It felt as though it turned straight to steam. I was immersed in my own sweat, jack straining as the blood ran so hot. The enemy had split into knots and eddies of men, mostly gathered around a knight or captain. We circled each company like wolves, ready to pounce, choosing our moment.

Our bills were bent and blunted; most had points snapped off. Body parts were everywhere, an anatomist's carpet. Then one of the Scots, clearly a gentleman from his bearing and gilded harness, stepped forward, his sword held at high guard, point about level with my eyes. He was helmet-less, had taken a few knocks, but otherwise serviceable. "The Bastard," he spat at me. "Are you the best they've got?"

I thought this a bit uncivil. "Probably not," I demurred, "but I will certainly see to you." From guard he swung a low cut, aiming to hamstring me. I side-stepped to the right and parried, low then driving upwards. He reciprocated with a low cut, which he made with the blade downwards. Next he cut at the back of my head, seen off with a sloping parry. Everyone around had taken a breather whilst we banged it out. Sweat cascaded from us.

We cut and swiped, circled and blocked, the blades ringing. He launched a glide, arms extended in textbook fashion. Pointless to resist, I let my own sword drift to the right. I had to be fully ready for his next move. He heaved straight in to empty my belly, springing forward on the right leg. This made me step back smartly, swinging around in a full circle to parry, then cut. We both missed our mark. He'd blocked using both hands on the weapon, then, reversing the point, attempted to rearrange my features with his pommel.

Some smart moves from me were needed before the crowd got bored. I used my right leg as a backwards pivot, blocking his pommel with my palm, grabbing the hilt and immobilizing him. His wild, dark eyes were full of hate whilst my point sheared up through his genitals deep into his gut, splitting a dark flood of blood and bile. England was still in the lead.

With a collective roar, more feral than human, my chaps skimmed forward, tearing into the enemy, hacking them down, shearing limbs, adding fresh meat to the pile.

All of a sudden, I found I wasn't feeling too bright. That last bout had pretty much finished me. As I paused and looked, I realized I was in worse repair than I'd thought. Some loon had managed to prick through my jack and I'd barely noticed. I say prick but I was bleeding quite heavily and the sweat running into my eyes was liberally mixed with blood – my own, too, which was mildly alarming. I thought about getting my helmet off but it hurt too much.

Another big Jock was coming at me. I really just wanted him to go away. He screamed and lunged but the blow went nowhere. He was batted aside in a mess of bone and brain as the good reverend swung his mace to very considerable effect.

"Truly, the Lord is a man of war. That's Exodus 15:3, I seem to remember. Now someone get this silly sod out of here before he gets himself killed and I've wasted all these years looking out for him."

Sir Thomas Howard fights his battle

In black dark of night, fitful candles shed narrow pools of light over Barmoor's ancient hall. The place looked better in the dark. My father was hunched on one of the battered trestles. I had never seen him look so utterly exhausted, shrunken, and grey. I am only half his age and had never felt so drained.

"Tomorrow," he said, stirring, voice sluggish, "hundreds of fathers will be mourning their sons. That's pain I understand only too well and I'd not wish such anguish upon any man, not even a Scotchman, and I've come too close to losing another."

"Well," I replied, embarrassed at the old man's emotion, him not normally being the demonstrative type, "Edmund will do very well. He's sleeping like a babe in the vault below us, alongside his deliverer."

That had been the worst moment, when I'd seen Stanley's men run. "Hume's wing was probably their best, all told," I continued. "Those poxy Swiss would have been proud."

The old man managed a smile. "Well, you had Dacre, the perfect antidote. I assume they'd already squared things between them?"

"Dacre's too canny to admit anything; just says he's a naturally brilliant officer. Frankly I've no intention of disagreeing. He did the business for us. When I saw their central block come stomping down at us, I thought we were surely finished. Their order was perfect. Not a peep came from their ranks; our arrows didn't even seem to slow them down."

"Thank God for Master Heron's local insight. It was the bog that did for them."

"It did that." I remembered that gut-wrenching moment when they spilled down from the ridge. They looked unstoppable. The arrow storm thinned them but didn't dent their momentum. Once they began to flounder, I sensed we had them. My lads marched down our shallow hill in perfect order, the pallid afternoon sun gilding harness and bill.

"You led them, of course – always helps."

"It didn't help King James," I observed drily. "He threw the battle away the moment he seized a pike."

"Being a general ain't like being an ordinary captain. You're not on the field to enjoy yourself. Couldn't trust his fellows, I imagine; the Scots never can. He probably thought he should set an example or some such. Besides, that's how the Swiss do it."

We went down and met them, the lines colliding, their long pikes disordered, mainly useless. I'd taken my place in the front rank but was careful to have a squad of chosen men around as close-quarter protection, so practised they moved as smoothly as a well-oiled fleece. We struck them like reapers, and like cornstalks they fell.

Only their officers gave us check and then not for long. I saw one well-built fellow, possibly a divisional commander, surrounded by his own affinity trying to regain momentum, get them going. We couldn't have that, so I sent in a full company, trained for just this type of operation. They made short work of the Scots, though their officer put up quite a fight, bills clanging from his harness till they finally brought him down.

"I'd the impression they didn't stand for long. Might be wrong, of course; you can never really tell, but I thought it was short – you got them on the run."

"Their backs were soon turned. Most that could ran off, abandoning their gentry and most of their kit. Our boys weren't in a merciful mood, gave 'em no quarter. Some begged, emptied their purses – little good it did them."

You will think me callous but we had no leisure for ransoms. Most of them had no estate and our task was winning. They seemed to vastly outnumber us, though it might not have been as unequal as it looked. The plain fact was our fighters got into a killing rage and there was no holding them. We'd already marched thirteen miles that day, we were near starving, and these vermin had sat there safe and warm on our ground, sucking their thumbs at us.

"When I saw the lion banner flanked by the saints, I knew I was facing James himself," the old man went on. "Well, no matter, though I knew it would put heart into them. There were a lot of them, two to our one at least. As they came on, it seemed nothing could stop them. Our guns hurt them; our bows hurt them. The bog slowed them but on they came – pretty damn disconcerting at my age."

"Giving ground was smart: draw them on and soak up their momentum."

"Didn't have much choice. We went back, well, must have been a full two hundred paces. I'd put my household men in the front line, like you did with your marines, half a thousand, and they did well, damn well – at some cost I might add. Darcy was on the left and certainly earned his spurs."

"We guessed you were under pressure – fairly easy deduction given how many of the sods there were."

"Pressure – more like on the bleeding rack; still, they'd made the cardinal error of packing *all* their best men into the front ranks. We were fresh and, fast as they came on, we just kept killing them. They were packed tight as sardines, flanks in the air."

"What exactly had gone wrong with Stanley?" I should explain that the right of our line should have been formed by Stanley's brigade but they'd not appeared as the fight began.

"The idiot locals managed to get the whole lot of 'em lost. Caused me a right headache, I can tell you. If their highlanders had come down on us as well, we'd have been in serious trouble. As it was, once Stanley had finally got his companies over the Pallinsburn, he decided not to wait for them to attack but try to turn their flank."

"Risky," I said.

"Right enough, but as they didn't move he was able to get around them into dead ground; hell of a steep climb but gave his fellows the chance to prepare a nasty surprise. Seems they never saw it coming – first they knew, our arrows were pinning them to the turf. That shook 'em; then the rest laid on with bills and that did the job. They ran like rabbits."

"That was pretty much the end for James, then," I continued. "His own reserves were piled in with nowhere to manoeuvre. Your fellows' bills were thinning them out in front, my lads on one side then Stanley on the other. Did you see him – the King, I mean?"

"Not sure I did. His banners were still flying almost to the end. By this point they were streaming away from the back, highlanders, lowlanders, everybody. King James was clear out of options. Darcy said his household launched one last charge: do or, in their case, die. I had the honour of being their prime target. I still didn't see him, mind you, but his standard seemed awfully close as it went down. Darcy has it, I believe."

"So," I asked, "is the King dead?"

"Most likely, though I can't prove it – not yet anyway. The man who would strut the world stage lies hacked and probably unrecognizable somewhere in the mess. Well, you've seen the field. I've never seen the like, not even Redemore Plain; Bosworth they're calling it now, a proper slaughterhouse. God knows how many they lost. More to the point, what about us?"

"Altogether, I'm not sure." As the sun dipped down over the western rim, cloaking the carnage, I'd had the heralds out to do a preliminary body count – time they earned their fees.

"On Edmund's wing we lost Bryan Tunstall, Christopher Savage, and one of my skippers, Maurice Berkeley." Poor old Maurice, one of my old faithful, he deserved better. "From your division, two knights, Harbottle and Gower; we think Lisle and Henry Grey are taken. Of the commoners, I'm saying four hundred or so, more very likely; double that wounded at least."

"What about theirs? Far as I know we only took a couple of gentlemen prisoners; the rest all went the same way. Understandable – our men were raging – expensive though. I'd like to have offered the King a few ransoms."

"As far as I can see, just about every magnate in Scotland is killed, the King almost for certain, half the clergy, a vast cull of the gentry. They won't need to start murdering each other for years to come. As for the rest, I'll take a guess; they've lost twelve thousand, maybe more."

"Ha, well, stick to those figures when you write to the Queen. Let little, fat swine Wolsey top that if he can. So far King Henry's taken two towns nobody's ever heard of and gone through half his inheritance, and we all know what a successful miser his father was. A sensible ruler by any standards. Clever and careful, I'll grant you, but I could never like the fellow."

The old man was brightening. The scale of our success was only beginning to penetrate. Now the gibbering poets will tell you victory rings bright with exultation. That's all wind and water; it's nothing of the sort. As the red mist ebbs away, all you're left with is exhaustion, a total numbness. You feel nothing. You know you're alive, of course, which is always a bonus but, that aside, there's nothing to brag of. You really don't care.

Now, in the gathering cloak of that late summer night, I began to perceive that we'd done all right. We had marched out to engage the Scots – no easy matter – and we'd accomplished that. We wanted to fight. We had and we'd won. No mere skirmish, we seemed to have annihilated their army, killed their King and everyone else who mattered.

"You'll be Duke of Norfolk yet," I suggested.

"Well, that was always my ambition, ever since we threw the title away for Crookback Dickon. Not that he was crooked, mind you; our Tudor masters just prefer it that way. Still, I'll grovel with the best of them, but I'll be smiling inwardly when I lick His precious Majesty's ring and I'll want to see the look on Wolsey's face. I've waited thirty very long years for this. I've simpered, crawled, kissed every proffered buttock in court and, by God, this old dog will have his day!"

I poured some more wine. It wasn't much, all that was left. Exhausted beyond words we'd marched back to camp; near midnight when we stumbled in to find our local hosts had stripped the place clean. We'd had little to start with – now we had nothing.

As we sipped our indifferent wine in the near dark, thick walls shutting out the sounds of the host outside, George Darcy appeared to make his report.

"Sir George, you are," my father beamed at the saturnine Yorkshireman. "We'll do all the formal stuff tomorrow, of course; be quite a gathering. I'm even going to knight Heron if he's recovered enough to stand."

"The Bastard fought a good fight," George confirmed. "I'd say he's earned that honour and more." He was pretty much knackered, as we all were. He stank as we all did, of blood and sweat and fear and death, the soldier's relish.

"How are things on the field?" I prodded him.

"Well, sir, you chose well leaving Sir Philip with your chaps. Scrope, Latimer, and Sir Marmaduke are there with their affinities; should be plenty."

"God," the earl interjected, "Old Constable's as ancient as me. There's life in us old hounds yet," he chuckled.

"A very valiant gentleman," Darcy tactfully replied, "none braver that I saw."

"Look here, lad," the old man leaned over. "You all did well today. You did flaming well, as well as ever Englishmen did. I won't pretend I'm not going to take my share of the plaudits. I'll lap them up and insist on more but I will also make damn sure that no gentleman who did his share today shall be overlooked where honours are concerned."

Darcy nodded his gratitude. "Our gunners hold their previous ground and we've a strong guard on the Scottish cannon. Their whole train is ours; seems their blokes just legged it and left everything."

"Now there's a prize," my father announced. "I rather hoped we'd nab their guns. We may not have ransoms for His Majesty but those cannon will be worth a shilling or two."

"I set men on collecting armour and weapons," Darcy continued.

"Good lad. You've the makings of a Howard; I'll see if I've any spare daughters. I intend to pay off the rank and file – most of 'em, that is, tomorrow. That's the thanks they'll have from a grateful sovereign but I daresay their packs will be heavier than when they came."

"We took their camp, of course," George went on. "The place was stuffed with loot. I've recovered a fair amount but, as you say, the men helped themselves. The place was a treasure trove, full of food and drink. Some thought the stuff might have been poisoned but I'm still here and…" he produced another bottle with a flourish, "by courtesy of the late King of Scots."

This vintage proved altogether superior to the dross we were drinking and we toasted His noble Majesty and all his enterprises in France. Might he do as well as we'd done.

"There's something else," George went on. "As we came up the ridge, towards their camp, we could see – well, just see I mean, as it was very near dark – their baggage train, what was left of it."

I raised an eyebrow.

"As I said, it was near dark but they'd been cut up pretty badly. None living, I don't think, and hundreds dead I'd guess, mainly women too. It looked pretty bad."

The earl and I digested this news. "This sort of thing's bound to happen from time to time, regrettable of course, reprehensible even. Were our troops responsible, do you think?"

"Impossible to say. I mean it might have been ours but could just as easily have been theirs, both or neither. I'd probably plump for the local reiving community."

"That fits," I said. "They turned this place over pretty thoroughly; it's all just business as usual as far as they're concerned."

"Exactly so," my father confirmed. "It's not as if any of these people *matter*. They're not going to be missed. We don't condone atrocities, of course, and we'll ensure the victims have a decent burial – decent and swift. No need for too many enquiries and, Thomas, I'd probably suggest you omit this from your official report. As for you, George, I'd just forget all about it."

"Forget all about what, Your Grace?"

"That's the spirit, lad."

Isabella Hoppringle fights her battle

We'd set the surgeons' lines up in a ruined farmhouse – can't remember the name. The place had been stripped to the bone, precarious spires of ruined stone, open to a clearing sky. A wind, not cold, brushed the drying green grass, lifting and flattening. If we'd not had thirty thousand armed men lined up in front of us, you'd have said it was a half-decent late summer's afternoon.

Behind, the baggage train waited, almost in some semblance of order: a great crowded convoy of wagons, carts, and pack animals, stacked high enough to bust with gear and loot; a host of women and bairns, drovers, sutlers, tradesmen, cobblers, and all. The army that follows an army; there were cattle and sheep, goats and geese, tools for every trade, from worn old wool and wooden utensils to silver and silks.

Dr Beaton puffed out his cheeks. "As hospitals go, this is perhaps not the best I've practised in."

"At least it's not raining," I cheered. My standards had become considerably more flexible in recent days.

"They'll easily sweep the English aside," Ellen breezed confidently.

"Thank you, general," I responded tartly. The girl was still young and daft enough to be taken in by the banners and drums. The steady tattoo of drumbeat, tum, tum, para-diddle, tum, was reassuring. The sound suggested there was order and logic and not just plain madness. It would be, it was, so easy to be seduced by this pomp of chivalry; but the sharp and gleaming array of surgeon's tools laid out – knives, probes, pliers, and oh so purposeful bone saws, my jars and phials of physick – suggested a rather different reality.

Paraded before us, the King's great legions did look impressive, their tall, ungainly pikes standing as high as bristling oaks, each grand division drawn up in well-formed bodies. Our Scottish guns were ahead and to our right, overlooking the valley below where we knew, but could not see, the English were deploying. I had the entire soldier's jargon by now even if my heart was still leaden with dread.

Our guns fired. It must have been around Nones. An apocryphal crack split the air and shook the trestles, buffeting our ears, and a great, rolling cloud of acrid, grey-black filth enveloped us like the devil's fog. We were half blind as this fearful cacophony continued, building to an intensity that must surely drive out all reason. We crammed wax and scraps into our ears to save them.

Noise and smoked billowed, crashed, and eddied. I couldn't be sure but I had an impression the fire from our cannon was slackening off. The first wounded began to appear. These were gunners, shorn of limb, bright white bone stark in mangled flesh, legs and arms taken clear off or mashed into bloody pulp. For the former, all we could do was to administer some basic pain relief and cauterize the wounds. We'd several braziers set up for this purpose.

"The use of the irons," Beaton explained as he expertly applied red-hot metal to a raw, jetting stump, "serves to close up tissue and veins; fights putrefaction as well." The screaming wounded were held down by orderlies while physicians applied irons. The pervading stink of sulphur was matched by the odour of roasting flesh.

I'd sequestered a fleet of lighter carts to take the movable cases back to Coldstream. Quite where we'd put them I'd no idea. These vehicles were soon filling up. Those who could walk or hobble, once we'd patched them up, clung to the tailgates of the wagons, a pilgrimage of the hurt and maimed. Beaton and his assistants carved and sliced, flensing away shattered limbs. We had only one treatment for such wounds to extremities.

It seemed not long, minutes perhaps, before the fire from our guns diminished and spluttered away. Theirs didn't, so it wasn't hard to work out who was winning. As we cut and cauterized, a sudden tide of refugees surged past. These were the rest of our gun crews. All had the wild-eyed stare of spittle-flecked terror. They slammed through us as though in flood, upsetting trestles, trampling their wounded comrades.

Now the whole of our vast line shivered, swaying like high trees in an autumn gale. I assumed, as the guns were still banging furiously, that the English were now firing on our boys. If proof were needed, several round-shot, sailing over the packed ranks, thumped around us. "That's novel," the good doctor noted, his cheery, untroubled face contrasting with his gore-splattered apron and arms reddened to the elbow.

Then the warden's men were gone; they marched down over the lip in front and disappeared into the valley. We could not see them. Like the flood, their next, right-hand division set off, then we saw the King's great, enormous phalanx move in turn. It was quite a sight. Now all we could see were the highlanders, way off to the east. I assumed they were just there to guard the flanks, or maybe nobody had told them what to do. Between us and them were the reserves; can't say how many this lot were. Bothwell, I think, commanded, arrogant little scroat; I didn't like him, the sort whose gaze never got above your neckline, about as subtle as a swineherd.

"Arrow-spoon if you please." Beaton dragged me back to the business of repairing broken flesh. Men were stumbling or being led back over the ridge. Once they began descending, they were in range of the English bows – the great and feared war bow which had, over the years, "killed more Scots than drink or the plague", the surgeon observed. "God only knows why we never manage to learn."

He'd told me it was an Arab physician who'd devised the arrow-spoon. The English use a range of arrow heads, long wickedly sharp bodkins, to punch through harness and just as nasty barbs against unarmoured men.

"The heads are often fixed to the shafts with beeswax," I confided to Ellen. "The wax holds the head just fine when it dries, but once shot into the body, is hard to draw. Often the head detaches and is left inside the wound – nasty.

"We use this," I indicated the spoon, "which we insert into the wound." I had a thrashing patient to demonstrate on. The shaft had entered between the third and fourth ribs, finding a weak spot in the padded jack. We'd stripped the coat, the soiled linen shirt, to expose a raw, ugly wound, gaping lips pulsing blood over pallid flesh. I'd given him henbane but two burly orderlies were still needed. "The device fixes around the head of the barb," I grunted, "just so. Then we can draw out the point," which I did manage, though it required a fair amount of probing and yanking. "Next, we, or in this case you, can dress the wound."

If we didn't lack for custom, as the battle was now banging on in the valley, we had a period of almost detachment. I'd sent for some of those with the train to help transport wounded. They came with bad grace and Hume's men had to use the butts of their lances to win cooperation.

I'd not really noticed – it didn't seem to matter – but our escort had shrunk. We were down from a troop to a mere handful, mostly older men or those less imbued with enthusiasm for doing and dying.

The train, this squalid crammed township on wheels, bunched only yards away, inert but still teeming, had almost a festive mood it seemed, a day at the races. No orders for movement had come so they did not move. I did not take it on myself to give any orders to shift the whole circus over to Coldstream. I assumed our commanders knew what they were about, complacent fool that I was.

This interlude didn't last. Quite suddenly, it seemed, a fresh swathe of running men hurtled through and past us. These were not borderers, not our folk or the warden's, but lowlanders, from Fife and Angus. They ran without looking at us. Some were hurt but most were whole, the infection of fear their only contagion. There seemed like an awful lot of them.

"That's the way of it," Beaton said to me. "I've seen men fight like lions, brave every hurt, then, all of a sudden, the rot sets in and they run faster than sheep. It's like their manhood, their courage, is a well, and all at once the bucket comes up empty." These men did not regard us but I could see there was scuffling for horses with the baggage, some pilfering.

Our few unwilling provosts studiously stayed blank, looking the other way. One fellow seized an armful of my physick, as though the stuff was liquor. I swatted him away, some bottles were broken. Our guards did nothing. My tongue lashing did not move them. They merely shrugged. Fear which labour had kept at bay came back to plague me. For the most part the train stayed where it was. The festive mood vanished.

We continued, bandaging and cauterizing, choosing those who might live and those who surely would not. A steady trickle had come in from the warden's battle. We understood this had gone well, with the English there seen off. Dacre was mentioned and I heard the Bastard named. I offered a silent prayer for my country's enemy.

"I know who you're thinking of," Ellen divined. She was as clotted with our patients' leavings as the rest of us but her green eyes still danced.

"Be still, girl," I mock chided, "or it will be a thrashing for you."

Now men were coming in from the centre, the King's division. Nobody was quite sure who was winning here. The left-hand mob, between James and Hume, had bolted apparently; all their officers were down. The King was hard pressed. We saw Bothwell's reserve move off, marching into the cauldron below. Whilst I'm no tactician, I deduced matters were deadlocked. Wafts of heat drifted up from the valley, brought by the shifting wind. It was just like lifting the lid of a hot pan. Battle brews up a furnace of heat.

Wounded men came in thick and fast – still plenty of arrow wounds but more with cuts from English bills: great tearing slashes or deep punctures. Most of those struck in the belly or chest cavity had little hope. I'd made up a pain-killing compound: lettuce juice, briony, hemlock, and henbane, bound with vinegar in a wine solution. We'd brought several flagons. Demand was high.

Afternoon blended into evening. The sun, which had fitfully brightened after a wet start, began to sink. I'd no idea how many wounded we had. Nobody was counting but it would have been several hundred. I'd drafted in yet more muttering conscripts from the train as unwilling orderlies, bullying them into compliance. Beaton and his surgeons worked on tirelessly, seemingly immune to fatigue.

As quickly as we replaced the blood-slicked baskets, they filled up with hacked-off limbs, an anatomist's work in progress. The pile at the back of the ruined steading grew bigger and smelled worse: sweet sickly stench of blood, spilt intestines, voided bladders and bowels. We hardly noticed, so long it seemed this had been our signature dish.

Towards Evensong there was sudden commotion away to the east. The highlanders, who'd stayed put all afternoon, were under attack themselves. So far, as best I could say, they'd played no part in the battle. No matter, it came to them: a deluge of English arrows, then the kerfuffle of contact. It didn't last long and they were sprinting too. I guessed they'd been taken by surprise and the shock had unmanned them.

"This could get very bad," Beaton observed, pausing in his labours. He wasn't wrong. This rout begat another as it seemed the whole of our centre was giving way. Some must have fled along the valley; others spilled back up the hill. They bolted this way and that, dumping harness and gear as a snake sheds its skin. There were thousands, must've been half the army. King James could never staunch so great a haemorrhage. The battle was lost. That was plain.

"Time to get moving," the doctor concluded. I wasn't about to disagree but the prospect brought hot bile rising up within me. I grabbed one of Hume's loons and tried to shake some sense into him. "Get up to the train," I insisted. "Take others; strip as many carts as you must to get the wounded away."

"They won't like that," he gaped.

"I'm not asking them to; that's the easy part. Take what we need and don't bother with please or thank you."

I got them moving; took hold of another. "You, ride down to the warden. Tell him I need some horsemen and foot loons up here and sharpish."

"What about all these?" Ellen gestured at the many rows of no-hopers.

"Leave them," I yelled urgently and saw her stricken look. "They wouldn't thank you for trying; moving them would finish them sure as a blade. Whatever happens to them is a kindness." I didn't utter such callous instructions lightly, but in cold, hard terms I was right. No point trying to save those already knocking at St Peter's Gate. They lay in their largely silent rows, pain at least at bay. More than a few had quietly gone; the rest, for the most part, lay quiet and uncomplaining, beyond hurt or aid.

We should have prepared for this from the outset. Nobody had foreseen defeat. Are all those vanquished taken so by surprise? There was no possibility I could make this work before the tide engulfed us. The men who came running knew neither friend nor foe. They paused only long enough to pillage. They pulled from the wagons whatever they could carry; beat any in the way aside. Mostly they'd dropped their swords.

But they had their knives. I watched as one, absorbed it seemed in his own salvation, paused, fleeing through our lines as though he'd recognized one of the wounded, drew his dagger, knelt, and stabbed the injured man in a fury of blows. "Ma brither-in-law," he confirmed conversationally to me, "cheatin' lyin' loser. Here's some guid from the day." Job done, he resumed flight.

All semblance of order had gone; leaderless men milled and squabbled over the wagons. The wounded went untended; half the orderlies and many of the women joined in the panic. A few of the wagons had moved off; the rest milled and swarmed and went nowhere.

Then they came at us. Where from I couldn't say; who they were I could not have said. Suddenly they were among us, raggedy men on raggedy garrons, women too but all armed. Were they English from the army? I don't know. Were they more Scots? I don't know that either. They might have been a nasty pairing of both or, most likely, the local riding names, Tynedale, Liddesdale, Redesdale too. They must have been there all along, just waiting for their chance. Now it had come and we were helpless.

The attackers struck like a hurricane, their lances lunged and jabbed, lunged again. The hopeless, useless tide of defeated men simply gave way, resuming flight, deluging away to the west. The train was a reiver's dream, packed high with loot and not a fighting man in sight. Those who stayed, or resisted, or could not run fast enough, were killed. Our women were part of the prize, to be stripped, used and disposed of. Children were valueless.

I ran into the storm – pretty stupid, but I did anyway. These people understood larceny. The train was being picked clean. Choice was so varied only the better gear was being lifted. A dismounted man was chasing one of our women; she ran like a crazed deer, panting in circles. He was a big, burly fellow – I could smell him – rank, tattered, but his dirk was gleaming.

So was mine. I'd grabbed one of the knives from surgery and just barged straight into him. He didn't see me coming, so intent was he on his sport. I was inside his guard before he realized, driving the very sharp point up into heart and lungs. He gave a long, surprised snort, foam of blood over my arm, and spewed more. I shoved him clear away. The girl ran on unknowing till a bolt thudded between her shoulders and she flailed on the red-smeared grass.

There were more. There always is. My next encounter was a woman – young, feral, knife-blade thin, quick as a ferret. She was yelling at me; couldn't understand a word but I guessed not complimentary. I suspect it was her partner I'd just gutted. I'd also carelessly left the blade in his innards. This fury had a long-bladed rondel dagger of her own and seemed very displeased with my features. She too received a surprise, though. A heavy, cast-iron griddle struck her neatly on the temple and she went down without a murmur.

"You're a gey bonnie fechter for a wee lassie; yi done reet weil in the stushie."

I think that's what she said. I recognized the braw highland harridan I'd felled earlier. She had a substantial black eye coming along but clearly bore no ill will. I still wasn't done. I'd no real idea what I was trying to do. Another of them, mounted this time, jerked his pony in front of me, his weasel eyes glittering with pure malice. This was rare fun. I swerved but he grabbed at my hair, dragged me along, then threw me down, winded.

My strength seemed to have gone as I scrabbled on hands and knees. He dismounted casually. He had all the time in the world. Ellen appeared out of nowhere, threw herself like a wildcat. "Get out of here, you stupid child," I tried to yell. I could live with getting me killed but not her too. He seemed to shrug her off, flinging her over the turf. He turned back to me, keeping the youngest till last, I supposed.

The pause had, however, enabled me to spot the ballistic possibilities of an abandoned half pike lying barely a foot from my right hand. The idiot had not. I hunched, gathered myself, and as he came forward, still grinning, launched up, taking the weapon in both hands. He wore back and breast so I drove upwards, the point shearing through his belly and bowels, spitting out through his great fat backside.

Ellen was sitting up on the grass. She looked dazed but otherwise unhurt. "Help me up," she said. "I'm a bit woozy." I knelt by her, gathered her close. "Just winded, I think," she continued, then coughed up her young life's blood and died in my arms.

Sir Thomas Howard writes to Queen Katherine

Barmoor, late evening, 9th September

God bless Your Gracious Majesty and be it known throughout your realm that your army has this day done its duty and right well. It is night and our camp here is miserable. Those dogs of borderers, our own, have stripped us bare of what little we had so we have neither shelter nor rations. Our horses, palfreys, baggage, and all are stolen from us. Truly, they do us greater damage than our enemies.

Let that be. Today, after a fatiguing march through wild and wet ways, we did come upon your enemy the King of Scotland with his entire great host and gave them battle. In short the day is ours and they are beaten from the field. Right hard was the fight and it did seem at the outset that their left would prevail against our right, for some of the Cheshire men fought not well but ran from the line.

Though he be my brother I do commend Edmund Howard to Your Majesty, for he did his duty most nobly against grievous odds and was saved from capture or worse by my Lord Dacre who remains Your Majesty's ever-valiant knight. Right hard against us in the centre did they press,

*their long spears contending against our bills, but
our brave fellows had the measure of these Scots
and laid so many breathless upon the ground,
the rest soon turned their backs and fled. By the
going down of the sun, the field was ours and not
one Scotsman remained alive upon it. Through all
this, our loss, grievous where it fell, was yet light.
Theirs is most heavy.*

*It is certain that the King of Scots and all his
cursed lords are killed, though the heralds have
not yet made their tally. Our army has been
maintained at a heavy cost to Your Majesty's
treasury but I know that the earl, my father,
intends, upon the morrow, to discharge the
bulk of the foot, which shall allay some of Your
Majesty's costs, and besides, all of the Scots'
great guns, with much powder and shot, are
taken, together with, as we now tally, some three
hundred and fifty sets of finest harness, the value
of which, even by auction, will considerably offset
Your Majesty's overall outlay.*

*His Grace will, as ever, have good cause to
celebrate that he did leave his realm in Your
Majesty's care, for we have brought great honour
to England's name. Privily I do confess me to Your
Majesty that should His Grace yet win great glory
in France, his triumph will scarce outshine your
own. It is a famous victory.*

Your ever loyal and loving subject, etc...

Chapter Ten: The Day After

To tell you plaine, twelve thousand were slaine,
That to the fight did stand;
And many prisoners tooke that day,
The best in all Scotland.
That day made many a fatherlesse childe,
And many a widow poore;
And many a Scottish gay Lady,
Sate weeping in her bowre.

Traditional verse

Lord Hume writes in haste to Queen Margaret

Morning, 10th September

Your Majesty,

The tidings I now impart are the most grievous
it has ever been my lot to set down; so dolorous
my pen near refuses to write, for never did pen
and ink perform so dread a chore. I will be blunt.
This news deserves no other course. Yesterday, as
I had feared, we were obliged to give battle. His
Majesty would have no other course and led his
own division in person, deaf to all entreaties. He
is killed and all of your lords and nobles around
him. Only I and the Earl of Huntly, who is with me,
now yet live.

*Amongst our dead are the Archbishop of
St Andrews, the Bishop of the Isles, abbots of
Inchaffray and Kilwinning; the Earls of Argyll,
Caithness, Crawford, Lennox, Montrose, Bothwell,
Cassillis, Errol, and Rothes; Lords Avondale,
Elphinstone, Hay of Yester, Keith, Maxwell (and
his four brothers), Ross, Seton, Darnley, Crichton,
Erskine, Herries, Lorne, Oliphant, Sempill, and
Sinclair; of gentlemen, so many I do not yet
have a full tally but our loss is terrible and far
surpasses any we have suffered before. Our
nation is now leaderless and rudderless.*

*Today, I shall at least attempt to recover our
great guns which stand abandoned on the field.
Thomas Borthwick and his men lie dead around
them. Once I have, as I hope, secured our train I
will return to you. Summon then, I pray you, the
council and acquaint them with these tidings.
Proclaim your son as King and yourself as Regent.
Our grief which will surely flow like the waters
of Babylon must yet wait awhile till the realm is
secured, for now we lie at your brother's mercy.*

*Further, I do beg you to write secretly to King
Henry and remind him of his duty to you as his
sister whom he has now widowed and entreat
that he should, as a chivalrous knight, forbear
from spoiling your realm yet further. I shall
return to Edinburgh as soon as I am able and
then shall I be at your side in this most desperate
hour. You may, as ever, count upon my absolute
fidelity...*

Alexander, Lord Hume

Hume then takes stock

Who loves a loser?

That was rhetorical. We all know the answer. To survive a catastrophic defeat when all others have fallen is even trickier than just losing. How can I explain why it was I lived, when most of my peers pulled off a collective coup by dying pointlessly, a stupid battle in an unnecessary war?

"You saved the whole division," Huntly concluded. "Scotland will need someone to hold the line, though I doubt we'll be getting any thanks."

"We've had plenty of disasters – a whole litany of failures – but this tops the lot. James wanted his battle and pulled us all into the fire with him."

This was at Coldstream. I'd led our fellows back to the crossing. We'd recovered the abbess and most of the medical train, though losses amongst the lower sort had been high – not that anybody would notice; a few dead camp followers amongst this day's butcher's list weren't going to matter.

Night was falling as we retreated. Isabella, God help her, was in shock, though Beaton managed to bring her round and they'd spent all night with the wounded, the handful we'd saved. As light faded, it had dipped into a glorious sunset, sinking over the impassive hills, as though God mocked us too.

Her house, that half-way haven between the two kingdoms, looked like hell's antechamber. Many of the attendants had run off as soon as news began to filter through. Her quiet courts and neat garden were stripped and despoiled. Squalid acres of torn canvas gave mean shelter to the hundreds of sick and wounded – bleeding, spewing, defecating where they lay, the stink of death as thick as fog.

Beaton and his crew worked by lamplight. Isabella looked like an apparition – mechanical, unseeing, her tranquil face a death mask, etched in grief. One of the novices had died, I think, the pretty red-headed girl; more waste. But she was one among thousands; King James had managed to blight a generation with his ambition – the idiotic, vainglorious fool.

We took counsel in the abbess's quarters, Huntly and I. In the circumstances I didn't think she'd mind a further raid on her depleted cellar.

"If you get the borders, I'll take the north. Argyll's heir will likely be offered the west."

"Seems right enough," I confirmed. "The Queen will be regent for as long as she lasts; I don't doubt the silly woman will make a fool of herself before long and then God knows what."

"I can't see Surrey following up though. Can you? King Henry won't sanction any kind of counter-invasion – I mean, what's the point? We're beaten enough as it is."

"Definitely not," I concurred. "That's the last thing he'll want. Old Surrey's victory will stick deep. He was just supposed to act the good shepherd, see us corralled and then off his land. Neither the King nor his man Wolsey wanted a Howard victory, especially while they're fooling about to no purpose and at huge expense over the water."

You'll think me callous, of course, a cynical opportunist, as the chroniclers might say, and you'd be quite right. Equally, in my own defence, nobody could say I hadn't warned them. I'd been against this whole sorry enterprise from the start. The "peace" party had been shouted down. Well, now we were the only ones left standing and we'd have our say. That's the real business of government – to keep things moving, to see that taxes get paid, that folks feel they can sleep safely so they don't mind paying their dues which keep civil servants like me in wages.

"Leave me a few companies of your men here. I'll keep a couple of brigades under arms. We'll march the rest back to Edinburgh, brief Her right royal Majesty, get Douglas and Elphinstone up to speed, make sure we've the right people appointed to council."

"At least there's plenty of vacancies."

Well, that's how politics works. For the rest it was less clear cut. All night stragglers had been slipping over the line, beaten men, vicious in their desperation. The townsfolk avoided them, just stared silently as they filtered through, no fanfares this time round. Huntly and I had no difficulty in keeping our affinities in hand: what was the loss of a few lowlanders to any of them? They'd had a pretty decent little war all told and, for my boys certainly, their homes were perilously close to the line. They knew what might be coming.

"Scotland generally is pretty safe," I pondered, "but not so the marches. If there's a backlash we'll feel it here, and it will come. King Henry will have Dacre beating us up before the autumn's out." Dacre would ensure I was forewarned, of course, but no need to spill that.

"The guns," I went on. "I'm going to attempt bringing them off in the morning, cavalry only. We'll ride to the field at dawn, take all we need and try to get them away."

"Tall order," Huntly grimaced. "They'll be guarded closer than the crown jewels. They're worth rather more and not already in hock. Howard isn't going to let that lot slip. With our train as prizes, his books will more than balance."

I shrugged; all true but I still had to try. The gain was worth the risk. If I could be seen to salvage at least something of our national pride then my own ledger would be in credit. That credit would be sorely needed in the coming months.

With a fine hint of irony, next morning dawned fair, a fine, clear light, smoke from the town curling past the rough timbered palisades. The abbey was unrecognizable, the central core of fine ashlar an island in a sea of ragged shanties, spilling down to the river, transient metropolis of pain and filth.

I took as many riders as I could muster, just under a thousand I recall. Men and garrons had got some rest and consumed what little fodder the abbess had left. I would have to make amends else they'd starve this winter. Isabella herself I'd not spoken to – too much the coward to face her, her silent agony. I, her sworn protector, had failed her. I'd failed to see the train needed cover, had left them exposed to the jackals. We'd lost a fortune in gear. All the best had gone, both what we had and all our loot. (I'd got my own kit well away beforehand, thank God.)

They tell you everything looks better in the light. That's not true of battlefields. It's not true of defeat; darkness is infinitely preferable. "That'll be the Frenchies." One of my heidmen[14] pointed to a slew of mutilated corpses: "Serves, 'em right, sneering, cocky sods." The Sieur D'Aussi, who'd dined at the King of France's table, now decorated a tree just south of Cornhill. I think it was him anyway. That's the other thing about losing: you need someone to blame.

Dregs from our defeat were still stumbling past. Most had already gone but these were the lamed and maimed. Some were helped along by comrades; most just stumbled, glassy-eyed. They paid us no heed. Many had cuts to face and

---

14 A "heidman" is the leader, almost a tribal chief, of a riding name or grayne.

limbs. Some nursed oozing stumps, flaps of scalp hanging loose, with no weapons or gear, without shoes; half had fouled their hose. They came singly, in knots and groups, driftwood on a lost shore. Some begged food; we swatted them away. We still had purpose and they weren't our people.

"Where's the damned English?" someone queried, Wat of Harden it was, I think, Scott heidman, great barrel of a bruiser.

"They heard you were coming and ran home," I yelled back. That raised a laugh. For men like him and me and the rest, this was just normal trade. I'd thrown out flankers and a strong guard behind. I wasn't going to endure any more surprises. Scott rode up alongside, heavy in the saddle but ready as an oiled blade. "Wonder how Johnny Heron's doing today?" he asked. "Be celebrating, I keen."

"He's probably in line for a peerage after yesterday. Howard will be doling out honours quicker than a pardoner."

Scott grunted, "Be a busy winter then?" That's a borderer's epitaph for their king and nobility. Within a month, Scott and plenty more here would be riding with Heron and preying on their own people. It's just how it is.

We came around from the west, hills behind. The English would normally leave a couple of strong companies to guard the spoils, hopefully no more, mix of bows and bills. I'd guessed the guns would still be where our gunners had left them in their rout. They were and we charged home in fine style, the valley floor below carpeted with a dense piling of yesterday's dead, mostly ours. I'd a train of draught animals, light carts, and palfreys to get all the guns and gear shifted. I was right: we were facing a double company and we'd achieved surprise. Trouble is, even if we got through the cordon, we'd need time to limber up cannon, and the hulking great things move exceedingly slowly.

Arrows thumped out and our latches replied. They formed a line; our lances poked at them. They jeered at us, showing us their behinds. After all, what did they have to fear from a few hundred after they'd hammered so many thousands of us yesterday?

"Cavalry," Wat motioned. "Who's the fancy banner?"

"The lord admiral himself," I confirmed. "He really doesn't want to part with our guns."

He didn't. The English horse piled into our flank. Their own guns, still on the damned hillock below, opened up, just to show us they could. They shot wide – too much risk of hitting their own blokes – but they had the range and wanted us to know it. This was never going to work.

"Pull back," I ordered. "We'll do no good here."

My lads are as nimble in exiting a scrap as they are to engage. We retired in good order. Their guns ceased firing. This battle was now definitely over. We skittered back smartly the way we'd come. Very few empty saddles, and at least I could brag I'd tried to remedy part of the late King's folly. Dead men carry a heavy burden and I fully intended to pour a lake of bitter bile over the memory of King James.

Now, and on that subject, there are still some who will mutter King James survived the battle only to be murdered by some of my affinity, out of fear and jealousy. That's all rubbish, of course. He could never have come off that field alive – his pride wouldn't allow it. If he lacked judgment he never lacked courage. If I had done for him, mind you, there'd be no apology.

"Was that a waste of time?" the heidman asked without rancour. "I mean, I'm all for a ride in the morning but we never really had much prospect, did we? Politics, I suppose?"

"We need to show the marches are still strong; we're not just sheep ready to be shorn. Dacre has to be able to report to King Henry that he can't just walk over the line and take possession. I need to make our case in court for a strong hand here, my own obviously."

"Sometimes, I'm grateful I'm just a simple reiver. Life at court makes our goings on out here on the edges look pretty dull, almost safe, by comparison."

No argument there.

There was no pursuit beyond a barrage of insults as we departed. Surrey had no need to attack. He'd win more kudos by paying his companies off and garnering his gains. I envied him the dukedom this would surely bring. I'd be lucky to keep my head.

We went back at a fair trot, past more human detritus on the way. These people had nothing. Folks would bar their doors and curse them. Wat and the other locals would pick off stragglers for sport and whatever they could steal. Who would want to boast he'd been at Flodden? Only the dead found their measure of glory, for what it was worth. We, the living, just bear a survivor's curse, despised by all.

"What a useless shower of no-hopers," Wat accurately confirmed. "Not even worth robbing."

Just before Coldstream, on the level flat past Cornhill, where ground dips gently towards the river, we came across another expedition. This one was very different from ours and as different again from the beaten horde. I recognized Isabella riding at the head; behind her was a whole convoy of carts, freshly scrubbed, and a gaggle of women trudging in their wake.

She was a ghost, a wraith of the powerful young woman I knew and probably loved (even though I'm her uncle – did I say?). Somehow she had steeled herself against all the terrors of the fight, all the horror swamping her once inviolate sanctuary. She was, I reflect now, the bravest of us all.

"Isabella," I greeted her. "Is this wise?"

She spoke firmly but with an edge of tiredness that seemed to reach into the depths of her formidable soul. "Someone has to recover the dead," she replied. "Lord Howard won't trouble us. He sent his safe conduct."

I could have said, "Fat lot of good that would have done you yesterday when you escaped by a miracle," but I could see there was no point arguing. Besides, we needed a full tally of our dead gentry. If I returned with this to the council, it would make me appear all the more diligent. I began to warm to the idea.

"Ca' canny," I said to her and we rode on. We, all armoured, booted, and spurred, rode away from the enemy; she, with her unarmed civilians, marched towards them. None of the women spoke; they simply plodded on.

It was some while later, a year or so, maybe more, I met a fellow begging in the streets of Edinburgh, by the tollbooth. He was ragged, shorn of left leg below the knee, hollow faced, emaciated. For some reason he looked familiar, and, in response to his mute plea, I dug in my purse.

"Did you lose that at Flodden?" I asked.

"Aye, my lord, I served under you. I was whole then. When I got back, my trade was gone: who needs a one-legged messenger? They ask me if I lost my leg in the battle. When I reply yes, thinking they'll be charitable on account, most just spit on me an' says, 'Good, serves you right for running away.'"

Like I said, nobody loves the defeated. Those who were never there urinate copiously on us and call it an epitaph.

Howard takes stock

"Is that him?"

"Aye, looks like, best I can tell."

"Are you sure – absolutely certain, I mean?"

"Well, if you were sitting for an artist's portrait, you wouldn't want to look like this but yes, I'm sure – this is King James IV of Scotland, what's left of him."

Dead kings on the battlefield look pretty much like anyone else – stripped naked and flung aside in the mass anonymity of violent death. This cadaver was red-headed, that much was clear, of average stature and reasonably well built, obviously well nourished. The face was livid and contorted, jaw shot through with a longbow shaft, one hand near hacked off by a bill and a flurry of other gashes – not a quick or an easy death.

"What about you – what do you two think?" I was addressing two of our meagre haul of captives; one at least, Andrew Forman, was a bishop. "You knew the man."

The bishop looked pretty grim. He'd been a biggish wheel in James's diplomacy. Identifying the remains was clearly something of a trial but time was pressing. "I don't have all day, my lord, and we've yet to talk of ransoms."

Forman flinched and Scott, the other captive, blurted, "Aye, that's the King right enough. I hope His precious Majesty roasts in hell," he added gratuitously but with sincere venom. The poor bishop flinched anew.

"There's this as well." Dacre motioned one of his affinity forward, typical rangy marcher type, sculpted in wind and fire, hands of steel. "That's the King's surcoat. Master Bowes here had it from this body and he's stripped a few in his time."

Without any undue show of deference the reiver thrust the shop-worn garment at me. It was heavy, silk-lined canvas bearing the royal lion, the genuine article no doubt, slashed and fringed in stiff, dried blood. "A nice trophy, I confess," I responded. The man remained where he was, relaxed but expectant.

"That wasn't a free gift," Dacre reminded me. I almost laughed as I fished in my purse, disbursing all the coin I had.

"It's the real thing," the borderer solemnly confirmed, as if a marcher would never dream of selling me a fake. It didn't really matter; for my purposes a convincing fraud would do just as well and I had a body.

"Right." I'd brought a team from the surgeon's lines with me. "You know what to do. I want him sorted – gutted, stuffed, whatever you need to do, and good to go by close of business today, nicely packed, leaded, and on his way to the Queen. Send this too." I passed them the coat. Her Majesty could post that on to the King in France, a very handy souvenir.

With hindsight, this probably wasn't such a good idea. The Queen wrote to Henry, as you'd imagine, laid it on pretty thick and sent the trophy on as well. She had every right to brag but not to King Henry VIII, especially when he'd that creeping little fox Wolsey pouring poison in both ears.

Our victory made us cocky; we'd waited a long time and we Howards aren't naturally retiring types. If Henry had stormed the gates of Paris, he could have afforded us our measure of triumph but we were his only success – made his measly gains look smaller still. The King of England was fickle, jealous, and petty. We'd not be forgiven for winning.

"Cheeky devil – Hume, I mean," Dacre went on, our primary purpose achieved, "trying to lift their guns under our noses – downright impertinent."

"That was pure policy," I confirmed. "He'd be shoring up his position in council. He and Huntly will be divvying the realm up between them. He was no fan of King James anyway so a regency council, headed I guess by Queen Margaret, will suit him just fine."

"Ah yes, the Queen of Scotland, our very own princess; England's loss is Scotland's burden. What are the odds she makes a mess of it and is out on her fat little rump before spring?"

"Your money's safe. So is she for the moment; the old man is paying chaps off as fast as you like. Far as we're concerned the war is over. The last thing King Henry wants or can afford is for us to cross the line – no point. They're beaten to a frazzle. That was our job; now we've done it – the end."

It was warm that morning. Thousands of blue-green flies were shrouding the piles of dead flesh in a luminous curtain. The air was still and you could hear the maggots, fresh about their work like rustling silk. "It's the smell," Dacre went on. "You never get used to it."

As the breeze stirred, a cloud of vileness blew through the valley, this charnel house we had created. Puddled and drying blood had turned the land dun, red, and brown; the burn was stiff and sluggish with it, rust-coloured water brushing by stripped, pallid flesh, corpses turning and swelling till their guts blew out, row upon row, rack upon rack. As the sun rose, so did the stink. Trails of eviscerated organs, hacked by blades, dragged out by human and other scavengers; colonies of rats were busily at work as though summoned by some diabolical piper.

"I'm getting them off the ground and into it, fast as possible, though there are an awful lot of them – more Scotchmen than I've ever seen before and all dead, praise God."

Aside from the bodies, many still twitching and writhing, clinging to life's last fitful embers, the field was a hive of industry. We had the guns safe in spite of Hume's little show. I had teams getting them sorted ready to be moved down to Etal for secure storage. More fellows were piling and listing the harness and gear we had. The heralds were out looking for deceased gentry or clergy; we had practically a whole synod it seemed.

"We recovered a fair few wagons from their supply train," Dacre continued. "Most of the dead there were women – looked a bit of a massacre. I got them buried quick; it seemed the decent thing." I nodded my thanks. Such details were best got out of the way before they could grow into rumours. Our enemies would be keeping a sharp lookout and I wasn't about to hand them any kind of gift.

"Your brother does well, I hope? He proved himself a bonny fighter."

"He does indeed. We're terrific bleeders, we Howards, but not easy to kill. Hopefully that bang on the head will knock some sense into him."

I have to say it never did. Edmund continued as a fool and a wastrel yet became one queen's uncle and father to another, though neither of them flourished. But I always loved my wayward younger brother, even though his endless debts cost me a fortune over the years. I'm glad he didn't live to see his daughter's fall, the brainless little fool – near ruined us all.

"I put our people in the church; about the only building round here the Jocks left standing. As we thought yesterday when I did the first tally, we got off quite lightly all considered – less than a dozen officers. They're still bringing in the rank and file."

"Under a thousand all told?"

"I'd say so, if it helps. I'd put their loss at ten to our one and hardly any of the quality escaped. Yesterday's casualties will set them back a generation."

"You know, I doubt it. Give our friends in the north one

thing: they're resilient. Besides, one man's loss is always another's gain. Sons who were fourth or fifth in line, destined for a life living on scraps, will find themselves lords, sudden heirs to estates they'd only dreamed of."

"Like enough, I suppose."

"I remember my father telling me how my grandfather told him what it was like to fight back in the old days, at Towton, if you remember. That was a bloodier show even than yesterday, yet it didn't end the wars between York and Lancaster; they went on for another twenty-five years."

"One of my own ancestors failed to return from that one," Dacre confirmed. "He was reckless enough to unhook his bevor[15] for a glass of water – was dead before he'd taken a swig. He's still buried in the churchyard there they tell me, he and his horse together! Still, at my age, I'd rather not have another day's work like this."

"Oh, I can't see them crossing the line again in any great hurry," I pondered, "and I suspect the French will do badly if they send for more aid – might even quieten the marches."

"Now that would verge on the miraculous."

"Johnny Heron did well yesterday, saved Edmund for sure. Not to mention this was all his idea."

"It's no bad thing for a fellow to have a chip on his shoulder – both in his case."

"He can afford to dispense with any old resentment," I confirmed. "The old man will knight him today, his percentage of the take will set him up nicely, and we'll make damn sure there's a decent cash grant from the King to follow."

"Just as well. We'll get his brother back as trade for George Hume, so Jono may have to find fresh digs or at least go back to his own. He'll need a new girlfriend too. I suspect he's quite keen on our friend the abbess."

---

15 A form of plate armour that covers the neck and lower facial area.

"Ah, Mistress Hoppringle... I was glad she survived the mess with their train yesterday. She's our best agent in Scotland by far. I sent over a safe conduct first thing; she's petitioned to claim their gentry."

"And you'll allow that?"

"Seems churlish not to. I owe her several favours after all."

As if on cue, Philip Tilney, whom I'd left in charge of the field, trotted over.

"There's a big posse of Scotch women come up, carts and all. Claim they're here for their dead and that we've allowed it. The one in charge, haughty piece but not bad looking, seems to have papers."

"It's perfectly in order," I confirmed. "Allow full and free access, give 'em every possible assistance, and send some labourers to help. Make sure they've food and drink. I think we can afford to appear magnanimous just this once."

Brian Tuke, Clerk to the Signet, writes to Richard Pace

Tournai, 22nd September

My Dearest Sir,

I have received reports as no doubt have you of the Earl of Surrey's victory over the King of Scots and his army in north Northumberland. This is a strange and barbarous place, their borderers and ours so alike in their fondness for larceny, licentiousness, and their endless vendettas.

The Queen has sent the King of Scotland's torn and bloodied surcoat to show that he is killed along with so many of their gentry there were insufficient carts to carry away the dead. In total our army killed ten thousand of theirs, and their loss was twenty times greater than ours. It is indeed a victory for a prince to boast of and let us pray God grants to King Henry a triumph equal in stature!

Around the King died the Archbishop of St Andrews, the earls of Caithness, Argyll, Morton, Montrose, Bothwell, Errol, Lennox and Crawford, Cassilis and Glencairn, a score of lords, lairds, and countless other gentlemen. The whole of the Scotch train is ours as is all their harness and gear. For sure, this will win Surrey his dukedom and fresh honours for the lord admiral and in faith these Howards have served His Majesty right well (and themselves no less so).

We lost few men of note. Sir Bryan Tunstall and Sir Christopher Savage both died nobly, as did others on our right flank where the blows fell most grievously. The earl has now paid off most of his soldiers, which is a great easement to His Majesty's purse. Rarely indeed does a campaign on those barren marches provide such a welcome dividend. For sure the Scots are ruined and do daily tremble in fear of an invasion, though they are yet safe enough; His Majesty may not be over keen to add yet more lustre to his subjects' laurels and must at least be mindful of his sister's distress.

Matters there will rest uncertain for the foreseeable future; that much is for sure. The new king is but a child and we may see fresh sport at the funeral games. Long may it remain so!

Your ever-loving friend, etc...

Isabella takes stock

I must not cry. I cannot sleep. I dare not think.

The narrow flame of candle flickers through this long night after the horror. I am huddled; one of the sisters is with me. She coaxes me like a child. She tried to feed me gruel but I threw it all back up. I am shivering but it is not cold. I am in fetters yet I am free; truth has loaded my chains.

Sometime in the crawling hours, Dr Beaton came to me. He poured some liquid potion down my neck. I do not ken what it was but it numbed me through. I could function, take charge again. It was what was expected, it is what defined me – until now. I worked, as I have these past days – bandaged the wounded, eased the sick, and comforted the dying. We'd need another field put by for further mass graves. My house will be defined by the extent of its inhumations.

I could barely remember what happened after Ellen died. I held her for a long time, the breeze lifting her long tresses, her pale lovely face cool and serene as marble.

"The warden's men got you away," Beaton told me later. "He'd realized we were under attack, sent his cavalry. We had many, many dead. You are mourning, I know, but your strength is needed. All Scotland will be in mourning tomorrow. I'm a connoisseur of military failures and this one's a humdinger. King James we think is dead and just about everyone else of consequence – lords, knights, and clerics. In short it's a total catastrophe."

"How many dead?" I managed to ask.

"Thousands. I've sent to Lord Howard for a safe conduct." I looked at him uncomprehendingly; the drug had slowed my overheated mind. "Isabella," he said, taking me by the shoulders, "you must go back there tomorrow. The dead must be looked for and brought back here. We cannot have it said we left the flower of Scotland as food for crows. It won't do."

"There'll be hundreds," I protested weakly.

"Quite right; the warden has given us all the carts we used for the wounded and his sergeants are assembling a company of goodwives and girls to assist. I'll send several of my fellows along in the vain hope anyone is left alive."

It's not fair, I wanted to wail. All I wanted was a dark corner, a bottle of brandy, and everyone else to leave me alone. These thoughts were plainly written on my face. "It has to be you," he coaxed me. "Nobody else here knows who's gentry and who's not. You're the only one who attends court; you know these people – knew them, I should have said."

He might have added "and you're related to many of them" but refrained, from tact I imagine, though I was long past that. "You might want to clean up a bit," he suggested.

I looked at the wild, haggard creature staring back at me from the glass. I didn't recognize her. She was much older than me, thinner. She looked like she'd escaped from the madhouse or was on her way back. Her hair was a riot, hands and face were begrimed, and she was saturated in blood – she reeked of it. She supposed she always would.

My current guardian eased off my stiff apron, rigid with others' blood, Ellen's blood. She peeled off my filthy kirtle, stripped me down to the cringing flesh, and commenced repairs. Firstly a wash: blood, snot, bile, grime gone, all traces scoured – why can't the rest be as easy? Next fresh shifts, clean kirtle, a sustained attack on the tangled hair, brush and smooth, keep a bowl of porridge down, all ready for the bright new day.

"Where's the warden?" I asked Beaton.

"Gone to salvage the guns, I believe. Rode out at dawn with most of his riders."

I groaned, "Hasn't he had enough?"

The good doctor shrugged. "I just fix the ones who get broken. I don't make the policy, for which I'm heartily thankful."

"And I'm just going to harvest the fruits of failure," I snapped, more bitter than I'd intended. Maybe I needed more physick. The stuff tasted like liquid fire. He'd cautioned me not to drink as well but I swigged down a hefty dram and took the bottle with me.

So we set off. I had over a score of carts, enough draught animals to pull them, enough carters to man them. Each would, I reckoned, hold at least a dozen bodies. We'd avoid the slopes so the gradients weren't too bad. Perhaps a hundred women and labourers trudged behind. They looked sullen, resentful, but then I probably did too. I'd decided to ride. My mare, sensible creature, had found her way home in the dark. I mounted astride. Decorum was amongst the dead.

Coming the other way were floods and eddies of survivors. No longer any kind of army, tattered, hollow, unseeing, they stumbled by, mostly without shoes, bereft of weapons or harness, many cut and slashed.

"Shirkers," somebody behind me yelled. "Cowards..."

My company of harridans began by pelting them with mud and curses, and then moved on to stones. The defeated made no reply; filth spattered them, rocks bloodied them more but they kept moving – that deep trance of exhaustion, pain, and despair. I knew the place they were in pretty well.

"Enough!" I screamed. "Let them go. Save your energy; you'll need it." Somebody answered back and I whacked her royally across the face with my crop. She cringed away. Drugs make you testy.

We passed the warden and his jolly cavaliers returning. I imagined they'd enjoyed themselves, another mad exercise in the mindless game of war. He was rather wary of me. Anybody with any sense would be.

"Have a care, Isabella," he warned me. "You've safe conduct but you know how much that can be worth."

"You surprise me," I retorted. I really should have given this bottle to somebody else to carry.

He had the grace to flinch slightly – only happens once a decade. "Yesterday was bad, I know," he persisted, "but even worse things can happen."

"Can they?" I riposted and spurred on whilst I was ahead.

I was feeling less sparky as we came nearer. Carrion crows were circling avidly, grating and raucous, and the whole valley was lifting with flies, a plague of them. Some of yesterday's furnace heat still clung. I wasn't afraid. Whatever Dr Beaton had poured into me was grand stuff. I suspected it would be easy to get too partial.

Mounted vedettes stopped us west of the field, cockily at ease. Dacre's men I guessed, they seemed welded to their garrons as though they'd sprung from the same womb. They took my safe conduct without comment.

"Can any of you read?" I enquired archly. They looked back at me, both appraising and sullen. "Get me the officer of the watch," I persisted. "Now – you dolts."

Arrogance has its place and I was past caring. The knight in charge introduced himself politely as Philip Tilney. He was courtesy itself; informed me he was the earl's brother-in-law and the army's paymaster. Perhaps he thought I gave a damn.

"The lord admiral has instructed me to offer you and your people every courtesy and not to impede you." He said this loud enough for the rest to hear. "And look," he went on, "that business up there yesterday..." He indicated

319

towards the ridge rising behind. "That wasn't any of our boys, you know. I mean a fair fight is one thing but women and children, that's not on. We don't do that sort of thing."

"That's a great consolation," I replied and rode on. Tell Ellen, I wanted to scream. Tell the murdered child who lies so cold beneath a sheet in my small chapel. Tell all the others piled on that flaming ridge, swimming in their own blood and their killers' seed. Time for another swig, I thought.

It seems to me, or certainly did at the time, that mankind has spent a fair proportion of recorded history trying to create an earthly version of hell. Flodden Field, at least in my experience, ranks as one of our better efforts. You smelt the place before you saw it, a stink of putrefaction and yes, of suffering, as though so much anguish could be somehow distilled into tangible odour.

Jen, the dark-haired goodwife I'd collected from the train, was with me still. Happily she'd survived.

"Did you know *all* the gentry?" she asked, walking alongside.

"Most, I suppose," I replied. "Never really thought about it. I'll get you an invite to court; be plenty of spare places."

"At least you look better than you did a few hours ago."

"One of the sisters helped me get through."

"That was me, actually; glad to be there though. You were in a pretty bad way."

"I still am," I confirmed, "but liquor and physick have their place. What about your husband?"

"He's all right – ran away. Not as daft as I thought. But I wanted to do something, do my bit you might say, before I scarpered off home."

We stopped and looked. Just below us where the stream had been, burial parties were at work. Like we were now doing, they'd tied cloths over their faces, scented against the stench. They'd dug great yawning pits and were laying bodies in neat rows, like fishermen after a good catch. Rigor had set in with most cases so the pioneers were using spades and axes to break stiffened limbs, the crack and dry snapping sharp in that rancid air.

"There's nobody that matters going under over there and we'll make sure proper words are said," my escort informed me. "We're not barbarians, you know." I wondered who he was trying to convince.

"Most of your better sort – those we've identified, from their arms and stuff – we gathered over here. They're not very pretty. We haven't really had time to clean any of them up. You know how it is."

Really I didn't but was prepared anyway. The better end of the dead flesh market, those who could be named, were dumped in unceremonious rows at the base of the little hill. Our carts drew up like carriages after the ball, though there'd be no dancing in Scotland for a while.

I'd dismounted with my new guardian at my side. I could tell by the way Jen stayed close that she was anticipating another collapse. I'd have said the odds were about even. What am I supposed to say about the flower of Scottish chivalry? The gloss was gone off their blossom.

"Lord," Jen breathed, "why are men so completely stupid? This lot all had wealth and status and bread in the larder. What the blazes was it all for?"

All good questions but irrelevant to current purposes; some faces I could recognize even in the sack-like indifference of death. I'd grown up with quite a few of them, a harvest of my own Pringle cousins. Twisted, contorted, and bereft of limbs, without faces – Scotland's aristocracy.

"We've begun making a list," Sir Philip, ever helpful, was beside me. "Couldn't find your herald chappie so got ours to do it – only a preliminary draft so far, but it should help get you started."

"What about King James?"

"Oh, he's not here. Well, sorry, I don't mean he's gone somewhere, not in this life anyway. He is in fact on his way to London, even as we speak, proper lead casket and all."

The corpses were stiffening in the strengthening sun, some shifting as they swelled. Down the line one burst noisily, probably a bishop, exciting the carpet of flies which lifted briefly then swooped down for the feast. The stink went up yet another notch. Jen voided her stomach of porridge. I took another swig.

"Let's get started." None of us present had ever undertaken a more dreadful labour. I do not intend ever to do it again. The only way I could sort them was by category. Earls to begin with, then bishops and lords, then knights and plain gentlemen; for just this once there'd be no complaints over precedence. They leaked everywhere. We didn't have anything like enough fabric for shrouds, so onto the boards they went, four deep as a rule, off the wagon went and up rolled the next.

Horror is like everything else. It soon becomes commonplace. It didn't take long for the banter to start.

"This one was a rich 'un for sure. Look at the size of his bleedin' huge gut."

"You can tell the bishops; they're the ones with choirboys attached." My bottle was getting pretty low. Jen had been helping, give the lass her due.

It took us hours. I chivvied the happy workers mercilessly. I wanted us and our cargo back at Coldstream before dark. I'd left instructions for grave-pits to be dug before I left. These magnates and gentry of the realm had done enough damage for one week; I didn't intend to let them add contagion to the score.

Heron takes stock

"Hybrid vigour," the Reverend Bell exclaimed. "You simply can't do better. If your blood was wholly blue rather than murky, you'd not heal the way you do. That's a great natural asset to have, especially in your case."

He was probing his own handiwork at this point; it felt like he was using a dirk. I whined feebly, consciousness dragging like a badly silted anchor. It seemed like I should attempt to sit up. Had I realized the effort involved, I might have reconsidered. "There you are," he boomed again, "back with us – bruised but not broken."

I wasn't so sure. My left shoulder felt like most of the King of Scots' army was jumping up and down on it. My right calf throbbed abominably. My head hurt – everywhere seemed to hurt to some degree.

"I'd give you something for the discomfort," he went on, "but I know how you fellows of reputation disdain such trivial balms."

We were in the basement at Barmoor. I recognized Edmund Howard lying in the cot next to me. "How's our local hero?" I managed to croak.

"Like you, he seems to have a remarkably thick skull and an excellent constitution. He will do very well, I think. And it's Sir Edmund now, to you. He's a knight; his dad says so. In case you think that's favouritism, you're one too. Sir John Heron, knight and, I should say, gentleman, whole and pure and perfect. You're no longer the Bastard, not in the sense of lineage anyway. If things continue this way I might yet end my days a bishop."

"Tell me we won?"

"Emphatically, I'd say: not a single Scotchman alive this side of the line but a very large number who aren't. Many in this category are or were gentlemen or whatever passes for gentry over there."

"And King James?" I queried.

"Among the deceased, we believe. Your boss is over there now looking for a convincing carcass. I hope the Scottish King enjoyed burning your – that is, your brother's – house down; you've paid him back with abundant interest. Speaking of cash, you'll be due some – your share of the spoils, which are substantial, what with all their guns and gear. Not only are you a gentleman, but you'll be able to live like one and stop stealing."

The good Father wisely deferred when we were joined by the earl himself, come to check on the welfare of his youngest son. I could see the previous day's exertions had taken their toll. The old man was as bluff as ever but the lines on his face were etched much deeper, tinged with grey, and he was walking with a stick. I'd not seen that concession to infirmity previously.

"Damn this gout," he began. "Plagues me worse than the Scotch, even worse than our own people – your own people, I might say, Sir John – who have left us pretty much bereft. Still, I think we can excuse you duty for today."

"They are gone for sure – the Scotch, I mean?"

"For sure, if not necessarily for good, but it will be a while before we see them on our side of the fence – a very long time indeed – and they'll think twice next time the King of France clicks his fingers. His Majesty will be most pleased."

I had sufficient wit to detect a hint of irony but thought it wise not to comment.

"What's the tally of their dead?" I enquired instead.

"Well, we'll say ten thousand, nice round number and not far off. Just about everyone who mattered is on the list, except Hume. He's much too canny; suits us of course. He's not the enemy. He and Lord Dacre have… well, let's say they have an understanding. You know all about that, of course, and we'll just keep the details to ourselves; no need to trouble the court."

The old man paused as though to gather himself.

"Now look here, laddie," he began. "I know you've had what could best be described as a colourful career, but that slate got wiped clean yesterday. King James cited you as one of his excuses for making war. Little good it did him and one more dead Scottish ruffian isn't going to be counted any more. Thanks largely to you, we turned a potential disaster into a win, a very significant win. I intend to do very well out of it and I'll make damn sure those who helped me do too. You're getting pretty close to the top of the list.

"You're Sir John now, a gentleman through and through. There's money in it as well, a fair bit if I've got my sums right. We'll swap one of our guests for your brother, so you may need to return to your own digs. If they're not to your liking buy somewhere better – you'll be able to afford it."

He paused again.

"I lost a son – you know that, of course. Had it not been for you, I'd probably have lost another and I don't value any victory that high. Not only are you a full gentleman, but you're a friend of the Howards. We're a venal bunch by and large. We make very bad enemies and can bear a petty grudge with the best. On the other hand, we don't forget our friends. Your quarrel is our quarrel. Your enemy takes us on as well. On current performance, I'd say 'God help him.'"

On that we shook, the old boy's grip still firm. As he rose painfully to his feet he looked at his still-sleeping offspring. "God bless you, boy," he said to me.

"Do I still possess a horse?" I asked the good Father sometime later.

"I believe so," Bell confirmed. "You rode back on him yesterday. You had some assistance to be sure but you did ride. Obviously, I should caution you against an undue amount of exercise in your parlous state but I'm confident you won't listen."

Edmund had come round, rather shakily. "Did we do all right?" he asked almost plaintively.

"Not bad for a southerner," I responded.

"I mean, did we win?" he persisted. "Did we beat the Scotch in the end? Half my brigade ran away."

"They were lacking in enthusiasm to begin with," I confirmed. "It got better later on. Most of 'em came back and then they got stuck in, good and proper as it happens."

"Story of my life – I always seem to miss the best bits. Where are you off to?"

I told him; he decided he would come too.

"Definitely not," Bell admonished. "One madman who may now be just a gentleman I can cope with but not a pair of you. Your brother, Sir Edmund, would have me keelhauled. Sailors do that sort of thing, I'm told."

We took the shortest route, back towards Wooler, past Watch Law and the easy ford below Fishes Steads. That place was gone, even the skeletal traces used up. We cantered up the soft eastern flank of Flodden Hill. It resembled something from the Old Testament, as though all the tribes had descended and consumed. An army is like a maelstrom: it devours everything.

That once green hillside was scorched by the ashes

of a thousand cooking fires, an acrid tang of burning still clinging to the air. Abandoned pots, mostly busted, piles of rubbish – nothing worth lifting was left. Our fellows had grabbed most of everything and locals had skinned what remained. The proud silken pavilions were gone. No banners or pennons flew. There were just the silent ghosts of abandoned earthworks as mute as the hill-forts of the old people. Perhaps their traces would endure as long; somehow I doubted it. "Let's call it King James's folly," I suggested.

"Not much of a testament," Bell commented. "Not much to say thirty thousand souls were here – not that we'll miss them." We trotted across the wide saddle of ground, tracks of the army's passage ploughed ahead of us – ruts gouged by their guns – yet no sound but that of the lone curlew.

"This got messy," he confirmed as we drew near the wreck of their baggage. Stripped and shorn carts lay at angles, still plenty of bodies maturing in the afternoon sun. The smell was getting pretty bad. "The abbess got out, you'll be pleased to hear. The admiral sent her a safe conduct to remove the better class of cadavers."

We ran into some of Dacre's scouts but they waved us on. It seems I was an attraction. Men cheered as we picked our path down the slope, a diversion from the mortality business. Looking at the state of the place, they'd be busy for a while yet.

"I'm not used to people cheering," I confessed. "Not used to crowds really. Whenever I'm near a group, they usually turn out to be hired assassins or a lynch mob."

"You're famous now, Sir John, as opposed to merely being notorious. Besides, you've only ever killed Scotchmen and this is your absolute masterpiece. This is England's masterpiece. No wonder the Howards, father and son, are looking so mightily pleased with themselves."

The poets will tell you a battlefield resembles a butcher's yard. That's not really true. Butchers tend towards order. There was none here and it was a very big yard indeed. As you'd expect the dead lay thickest by Piper's Hill and just east where the fighting was heaviest. I knew we'd racked up a fair score but this was impressive. At the base of the hill stood a convoy of carts, bodies being sorted, loaded, and stacked.

"She's down there." The vicar had guessed who I was looking for, and yes, there she stood, seemingly apart and oddly aloof, out of place. She was out of place; her world was one of serenity and order, continuity, and a measure of security. "I'll leave you to it. I'll ply my trade amongst the grave-diggers." He turned tactfully away. I eased down from the saddle. Damn, I was sore.

I looked at her, tall and lithe in afternoon light. She looked thinner. Closer, she was even paler and drawn tight as a drum-skin, her dark eyes huge and suffering with grey-black smudges beneath. She had aged without changing. For all of that, anguish could not diminish her. The etching of sorrow only made her glow more luminous.

She had not seen me. Her movements were automatic, unfocused. I saw that the raven-headed doxy with her was holding a near empty bottle. I assumed they'd been sharing. Isabella reached out for another swig and grimaced, as there was none. Ever the gallant, I was able to offer my flask, damn near full and with the lord admiral's best.

She took it automatically and then noticed. She stared for a moment, as though she didn't quite trust her own eyesight. Judging by the state of the brandy ration, I wasn't entirely surprised.

"Johnny," she managed at last. If it was possible, she'd gone a stage paler. She seemed to sway and I thought she might pass out. I reached out a hand to steady her. Her buxom companion regarded me intently. She'd been around the houses, I guessed, wrong side of thirty, but her kirtle bulged in the right places and her teeth at least looked sound. She was trying to work out the dynamic here. As ever with Isabella, so was I.

"Walk with me," I suggested and led Isabella off. She seemed to be in a kind of trance but my flask was helping.

"I should stay," she began but did not resist.

Raven-hair waved us on. "I'll mind the shop," she offered. "Won't be many complainers."

In spite of my generally distressed condition, my kit was still stiff with the blood of several, yet certain parts seemed refreshed and raring for a fresh objective. Jen, as I discovered her name was, might easily have been persuaded to begin the reconciliation process. Timing might prove problematic and I suspected Isabella's reserves of humour were running dangerously low.

We drifted towards the chapel, only building standing. Some of our chaps were preparing fresh graves while their soon-to-be occupants waited inside. Nobody paid us any heed. We squatted down by the wall, afternoon sun slanting warm on our upturned faces. For a while we didn't speak. She was leaning against me, her face on my shoulder.

"I'm not hurting you, am I?"

"Not at all," I lied. In fact, sharp needles of agony were toying with my wound but we have to bear such things.

"I'd ask you to dinner," she continued, "but we've none to offer."

"Well," I replied, "at least it would make asking you back easier; we've even less."

"You stole everything from us," she said without rancour.

"It is what we're good at," I admitted. "We're non-partisan really. Once our fellows had finished clearing your side out, they did the same for us; reiving's impartial."

"Just about everybody died," she went on. "You wouldn't recognize my house; it's a city of the dead – no food, no drink, no home, no hope; just corpses."

We rested awhile. She was still rigid against me. I was aching and not just from my wounds.

"What happens now, Johnny? Where do we go from here?"

"God knows," I replied. "You'll be safe enough; I'll make sure. I'm a gentleman now so people have to listen to me and I've still got the warden's brother, even though he has mine."

She didn't reply. She had begun to relax slightly; I could feel some of the tension leeching out of her. She moulded more against me. Despite the pain, this was a pleasant sensation. I could feel her drifting off – she was completely done in. Her breathing eased, became less ragged. She dozed, then slept. Above us the larks still sang, indifferent to the excesses of human folly below. "All right for you," I said to no one in particular, "try living down here for a while."

Isabella slept on; the dead will always wait for you.

Correspondence (Inventory) sent by Master Edward Ripley, dealer in quality used arms and armour, ordnance, and all accoutrements thereto, to Thomas Howard

Etal, 12th September

My most noble and illustrious Lord Admiral,

Pursuant to your instructions, I and my valuation team have made a full, thorough, and diligent inspection of that quantity of great guns, accessories, sundry arms, and harness recently taken from those rogues the Scotch in the course of your lordship's most prodigious and resounding victory lately won at Branxton.

May it please your munificence, the full tally of these may be summarized as set out for your most kind and benevolent attention hereafter, viz: Iron Courtaulds (so called murtherers) in number seven, 6,000 lb dead-weight, all upon wooden wheeled carriages (two of which need minor repair, one written off and to be replaced); four bronze gros culverain in good and serviceable repair, minor pitting to bores, all on wheeled wooden carriages (note damage to wheels in several instances); four sakers ditto; four culverain moyene cast in bronze ditto (one with split barrel); quantity of falcons, mounted on carts with breech mugs, together with numerous carts and two cartloads of pioneer tools, one cartload gunner's tools, numerous barrels of well-milled powder, quantities of shot in all calibres, rammers, spikes, spongers (some damaged). In addition, almain rivet harness (munition quality), five hundred and seventy-two sets, comprising breast, back, and tassets (evidence of wear), large quantity munition-grade sallets (several holed), three hundred and twenty-eight first quality gents' Italian/Almain harness, all sound (though some repairs needed in places), together with armets, wrappers (many damaged possibly beyond economic repair), approx twelve hundred good-quality bastard swords and Scotch highland two-handed swords, sundry rondels, dirks, ballock knives, large quantity of pikes, some with damaged heads (twenty cartloads), numerous quality leather gentlemen's boots (various sizes), purses, belts, personal effects, rings and charms, etc.

As to valuation, I would submit for your illustrious attention that the whole of the above, subject to fluctuations in the market occasioned by so sudden a glut and the absence of Scottish buyers, might be valued in the region of some twelve thousand, four hundred pounds, eight shillings and thruppence, subject only to my commission to be deducted from gross sale proceeds, though of course after those monies due from me to your agent (as per our previous memorandum). With Your Excellency's most kind permission I shall tomorrow by first post dispatch for Your Grace's esteemed attention a full and whole inventory of all tentage, ropes, carts, conveyances, cooking and domestic utensils, tools, hardware, and insight gear recovered from the former encampment of the Scots.

Assuring you of my best and most constant attention, I hope I may have the honour to remain, etc...

Postscript: Sir Thomas Howard, formerly 3rd Duke of Norfolk, has time to reflect

There's an east wind that comes up the Thames. It blows constantly, sometimes whispering, sometimes howling.

Tonight it's just there, worming through badly filled joints and ageing casements. The Tower is not a good place to be at the best of times, assuming you have a choice. Most don't and I'm one of them, older by four years than my father when he fought at Flodden but stripped of titles, honours, and position. Two of my nieces became Queen, each as foolish as the other. Both paid the same price.

My own long, sometimes glorious, latterly inglorious career is very near its ending – at dawn in fact. The King is on his deathbed but found strength to sign the warrant. It seems fitting enough. I could scarcely expect more. It was I who raised the Howards' star into the regal firmament and now I who must carry the burden of failure. Nobody could say God doesn't have a sense of irony.

It is that night, over thirty years since, that my thoughts return to. My finest hour, I the general who had won the greatest victory ever fought against the Scots, laid low their King, his lords, and bishops and knights and unnamed kerns by the gross. I still have a copy of the dispatch I wrote to Queen Katherine, blood hot in my veins, the red shift barely lifted. There, in the old hall, stripped by the bastard reivers, I wrote my dispatch. Did I boast? No, I was modesty itself, the dutiful subject. It was she, the Queen, then regent, that sent my trophies on to the King, the bloodied surcoat of his dead brother-in-law. Henry made much of us and feigned joy but the plain fact was he raged with jealousy.

His own glorious campaign was a stillborn thing. He won a petty skirmish and called it victory. His ally deserted him and the French were left laughing. We were grudgingly given greater titles, but that year will be remembered as the year of the Howards. Overall, our memory may need some highlights. I suppose I'm the only one left aside from that diseased hulk, the shell of a King who could have been great. The Queen is gone of course, treated abominably and cast aside for a heretic whom, admittedly, I did sponsor. My brother's life was a sad parody. He should have died on that field, though his daughter became Queen, briefly. I'm glad he didn't live to see her head upon the block – nobody deserves that.

Heron, the swashbuckler, gained a knighthood, as you know, plus a handsome pension and his past sins forgiven. Not that he desisted, of course; he kept on brawling till his luck finally ran out. Dacre is gone too – all that generation. Hume, for all his slipperiness, was never trusted after and died a traitor's death. Wolsey also – I did well to see his fall. I wonder sometimes if the abbess still lives. I rather hope she does. If so, her retirement should be comfortable enough.

Can you hear them? The bells are tolling. Not for me; rather for King Henry. By that stroke of providence, I am spared. Even if I don't see daylight again, I will live, and who knows, who can tell? England may yet have need of Old Tom again.

Finis

Historical Note

Few battles in British history have produced a mantle of such romantic gloss, perhaps most markedly on the Scottish side, where Flodden, understandably, still rates as a major calamity. James IV who, had he decided otherwise on the day, might well have been remembered as one of the nation's most successful, rather than rashly quixotic and foolhardy, monarchs, has been blamed ever since. This is, in fact, unfair. James was an excellent ruler in many ways and his failure at Flodden did involve a fair measure of sheer bad luck.

The Flodden tradition, ably abetted by Scott and other nineteenth-century romantics, has woven itself into the consciousness of a nation. As ever with history, the reality is both more complex and multi-layered. The contemporary sources are patchy, so we are frequently thrown back upon heroic assumption. Both James IV and Henry VIII are fascinating characters, and it is the underlying dynamic between these two aggressive and able monarchs that lies at the root of this conflict.

James was both more mature and in many ways more astute. Henry VIII's campaign in France was a vainglorious puff that emptied his father's wonderfully hoarded treasury and achieved nothing in strategic terms. The only laurels won in 1513 were garnered in cold and distant Northumberland, not the universal cockpit of Flanders and Artois. Henry's vaunted victory – the "Battle of the Spurs" – was an insignificant skirmish whilst Flodden proved the bloodiest fight in three centuries of savage and bitter cross-border strife.

Less certain is the extent of the consequences. Some writers, notably Peter Reese, see the consequences as far reaching and damaging, weakening the northern kingdom for the remainder of the sixteenth century. Whilst the evils of minority kingships were frequent visitors to Scotland, other chroniclers see the battle, despite the level of loss, as having remarkably few long-term consequences. What is remarkable is the manner in which the Scottish polity bore the loss, steadied and continued, even fighting back later the same year.

It was on a wet, blustery afternoon in late summer that King James IV of Scotland committed his army to battle against an English force led by Thomas Howard, Earl of Surrey. Only the monument atop Piper's Hill by the pleasant if unremarkable north Northumbrian village of Branxton marks the site of the epic clash of arms which followed. The village is so small that the "Remembering Flodden" project is constructing a visitor centre in a disused phone box, the smallest information point in Britain!

This proved one of the bloodiest days in British history, the most prodigious slaughter in three centuries of border warfare between England and Scotland. Despite the level of carnage, Flodden is barely remembered in England; some distant battle that no longer features on any school curriculum. In Scotland the situation is very different. Here echoes of that day still resonate, distorted by successive overlays of romance and myth – perhaps more so now than ever, as the independence debate gathers increasing momentum.

Sir Walter Scott has much to answer for in this. He relates how, on the eve of battle, the young Earl of Caithness, with three hundred of his affinity, presented himself before King James. The earl was under something of a cloud, having been outlawed for recent misdemeanours. The King, nonetheless, allowed expediency to triumph over form and admitted the Caithness contingent to his rank – decent of him but unfortunate for them, as they fell to a man on the field. The earl's affinity wore green and the colour was, even at the time of Walter Scott's celebrated *Minstrelsy*, still considered unlucky in Caithness. Such Flodden traditions have a romantic ring and yet many may be true; no fewer than eighty-seven Hays fell around the banner of their chief.

The bare facts of the campaign and battle of Flodden may be summarized quite succinctly. It was fought as a consequence of strategic decisions made by Henry VIII of England, principally his intention to invade the realm of France in 1513 in support of his ally, the Habsburg Emperor. In so doing, he was fully aware this would antagonize his brother-in-law, James IV of Scotland, who might, in support of his French ally, launch an attack on northern England.

James, stung by Henry's contemptuous rebuttal of several ultimata, pushed ahead with his plans for an invasion of Northumberland, his efforts boosted by supplies of bullion, arms, and a cadre of military advisors from France. James, under the influence of his French advisors, had resolved to drill his raw levies in advanced pike tactics developed and practised with great élan and success by redoubtable Swiss mercenaries and imperial *Landsknechts*.

Thomas Howard, Earl of Surrey, latterly 2nd Duke of Norfolk – England's venerable senior commander, who had started his long career in arms as a Yorkist – led the English host. His available forces were undoubtedly inferior in numbers to those of the Scots. Most contemporary commentators give the English between sixteen and twenty-six thousand effectives. These troops were made up mainly from retainers of the magnates and shire levies from those counties north of the Trent.

Surrey's eldest surviving son, the lord admiral, brought a stiffening of twelve hundred marines from the fleet whilst Lord Dacre furnished some fifteen hundred border horse. Surrey also had an artillery train (though his was made up of lighter field pieces). These English guns could not compare with the Scots' train in terms of weight of shot but were faster firing and more manoeuvrable. On the field, English gunners did briskly murderous service and emerged victorious from the opening artillery duel. This virtually decided the outcome.

After the initial Scottish muster on Burgh Muir, the host moved southward to the border to commence the siege of Norham. This was the prince bishop's great hold by the Tweed – "Queen of Border Fortresses". The castellan had advised Surrey he could hold out until relieved, echoing the earlier siege of 1497, but this time the Scottish train was vastly more formidable.

Following a mere five days of bombardment and infantry assault, the fortress surrendered on terms. Wark soon followed. James went on to take lesser holds at Etal and Ford, both of which were then slighted (the legend that James was beguiled by the lascivious charms of Lady Heron at Ford is undoubtedly a romantic myth). There is no indication that James intended to seek battle. His objectives could have, and indeed largely had, been attained without the hazard. He may, however, have wished to put his army to the test but the first position he chose, astride Flodden Edge and overlooking Millfield Plain, was entirely defensive. His guns were well dug in and the ground favoured the Scots.

There is magic in these otherwise unremarkable hills. Scottish campfires above plundered Fishes Steads were laid on top of Iron Age cooking pits, older to them than they to us. The landscape remains essentially unchanged, though far more is now beneath the plough, and generations of patient drainage have drawn the sting from fatal mosses.

We can walk the same ground as the combatants of five centuries past, happily devoid of the irritating accretions that besmirch so many of our over-regulated heritage sites, dumbed down to the point of derision. To do so is a remarkable experience; to attempt to visualize the great Scottish army bivouacked by the farm, aptly named Encampment, to clothe these regular fields with a swarm of crude bothies for the commoners and proud pavilions for the gentry, the smoke of several thousand fires, the pungent aroma of cooking, human and animal waste, wet wool, sweat, and the acrid tang of spent powder as the great guns practised their killing reach.

Surrey's decision to attempt an outflanking manoeuvre and occupy Branxton Hill was a bold one which nearly came unstuck, as a significant gap opened between his and Thomas Howard's division. James chose not to exploit the opportunity but to await his enemies' full deployment. This was entirely consistent with Swiss doctrine. Combat began with a brisk artillery duel. The heavier Scottish ordnance, having been dragged over the intervening saddle, could not be properly dug in. Nor were the gunners necessarily Scotland's best, as many of these were attached to the fleet. Very quickly the English gunners established fire supremacy, their Scottish counterparts fell or deserted, and round-shot began to fall amongst the densely packed ranks of pikes.

For James this was intolerable: he unleashed Hume and Huntly's powerful division on the Scottish left. At the outset, his choice of tactics appeared fully validated. At this point on the ground the lateral burn, running by the foot of Branxton Hill and which was to bring ruin to the King, was a far lesser obstacle and Edmund Howard's weak brigade on the English right almost instantly folded. Only Howard himself with a handful of knights stood his ground and fought on against hopeless odds. A timely intervention by Dacre's horse restored the position, shoring up this crumbling flank. Hume's unwillingness to continue the fight smacked to many of both treachery and collusion between the wardens – scarcely an unusual arrangement in border warfare!

Meanwhile, the division of Errol, Crawford, and Montrose hurled themselves downhill, followed by the King's vast, bristling phalanx, to smash the English centre. Ground, however, proved far more difficult than a view from the hilltop might suggest. The burn ran deeper and its banks proved more slippery than either appeared. Momentum, key to success with pikes, was lost and with it cohesion. The Scots struggled through wet and mire to find themselves slogging up a rise to meet an English line which surged forward to engage. Now crucial impetus was lost, their pikes proved no match for the formidable English bill. Most dropped staves to draw swords, and Howard's men swiftly gained the upper hand. D'Aussi's reserve merely added to the scrum and many Scots began filtering away.

Only the highland division under Lennox and Argyll remained uncommitted, and the clansmen were scattered by Edward Stanley's brigade. Though Stanley's men came late to the fight, an opportune, brilliant flank attack broke the highlanders and killed their chiefs. Appeals to Hume to bring his and Huntly's men into the ring fell on deaf ears. James had, in fact, battered a salient into the mass of the English centre, one which was in danger of being annihilated as the bills closed in. King and nobles, encased in fine harness, fought on doggedly, whilst many of the commoners decided upon discretion.

In a final quixotic gesture, James and his household men flung themselves upon Surrey's banners. The King of Scotland died almost unseen in the ruin of his proud army. As dusk fell, the English were left masters of the field. Perhaps as many as eight thousand Scots fell. English losses were far less, maybe a thousand in all.

Today there is a car park in Branxton and the church certainly repays a visit. The monument, erected in 1910, is in the form of a large granite cross set on Piper's Hill, roughly on ground held by the English right and is now well furnished with good-quality interpretation panels. This slight eminence gives an excellent view of the field. Directly ahead of you stands the ridge itself and one can see the commanding nature of the Scottish position. Although the burn has been diminished as an obstacle by subsequent field drainage, we can easily perceive just how difficult this would have proved at the time coupled with the unexpected extent of the slope leading up to the English position.

Stand at the top of the ridge, however, and these obstacles are far less apparent. We can see why James, with no scouting, could have been so dangerously misled. Flodden Edge, south of the Branxton position, over the undulating saddle which links the two, is also interesting, as evidence of field fortifications remains and these are now being exposed by the spade. Standing here, looking over the plain below, one can easily discern why Surrey would shudder at the thought of a frontal assault. There is now a series of excellent footpaths over the ground, which is mainly under the plough. Take the track beyond the cross towards Branxton Stead and then ascend Branxton

Hill, turn left by the farm and pick up the road back down to Branxton. Marden Farm is to your right and a footpath links this to the settlement.

Nearby, at Etal Castle, English Heritage has mounted an excellent display and interpretation of the battle. The castle itself, of course, featured in the action of 1513 and the site is well worth a visit. Norham Castle should also be on anyone's itinerary. The castle still dominates the river crossing and the pleasant village below. The magnificent stone keep still offers note of the importance of the prince bishop's great fortress in border warfare.